CRUSADER

BEN KANE

ORION

An Orion paperback
First published in Great Britain in 2021 by Orion Fiction,
an imprint of The Orion Publishing Group Ltd.,
Carmelite House, 50 Victoria Embankment
London EC4Y 0DZ

An Hachette UK company

1 3 5 7 9 10 8 6 4 2

A CIP catalogue record for this book
is available from the British Library.

ISBN (Mass Market Paperback) 978 1 4091 9781 2
ISBN (eBook) 978 1 4091 9782 9

Typeset by Input Data Services Ltd, Somerset

Printed and bound in Great Britain by Clays Ltd, Elcograf S.p.A.

www.orionbooks.co.uk

For Ferdia and Pippa.
You are my everything.

Naples
Messina
Bagnara
Reggio
Palermo
Catania
SICILY
SOUTHERN ITALY and
SICILY in the LATE
TWELFTH CENTURY
N·G

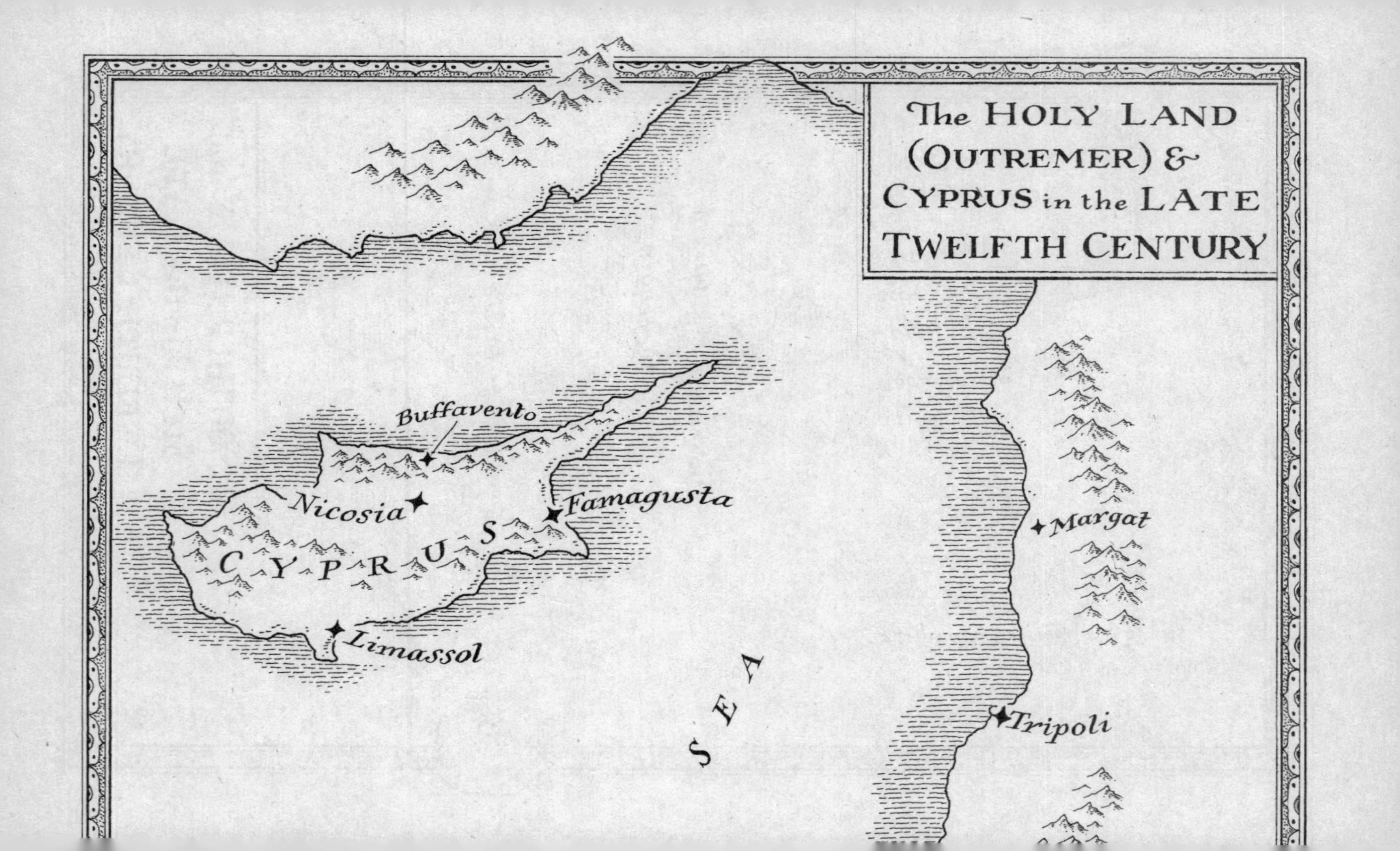
The HOLY LAND (OUTREMER) & CYPRUS in the LATE TWELFTH CENTURY
Buffavento
Nicosia
Famagusta
CYPRUS
Limassol
SEA
Margat
Tripoli

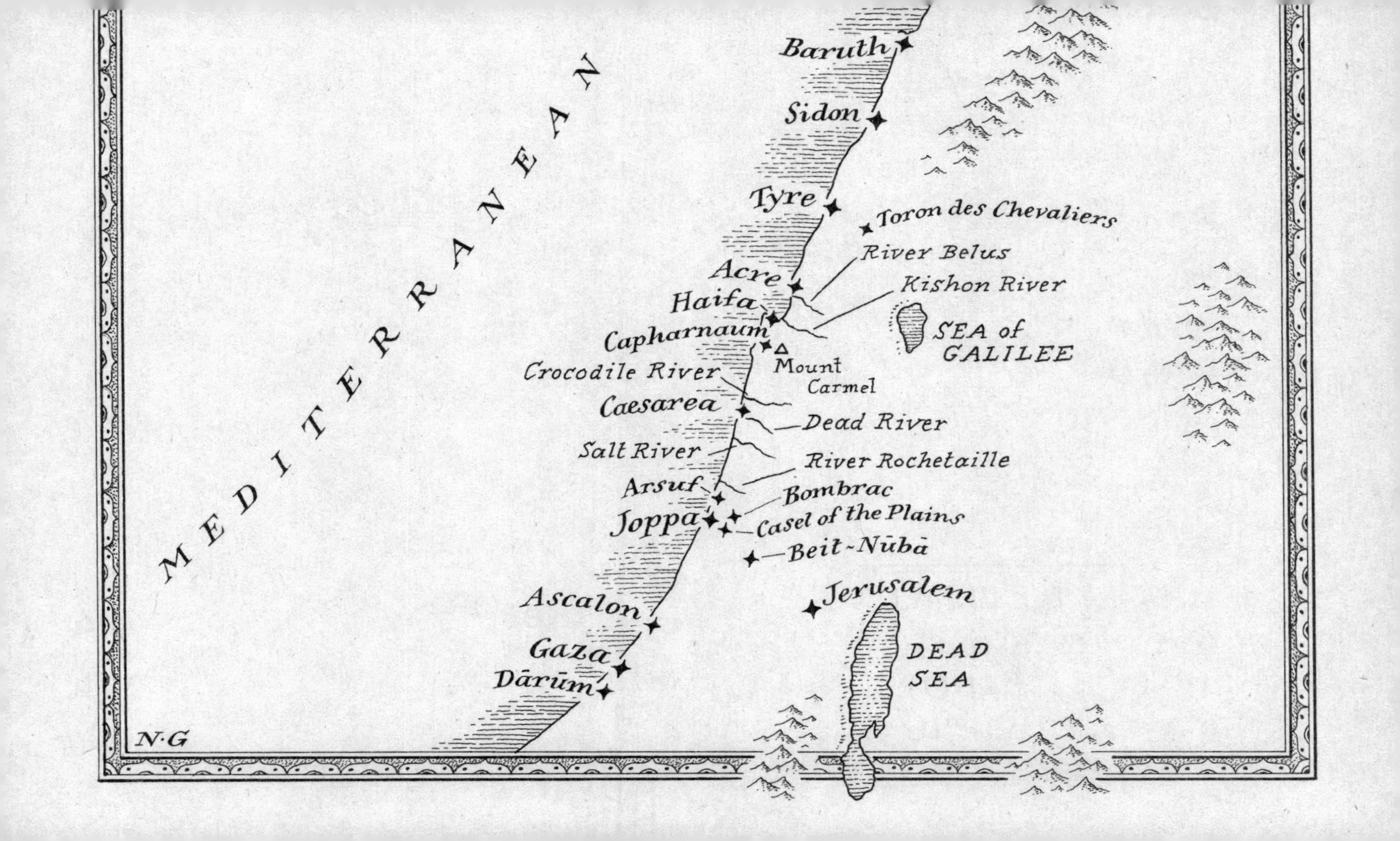
MEDITERRANEAN
Baruth
Sidon
Tyre
Toron des Chevaliers
River Belus
Acre
Kishon River
Haifa
SEA of
GALILEE
Capharnaum
Mount
Carmel
Crocodile River
Caesarea
Dead River
Salt River
River Rochetaille
Arsuf
Bombrac
Joppa
Casel of the Plains
Beit-Nūbā
Jerusalem
Ascalon
Gaza
Dārūm
DEAD
SEA
N·G

LIST OF CHARACTERS

(Those marked * are recorded in history)

Ferdia Ó Catháin/Rufus O'Kane, an Irish noble from north Leinster in Ireland
Rhys, orphaned Welsh youth
Robert FitzAldelm, knight, and brother to Guy FitzAldelm (deceased)

Royal House of England:
Henry Fitz Empress*, King of England, Duke of Normandy, Count of Anjou, (deceased)
Alienor (Eleanor) of Aquitaine*, Henry's widow
Henry (Hal), eldest son of Henry (deceased)
Richard, King of England, Duke of Aquitaine* and second son of Henry
Geoffrey*, third son of Henry, Duke of Brittany (deceased)
Arthur*, Geoffrey's young son
John*, Count of Mortain, youngest son of Henry, also known as 'Lackland'
Joanna*, Queen of Sicily, daughter of Henry

English Royal Court:
Beatrice, maidservant to Queen Alienor
André de Chauvigny*, knight and cousin to Richard
Baldwin de Béthune*, knight
William Longchamp*, Bishop of Ely, Richard's chancellor
Hugh de Puiset*, Bishop of Durham
Geoffrey*, bastard son to Henry, Archbishop of York
William Marshal*, one of Richard's justiciars
Bardolph*, FitzPeter* and Bruyère*, also Richard's justiciars
Philip, squire and friend to Rufus

Religious: Archbishop Walter of Rouen*, Archbishop Gerard of Auxienne*, Bishop Hubert of Salisbury*, Bishop John of Evreux*, Bishop Nicholas of Le Mans*
John d'Alençon*, Archdeacon of Lisieux and a former Vice Chancellor of England
Hugh de la Mare*, clerk
Ambroise*, cleric and author of the extant *Estoire de la Guerre Sainte, The History of the Holy War*
Prior Robert of Hereford*
Ralph Besace*, medical cleric
Nobles: Robert, Earl of Leicester*, Count de Pol*, Count Robert de Dreux*
Knights, Robert de Turnham*, Geoffrey du Bois*, Peter and William de Préaux*, John FitzLucas*, Bartholomew de Mortimer*, Ralph de Mauléon*, Henry Teuton*, Henry de Sacey*, William de l'Etang*, Gerard de Furnival*, James d'Avesnes*, Matthew de Sauley*, Peter Tireproie*, de Roverei*, Richard Thorne
Guillaume de Caieux*, Flemish knight
Richard de Drune, Hugh de Neville*, men-at-arms

Other characters:
William*, King of Scotland
Philippe II*, King of France
Alys Capet*, Philippe's sister, betrothed to Richard in childhood
Henri of Blois*, Count of Champagne and cousin to both Richard and Philippe Capet
Philippe, Count of Flanders*
Guillaume des Barres*, a famous French knight
Raymond, Count of Toulouse*
Hugh, Duke of Burgundy*, cousin to the French king
Joffroi, Count of Perche*
Peter, Count of Nevers*
Bishop of Beauvais*, cousin to the French king
Drogo de Merlo*, nobleman
Aubery Clément*, knight

Sicily:
William II de Hauteville*, King of Sicily (deceased)

Constance de Hauteville*, William's aunt and heir, wed to Heinrich von Hohenstaufen*, King of Germany and heir of the Holy Roman Emperor, Frederick Barbarossa*
Tancred of Lecce*, illegitimate cousin of William
Reginald de Muhec*, a local nobleman
Hugh de Lusignan*, nephew of Guy, Geoffrey and Amaury
Del Pin*, the governor of Messina
Margaritone*, the admiral of Tancred's fleet
Berengaria*, daughter of King Sancho VI* of Navarre, Richard's betrothed

Outremer:
Guy de Lusignan*, King of Jerusalem
Sibylla, Queen of Jerusalem*, Guy's wife (deceased)
Isabella of Jerusalem*, Sibylla's half-sister
Humphrey de Toron*, her husband
Conrad of Montferrat*, Italian-born ruler of Tyre, cousin to the French king Philippe
Geoffrey* and Amaury* de Lusignan, Guy's brothers
Robert de Sablé*, grand master of the Knights Templar
Garnier de Nablus*, grand master of the Knights Hospitallers
Balian d'Ibelin*, Lord of Nablus
Reynald of Sidon*
Leopold, Duke of Austria*
Joscius, Archbishop of Tyre*
Saladin*, Al-Malik al-Nasir Salah al-Dīn, Abu' al-Muzaffar Yusuf ibn Ayyūb, Sultan of Egypt
Saphadin*, Al Malik al-'Ādil, Saif al-Dīn Abū Bakr Ahmad ibn Ayyūb, brother to Saladin
Mestoc*, Saif al-Dīn 'Alī ibn Ahmad al-Mashtūb, Muslim commander in Acre
Karakush*, Bahā' al-Dīn al Asadī Qara-Qūsh, Muslim commander in Acre
Reynald de Châtillon*, nobleman (deceased)
Abu, Muslim youth in Acre
William Borrel* and Baldwin Carew*, Hospitallers
Ibn an-Nahlal*, secretary to Saladin
Rashīd ed-Din Sīnān*, the Old Man of the Mountains

PROLOGUE

Southampton, November 1189

Deep gloom blanketed the one-roomed house in which Rhys and I waited, our nerves wire taut. We stood in silence against the wall by the hinges of the rickety front door; that way our quarry, entering, would see us when it was too late. Dagger clutched tight, one eye against a hole in the wattle and daub, I peered into the alleyway outside, trying to keep my breathing slow, measured. Trying to convince myself that this was the right course of action.

Night had fallen some time since over the stews, the poorest part of the town, and there was little activity outside. A pig had been slaughtered in the butcher's yard soon after our arrival, its high-pitched squeals setting my teeth on edge. A pair of gossiping women, neighbours, had walked by after that, but no one else. Unease pricked me. I could not be sure if my quarry, a spade-bearded man-at-arms by the name of Henry, would return here before his wife. I had no wish to involve an innocent in my dark business. I steeled my resolve. If the woman came back, we would gag and blindfold her, and wait on for her husband. I tried not to think about the babe I had been told of.

I shifted position, rolling my shoulders against a threatening cramp in my muscles. My gaze wandered the room. The dim orange glow of a low-smouldering fire in the central hearth outlined two stools, a trestle table, a wooden clothes chest and a blanket-covered straw pallet in one corner. The dog tethered to the back wall was quiet – it had wolfed down the bread I had brought with me for just such an eventuality and now seemed content with our silent company.

Our wait continued for I do not know how long. I grew cold; more than once, I had to pace about, cat soft, to get the blood flowing again. Rhys did not stir. Only the movement of his eyes, watching me, betrayed that he was not a statue. Faithful heart he was, I thought, my heart warming to have him on this difficult mission.

At last footsteps came, approaching the house. I slipped back to my spyhole, a tiny part of me hoping they would pass by.

They came to a halt outside.

I nudged Rhys, hard.

He nodded. Closer to the door, he was poised; ready to spring.

The hook rattled, and I tensed. I had been unable to fasten it to the staple on the jamb from the inside.

A curse. 'She left it open, as usual.'

With a creak, the door swung inward. The dog whined and strained at its tether, tail wagging.

A figure hove into sight. He had a beard, although I could not see its shape in the poor light. Rhys leaped forward, wrapping one arm around the man's right shoulder, and with his other hand, grabbing for the man's flailing left arm. Blade at the ready, I darted around to the front. Rhys's grasp slipped, and I took the man's bunched fist on my cheekbone. Stars burst across my vision, and I staggered.

Thank Christ our victim fought back rather than shouted. While I tried to unscramble my wits, he and Rhys tumbled to the floor, wrestling and trading blows. A flying kick struck the pot hanging from a chain over the fire. Its lid flew off, hitting a wall with a dull clang, and hot pottage sprayed the room. The dog barked.

Head clearing, I drove a punch into the man's belly. Mouth gaping like a fish in a net, he sagged back into Rhys's embrace. Quickly, Rhys hooked his arms under the man's from behind, bringing his hands up and around the back of the other's neck, where he clenched them together. This vice-like hold was almost impossible to break, but I laid my dagger tip under the man's left eyeball, nonetheless. Chest heaving, he stared at it, at me, at it again.

'Shout, and it will be the last thing you do,' I hissed.

His spade-shaped beard went up and down as he nodded, terrified.

'You are Henry, a man-at-arms?'

Again he indicated yes.

'Do you know me?' I demanded, shoving my face into his.

He shook his head, but I had seen the flicker of recognition. He was lying.

'You had words with Robert FitzAldelm, a knight, a few months ago.' The royal party had passed through Southampton before the king's coronation; my enemy had used his time here well. If there had been any doubt in my mind, the naked fear I saw in Henry was my answer. He *was* the man I sought, I decided, continuing, 'FitzAldelm was asking about the death of his brother, seven years ago, outside a nearby inn.'

That night, I had slain one FitzAldelm brother, and earned the lifelong enmity of the other – Robert. I was here to ensure that his witness, Henry, could not threaten my position at the royal court.

I pricked Henry with the dagger tip. 'Well?'

'I spoke with FitzAldelm, yes, sir.'

'You claimed to have seen me – *me* – near the same inn.'

'Y-you, sir?' He could not meet my gaze.

I seized his chin and forced his head up. 'So FitzAldelm says.'

His eyes flashed to mine, and away. 'I was m-mistaken, sir. It was a long time ago. My memory is not what it was.'

'You have never met me in your life, and so you will swear if anyone asks.'

'Gladly, sir,' he babbled. 'Gladly.'

'This shall be payment for your silence.' I tugged free the purse that had been on my belt since London and dangled it before him. 'Three years' pay for a man-at-arms it holds.'

For the first time, the trace of a smile. 'Not a word shall pass my lips, sir, I swear it on my soul. Satan take me if I lie.'

The moment was here, the one I had dreaded since deciding to hunt down the only witness – apart from FitzAldelm – who knew or suspected my deep-buried secret. Yet reluctant, I glanced at Rhys. Face dark with suspicion, he gave me an 'I do not believe him' look. I moved my attention back to Henry, who gave me an ingratiating smile.

I thought of FitzAldelm, and his burning malice. He would not meekly accept Henry's changed position. 'You have a wife and child,' I said, thanking God that they were not here.

Utter terror blossomed on his face. 'Yes, sir. The babe is but three months old. Our firstborn, a boy. They have gone to visit her mother.'

'How close?'

'The other side of the town, sir.'

'When will they be back?'

'Not until the morning, sir.'

Relieved beyond measure, I asked, 'Do you care for them?'

'Yes, sir.' His voice shook. 'They are everything to me. Do not hurt them, I beg you!'

Revulsion filled me, that he thought I was capable of threatening two innocents' lives. I reached a sudden decision. 'They shall come to no harm,' I said. 'I swear it, by Christ on the cross.'

As Henry sobbed with relief, I exchanged an odd look with Rhys.

Then my dagger swept across Henry's throat, left to right.

His eyes – bright with shock and pain – met mine. He could not speak. Nor could I. Warm blood showered me. Henry bucked and strained, but Rhys held him fast. The life in him faded, and he sagged towards the floor. There was a soft thump as Rhys let go.

As if it knew its master's fate, the dog whined.

Now Rhys and I stared at each other over Henry's corpse. My hands were shaking. 'I killed him.'

'You did.' Rhys's tone was matter-of-fact.

'I—' I looked at my red-stained hands, my blood-soaked tunic. I touched my cheek, and my finger came away sticky. Shame and grief lashed me. 'What have I done?'

'Sir.'

Rhys had never addressed me so. I looked at him, stunned by the ruthless determination in his face.

'FitzAldelm would have put Henry's feet in a fire if he had gone back on his word, you know that. He would have sung like a caged bird.'

Miserable, I nodded.

'The purse of silver was a sop. A pretence.'

I listened, like a child having something simple explained to him.

'Killing him was the *only* choice we had.'

Not true, I thought. I could have done nothing. FitzAldelm's attempt to blacken my name with Henry's testimony might have failed. Rhys would have made a plausible witness in my favour; he was also known to the king. Henry, on the other hand, was a nobody. A nobody with a wife and baby son, my conscience screamed.

Dragged back to gory reality by Rhys, I did as he ordered. The deed was done, he said, and it served no one if we took the blame. I made no argument as we cleaned up the worst of the blood, and wrapped Henry in the blanket that covered his straw pallet. Then followed the grimmest of times, a wait by his cooling corpse until we could stir abroad without being seen.

Mind numbed by the horror of it all, I continued to let Rhys lead. Never before had I entombed a man in the depths of a midden, and returned, dressed in his spare clothing, to bury my own. Never before had I fed the dog of a man I had murdered. I stood in the little house, watching it devour a hunk of cheese that had lain on the table.

'We must go.' Rhys, calm as ever, was at my elbow. 'Dawn is not far off.' He handed me my mantle.

This was some small blessing, I thought. We had both taken ours off earlier, accidentally ensuring that our outer clothing was free of tell-tale bloodstains. I swung mine around my shoulders.

Its bread finished, the dog gave me an expectant look.

I thought of Henry's wife, who with her man dead, would soon go hungry. With a soft chink, I laid the purse on the table. It would last more than three years if she were careful. The coin would not bring her husband back, I told myself, but it was better than nothing.

The knowledge lessened my guilt not a whit.

PART ONE

NOVEMBER 1189–JULY 1190

CHAPTER I

London

Richard looked up from the mound of documents on the table before him. His mighty frame was ill-suited to perching on a stool, yet still he appeared kinglike, clad in a dark red tunic, fine hose and leather boots. Weak sunlight lanced in from the windows, burnishing his mane of red-gold hair. He frowned. 'God's legs, Rufus, you look terrible! Are you ill?'

I hesitated. In truth, I had been plagued with guilt since Henry's death. Royal business completed in Southampton – the delivering of important messages from Richard to his ships' captains there – Rhys and I had ridden back to court. Now all eyes were on me: the king's, those of William Marshal, one of his trusted advisers, the justiciar William Longchamp, my enemy FitzAldelm, several clerks. Even the pages standing by with flagons of wine were staring.

'I am well enough, sire, thank you. It is poor weather for travelling – I caught a chill.' I coughed, realistically, I hoped.

Satisfied, Richard asked, 'You delivered the letters?'

'I did, sire, and brought the captains' responses.' I handed the rolled parchments to a page, who ran them over to the king.

'Get you to bed then. I cannot have one of my best knights taken ill.' Richard's secretary had cracked the first seal and was already unrolling the letter, preparing to read it to the king.

Since his coronation in September, his only focus had been the raising of funds, and the organisation of his long-planned campaign in the Holy Land. The joke went that everything in his kingdom was for sale: powers, lordships, earldoms, sheriffdoms, castles, towns and manors. Not a day passed without his palace being thronged with lords and bishops seeking to retain what they already had, or trying to better themselves by securing new titles and lands.

Grateful that his attention had moved on, I muttered my thanks and withdrew.

FitzAldelm, fresh-returned from a mission to meet the new Scottish king William, threw me a look of pure spite. My hatred pricked, but not as it had before. Guilt savaged me next. Murderer, I thought. I am a murderer. I was doubly damned, because I had no wish to undo Henry's killing. FitzAldelm now had no grounds to accuse me of killing his brother.

Richard called after me to rest as long as I needed.

I needed a priest, not my bed, I thought. So great was my burden, however, that I could not contemplate confessing. My guilt was my own, deserved punishment for what I had done. Something to be borne in silence.

For his part, Rhys was unaffected by our actions, but he knew my mind. He guided me to a tavern in the stews, where he bought jug after jug of wine. Southampton was not mentioned. We spoke instead of Outremer – the Holy Land – and the battles to be won there. We sang too, bawdy tunes plucked out by a minstrel on a gittern; these lifted my mood somewhat. Rhys's steady arm supported me as I staggered back to the palace. I do not remember him putting me to bed, but he must have done, for that is where I found myself the next day with a pounding head. Grateful not to have to attend the king – his command had been to get well, and I was not – I stayed under the blankets and felt sorry for myself. Rhys's patience ran thin in the end. Leaving a chamber pot and a jug of water by the bed, he left me to my misery. I had not the energy or the heart to call him back, still less issue a reprimand.

I fell asleep again, to be tormented by Henry's last words, endlessly repeated, 'They are everything to me. Do not hurt them, I beg you!' Again I saw him in Rhys's tight grip, and my knife opening his throat. Jerking awake, my stomach heaving, I lunged for the pot and brought up the water I had drunk not long before. Face cold with sweat, drool hanging from my lips, I remained slumped over the side of the bed, too miserable to stir.

Not even the pad of footsteps entering the room made me lift my head. It would be Rhys, I thought blearily, or perhaps the man-at-arms Richard de Drune, another friend and comrade. He would poke fun, as would Philip, if it were he who had come. Squire to the king as I had been, he was the closest of my friends, someone I shared almost everything with. I wondered if I could tell him about Southampton, but imagining his shock and revulsion, I decided against it. Henry's murder was my dark secret, and Rhys's.

'Drank too much again, did you?' A soft laugh.

Surprised – Beatrice did not often risk coming to my quarters alone, for to be seen without a chaperone risked her reputation – I lifted my head. 'My lady.' I wiped my mouth, and tried to smile. 'One cup too many perhaps.'

Chestnut-haired, possessed of a voluptuous figure and a wicked smile, Beatrice was servant to one of Queen Alienor's ladies. I had begun courting her two years before. Despite the periods when we were apart, she with her mistress and I with the king, we had rekindled our passions each time fortune brought us together. Meeting in secret, in stables or rented rooms above inns, we did everything but lie together as man and woman. On this final barrier Beatrice would not budge. 'When we are wedded, Rufus,' she had been fond of saying. Her eyes would search mine, and I, God forgive me, would murmur in her ear that if we were to be husband and wife, then we could—

'Rufus?'

I had not taken in a word of what she had been saying. 'My lady?'

'Rufus!' She stamped her foot. Normally I found this attractive, but now it seemed petulant. 'You are in no fit state to talk of important matters.'

Her tone reminded me that of recent months, we had argued frequently. She had become obsessed with marriage, and I, the stark realisation that she was not the woman for me loud in my mind, had come up with every conceivable excuse to avoid committing myself.

I sat up, assumed a serious face. 'I am, my lady. Your pardon.'

Mollified, she said, 'I said, you will be leaving soon. For the Holy Land.'

To my relief, the nausea was subsiding. 'Spring at the latest, but probably sooner.' The king was talking of meeting Philippe of France before the year's end, to plan their journeys to Outremer and to deal with many other concerns. Once we had travelled to Normandy, it was unlikely we would come back to England. It was by no means certain that Queen Alienor would join us.

'I will not see you again for at least a year. Or longer.'

Her voice caught, tugging at my heart. 'That is true, my lady.'

'There *is* time for a betrothal and a wedding.' She continued coyly, 'As man and wife, we could *know* each other at last.'

'We could . . .' Bleary-eyed, furry-tongued, I stared at her. Pretty though she was, there was a possessive slant to her expression that I did not like.

'Do you think the king would attend?' she asked.

My mind was still fuddled. 'Attend . . .?'

'Our wedding!'

Sweet Jesu, I thought. I had previously had the feeling that she valued my relationship with the king, my position at court, more than what we had together. This was proof. My impending departure for Outremer afforded me the opportunity to end our dalliance. The thought of that pricked my heart, not from grief but the memory of Alienor, my first love. Her I would have sworn my troth to, in a heart-beat, and wedded her upon my return from the Holy Land. Sadly, there was no chance of that. She had followed her mistress, Richard's sister Matilda, to Germany years before, and the death earlier in the year of Matilda made the slim chance of ever tracking her down all but impossible.

'Say something!'

'Beatrice, I—'

'You do not *want* to marry me?'

I hung my head, which was of course, exactly the wrong thing to do.

'Well?' Her voice was waspish.

Even at my best, I struggled to deal with Beatrice – or any woman – when they became emotional. My head pounding like a drum, I flailed for what to say. Tell the truth, and I would break her heart. Murderer though I was, I recoiled from that. Gently, I lied, 'I could wish for nothing more, my love, but there is a good chance that I will fall in battle.'

'Do not say that!' She sat by me on the bed, and took my hand. There were tears in her eyes.

'It is true, my lady.' Speaking the truth hardened my resolve to end things between us, and this seemed a promising way. 'I would not have you a widow mere months after our wedding.'

'Other knights are marrying before you leave!'

She was right. I could name two without even thinking. Let her accept it, please, I thought. 'Are they as close to the king? You know what a lion he is in battle, Beatrice. Wherever the fighting is thickest, Richard will be there, and so will I. Death and I will walk hand in hand in Outremer.'

Her face paled. 'You are scaring me, Rufus. Do you seek to die?'

How strange it is when someone, unknowing, almost places a finger on the truth, harsh though it might be. 'If Death should find me, my lady, I shall meet it face-to-face.' It is what I deserve, I thought.

'Rufus!' Now her tears fell.

'Going our separate ways would be best.' I patted her shoulder as she began to sob. Uncomfortable with my dishonesty, I could not have been more grateful when de Drune walked in.

Beatrice pulled away. Composing herself, she threw me a venomous glance and muttered something about my wasting her time before stalking out the door.

De Drune began whistling, his face angelic. 'Did I disturb you?'

'In a manner of speaking.' I felt drained, spent.

He handed over a costrel. 'Hair of the dog.'

I swallowed a good quarter of it ere he stopped me. 'That cost a pretty penny,' he protested. 'It is none of that English vinegar that a man has to drink with closed eyes and clenched teeth.'

'You deserve to lose the lot for strolling in like that,' I growled in mock anger.

'How was I to know you were hoping to make the beast with two backs?' Like Philip, de Drune knew of my romantic strivings with Beatrice, and my lack of success with the final hurdle.

I snorted.

'That was not about to happen?'

I sighed. 'No.'

He made an apologetic face. 'A shame.'

'I think not.' Passions subsiding before my headache, common sense was seeping back.

'How so?'

'If I had ever lain with her, she would have sunk her claws into me for good.'

De Drune gave me a searching look.

'Beatrice wanted us to wed. Before we leave for Outremer.'

'And you are not of the same mind.'

I shook my head as vehemently as the pain would allow. 'I had just told her so when you walked in.'

'A wise move. God knows how long we shall be gone.'

'If we come back at all,' I said, thinking of Henry, and the release death would grant me.

He scowled. 'Less of that kind of talk. I for one have every intention of returning from the Holy Land. I shall be a wealthy man, God willing.'

Glad to be taken from my dark thoughts, I asked, 'What will you do?'

'Time waits for no man, they say.' He cast me a look. 'I have a mind to settle down, open an inn, maybe.'

I grinned. 'With free ale for old comrades?'

'I did not say that.'

We laughed, and he made no protest when I reached for the costrel again.

If only relationships with women were as easy as those with sword comrades.

Richard's preparations continued apace as Christmas drew closer. His attention to detail continued to astound me. He could remember the number of horseshoes ordered from such a town, 'Fifty thousand from the ironworks at the Forest of Dean,' and how many wagon wheels another lord had promised to supply. Possessed of a boundless energy, he would pace up and down, reeling off lists of figures, names of ships, their crew sizes and the provisions they needed, while his clerks and officers desperately rummaged through scrolls and parchments to corroborate the information.

Taken piecemeal, I could relate to the constituents of the king's upcoming campaign. One hundred thousand nails here. Twenty score barrels of salted pork there. Two palfreys and two sumpter horses from every city in England, and half that number from every manor. A dozen knights and ten score archers, and the quantity of their weapons and arrows, from that baron; ten knights and a hundred and fifty men-at-arms from another. One figure stuck in my mind long after the rest. Fourteen thousand pounds, more than half the annual royal revenue from England, was the sum paid for Richard's fleet of one hundred ships. The sum was beyond comprehension, but it brought home the sheer size of the enterprise I was part of, and increased my belief – already strong – that we would succeed.

Provisioning his army was not the last of Richard's concerns. The kingdom had to be maintained during his absence. His lady mother Queen Alienor would oversee affairs: the king met with her often, and she sat in on many a meeting with his lords and advisers. She intervened directly when needed – on one recent occasion preventing an unwanted papal legate from leaving Dover without the king's permission – and acted as a steadying presence in the background. The majority of the work would be done by Richard's two new justiciars, however. Replacing his father Henry's long-serving chief minister, Richard had stamped his own authority by appointing as justiciars Hugh de Puiset, bishop of Durham for many years, and William Longchamp, the bishop of Ely.

One blustery morning, several days before we were to depart for Normandy, I was attending the king, who had summoned the pair. They arrived almost at the same time, and their entrance boded ill. De Puiset, tall and lithe, made to pass the threshold first, but Longchamp, short and stout, did the same. For a moment, they both blocked the doorway, each casting hostile sidelong glances at the other, and then Longchamp pushed past, leaving de Puiset glaring at his back.

'Mark them. Like two squabbling children,' said Richard.

'I am minded of my brothers, sire.' My heart twinged for my long-dead kin. It was scant consolation that Guy FitzAldelm, the man responsible, and whom I had slain in Southampton, was also mouldering in a grave. This was no time to brood, I told myself. I studied the two justiciars, de Puiset hurrying to catch Longchamp so he should not reach the king first. 'There is little love lost between them.'

Richard let out a sigh. 'Yet these two are to share the rule of the realm while I am in the Holy Land.'

I made no reply. It was not for me to pass further judgement on men who stood higher in the king's favour than I.

Richard acknowledged the pair's bows, and gestured at the stools which had been placed opposite him. 'To business, my lords,' he said.

I listened with more than my usual interest. Their discussion involved not barrels of nails and horseshoes, but the king's half-brother

Geoffrey and his youngest brother, John, formerly known by the mocking name of 'Lackland', but since the coronation as the Count of Mortain in Normandy.

Geoffrey, some five years older than Richard, had remained loyal to their father Henry right to the end. An illegitimate son, he had no claim to the throne, yet, I thought, it would not be strange if Geoffrey had aspirations beyond his station. Had not William the Conqueror begun life as William the Bastard?

John was different. As Richard's only living brother, he was closest to the throne. He was a spiteful and unpleasant individual, forever scheming or whispering in men's ears. I had disliked him from the first moment we locked eyes; unfortunately, the feeling was mutual.

The matter was not quite as black-and-white as I saw it, however. Richard was unwed, and had no recognised children. It made sense to make his peace with oily-tongued John, but as with Geoffrey, his trust – and for certes, mine – did not go far.

My attention was drawn back to the conversation.

'Geoffrey may not have wanted to become a priest, sire, but he did allow himself to be ordained,' said Longchamp.

'Protesting loudly,' De Puiset added. 'I seem to recall he once said that he preferred horses and dogs to books and priests.'

This amused me, for I felt the same way.

'You speak true,' said Richard, with a dangerous glint in his eye. 'Once also he placed the lid of a golden bowl on his head and asked his friends if a crown would not suit him. It is well that Geoffrey is now a priest and archbishop both.'

'Nonetheless, it is wise to consider banning him from England for the duration of your absence, sire,' said Longchamp.

'And John? Would it be right to do the same to him?' demanded Richard.

The justiciars shared a look. I understood the wariness in it. Although Richard had spoken much of also banishing John, this suggested he might be having doubts. Few men liked to disagree with the king, however.

'Well?' Richard barked, his gaze roving from one to the other.

'Has doubt crept into your mind, sire?' asked Longchamp, subtly turning the question back at the king. 'I wonder if you have talked of this with your lady mother.'

'I have,' admitted Richard.

De Puiset was quick-minded too. 'It would not surprise me, sire, if she, with a mother's love, thinks that John should be given a second chance.'

Richard snorted. 'Were you eavesdropping?'

'Nay, sire.' De Puiset let out a polite laugh, but he looked pleased.

Longchamp would not let de Puiset keep the initiative. 'Mayhap, sire, the queen worries what might happen if something were to befall you in Outremer – God forbid – and John were languishing in Normandy or Anjou instead of England. An empty throne would tempt many's the man.'

Richard chuckled. 'God's legs, you were listening as well! I tell you, nothing will happen to me during this campaign.'

His conviction was infectious, but the tribulations and dangers that lay ahead were myriad: storms at sea, disease, injury, capture, even death. Silently, I asked God to keep his hand over my lord and king.

'Nonetheless, sire, it is best to plan for all eventualities,' said de Puiset, with Longchamp muttering his agreement. De Puiset continued, 'And if anything untoward should occur, John would presumably be your heir, sire.'

'Correct.' Richard frowned. 'Yet he has not earned my trust. I can understand, though, why some think it wise that he return to England when I leave.'

De Puiset nodded, but Longchamp looked less than happy.

He does not wish his power diminished, I thought.

'I – we shall follow your every wish, sire,' said Longchamp. 'Whatever you decide, fear not. Your kingdom is in safe hands.'

'I am glad to hear it.' Sarcasm dripped from Richard's voice.

Longchamp gave him a pasty smile. De Puiset's face remained expressionless, but the rebuke had brought a flash of pleasure to his eyes.

A silence fell, which neither justiciar chose to break.

'I shall continue to think on it,' Richard declared at last. 'Time is on our side still. You may go.' A glance over his shoulder. 'Rufus, let us ride out together. My head is filled with cobwebs. Only fresh air will suffice to clear it.'

'Sire.' I was delighted. A mountain of parchments now awaited the king's attention, and the queue of nobles and officials outside the chamber numbered a score at the least. Hours of dreariness faced us.

Bidding farewell to the justiciars, the king and I made for the stables. We had no need of our destriers, being unarmoured, but they needed regular riding out. Being kept inside all winter was good for no horse, Richard declared, let alone the magnificent beasts that we rode to war. I took Pommers, and the king the destrier he had been using since the death of his favourite Diablo. A mighty, high-spirited bay with feathered fetlocks called Tempest, he was fond of nipping anyone, man or horse, who came near.

Hoods of our mantles raised, the plumes of our breath whipped away by the wind, we clattered out of the still-frosty courtyard and down towards the river. Rhys and Philip rode behind us on Oxhead – my second warhorse – and another of the king's destriers. Those on foot scrambled to get out of our way; more than one curse was thrown after us. I hoped that Richard had not noticed; I had no wish to punish someone for their ignorance of who had passed by. He laughed, however, and I realised he enjoyed the all too rare anonymity.

We rode in silence, I content not to speak if the king did not, and he in a contemplative mood. Close to the river we passed, aiming for the city walls, and soon reached open countryside. Clouds raced overhead, glimpses of blue a reminder that the sun was up there somewhere. Smoke trickling from the roof of a farmhouse was snatched away. Although the trees were leafless and brown, the hedges a muted green, and the road a sea of mud, there was a freshness in the wintry, yellow-tinged air. A dog barked in the distance. Jackdaws chattered and scolded one another from a nearby copse, and a bright-eyed robin watched us from a holly bush laden with berries. A hare picked a path through the stubble in a field. Two red-cheeked boys collecting fallen wood waved at us.

''Tis good to be away from it all, Rufus,' said Richard. 'A day like this is food for the soul.'

I stared at him in surprise, for he did not often wax lyrical.

'It is easy to love the land in spring and summer, when everything is green and flowering, but wintertime also has its beauty.'

'It does, sire. A crisp day like this makes the rainy days more bearable.'

'Remember it well, for we shall not see a proper winter again for God knows how long.' Richard's mood had become business-like again. 'Our jaunt needs must be brief, sadly. Let us to the wood before we turn around.'

We rode on. My gaze went back to the hare, which had not yet reached the field's edge. 'If the wind calmed but a little, it would be a fine day for loosing a hawk at yon creature.'

A smile. 'You are becoming one of us, Rufus.'

He had not meant to discomfit me, but I shifted in my saddle. More than a decade had passed since my forced departure from Ireland. Dreams of returning came less often. I wanted to become Lord of Cairlinn, my family's former lands, but that desire no longer coursed through my veins as it once had. A different type of guilt battered me. This was no way to honour my father and mother, who had been so foully murdered.

'I spoke not to chide you, Ferdia, but in affection.'

'Yes, sire.' There was more, I thought. He tended to call me by my given name only when he was in a serious mood.

'You are my sworn man, Ferdia; you have also taken the cross. Unless you are without honour – and I know you are not – there is no way back to Ireland at this time.'

Startled by his insight, I met his gaze. 'You knew I was thinking of Cairlinn, sire?'

'Most of the time, your face is like an open book.' He laughed, that infectious belly laugh which erupted from him when he was much amused.

I felt my cheeks flame as they had when I was a stripling youth. I had always tried to copy Richard, a master at concealing his emotions, but it was plain I had much yet to learn.

'God made you that way, Ferdia. It is no bad thing.'

This was how Beatrice saw through me with such ease, I thought ruefully.

'My brother John, now, he is cut from different cloth.' Richard's voice had taken on a weary note. 'He has sworn fealty to me, like you. You, I would trust with my life, for example, but he . . .' His words tailed away.

I could not have agreed more: to me, John was a snake.

The king gave me a questioning look.

I hesitated, torn, but forced to make a decision on the instant, I swallowed my opinion. My dislike of John was personal, I told myself. He had never actually done anything to me. 'If your lady mother trusts him, sire, maybe you should too.'

'Ha! I know not if even *she* trusts John, but she believes he ought to be given a second chance. Mother's love, Ferdia. There is nothing stronger, and at times, nothing more blind.'

If the king had any children, I thought, John would be less of a concern. It was a delicate subject, for Richard had been pledged to Philippe Capet's sister Alys for many years, but never seemed inclined to complete the arrangement. 'If you were to marry, sire, and have a child of your own . . .'

'God's legs, art as bad as my mother,' cried Richard, but he was smiling. 'But it is true that a king needs a wife and more important, an heir. Happily, I have high hopes in that regard. An arrangement with one of the northern Spanish kingdoms would kill two birds with one stone, bringing me a wife, and giving me an ally in the south against the Count of Toulouse. I am told that Sancho of Navarre has a daughter of suitable age. We shall soon travel south to meet with him. God willing, I will be betrothed to his daughter ere we part company.'

'And Philippe, sire?' I had no need to mention the name Alys.

He shot me a keen glance. 'I will deal with him when the campaign is well underway, and he has no means of reneging on his promise and returning home.'

'He will not be pleased, sire.'

'Nor will he, but every man has a price. I shall have to find what Philippe's is.'

I decided that my concerns with Beatrice were trifling in comparison with the king's.

'Here is the wood,' Richard announced. 'We must get back.'

'To books and accounts,' I said wearily, wishing I was already in Outremer.

He chuckled. 'They are a curse, it is true. I would have liked nothing better than to set them aside and leave for the Holy Land the day after my coronation. But careful planning is vital in war, as in everything else.'

'I would prefer to charge a line of Saracens alone than deal with the mounds of parchment on your desk, sire.'

'So would I.'

I grinned.

'When the day comes to face the Turks, as it will, we shall ride at the enemy together.'

Basking in the king's favour, mind full of glorious images of battle, I forgot about Beatrice. FitzAldelm. Henry.

All that mattered was the war against the Saracens.

CHAPTER II

Nonancourt, Normandy, March 1190

Spatters of rain hit my face as Philip and I reached the bottom of the stairs that led up to the great hall, and I glanced skyward. I had decided there was time to reach the kitchen without a cloak. Now I was not so sure. A great bank of black cloud loomed over the keep; thunder rumbled. Apart from a lad hurrying a horse into a stable, the bailey was empty. Faces peered from the forge, the workshops, awaiting the deluge.

'Best hurry,' I said.

Philip needed no encouraging, for like me, he was clad in tunic and hose. He took to his heels, and sensing the challenge, I leaped after him. In a heartbeat, we were like small boys, running pell-mell in an impromptu race. Thanks to his head start, I was unable to catch him, and he crowed with delight to reach the kitchen door first. I was glad just to gain cover as the heavens opened.

'Too much time spent at table, Rufus, and not enough at the quintain,' he said, entering.

I shoved him. 'You cheated! We did not start together.'

'Is that a paunch I see?' He poked at my midriff.

Stung, for there was a little more flesh there than before, I growled and wrapped an arm around his head. 'I still have the beating of you, you pup!'

He wrestled free, laughing. 'With a sword perhaps. In a footrace, never.'

He was probably right, although I did not like to admit it. There had been little time since London for exercise or weapons practice. As a squire, Philip was freer to attend to his own training, while I, a close companion to the king, was busy from dawn to dusk with meetings, messages to be carried, and officials to instruct. Not only that. We rarely stayed anywhere for more than a sennight. I could scarce remember where I was each morning. In other circumstances, this constant change would have soon palled, but the rising excitement in the court about our departure for Outremer was infectious.

On the eleventh of December we had crossed the Narrow Sea from Dover. Christmas was spent at Burun in Normandy; an enjoyable time of overeating and drinking. A few days after, however, there had been a tense meeting with Philippe Capet. Both kings had agreed to a lasting peace while they were away, making no attempt on one another's territory, and binding their barons to do the same. Richard had again pledged his troth to Alys, Philippe's sister, this just days after he had told me of his plans to wed King Sancho of Navarre's daughter. He was walking on a knife edge; one slip, and the French monarch might withdraw from the campaign, and after that, declare war. Richard seemed convinced that he could pull it off, however, and I told myself he knew best.

By Candlemas, we had moved south to La Réole on the banks of the Garonne, where Richard received anew the allegiance of his Gascon lords. Planned discussions regarding the king's intention to marry Sancho VI of Navarre's daughter Berengaria had been prevented by the snows that blocked the Pyrenees mountains, but overtures had been sent by ship. From La Réole we had ridden here to Nonancourt, arriving two days before. Richard had called a great conference, which was to be attended by his mother Queen Alienor, his brothers Geoffrey and John, William Longchamp, Hugh de Puiset and a host of other bishops. Almost everyone was here. The great hall was full to bursting. Not an hour since, I had spied the two justiciars squabbling; Richard's concerns about their rule of England was well-placed.

Threading our way past the servants washing pots and pans at the sinks, we made for the ovens. We were well-known, often coming down in search of fresh bread or pies. I had made sure of a constant welcome by slipping the head cooks a few silver pennies each the day of our arrival. Securing chicken and raisin pastries for ourselves, we retreated to the side of the doorway, there to watch the rain as we ate.

A hooded figure came down the steps. Near the bottom, a gust of wind tore back the cowl, revealing for an instant the block head of FitzAldelm. Rather than approach the kitchen, however, he slipped through an entrance that led to the basement under the great hall. There lay cellars for wine and foodstuffs, storage rooms, and cells that served as dungeons. It was odd that FitzAldelm had come outside, thereby risking a drenching. Anyone else would have taken the internal staircase from the great hall. I said as much to Philip, who agreed.

'I will go and see,' he suggested.

Touched, for FitzAldelm was his enemy only because he was mine, I gripped his arm in thanks. 'If he saw me in there, he would know I was spying on him.'

'Whereas I, a squire, could be there for any number of reasons,' said Philip, winking. Munching on the last of his pastry, he dashed out into the rain.

A short wait, and the cloud burst that had turned the bailey into a sea of puddles had finished. Keeping close to the wall, I reached the steps with my feet still dry. From the nearby abbey, the bells tolled tierce. Up I went, two and three stairs at a time. There was plenty yet to be done before the conference called by Richard began, enough to take my mind from FitzAldelm and his devilry.

The great hall had been cleared, all the tables moved by servants to the side walls, save a long one in the centre of the room. Cushions on the benches meant that royal and bishop alike did not have to sit on hard wood. Fresh rushes and scatterings of dried herbs covered the flagstones. A fire roared in the huge central hearth, keeping those close to it pleasantly warm, even too hot. Those further away would feel draughts aplenty. Wind rattled the shuttered windows, and each time the door at the far end of the hall opened, a great waft of cold air swept towards us.

Almost everyone was here. Richard's place was empty, for he was pacing about with Henri of Blois, the Count of Champagne, a fair-haired young man in the odd position of being nephew to both Richard and Philippe Capet. Amiable and quick to laugh, he seemed a good type, and the king liked him. Henri was to travel to the Holy Land within days, his task to aid the siege of Acre, the coastal city lost to the Saracens almost three years before. Like almost every Christian-held stronghold, it had fallen soon after the disastrous battle at the Horns of Hattin.

Spaces had been kept for Richard's mother and Alys, his betrothed, to the right of where he would sit. Unobtrusive, Philip waited a few steps to the rear. Beyond the empty places was Geoffrey, the king's half-brother and Archbishop of York. He was deep in conversation with the bishops of Norwich, Bath and Winchester, and studiously ignoring Hugh de Puiset, the bishop of Durham, seated opposite. He in turn pretended not to see William Longchamp the chancellor, bishop of Ely and his fellow justiciar, who was seated just past Hubert, the bishop of Salisbury, and talking to William Marshal and *his* brother John.

The presence of so many high-ranking clerics scraped raw again the weeping wound on my soul. I had considered confessing to Henry's murder to one of the bishops, but swiftly set the idea aside. My repentance might convince a cleric, but God would know me for a liar. Feeling wretched, I diverted myself by again studying those present.

To the left of Richard's place was John, his brother and Count of Mortain. Dark, red-haired, slight, and with a tendency to paunchiness, he retained none of the king's presence or majesty. John was keeping his own counsel, supping often from his cup as his snake eyes wandered around the gathering. The bishop beside him seemed content to leave well alone, instead speaking with his fellow religious and the nobles on the other side of the table.

John made me think of FitzAldelm, and I moved my own gaze casually to my enemy. He, like me, stood with Baldwin de Béthune, André de Chauvigny and a group of mesnie knights and officials, facing the king's place at the table, and a respectable distance back from it. We were to be allowed to witness the conference, but not participate. FitzAldelm was talking to Odo de Gunesse, a crony of his who had joined the mesnie. Charming, and a fine fighter, which explained his invitation from Richard, de Gunesse was also as sly as a fox. That was a side I doubted the king had ever seen. I only had because I had once overheard him and FitzAldelm talking. There was no doubt in my mind that de Gunesse would also be capable of murder.

The door from the private quarters at the near end of the hall opened. A steward emerged, crying, 'Queen Alienor!' in a loud voice. He also announced Alys, sister to Philippe Capet.

There was no mention of her betrothal to the king, a detail I noted. Before Richard could marry Berengaria, he had to disengage himself from the twenty-year-long arrangement with Alys, a thorny prospect that risked war with France. This legal quagmire, I had heard Richard disclose to de Chauvigny, was the reason for inviting so many bishops to the conference. To solve his dilemma, every aspect of dynastic marriage and the minutiae of canon law would have to be discussed. 'They will stay at the table until I get what I want,' the king had declared. Of Alys's feelings, he made no mention, but I knew that they had spoken in private since her arrival. I did not envy her her position, a pawn between two kings.

Everyone at the table stood. Richard hurried to accompany his mother to her seat. He made a quiet greeting to Alys, who walked demurely behind Alienor. We all bowed as the queen reached us, a vision in a dark green gown, with her hair held up by a gossamer-fine gold hair net. Still a beauty despite her age, the picture of dignity and majesty, she smiled as the king fussed over the placing of her cushion. He paid the same attention to Alys, pretty but reserved in a sky blue dress. I wondered if the rumours about her having an affair with the king's father Henry when he was still alive were true.

Taking his own place, Richard began without preamble. There was much to talk about, he said, but he would start with the most pressing matters.

'Since my departure from England, it seems that my justiciars have been, if not at each other's throats, then strongly disagreeing.' He stared at de Puiset, and then Longchamp. The former flushed, but the latter looked unsurprised.

He knows what is about to happen, I thought. Richard has told him.

'The thing that pleased one of you, I am told, always displeased the other,' said Richard.

De Puiset coughed. 'It is true to say, sire, that we have not agreed on much.'

Richard's eyes moved to Longchamp.

Smooth as oil, he said, '*I* concurred with several of de Puiset's plans, sire, whereas he—'

Richard raised a hand, silencing the chancellor. 'I have not the time or patience to listen to either of you. If this is how matters stand when I am only across the Narrow Sea, I dread to think what might happen by the time I reach Outremer. From this day forward, the rule of my kingdom shall be divided in twain. You, de Puiset, shall be justiciar from the River Humber north to the Scottish border. Longchamp, you shall have authority of the rest of England.'

While Longchamp, smiling like a cat given a bowl of cream, offered his gratitude, de Puiset's face turned bright red. 'Have I displeased you, sire, to be given this position?' He made the last word sound contemptible.

'Are you saying that you do not want it?'

Wrongfooted, de Puiset stammered, 'N-no, sire!'

'Take what you have been given then, and be grateful.'

Impotent before the king's authority, de Puiset muttered his thanks. He shot a murderous glance at Longchamp.

The chancellor's star continued its ascent as Richard declared that messages would be sent to Pope Clement, requesting he be made legate of England and Scotland, the highest church position available. The king also ordered Longchamp to have a deep moat dug around the Tower of London, to augment its defences.

Matters moved on to Geoffrey, Richard's half-brother, and the king's manner grew even brusquer. It was no surprise. Just a few months before, on the eve of our departure from England, he had had to resolve a bitter dispute involving Geoffrey, de Puiset, and several other bishops and high church officials. Since Christmas, the argument had rumbled on and on, incensing the king so much he had confiscated some of Geoffrey's estates.

'If this is about the monies I owe you,' Geoffrey began.

'It is not,' said Richard, cutting across him. 'There is no other way to say this, Geoff. I want you to take an oath on the Holy Evangelists that you will not set foot on English soil for the next three years, except with my permission.'

Geoffrey all but spat out a mouthful of wine.

'Accept my will, brother. I shall have it no other way.'

'Yes, sire.' Geoffrey's voice was strangled, his face anguished, but he dared not protest.

Richard leaned forward to regard his younger brother. 'You shall make the same pledge.'

John looked pained. 'You would have me remain in Normandy or Anjou for the entire time you are away, sire?'

'I would.'

'You go to war, brother. Apart from injury or death in battle, you will risk storms at sea, disease in camp and capture by the enemy.'

'I go not just to war, but to free Jerusalem from the Saracens,' Richard chided.

'And we all here hope and pray you succeed,' said John, sounding remarkably genuine. 'Nonetheless, the risks are considerable. God willing, none of these misfortunes will befall you, but *if they should*, you will need loyal servants in England to secure the throne.'

'And I have them,' said Richard. 'Longchamp, de Puiset, Marshal, Bardolph, FitzPeter and Bruyère.' In addition to the two senior justiciars, he had named William Marshal and his three co-justiciars, all of whom were present.

John's cheeks were pink. 'They are not your flesh and blood, sire!'

'Indeed they are not,' replied Richard. 'Our lady mother the queen is, however. She shall remain in England.'

Taken aback, John soon regained his composure. He glanced at Alienor. 'Is this decision to your liking?'

Looking uncomfortable, Alienor made no immediate answer.

'Your silence suggests you do not agree with Richard, Mama,' coaxed John.

Richard frowned.

'It is true I have reservations,' said Alienor. 'Your brother the king and I have spoken about this. We shall continue to take counsel, but in the meantime, I bid you to follow his command and take the oath.'

John's eyes glittered, but he nodded. 'Even so, Mama.' He glanced at Richard. 'I will swear your vow.'

Richard seemed satisfied.

There followed the beginnings of a discussion of canon law in relation to the king's betrothal to Alys, Philippe's sister. It was apparent from the outset that the intention was to extricate Richard – legally – from the arrangement. Alys soon grew discomfited. The king had the grace to look embarrassed when she mentioned not feeling well and asked his permission to retire; he granted her request at once. Alienor whispered in Alys's ear as she rose, and Alys managed a strained smile.

The poor creature, I thought, as she slipped away.

Philip poured more wine for the king and then made his way towards the buttery, at the far end of the hall. Wearied by the droning voices of bishop after bishop, I quietly went to join him.

Under the disapproving stare of the butler, who kept charge of the buttery, I helped myself to a silver beaker. Philip, knowing full well what I wanted, filled it to the brim from his renewed jug.

'God's toes, I will die from boredom ere the day is out,' I said, throwing back a mouthful.

A sniff from the butler. I glared at him, and he took a sudden interest in the slattern pushing a broom along the floor nearby.

'At least you can drink,' said Philip. 'I must needs stay sober.'

'My commiserations.' I saluted him with my cup.

He pulled a face. 'Taunt me again, and I will not tell you my news.'

His offer to follow FitzAldelm came flooding back. I moved away from the butler and the unfortunate girl with the broom, who was now on the end of a tongue-lashing. 'What did you see?'

Philip's expression grew conspiratorial. 'The reason FitzAldelm took the staircase was that John, no less, came down the internal one.'

'They did not want to be seen together!'

'Such would be my guess.'

'What were they talking about?'

'That was the most frustrating part. I followed them into the wine cellar, but I could not get close enough to hear a word.' Philip made a face. 'I am sorry, Rufus.'

I smiled my thanks. 'Apologise not – I could have done no better.'

'It does not look good. Why would they have need to meet in secret?'

Philip was usually a trusting soul. His suspicion gave credence to my own. 'Treason,' I said.

'Surely not?'

'A man like FitzAldelm is only out to feather his own nest. John is cut from the same cloth. Remember how he abandoned his dying father at the last, when Richard's victory could not be denied?'

'It was despicable.' Philip shook his head. 'Why did Richard accept John's fealty?'

'He shares the same weakness his father had. Henry forgave his sons time and again – Richard among them – when they rose against him. Letting John return to the fold is no different.'

'Do you think the king will allow John to travel to England?'

I thought of Richard's conversation with de Puiset and Longchamp in London. Of the regard he held for his mother. Of her hesitation when John had asked her opinion of the ban. 'Yes,' I said wearily. 'I think he might.'

It seemed as if the obstacles in Richard's path would never come to an end.

As if we might never be able to leave for Outremer.

*

Some days later, Richard met again with Philippe. I was there. The two kings' pledges not to threaten each other's kingdom while away at war were renewed, and the bishops vowed to excommunicate anyone who broke this agreement. Both sides were experiencing delays with their preparations to leave for Outremer, so it was agreed that instead of the first of April, the armies would meet at Vézelay on the feast of John the Baptist, the twenty-fourth of June. The meeting came to an unfortunate and unforeseen end thanks to the arrival of a mud-spattered, exhausted messenger. He had ridden with all speed from the French court, carrying terrible news. Queen Isabelle, Philippe's wife, had died in childbirth after delivering twin stillborn sons.

The French king left without even saying farewell. A sombre-faced Richard had watched him go. 'He is no friend of mine, Rufus,' he said to me. 'But I would not wish such tragedy on any man. May God watch over him.'

Few people ever saw the gentle side of Richard, but it was there.

Wrath replaced the king's sympathy not long after. We rode again, through Maine, Anjou and Poitou to Gascony, and the castle of a lord whose men had been preying on and robbing pilgrims on their way to Santiago de Compostela in Spain. After a brief siege, we stormed inside, killing any who gave resistance. The lord surrendered easily enough, expecting as a nobleman to be granted clemency.

Richard had him hung from his own battlements.

Royal justice dispensed, we resumed our journey south. We had ridden for less than a day when a messenger caught up with us. It was a common enough occurrence; with Richard ever on the move, important news had to be taken to him. Spending most of my days with the king, I was often party to the information they carried. In the main, it was boring, administrative concerns such as the allocation of an estate or forests to a lord, the appointment of a bishop, or the crewing details of ships that would carry us to Outremer.

Not that evening in April.

A letter from Queen Alienor arrived, detailing the brutal massacre of hundreds of Jews in York. For all that most people did not like them – Jews being the murderers of Christ – it was shocking news.

Richard was incandescent with fury, ranting about Longchamp's incompetency. 'He must deal with this, and severely! I cannot return to England, not now!'

I looked around. Men were talking in hushed voices, wary of the king, the horror of York weighing on their minds. FitzAldelm it was who I heard whispering none-too-quietly, 'More pity it is that every bloodsucking Jew in the realm was not slain so.' He glared when de Gunesse uttered something in reply. I pricked my ears, managing to hear de Gunesse say again, 'Your debts.' FitzAldelm told him to shut his mouth. I stored the little nugget of information away for another time. FitzAldelm was in debt to a Jewish moneylender somewhere in England.

The next morning, after a calmer Richard had finished penning several letters, to his mother, to Longchamp, de Puiset and his seneschals in Aquitaine, Normandy and Brittany, we broke camp. For days we travelled, further south than I had ever been before, to the steep and beautiful Pyrenees mountains. Home to bears, wolves and eagles, their slopes dense with trees, they marched from western to eastern sea, dividing Aquitaine and the County of Toulouse from the Spanish kingdoms. In a sleepy town on the border between Gascony and Navarre, Richard met with King Sancho VI, a gaunt-faced little man with prominent eyes.

Beauty was not everything, I said quietly to Philip, but if Sancho were anything to go by, Berengaria would turn few heads. Winking, Philip declared that a man gazes not at the fireplace, only the fire he is stoking. As long as Berengaria bore Richard a son, Philip continued, her looks mattered not a jot. This last was impossible to argue with; love and attraction came well after the kingdom's needs.

None of us were privy to the conversations between Richard and Sancho, which went on for several days. The king of Navarre drove a hard bargain, for more than once I heard from behind the chamber's locked doors an exclamation of 'God's legs, how much?' In the end, however, the deal was done. Richard laid it all out to William Marshal, who was with us, and I heard every word.

The king would set aside Alys, so that he and Berengaria might wed. But with Philippe Capet still unaware of the new arrangements, the marriage could not proceed before the monarchs set out for the Holy Land. With Richard likely to be gone for at least two years, a solution had to be found, and it was this. He and Sancho had agreed that Alienor would journey to Navarre. Then, with the queen acting as Berengaria's chaperone, the pair would travel to Sicily, one of Richard's planned stopping points on the journey to Outremer, allowing the wedding to take place in Messina.

I wondered if Beatrice would accompany Alienor; I might see her in Sicily. The embers of that fire were cold, I told myself. I would meet any attempt to rekindle them with a firm rebuttal.

I was going to war, not trying to find a wife.

CHAPTER III

Chinon, Touraine, June 1190

Midday was not far off, and the land was baking in summer sunshine. High in the blue sky, a kestrel hung, watching for small prey in the fields below the castle. Rhys and I were in the courtyard, which had been emptied by the king's order. Instead of the usual throng of servants, soldiers, horses and wagons, straw targets had been set up against the wall opposite the keep. Facing them stood a dozen of Richard's sturdy Pisan crossbowmen. Cocksure, full of banter, they had been whiling away the time until the king arrived by competing against one another. They paid little heed as I took a position at one end of the line, and Rhys, who had invested in a crossbow of his own long before me, did the same.

More than a month had gone by since the king's secret meeting with Sancho. Still we had not departed for Outremer, but my patience, worn to the nub, had finally been rewarded. Richard's troops were to assemble within days at Vézelay. There, as planned, we would meet King Philippe. Marching south to Lyon together, the two armies would cross the River Rhône and after, part company. The French monarch intended to travel overland to Genoa, while we took ship at Marseilles. Reunited in Sicily, our voyage would continue to the Holy Land.

I could not wait.

Click. The sound of a crossbow trigger was innocuous, but always sent a nervous thrill through me. The steel bolt penetrated mail at close range with ease. Clad as I was now in just tunic and hose, it would kill me for certes. I glanced from Rhys to his target, some four score paces away. A black dot in the centre marked his effort. 'Not bad.'

He grunted, already placing the end of the weapon against his belly and pulling back the string.

I took aim and shot.

'Ha!' cried Rhys. 'You almost missed the damn target.'

'If it were a man, I would have struck him in the shoulder.'

'My enemy has been hit in the chest.' There was no mistaking his smugness.

He was a better shot, and we both knew it. Use of the crossbow was frowned on for knights, and so when Rhys had shown an interest some while before, I had not. Richard's recent declaration that crossbows were a weapon for every soldier in Outremer had changed everything. I had begun to practise regularly.

'Let us shoot again,' I said, reloading.

My second effort was better, and as good as Rhys's. So was my third, but the next quarrel flew over the target altogether. Rhys could not contain his delight, and I glowered at him. So it went, I occasionally shooting as well as he, but for the most part not, and he doing his best not to crow. I made a show of grumbling under my breath, but I was inwardly pleased. I could outfight him on a horse, and on foot; why should he not be better at something else?

Despite my equanimity, an unspoken contest lay between us. Engrossed, we did not see the king arrive. Alerted then by the buzz of excitement, I saw him mingling with the Pisans. Passably fluent in Italian, he was laughing and smiling, here admiring one man's crossbow, there watching another shoot at the targets. Philip was with him, carrying a massive crossbow and a bundle of quarrels. Richard's cousin, André de Chauvigny, was loading his own weapon and bantering with Baldwin de Béthune; other household knights were there too, crossbows in hand. FitzAldelm, who had not seen me yet, was holding forth on some point.

'The ladies are watching,' said Rhys.

I looked up behind us. Queen Alienor stood framed in one of the larger windows that opened into the royal quarters. One of her ladies was beside her, and over *her* shoulder I spied Beatrice. She turned her head away before I could acknowledge her. My heart twinged. Apart from a short, stilted conversation at Nonancourt, there had been no contact during my time away with the king, and since Alienor's arrival at Chinon, we had exchanged only a few cold words. My bed was made, I thought, and now I had to lie in it.

Rhys's gaze was heavy on me, but I said nothing, and bless him, he did not ask.

'I do not understand, sire, why we should learn the use of such cowardly weapons.' The loud, nasal voice belonged to de Gunesse.

'Cowardly, how?' asked Richard.

'The crossbow kills from a distance, sire. It compares not at all with the sword or lance.' De Gunesse tittered, and looked around for support. A few heads nodded. FitzAldelm said, 'I confess I am of the same mind, sire. They do not seem chivalrous.'

This, from a man who had attempted to kill me, was laughable, but I held my peace. Still waters run deep, the saying went. Lie still for long enough, and perhaps FitzAldelm would let down his guard, granting me an opportunity to unmask him for the faithless caitiff he was.

'Chivalrous the crossbow may not be, but to a soldier on foot faced with a charging knight dressed in full mail, it is the difference between life and death,' said Richard. 'There may be times in the months and years to come when we cannot ride into battle. For all we know, the Christian siege of Acre – going on as I speak – will linger until our fleet reaches the shores of the Holy Land, and if it does, I will not wait until the walls are breached.' He took his crossbow from Philip and brandished it. 'This shall be my weapon, just as it is for the poulains, the Franks of Outremer. It matters not how we kill the heathen Saracens. One way to Hell is as good as another!'

A loud cheer went up. De Gunesse, chastened, nodded.

Richard spanned his crossbow and loaded it. Raising it to his right shoulder, he took aim and shot at once. All eyes followed the quarrel. A second cheer erupted as it hit the centre of a target.

'You should each be able to do that,' said the king. 'Go to!'

The knights took up positions, each aided by a Pisan, who could offer instruction and advice. I busied myself with loosing at our target; Rhys did the same. Every so often, the order to stop would ring out, allowing him and the Pisans to retrieve quarrels, and the practice to continue.

Time passed. The sun climbed in the sky, and the temperature in the courtyard soared. Sweat darkened my tunic; I could feel my face beginning to burn. I thought of the rare hot summers of my youth, and how red my skin had been then. In Outremer I would be cooked alive.

'Do the Saracens use crossbows?' asked Rhys.

'Nay, but almost every man uses a bow and rides a horse.'

Richard's voice made us turn, I bowing and Rhys dropping to one knee.

'The Saracens have no knights like us,' the king continued. 'They rely instead on thousands of mounted soldiers called mamluks. It is said they have four eyes, two in front and two behind, so acute is their vision! Trained to ride from childhood, the mamluks are skilled in all aspects of horsemanship. Expert with ropes, inveterate hunters, they can withstand every extreme of weather, and loose their arrows in any direction while their horses are at the gallop.'

Everyone had stopped shooting. I could tell by Queen Alienor's rigid stance that she too was listening. Richard's vivid description had brought alive our enemies.

'Every mamluk is at one and the same time a herdsman, groom, trainer, horse-dealer, farrier and rider,' said the king. 'He can ride for days, sleep in the saddle, and change mounts at full tilt. Over the course of his lifetime, he spends more time astride his horse than with his feet on the ground. It is men such as these who will be our foes in Outremer.'

Curiosity pricked me. 'How do you know this, sire?'

'A man called al-Jahiz wrote those words centuries ago. I cannot read Arabic, but his words have been translated.' Richard was not only a king and a war leader, but a reader with voracious interest.

'They will break before our charge, surely, sire,' I said. A massed group of knights on the attack was a terrifying, ground-shaking event. I had done it once, at Châteauroux, but the memory was still vivid. Nor was it any surprise that men said that a Frankish knight could batter a hole in the very walls of Jericho.

A number of voices agreed with me.

'Aye, the way a cloud of gadflies recoils from a swinging arm,' answered the king. 'And the next instant, they swarm in again, biting and stinging afresh. The mamluks will shoot even as they flee. Their arrows cannot penetrate our mail, but they *will* bring down our horses, and knights on foot, far from their own army, are easier prey.'

'How shall we best fight them, sire?' asked de Chauvigny.

Richard twisted, realising that everyone was hanging off his words. He laughed. 'With discipline.'

We stared at him, not understanding, and his smile grew broader. 'All will become clear in time, messires. For now, practise your aim.'

Richard stayed by my side with Philip as the practice resumed, shooting at our target. Rhys's skill was plain, and the king complimented him on it. Grinning like he always did when Richard acknowledged him, he felt bold enough to enquire, 'Are these *mamluks*—' his Welsh-accented French mangling the word even further '—really so dangerous, sire?'

I saw eyebrows lift and lips curl, that he should have the temerity to question the king so, but Richard was ever a man to take as he found, and he liked Rhys.

'It *is* hard to believe, lad, how such light-armed men can be so lethal. I was inclined to disbelieve al-Jahiz initially – he would not be the first writer to lie – but I fell to thinking about the lands conquered by the Saracens. It is not just the Holy Land,' said the king, handing his crossbow to Philip so he could spread his arms wide. 'Over the last five hundred years, they have taken Egypt, Syria and Outremer, and swept deep into the eastern deserts beyond. Turkey lies under their thrall; Constantinople itself is threatened. The armies who won these vast swathes of territory, equivalent in size to Europe, were not made up of knights, but mamluks.'

Rhys scowled, and sent a bolt at the target.

I could not help myself. 'Can we win then, sire? Is it possible to beat the mamluks?'

'God willing, it is, as I said, with discipline. We will need stout hearts too, and carefully laid plans,' said Richard, taking aim. His bolt landed so close to Rhys's it was impossible to make them apart. He gave Rhys a great buffet. 'How about that, master squire?'

'Sire.' Without another word, Rhys spanned his weapon, loaded and shot. A metallic click reached us as his quarrel dinked off the first two and sank into the straw. He looked at Richard and grinned. 'Your turn, sire.'

The king's eyes gleamed. Taking a bolt from Philip, he aimed and almost at once, pulled the trigger. Thunk. The bundle of half-buried quarrels moved again. Incredibly, he had hit them as well.

'A magnificent shot, sire,' I heard FitzAldelm say.

I ignored my enemy and gave Rhys a meaningful stare. Oblivious, he was already reloading. Unable to say anything without being heard, I swore inwardly. Richard was still enjoying what had become a contest, but if Rhys won, the king's volcanic temper might be unleashed. He did not like being bested at anything.

Rhys landed another bolt right beside the others.

So did Richard.

I ground my teeth as they reloaded, and tried once more to gain Rhys's attention. My efforts were in vain. He raised his crossbow. I waited until his forefinger whitened on the trigger. 'Rhys!' I cried.

My timing was perfect.

His bolt missed the target entirely, knocking stone chips off the wall behind. He shot me a furious look.

'That was not knightly, Rufus.' Richard's tone was reproving. 'Anyone would swear you thought he might beat me.'

'I was merely testing his mettle, sire,' I lied. 'During a battle, there will be many distractions – men shouting or screaming to name but two.'

'It strikes me that that was not your purpose,' said the king dryly, 'but I will continue the pretence. You must do the same to me as to your squire. Not this shot, for I will be expecting it, but perhaps the next or the one after that.' He stared down his crossbow at the target.

My worries abated. So confident was Richard of his skill that in his mind, there was no possibility of losing to Rhys. I shot *him* a look, and mouthed, 'You must lose!'

Seeing my urgency, some realisation sank in. There was still a mulish cast to his face, however. I did not trust that he would deliberately shoot with less accuracy. Caught in the horns of a dilemma – to shoulder barge him 'by accident', say, would anger Richard, but to do nothing would see the contest's intensity surge – I hesitated.

The king's bolt landed a little to the left of the target's centre. He made an exasperated noise. 'Go to, young Rhys. Do your worst.'

To my intense relief, John entered the courtyard, loudly demanding to see the king. Richard's head turned. Men stopped shooting, and whispered to each other. It was rare for the Count of Mortain, to seek out the company of his royal brother in public. He will not have come to practise his skills with the crossbow, I thought. John had none of Richard's interest in war or weaponry.

'Where are you, brother?' called John, brash and confident. Since Richard had partly rescinded his ban on entering England – largely thanks to the efforts of Alienor – John acted as if free to do what he wanted. In fact, the decision about whether or not he could return to England had been left to William Longchamp.

Richard's mask slipped back into place. 'Another time,' he said to

Rhys, who bowed deeply, and walked away. 'Johnny! Are you come to shoot against me?'

John muttered something. Richard laughed, and they fell into conversation. The contest was over, I decided. My mouth opened to rebuke Rhys for his foolishness. I took a step towards him.

I barely heard the click, but a giant punched me in the back of the head. Knees buckling, I stumbled. Rhys caught me in a strong grip before I fell. Vision blurred, my senses spinning like a top, I looked up at him. His face contorted with rage. 'FitzAldelm, you dog!' he cried.

'God forgive me, it was an accident!'

I got my legs under me again and stood. A stinging sensation, as if a hundred wasps had stung me at once, came from the back of my skull. I reached around to feel, and my fingers came back bloody. Not quite believing what had happened, my gaze swivelled.

FitzAldelm was ten paces away, a crossbow dangling from his grip. Again he made a loud, convincing apology that he had been struggling with a stiff trigger, and had not looked where his weapon was pointed. 'I beg pardon, sir,' he said to me beseechingly. 'The wrong is all mine.'

We locked eyes. He had tried to murder me again, in plain view of half the court. I knew it. He knew that I knew. The twitch of his lips told me that what happened next was up to me. As my vision cleared, I searched the nearest faces, hoping – *praying* – that someone had seen FitzAldelm's heinous act. My hope was in vain. Everyone seemed shocked and concerned, but nothing more. Alienor was no longer at the window above, but Beatrice was. It was fleetingly pleasing that she looked stricken.

'Are you hurt?' FitzAldelm asked.

I felt again for the wound, which was at the base of my hairline. About three inches long, it was not deep, but I had had the luckiest of escapes. But for the step I had taken towards Rhys, I would have been choking out the last, bloody moments of my life on the flags of the courtyard.

Icy fury took me that FitzAldelm could be so coldblooded. I was sorely tempted to raise my crossbow, pull the trigger and pulp his hated face into red ruin. Seductive though the idea was, to shoot him down in such a manner would see me named a murderer. No one apart from Rhys knew that FitzAldelm had just deliberately tried to kill me – or that he had done so once before, at Châteauroux.

So I smiled a smile I did not feel, and said, 'No matter. It is not uncommon for novices to make such mistakes.' My condescension saw hatred flare up in FitzAldelm's eyes, but he was as bound by the situation as I, and muttered something about needing more practice.

Hearing the commotion, Richard came over. I allowed FitzAldelm to explain what had happened. The king rounded on him in disgust. 'Have a care, Robert! Knights like Rufus do not grow on trees. Did I not know you better, I would mark you as an Assassin, sent by Saladin to deprive me of a fine knight!'

Everyone laughed, even me, for without knowing, Richard had touched in part on the truth. There were no deadly killers from the mountains east of Outremer in Chinon, but FitzAldelm *had* tried to murder me. I longed to tell Richard but decided to remain silent. Despite Rhys's testimony, my accusations could easily appear baseless and false. When I denounced FitzAldelm, I wanted incontrovertible proof.

Rhys, spitting with rage, took me to the surgeon. 'I'll kill him myself,' he whispered the instant we were away from the crowd. 'As God is my witness, I will slit his throat tonight.'

I seized his wrist. He glared at me. I said, quiet but savage, 'You will do nothing of the kind.'

'He tried to murder you, *again*!'

'Aye, he did. And if you slay him, who do you think will be blamed?'

A snort of disgust. 'Are we ever to do nothing? Better you just offer yourself to him, surely?'

'You are angry, Rhys. So am I, believe me. He will not get away with this, I swear to you.'

'When shall we act?'

'I want to fight him in single combat.'

Rhys looked at me as if I had gone mad. 'Why show the cur any respect? He does not treat you with honour.'

'You know why.' I hesitated, and said, 'Southampton.'

'In that case, let me do it,' Rhys pleaded. 'Nothing would give me more pleasure.'

'His life is mine to claim, not yours. He cuffed you about several times, and verbally abused you, but that is about the height of it. He and I have a great deal more history.'

Confounded, for I was right, Rhys subsided into a glowering silence.

I was none too happy with myself. I had spoken of a duel, but the king took a dim view of his mesnie knights fighting. If I killed FitzAldelm in such a contest, my hard-won position would be in jeopardy, and that was not something I was willing to contemplate. Murder seemed the only avenue open to me, but shame-scourged by memories of Henry, I was not prepared to take it.

My mood blackened further later that day, during Richard's final council before our departure. It was as if he had somehow discerned my desire to harm FitzAldelm.

'Any man who kills another on the journey to Outremer,' declared the king, 'shall be bound to the dead man, and if at sea, be thrown overboard. If on land, they shall be buried together. If it be proved by lawful witnesses that any man has drawn his knife on another, or has struck him and drawn blood, his hand shall be cut off.'

As Richard continued to list the punishments for other crimes, I turned to look at Rhys, standing behind me. 'He is not worth any of those punishments,' I whispered.

Rhys gave me a sullen nod.

Oddly, I felt a sense of relief. Henry already haunted my nights; I often woke drenched in sweat, mind bright with the final moments when he had pleaded for his wife and child, and I had ended his life in the most brutal fashion.

Much as I hated FitzAldelm, I had no wish for him to join Henry in my nightmares.

It was a glorious morning when we set out for Vézelay. Above Chinon, the dawning sky was a brilliant cerulean blue. The air, cool but with the promise of coming warmth, carried with it the scent of fresh-cut grass from the paddocks over the river. Two cocks crowed at one another from a nearby farm. It was not every day that a king set off for Outremer, and every inhabitant of the castle had come to see us off. Workmen and stable hands in drab, stained tunics. Cooks and butchers. Carpenters, stonemasons, apprentices. Mercers, coopers and bowyers. Washerwomen with chapped hands. Maids, done up in their finest.

There were snot-nosed infants in their mothers' arms, and small boys holding toy swords made from sticks. I saw clerks with ink-stained fingers, and a group of tonsured monks. The seneschal stood with his underlings. Soldiers of the garrison, men-at-arms and knights were ranked by the gate and on the battlements above. The faces of these last held a mixture of resentment, at being left behind, and relief, at not having to undertake the dangerous journey we were all about to begin.

Magnificently dressed, Queen Alienor stood with John by the doors that led into the great hall, her ladies around her. Many were in tears, for their husbands or suitors were among our number. Beatrice was absent, which pricked my conscience, because I had not gone to say farewell. It was cowardly, I admit, but easier. I hoped that any feelings she still held for me would dissipate with time. John's face was impassive; just a moment before, he had bade Richard farewell with a cool respect that offered no indication of his true emotions. For his part, the king was stern, advising his brother to do his duty and to keep the kingdom safe until he should return.

While I and the rest of his mesnie waited, Richard was talking with his mother. This was not their first meeting today. He had closeted himself with her earlier while I stood guard at the door. He had emerged with flushed cheeks and traces of moisture at the corners of his eyes – I did my best not to notice. From Alienor's chamber, the sound of quiet sobbing had carried. Now, an hour later, both were in full control once more.

'God's blessings be upon you,' said Alienor.

Richard dipped his chin. 'And on you, Mama.'

'We shall meet again soon, at Messina.'

I looked at the queen with newfound respect. She had agreed to Richard's request, to accompany King Sancho's daughter Berengaria from Navarre to Sicily. It was a considerable distance to travel, and she was almost seventy. True, she had been to Outremer previously, but that had been more than forty years before, when she was a young woman. Rather than seem daunted, however, Alienor appeared invigorated, even excited by the prospect. If all the men in Richard's army had her backbone, I thought, Jerusalem would fall in no time.

'At Messina, Mama. I will count the days until then.' Bowing, Richard took her hand and kissed it. They stared at one another briefly, and then he walked to his rouncy, held by Philip. He did not look at John.

I did, sidelong, and almost wished I had not. Although his pudgy features were smoothed into a bland expression, his eyes – the window to the soul – were dead and black, like those of a serpent. If he held any affection for his brother, it was buried deeper than a corpse. Most probably, I thought, he was rejoicing inside at Richard's departure.

From his position by my horse's head, Rhys was watching too. 'While the cat is away, the mice will play,' he said to me as I prepared to mount up.

'I hope you are wrong,' I replied, stroking the rouncy's neck. 'Not just for the king's sake, but ours. John is no friend of mine.'

'Nor of mine.' Rhys's gaze was flat and hard, as it was before a battle. He clambered onto his horse's back, who, impatient, jinked about, his shoes ringing off the cobbles.

Like Philip, Rhys had no particular reason to dislike the Count of Mortain, but loyalty meant everything to him. 'It is good to have you by my side,' I said. 'Like a younger brother you are to me.'

'And you, sir, are the older brother I never had.' It was rare for Rhys to show emotion, but his voice had caught.

'As brothers we shall go to war then.'

He gave me a fierce, grateful smile.

Richard saluted Alienor, who inclined her head in recognition. A look passed between him and John, but no words were spoken. Then, with a loud shout of 'To Vézelay,' the king rode towards the gate.

We followed.

My skin crawled, the way it did when someone was staring at me. I glanced over my shoulder. I stiffened, for it seemed John was gazing in my direction. Then I realised that his attention was fixed on someone just to my rear.

'Where is FitzAldelm?' I muttered to Rhys.

He was perfectly situated to see. 'Two men back.'

'What is he doing?'

'Looking back at the queen.' Rhys paused. 'Or John. I cannot be sure.'

It was the king's younger brother – I knew it in my gut. Memories flooded back. FitzAldelm sauntering out of the infirmary at Bonsmoulins, and a short time after, John. Several occasions in the months before Richard's coronation when I had seen the pair in conversation. The time they had met in the wine cellar at Nonancourt. I cursed myself. Busy with duties for the king, and with months passing between each incident, I had paid them little heed.

Now, they added up like the simplest of equations.

John and FitzAldelm were in league. I would stake my soul on it.

Without a way of proving it – and this seemed unlikely indeed – I could do nothing.

Nothing but watch.

Wait.

And keep my sword sharp.

Our camp at Vézelay was vast, its hundreds of tents dwarfing the French encampment. We arrived on the second of July, and already many of Philippe's lords had departed for Outremer. The two kings were in fine mood when they met, exchanging the kiss of peace and talking with excitement of the impending campaign against Saladin. They swore afresh to remain allies, and pledged that whatever they gained together would be shared loyally. This detail I had cause to remember later. It was also agreed that whoever arrived first at Messina would wait for the other.

'He does not look like a king,' Rhys said quietly. 'He more resembles a peasant.' Together with many others from the mesnie, and with French knights and nobles doing the same, we were watching Richard and Philippe talk.

I swallowed a laugh. It was hard to argue with Rhys, for Philippe was not handsome. A well-built but ungainly man, he had a shock of brown hair that forever looked uncombed. He was also blind in one eye, and his clothes, though richly cut, were rumpled and foodstained. 'Appearances deceive, Rhys,' I said. 'He is as wily an individual as you will ever meet.'

'Trust him not,' agreed de Drune, appearing by my side.

'Where have you been?' I asked.

'Here and there.' De Drune winked.

'Where?' I pressed.

'Counting the Frenchies' tents. Drinking wine with a group of their crossbowmen. Talking.' De Drune looked pleased with himself. 'Even with the soldiers who have left, Philippe's army is tiny in comparison to ours. We have, what, ten thousand men?'

'Give or take.'

'Philippe has less than half that.'

'You are sure?' This we had suspected, but it was pleasant to have the information confirmed.

'I would bet my wife's honour on it, if I had one.'

I rolled my eyes. 'Whatever deviousness Philippe may plan, he shall not overcome us by force of arms at least,' I said.

'It would not come to that, surely?' said Rhys. 'We are going to free Jerusalem together.'

I smiled. In some ways, Rhys was still a boy. 'He is unlikely to resort to violence in Outremer, true enough. He will ever seek to gain advantage over Richard, however, not least in the matter of his sister Alys.' I wondered when the king would tackle that thorny issue.

De Drune offered me his costrel. I hesitated, but seeing everywhere men from both sides drinking and laughing together, I put away my worries and took a sup.

After two days at Vézelay, the combined armies of Richard and Philippe marched out, passing through Corbigny, Moulins and Belleville-sur-Saône on their way south. It was a pleasant journey, sunny spells interspersed with cloud ensuring the temperature remained comfortable. Occasional rain showers could not dampen our high spirits. Another reason to be content, and less on guard, was FitzAldelm's absence. An expert at securing supplies, he had been sent by the king to find food for men and beasts both.

At Lyons, where a bridge took our path over the mighty River Rhône, I saw him again at the head of a train of wagons. A small brindled terrier ran close to his horse, leaping at the morsels of food he threw to it. Thus occupied, he did not spot me. With luck, I thought, we would not meet each other for the rest of the day. Once he had finished his duties, however, he would return to the mesnie, and our simmering hostilities would resume.

The crossing of the Rhône proved eventful, tragically. Part of the bridge collapsed under the weight of men and horses. By God's mercy, only two men were drowned. To my regret, FitzAldelm was not one of the twain. I rescued from the water a big knight from Romford, a pleasant individual called Richard Thorne. Several horses also had to be destroyed after breaking their legs, but the principal effect was to delay our journey. Only a part of the English and French hosts had crossed; the rest, thousands strong, remained on the far side. The river's width of twenty score paces felt like a gulf many times that distance.

Philippe was bemused and dismayed by what had happened, but Richard threw himself into the challenge. Ordering both banks scoured for craft of any kind, he ordered trees felled and boats constructed. Before sundown the following day, we had more than a hundred. The morning after, the king took charge. Under his direction, the largest craft rowed into the current one after another and dropped anchor as near to ten paces apart as they could manage. The anchors were either heavy rocks or wicker baskets filled with stones, and all attached to cables. There were accidents: men falling overboard, baskets bursting asunder, and an occasional boat capsizing, but the work continued regardless. By mid-afternoon, a line of craft spanned the Rhône in a roughly straight line, held in place by their anchors.

Our carpenters had been hard at work too, fashioning planks from hewn-down trees. These were laid down from boat to boat, and secured together by ropes. There was no siderail and the whole structure moved gently in the current, but it was a road. Taking great care, leading their horses, the first men crossed just before sunset.

Watching from his pavilion, Richard beamed from ear to ear. 'The rest can come over in the morning, Rufus,' he said. 'Three days we will have lost, that is all.'

It seemed an acceptable delay. We would be able to set sail within the next two weeks.

Everything was still going to plan.

PART TWO

SEPTEMBER 1190–JUNE 1191

CHAPTER IV

Southern Italy, September 1190

I breathed deeply, savouring the crisp autumn air. I was riding in thick-forested hills with only Richard for company. Nine days south of Salerno, beautiful, wild and remote, here steep and there rolling, they had few inhabitants. Leaving our companions early that morning, we had spied a number of deer and boar, and even the tracks of bears. Now and again, in the gaps between the trees, I spied a hawk far above.

The impatience I had felt since July, and our embarking at Marseilles, was dissipating with every passing hour. Although half the army had set off for the Holy Land by then, under Archbishop Baldwin of Canterbury, while we had taken a meandering voyage down the Italian peninsula, we were close to Sicily – a real milestone – at last. Warm sun on my face by times, cool tree-cast shadow at others, riding at a gentle pace with the king, I could not have asked for more. Blankets and bags of food were strapped behind our saddles; I also carried a small tent in case we did not find lodgings at night. Bandits were rare in these parts, and we had helms, swords and shields as protection.

Two days, our journey to Bagnara would take; meeting the fleet there, we would embark. Philippe Capet was already at Messina, having won the game of leapfrog we had played with him down the coast. Richard's sister Joanna was also on Sicily. As he had told me more than once, he and Joanna had not seen one another for more than fourteen years.

I cast a sidelong look at the king. It pained me to note the bags under his eyes, and the amount of weight he had lost during his recent illness, a bout of quartan fever. There was colour in his cheeks, however, and his eyes had regained their usual sparkle.

He noticed my glance. 'This is a happy day, Rufus! Sicily awaits us. And Joanna.'

'Your sister was wed to King William of Sicily, was she not, sire?'

'Indeed, but he died some months before we set sail.'

I remembered Richard's shock at the news, which for reasons unexplained, had only reached him in Marseilles.

'Sadly, William and Joanna had no children. His next of kin is his aunt Constance, but the Sicilians do not want her on the throne. She is married to Heinrich of Hohenstaufen, the son and heir of the German emperor, Frederick Barbarossa – a man much reviled on the island. Not that Constance could have taken power; she lives in Germany.'

'William's death left the throne ripe for the seizing then, sire?'

'Even so. I understand that a cousin of William's, Tancred of Lecce, took his opportunity some weeks since. A dwarf born out of wedlock, and ugly to boot, he is nonetheless the current king of Sicily. They say he looks like a monkey with a crown on his head.'

'It is worrying that there has been no news of your sister during this time, sire.'

Richard's jaw worked. 'Tancred has her captive somewhere, I wager.'

'If that is the case, we must free her, sire,' I cried.

'Indeed we must.' A grim smile. 'I would not want to be in Tancred's little monkey shoes if he has harmed a single hair on Joanna's head.'

'How strong are his forces, sire?'

'They will be weaker than mine, for certes, but Tancred may not be without allies. I wager he is pouring honeyed words into Philippe's ear even now. Trouble awaits us.'

His words rang true. The French king, a lover of scheming and deviousness, would want to gain whatever advantage he could from the prospective hostility between Richard and Tancred, while the latter would seek help in whatever quarter he could.

'Might it then not make sense to travel with more haste, sire?'

'Today and tomorrow are the last days of freedom I will have in many a month, Ferdia. Two days matter little. Once matters are settled in Sicily, I am to be wed. After that, we must sail for Outremer and the siege of Acre. War will meet us there as our feet hit the shore. It will not end until, God willing, we enter Jerusalem. Do you see my reasoning now?'

'I do, sire.' There was more to it, I thought, noting the little pricks of red on his cheeks. The king was also marshalling his strength for the confrontation with Tancred.

We passed the morning in light mood, swapping hunting stories, reliving battles and cracking jokes. I also found myself telling the king about Beatrice, and how I had ended things.

It was better that way, he told me. 'There is no place for women in war. They are a distraction, Ferdia.'

This explained in part his setting aside his bed companions, I thought. There had been a few since Marseilles – mostly the daughters of landowners with whom we had stayed – but none after Pisa. He was single-minded in his determination. 'Will your new queen return to Aquitaine or Touraine after the wedding, sire?'

'That is what I would prefer, aye, but Berengaria will be accompanying me to Outremer.' A frustrated bark of a laugh. 'Begetting an heir is all-important, and that can scarce happen if she is in Chinon and I am at Acre.'

I wondered what chance of contentment their marriage might have. The purpose of their union was to have children, but without happiness, a life of dissatisfaction beckoned. Or maybe it did not, I thought, for Richard at least. I pictured the fierce joy that transfigured his face in battle, and decided that was his true passion. Beside that, the love of a woman could not compare.

'I am famished,' the king declared. 'Do you smell that bread?'

'I do, sire.' My own belly was rumbling.

Hours had passed since leaving the abbey, and we were entering a village. Small, one-roomed houses with thatch roofs were separated by patches of cultivation. Women stood knee deep in a stream to our left, beating clothes off rocks. On the bank, a girl cradled a swaddled babe. Smoke trickled skyward from a forge roof. Hens pecked in the dirt. A greybeard sat in the doorway of a hovel, watching us through rheumy eyes.

Led by our noses to the bakery, a detached building slightly larger than the rest, we halted. I went inside – Richard never carried money – and purchased two still-warm loaves. Mouth watering, I emerged to find the king staring across the street, if it could be called that.

'What is it, sire?'

'I can hear a hawk in that house yonder.'

I stared at him, not understanding.

'Churls are not allowed to own hawks – they are reserved for the nobility.'

In England, perhaps, I thought, and Aquitaine, but this is Italy.

To my surprise, Richard next leaped to the ground and tossed me the reins. 'I will not be long.'

He ignored my protest, instead making a beeline for the house from which the piercing cry – surely that of a sparrow hawk, I thought – came.

Ill at ease, one arm holding the loaves against my chest and the other hand gripping the king's reins – my own horse was standing quietly – I wondered what to do. Go after Richard, and I risked not just his wrath, but the horses being stolen. The ill-favoured youths lounging by the bakery's entrance would never dare attack me, armed as I was with sword and shield, but they might steal a pair of fine mounts if the opportunity presented itself.

Deciding to follow the king's command, I stayed put, listening with all my might to what happened across the street. The smell of the bread filled my nostrils, turning my hunger into a ravening beast, but with no hands free, I could not take as much as a bite.

One of the youths sauntered in my direction. He said something, using a local dialect that meant nothing to me.

Sure he was up to no good, I gave him a hard stare. 'No speak . . . Italian,' I said, exhausting my vocabulary in that language.

He leered. What teeth he had left were half-rotted and brown. Again he spoke, and there was a querulous note to his voice that I did not like.

I tried again, in French. 'Do you understand?'

He frowned, no comprehension on his face. He spoke to his companions, who sniggered.

My skin crawled. I was tempted to lay a hand to my sword, but told myself I was overreacting. They are just peasants, poking fun at the stranger, I thought.

Richard's voice, loud and angry, carried from the other side of the street.

A man shouted back. A woman joined in.

Richard yelled; the hawk let out a piercing cry.

More shouting. The youth lost all interest in me. Together with his three companions, they went to investigate. I was left alone, feeling more and more uncomfortable.

I could not stand around and do nothing. As my stomach growled in protest, I dropped the loaves to the ground and seized my own horse's reins. 'Come on,' I said, leading it and Richard's mount away from the bakery.

I walked round the corner of the house to find the most bizarre situation unfolding. Outside the back door stood a wooden perch. Half-fluttering above it, restrained by a leash attached to its jesses, was a magnificent sparrow hawk. An indignant Richard stood by the perch, his naked sword in his fist. Confronting him were a stout, middle-aged man with a florid complexion, perhaps the householder, and a shrewish-faced woman of the same age, his wife, like as not. Neighbours, or other villagers, were there too: a soot-marked, muscly man who looked like a smith, a bony youth in a leather apron – his apprentice – as well as an old woman in a filthy dress and the youths who had accosted me outside the bakery.

Mouth open in amazement, I confess I did nothing at first.

Richard reached for the hawk, which dodged his grip. It pecked savagely at his wrist, and he swore. He shouted in Italian, something like, 'I *will* take this bird!'

The stout man yelled back – I did not understand what – and took a step forward.

Richard pointed his sword at him.

The man stopped.

A stone flew through the air, just missing the king's head.

It was like the pebble that starts a landslide. Suddenly, the air was full of rocks. From nowhere, the youths produced sticks, and closed in on Richard.

Noticing a ring in the wall – it seemed in the moment as if placed there by God – I looped the horses' reins around it, and drew my sword. I ran towards the mêlée, roaring at the top of my voice.

The stout man now had a knife in his hand. He lunged at the king, who could easily have used a killing blow, but instead struck him across the head with the flat of his blade. As the stout man dropped, senseless, Richard's swing continued. His sword clashed off the wall of the house. Sparks flew, and the blade snapped in two. Richard cursed and faced his other attackers even as a fresh barrage of stones rained upon him. Those with sticks moved forward, although two at the back had turned at my first shout.

'Dex aie!' I cried, knowing the louder I was, the more likely fear would kindle in the villagers' hearts. I repeated the English royal war cry. 'Dex aie!'

The pair facing me took to their heels, and I let them go.

Richard caught one of the youths in the mouth with a stone and burst his lip. Blood sprayed; he screamed and fled. The king felled another with a mighty punch; the others retreated, all except the stout man's wife, who, shrieking insults, pummelled Richard with her bony fists. He pushed her aside. Squawking with rage, she went at him next with a three-legged stool. The king snatched it from her, and hurled it back into the house. Off she went to fetch it, still gabbling in the local dialect.

I reached his side. 'Are you hurt, sire?'

'My pride only.' He glanced back at the hawk, which was still flapping up and down off the perch.

A stone whizzed past my ear. I looked. The youths had retreated to a small shed opposite the house. They were egging each other on. Another rock came flying in. I ducked. I could see people peering from other dwellings. Two men were talking together by the edge of a vegetable patch. Raised voices came from the street.

'We had best leave, sire,' I said.

Richard glanced at the hawk, then at me. He swore. 'That bird should not be here.'

'In Italy, sire, the law must be different. The stout man clearly believes you are trying to steal his property. So do the rest of these peasants.' We both stooped to avoid the fresh stones that came humming in. One of the youths, I saw, had armed himself with a sling. A missile from that could kill. 'How would it be, sire, if you were to be slain here, and never reach Outremer?' I said. 'I *insist* we go – *now*.'

His intense blue eyes, which could terrify most men, bored into me.

Somehow I did not look away.

Incredibly, he chuckled. 'Very well, Ferdia of Cairlinn. It shall be as you say.'

A stone thwacked into my ribs as we ran for the horses. Thank Christ it was not from the sling, but it stung like a hornet, nonetheless. We leaped into the saddle, and cantered onto the street, leaving a tide of angry villagers in our wake. I had time to glance regretfully at the loaves I had bought – now being eaten by a couple of ribby mongrels – and then we were gone.

Angry shouts followed us down the road. I looked back. The shrew-faced woman was waving the stool at us, and yelling something incomprehensible. A chuckle escaped me.

'God's legs!' Richard's belly laugh split the air.

The floodgates opened. Gales of hilarity consumed us, and we had to slow our horses to a walk. We laughed until our sides hurt and tears streamed down our faces. Richard would say 'the harridan with the stool', and I would cackle. Each time I mentioned the bread, and the dogs eating it, he would hoot with mirth.

The joking went on until long after the village had vanished into the distance.

Trumpets blared again and again, a deafening clarion that carried far over the water beyond us. As it was supposed to. Two days had passed since the incident with the hawk. South from Bagnara, where Richard and I had rejoined the fleet, we had come, part of a mighty armada that filled the Faro, the narrow strait between Italy and the island of Sicily. I was with the king in the lead vessel, the largest of the galleys, a sleek beast with a single mast and a bank of oars. To either side, a short distance back, were a dozen more, brightly-painted, with glittering shields hanging from their sides. Pennons and standards fluttered from every mast. Behind them came the heavy-bellied dromonds, and score upon score of snacks, the transport craft.

The trumpets sounded again, relaying the king's order. Waves foamed off our prow as the oarsmen pulled harder, powering the ship towards Messina. We were close now, and Richard wanted to arrive in style. It was the twenty-third of September, the year of our Lord 1190; we were approaching the first important staging post on our journey. Because we needs must wait for Alienor and Berengaria, it was probable that we would have to overwinter on Sicily. It was galling, but there was nothing the king, or anyone, could do.

'This is a fine way to reach a city!' Rhys was standing beside me at the rail. Sea voyages were not his favourite, but today's calm conditions and the grandeur of what we were about had him in a good mood.

I gazed back at the fleet, and laughed. 'Truly it is.'

'I heard Philippe came into Messina in one ship,' said Rhys.

'As did I.'

'But he too is a king. Does he not wish to appear like one?'

'Perhaps he did not want to outshine Tancred, who is only new to the throne,' I said, repeating what I had heard de Béthune say.

'Our lord is not worried about that.'

'He is not.' We looked towards the prow-mounted platform before us, where the king stood. Clad in shining mail from neck to foot, a white cross on his surcoat, he bore a red heater shield emblazoned with his single Angevin lion. A golden circlet held his mane of reddish-blond hair in place. He was the very image of a warrior king.

He is also unconcerned with what Philippe thinks, I decided. It seemed plausible that Richard's intention was actually to annoy the French king, for it was *he* who would witness our grand entrance. Tancred would hear of it, of course, but he was in Palermo.

In truth, the pomp and ceremony was unwarranted, and more cautious heads like André de Chauvigny had argued for a quieter end to our voyage. There was no need to antagonise Philippe or the local population. Tancred already knew that Richard's forces greatly outnumbered his.

'Why rub his nose in it, sire?' de Chauvigny had asked, voicing all of our concern.

The king would have none of it.

Usually, I brooked no criticism of Richard, but it was hard to argue that on occasion his pride got the better of him. I hoped that in Sicily, we would not live to regret it.

CHAPTER V

Messina, Sicily

By nightfall, we were ensconced in the house of Reginald de Muhec, a noble Lombard – as we termed the local Normans – who had been on the quay to greet Richard. A spacious dwelling in the suburbs of Messina, with a mosaic-floored central courtyard, trellised vines and pattering fountains, it was more opulent than many castles in England. Over the walls, I could see palm trees and a church which had been a mosque, which only emphasised the foreignness of our situation.

Inviting Richard to stay for as long as he wished, de Muhec had diplomatically withdrawn after we had eaten a delicious meal together. The repast was finished off with plates arrayed with exotic melons, figs and pomegranates, surrounded by sugar-coated almonds and hazelnuts.

Rhys, who had a sweet tooth, thought he had died and gone to Heaven when the unfinished trays were taken away by servants and came within his reach. Cheeks bulging with what he had already stuffed in, he loaded a platter until it could hold no more. I watched with amusement as he followed the dark-skinned servants down the kitchen passage. It was odd to see Saracens as domestics, not enemies, but it was normal in Sicily. Here Saracen dwelt alongside Lombard and Greek.

Richard had changed out of his mail. Clad in tunic and hose like the rest of us, he sat at the table, a goblet of wine before him. He was in thoughtful mood, the confident, outgoing air of earlier put away now that he was no longer in public.

I was there, so too were de Béthune, de Chauvigny, FitzAldelm and a handful other favoured knights. Garnier de Nablus, grand master of the Knights Hospitaller sat beside the newly appointed Templar Grand Master, Robert de Sablé. De Nablus was less grim than de Sablé, but only by a fraction. Their demeanour was not surprising, I decided.

These were men who had dedicated their lives not just to God, but to war, and the defence of the Christian realm of Outremer.

Walter, the archbishop of Rouen, and Gerard, the archbishop of Auxienne were also present. Walter was as round and shiny-cheeked as an apple, but behind his affable exterior lurked a sharp mind. Gerard was as thin as a rake, a severe man who did not drink. These men were fiercely loyal to the king, which explained why they remained in the company when other religious had gone to their respective lodgings.

FitzAldelm was bitching to de Chauvigny about his room, which he did not think was large enough. De Chauvigny, a relaxed type who would happily have slept on the floor, gave little by way of reply. FitzAldelm's attention moved to the king. 'I still think it is not right that you must stay here, sire, while Philippe lounges at his ease in the royal palace within the city.'

'If his attempt to leave had not met with abject failure, it would have been mine for the taking,' said the king with a smile.

He was referring to Philippe's petulant decision to depart for Outremer moments after he had met with Richard on the dock. In an odd twist of fate, the winds had changed as Philippe's ships put to sea, preventing them from making any headway. An embarrassing return to port had resulted. Our sailors had made the most of it, whistling and jeering as the French vessels docked.

Richard had been highly amused, calling to Philippe that God meant for them not to be apart. The French king stormed down the gangplank without reply. We had not lingered either; the locals, amazed at first by our fleet and then by the mighty destriers disembarking, had grown unhappy with the numbers of troops coming off the ships. It was no wonder, for we looked like invaders.

My attention was drawn back to the table, where FitzAldelm was like a dog with a bone. 'Still, sire,' he said, 'what right has Philippe to a palace when you, our king, has none?'

'He was here first.' De Chauvigny, confident of his position, and probably disliking FitzAldelm's real reason for complaining, winked at Richard.

Everyone laughed except FitzAldelm.

'You speak truth, cousin,' said the king. 'Your indignation is appreciated, Robert,' he went on, addressing FitzAldelm, 'but the right or wrong of it matters not at this point. To demand Philippe move would be deeply insulting, not least because of his offer to stay in the palace with him.' He waved a hand. 'Is this house not to your liking?'

'It is more than adequate, sire,' said FitzAldelm, now unable to mention his discontent.

'Is my sister being held in such luxury, I wonder?' Richard muttered.

'Unless the monkey Tancred is a complete imbecile, sire, Joanna is being well-looked-after,' said de Nablus.

'And he will send her to you with all speed, sire,' I added.

The king's note, sent to Tancred at Palermo within an hour of our landing, had made his position clear. Joanna was to be delivered at once, together with her considerable dowry, or Tancred would suffer the consequences. With Richard's army disembarked, there was no need to be more specific.

The king drummed his fingers on the table. 'He had best do so, or by God, I will hew his head from his shoulders myself.'

'Let us hope that will not be necessary, sire,' said Archbishop Walter.

Richard grunted, but made no apology.

'Have you given thought, sire, to the supplies needed by your troops?' Walter asked.

'The local traders will cope in the short term with the demands we place upon them. Should we need to stay longer, measures will have to be set in place. Bulk orders of grain and wine from estates and towns on the island, and so on.'

'Soldiers are rough creatures, prone to drunken and licentious behaviour, sire,' said Archbishop Gerard. 'The local Christian women are likely to be accosted in the street.'

'If that happens,' said the king, 'it will be because the men want not to seduce them, but to annoy their husbands.'

Into the chuckles and smiles, the archbishop ploughed on. 'With thousands of soldiers in Messina, sire, it is impossible that no crime will be committed.'

He spoke the truth and we all knew it.

'Strict orders have been given to keep the peace. Any crimes committed will be severely punished,' said Richard. 'Short of caging my troops, I can do little more.'

Gerard nodded. 'We shall encourage everyone to attend mass daily,' he said.

Imagining de Drune's ripe reaction to that suggestion, I hid my smile behind my cup. Like most men in the army, I suspected, he was getting uproariously drunk, a theme that would repeat nightly until his coin ran out. Each morning would see him not in a church, but snoring on his straw mattress.

I had high hopes of joining the revelries soon. Richard's every waking moment was to be taken up by matters of high state – meetings with Philippe and Tancred and so on – but with luck my presence would not be required. De Drune's invitation, to find the finest hostelry in Messina and drink it dry, was attractive indeed. Rhys would not be left behind, and if I could prise Philip away from his duties, he would enjoy it too. I would also send word to Richard Thorne. Since his near drowning in the Rhône, we had become fast friends.

My opportunity did not come at once. For two days after our arrival at Messina, the king held meetings with Philippe. Appearances had to be kept up, which meant Richard wanted his best knights as his personal bodyguard. While de Drune took a delighted Rhys out drinking – I had given him permission – I had to attend the king. The meetings were never long, thank Christ, but worryingly, they were ill-tempered affairs during which Philippe made frequent sniping comments at Richard. The king responded with barbed comments of his own. It did not bode well for our time in Outremer.

The king's behaviour was out of character; normally, he was the picture of composure when formal occasion demanded it. His frustration, as he admitted himself, arose in part from his inability to agree on a leaving date. Philippe used this prevarication to imply, none too subtly, that Richard's zeal for the campaign was fading. He could protest little, because *he* was waiting for Berengaria to reach Messina with his mother Alienor – an arrival the French king still knew nothing about. This twist to the tale had to be dealt with as well, although quite how nobody knew.

On the fifth morning, the twenty-eighth of September, word came that the ship carrying Richard's sister Joanna was about to dock. The king's mood was entirely transformed. Beaming from ear to ear, he rushed from the breakfast table. I grabbed a final marzipan torte and went after him. Delayed in the courtyard by a faulty bridle, I sent a red-eyed Rhys in search of another. Richard was about to wait for no one, however. Crying that after fourteen years he could not tarry for even an instant, he rode out with de Béthune, de Chauvigny and a handful of others. FitzAldelm, curse him, was among their number.

I paced about impatiently, waiting for Rhys to reappear, my eagerness to see Joanna at fever pitch. Although a widow, she was only twenty-four years old, and by all accounts a great beauty.

'Ready, sir.' Despite the sheen of sweat coating his pale face, Rhys was grinning. 'I borrowed a bridle from Usama.' He had become fast friends with one of the grooms, a friendly Saracen lad who spoke Latin and some French.

'Come on then,' I urged, swinging up into the saddle. 'The king is halfway to the port by now, like as not.'

Out the main gate we went, and down the lane that led to one of the city's main streets. I already knew Messina well, or it felt like that. The former-mosque-now-church I had spied on the first day stood adjacent to our lodgings. On its other side was a small Benedictine monastery. Opposite were large residences with courtyards, similar to de Muhec's home. An ox cart trundled by, laden down with planks of wood. Reaching a crossroads, I saw two women emerge from a house. They adjusted their veils, and I thought, it is hard to know Christian from Saracen here. The Lombards had adopted many customs from the Saracens, the people who had ruled Sicily before their invasion a century and a half before.

Leaving the residential quarter behind, we entered a more commercial one. The street was thronged with pedestrians, and our pace slowed to a walk. Of Richard and his party there was no sign, and there was little point in trying to force a path through. Most of those around us were Greeks, the majority of Messina's population – Griffons we called them somewhat insultingly – but some were Saracens, of every skin colour, dark brown, light brown and deepest black. These last I had heard came from Ethiopia and Sudan, lands far to the south of Egypt. Jews there were too, with skullcaps and ringlets dangling down in front of their ears, and Armenians in curious pointed hats.

Every building was a business of some kind. Bales of cotton were being unloaded from a cart and carried indoors. Elsewhere, tiny songbirds trilled at each other from behind their cage bars. A silversmith tapped with a fine hammer on a little table-mounted anvil. Lengths of sugar cane – something I had seen for the first time here – were propped against the wall of another shop, with sacks of crystallised sugar occupying every inch of the floor. Fruit vendors called out, offering from their little stalls freshly-squeezed pomegranate and orange juice. Two youths chivvied sheep into an alleyway. I glanced within; a pen awaited, and after, from the odour of blood and shit, the butcher's knife.

A tantalising aroma, that of hot, fresh bread, replaced it a distance down the street. Recognising the bakery I had purchased from before, and still hungry, I said to Rhys as we reached it, 'A few moments longer will not make any difference. Wait for me.'

Yet suffering the effects of the previous night, he seemed grateful to slump in his saddle, a listless hand on my reins.

Heat beat at me as I approached the bakery, a small building with a counter spanning the width of the entrance. Loaves and various pastries and pies were on offer. At the back wall were two domed brick ovens, in the open maws of which I could see charcoal glowing. Workers with long wooden paddles stood by, peering in now and again to check nothing would burn.

I smiled at the proprietress, a striking Griffon woman with long black hair, and pointed to the medium-sized loaves that I had enjoyed over the previous few days. My Greek was still non-existent, so I held up two fingers: one for me, and another for Rhys.

She answered, harsh words in her own tongue.

This was different, far less friendly than before. I gave her a polite smile and held out four trifollaro coins, the coppers that were the lowest denomination of currency on Sicily.

She shook her head angrily, and held up a hand, fingers outstretched, as well as the thumb on her other.

'Six trifollaros?' I cried. 'Yesterday they were two each, and now they are three?'

She met my stare. There was fear in her eyes, but obstinacy too.

I rummaged in my purse, and slapped down half a dozen coins. 'There will be men more unhappy than me about this,' I said.

My only answer was a scowl.

Rhys was unsurprised by my story, and revealed that the price of wine had also climbed sharply since our arrival. 'The locals do not like us,' he said. '"Malodorous dogs" they call us.'

'There is some truth to that,' I replied with a chuckle. 'Most men are not overfond of washing, while the Griffons and the Lombards seem to bathe at every opportunity. Even the ungodly Saracens do so, by all accounts.'

'Longtails we are to them all,' said Rhys darkly. 'Devils.'

That insult I did not like, nor the rumour he then told me of a crossbowman being murdered and his corpse thrown in the latrines. 'Word of that killing has not come to the king,' I said, 'which makes me think it is a lie.'

Rhys nodded, but the glances he was giving anyone in our path were not friendly.

I too began to pay more attention to my surroundings as we continued towards the port. Perhaps it was my imagination, but the atmosphere seemed more hostile than it had been. I saw fewer smiles. Could not hear innkeepers asking soldiers to enter and sample their wines. The moment I spied ships flying Tancred's colours at the dock, however, my concerns vanished like mist under the morning sun.

Joanna had arrived.

She was every bit as beautiful as she had been described. Tall for a woman, statuesque, with red-blonde hair like her brother, she was captivating. Full of laughter, obviously happy to be reunited with Richard, she had a musical, enchanting voice. I was entranced, but there was no introduction for me, or for any of us immediately: the king was consumed with reacquainting himself with the sister he had been parted from for so long.

'You were but a girl the last time I saw you, lass,' he said, beaming. 'Now you are Venus come to Earth!'

Joanna batted away his compliment, blushing, but I could see she was delighted.

They did not stop talking all the way back to de Muhec's house, Richard leaning down from his horse, and she peering out from the litter he had commandeered.

I treasured every glimpse I got of her.

Philippe was also eager to meet Joanna. The very next day, he paid a visit. To my great annoyance, he was most taken with Richard's sister, and she seemed interested by his conversation. I was relieved to hear Richard telling Joanna after Philippe had left that there was no question of his marrying her, and even more pleased when she made a face and said, 'Sweet Jesu, brother, marry *him*? I would rather enter a convent.' Seeing his confusion, she let out a tinkling laugh. 'My laughs and smiles were an act, to help your cause.'

Richard gave her an astonished look.

Ah, the wiles of women. I had also thought Joanna was being genuine. Wary, I held back while the knights of the mesnie vied with one another to speak with her. She appeared to enjoy their company too, which could have been an act, but drove me to unexplained jealousy. Discomfited by my surging emotions, I was glad when Richard took me with him the following day, back to Bagnara and the fortified monastery from where we had prepared to cross to Sicily.

Occupying it temporarily – the chief monk's protests to Richard fell on deaf ears – the king left orders that quarters were to be found for half a dozen knights and fifty men-at-arms.

My pleasure at being away from Joanna's attractions was then replaced by dismay, for Bagnara was to be her new residence. Not feeling able to talk with her was bad, but not to see her at all was worse. Terrified that Richard would discern my feelings and be angry, or worse still, amused, I assumed a mask that until now I had rarely managed. In fine humour thanks to his day's work, he had no idea of my inner turmoil as we returned to Messina on the evening of the last day of September.

The following day, Joanna was transferred to Bagnara with her ladies, much to her displeasure. Richard would not listen to her protests. 'It is for your own safety, lass,' he told her. When she asked what he meant, the king made reference to the tensions rising between his soldiers and sailors and the local population.

'It is not going to come to fighting, surely?' Joanna asked, horrified.

'I hope not, but I must plan as if it will.' Richard kissed her and said that her sojourn in Bagnara would not be for long.

Selfishly, I hoped he was right. I had decided when next I was granted the opportunity, I *would* try to talk to her. The idea was almost as terrifying as it was appealing.

On the second of October, we seized a Griffon monastery on an island that lay in the Faro strait between Sicily and Italy. Richard's distrust of the locals had grown to the point of wanting a secure place to store equipment and siege weapons, and to stable horses. Monks being monks, they did not resist being evicted, but they were deeply unhappy. Word of what we had done spread from the moment they reached Messina. Crowds gathered in the streets that evening, and the king judged it wise to have the entrance of de Muhec's house barred. As the night drew in, we saw some of the bolder Griffons on the city's battlements, drinking wine and shouting insults at our main camp. It would come to nothing, God willing, I said to Rhys, but I had a bad feeling in my belly.

The next morning, we went to the courtyard after breakfast; this had become the mesnie's habit. At sea, and travelling through the Italian countryside, there had been less opportunity for sword practice, but here we had time on our hands. Richard's suggestion that the knights practise together daily met with uniform approval.

So it was that some dozen of us were fully dressed for war and hammering away at one another when a bloodied figure came hurrying down the passage that led to the front door, one of the sentries at his heels. To my surprise, I recognised the tall shape of Richard Thorne.

'I must speak with the king!' he cried.

Richard, who was quite near, heard. He lowered his blade. 'Who comes?'

Thorne took a knee, his middling brown hair falling over his face as he did. 'Richard Thorne, sire, of Romford.'

'Up, man,' said the king impatiently. 'What news?'

It all poured out. How Thorne had been near the entrance to the army's camp, and seen an archer complain bitterly to a Griffon woman about the price of the bread she was selling. Three times the price it had been not a week before, he had shouted to his companions. Furious, the woman had launched into a screeching tirade. It had not taken long before the other stallholders, Griffons all, attacked him. When the archer's companions managed to pull him to safety, he was battered, bruised and missing great chunks of hair.

'Naturally enough, sire, his friends did not hold back,' Thorne went on. 'They laid about them with fist and boot, which drove the Griffons to even greater extremes. Knives were drawn, and cudgels seized, and the men-at-arms had to defend themselves with even more vigour. Blood is being spilled even now. I fear the violence will spread. Mobs of Griffons are descending from the town towards the camp, and even a few Saracens.' He gestured at the cuts on his face. 'I was lucky to get through so lightly scathed.'

'God's legs!' Richard shouted. 'I will teach those thieving Griffons and enemies of Christ a lesson. With me!'

We leaped to our feet and scrambled for our war gear.

CHAPTER VI

We prepared to depart as soon as possible. Thorne insisted on coming too, dazed though he was. A gambeson and shield were found for him, and an old pot helm covered in rust spots. There was a spare horse too, which meant we were fourteen knights, including the king, and the same number of squires behind us. The latter did not often ride into battle, but there was no time to rally more knights.

Angry Griffons filled the streets, but our charge saw them scatter like mice before a cat. Not a man had to raise his sword during the ride from de Muhec's house. Missiles aplenty were hurled at us once we had ridden by, but no one was badly hurt. To my delight, FitzAldelm was one of the few victims. He had neglected to don a helmet, and a piece of jagged roof tile opened his cheek nicely. He bled like a stuck pig.

The mob outside the camp took a little longer to break, but they were soon running for their lives. We thundered after, up the street that led to the city's main gate. Even though the Griffons had scattered into alleyways and lanes, our number was still small in comparison to the fleeing crowd. All the impetus was with us, however, because we were on horseback. There can scarce be a man in Christendom whose bowels do not turn to water when facing a cavalry charge unarmed and on foot. If there is, his wits are curdled in his skull.

'Use the flat of your blade!' Richard kept shouting. He had contrived to snatch up a stout cudgel. This he cracked with liberal abandon on pates, shoulders, arms and chests.

My initial excitement had been diluted by this point. I had no wish to fight unarmed townspeople. My mind changed soon after when a lanky figure came screaming at me from a side alley, a thick length of timber in his hand. Fortunate to have reacted in time, I sawed on my reins, turned and drove my horse at him. Terrified, he stepped to one side and I sent him spinning to the ground with a blow from the flat of my sword. I then had to help Rhys, who was being assailed by three youths. After that, I struck out at each and every Griffon and Saracen.

We galloped up the street. Before long, all resistance had vanished. The mob had vanished. Those few who were still before us were now running in blind terror. Nearing the gate, I slowed up. There was a mixture of soldiers and ordinary townspeople atop the battlements. 'Sire,' I cried. 'If they are on the wall, they are manning the gate too, like as not!'

Richard's eyes followed my outstretched arm. 'You have the right of it, methinks. Halt!' he shouted at the few riders who were in front.

Three squires and two knights did not hear. Laying about them with their swords, the battle lust in control, they cantered through the entrance to the city.

An instant later, the doors were heaved to with a great creaking and groaning. A mighty slam and the falling thump of a locking bar announced to one and all that the way was barred.

'The hellspawn!' cried Richard, riding closer.

One eye on the rampart in case anyone should shoot at the king, I glanced about. There was no sign of FitzAldelm, and hope flared in my breast. Sure enough, when a headcount was made, it was revealed that my enemy was one of the twain who had foolishly charged inside the city. The other was Peter Tireproie, an excitable type who was friendly with de Béthune. Their respective squires and one other – thankfully not Rhys – had followed. From the shouts and clash of arms on the other side of the gate, they were giving a good account of themselves.

It was a bad situation, however, and we knew it. Five armoured men could not hold off a huge crowd for long. Richard took the initiative, somehow attracting the attention of a captain of the guard. Announcing that for each of his men were killed, ten citizens of the city would hang, the king retreated. A barrage of abuse followed – I heard in French, 'Piss off, you long-tailed king!' – but the captain vanished from view, and a little time after, the sounds of fighting diminished and died away. Hooves rang off cobblestones, which told us that our comrades had ridden off, with luck to a place of safety.

Furious at the insults sent his way, but aware we could do no more, Richard led us back down the street.

I prayed as I had not done for months. Let FitzAldelm have taken a mortal wound, I pleaded. I cared not a whit that my request was sinful.

If I could not strike him down, maybe God would.

Sad to say, my request was not granted. FitzAldelm, Tireproie and the squires were allowed to leave the city a few hours later. They found us at de Muhec's residence, where we had retreated. Rioters were still roaming the suburbs, and the king judged it wisest to let tempers settle overnight. His decision to send Joanna to Bagnara, which I, smitten, had not liked, now seemed wise.

Tireproie had the grace to look chastened by his escape, but FitzAldelm began crowing about the yellow-livered Griffons running from five men. At first he did not notice the glances and mutters around the table.

I looked at Richard, who had a little smile playing around his mouth. He said nothing. Nor did I.

De Chauvigny it was who shattered FitzAldelm's fantasy. 'Come now, Robert,' he said. 'Did you not hear the king talking with the captain of the guard?'

FitzAldelm, who was still expounding on the numbers of rioters who had run from his sword, stopped. His eyes flickered to Richard, and back to de Chauvigny. 'The king?'

'He told the captain that for each of you who were killed, ten Griffons would be executed. No doubt you were fighting valiantly, but his threat is the reason the mob retreated.'

There were muffled chortles around the table. I made no attempt to conceal my amusement.

FitzAldelm's one cheek flushed red with embarrassment – the other half of his face had a dressing on it – and he shot me a murderous look.

I saluted him with my cup.

The next morning, Richard held a conference to try and secure peace. He summoned Tancred's officials who were in the city, and invited King Philippe also. So many of the great and good were to attend that the only space large enough in de Muhec's house was the courtyard. Tables were set up, forming three sides of a square, with the king and his officials occupying the central one. Philippe and his followers were to sit to his right, a position of honour, while the Sicilian deputation took the least important seats.

Philippe arrived before Tancred's men. I knew some of his men

– Hugh, the duke of Burgundy, Joffroi, the count of Perche, and Peter, the count of Nevers – but de Béthune had to tell me who the bishops of Chartres and Langres were. The lot of them huddled together, making no attempt to speak with Richard's party. Archbishop Walter broke the ice by walking over with Archbishop Gerard; a stilted conversation began. The French nobles made no attempt to emulate this example, and nor did the rest of ours. We were allies, but not friends.

Richard greeted Philippe, who approached with no great hurry. The kings exchanged the kiss of peace, but there was little amity in their faces. Philippe accepted the wine Richard offered politely enough, however, and agreed that a repeat of the previous day's violence had to be prevented.

The sooner peace was restored, I thought, the sooner Joanna could return. Amusingly, that prospect was more fearsome to me than the threatening unrest. Battle knowledge I had, yet in the art of love, I was a poor student.

'The Sicilians are not to be trusted, my lord,' said Richard. 'I have it on good authority that del Pin and Margaritone instigated the rioting.' Del Pin was the governor of Messina, and Margaritone the admiral of Tancred's fleet.

'I have not heard that, my lord,' said Philippe coolly. 'The unrest started over a loaf of bread, I thought?'

Richard's mouth tightened. 'That was but the final spark.'

Philippe said nothing.

'It is best if we present a united front to these Griffons and Saracens,' Richard declared. 'Will you support me, my lord?'

'There was no trouble before you and your army arrived,' said Philippe. 'As I see it, the trouble began with your men and their unruly behaviour.'

'Who is the enemy here – me or the Sicilians?'

'I could ask your soldiers the same thing, my lord. I thought we voyaged to fight the Saracens, not the inhabitants of Messina.'

'It is not as simple as that, and you know it!' said Richard, bristling. 'I too wish reach Outremer at the earliest opportunity.'

Philippe raised an eyebrow, but any further conversation was prevented by the arrival of the Sicilians. Del Pin, a sallow-skinned, aloof man, led the deputation. He seemed thick as thieves with Margaritone, a thick-middled figure with gold rings on every finger. There were three archbishops with them, and a host of others, whose names I did not even attempt to remember.

Much bowing and scraping followed as the Sicilians paid their respects to the two kings. Everyone took their seats, and the squires and servants poured wine. Richard made a toast to peace, which went down well. Compliments were paid him on the wine. He did not catch, as I did, the French noble mutter how fortunate it was that the vintage offered was not English.

The talks went on in French for the main, but a number of the Lombards spoke only Latin, so an interpreter was needed. Having little interest in the negotiations, my attention soon wandered. I mostly thought of Joanna, as I had done since her departure for Bagnara. I was a fool even to dream about her, but I could not help myself. I had memorised every detail I could. Her long hair, and how it framed her heart-shaped face. Her skin, which looked so soft, and which I longed to caress. Her figure, hidden and yet so apparent under the contours of her gown.

My head snapped round as a loud banging came from the front door. I was not alone in laying a hand to my sword hilt.

A panting messenger was brought in, a man-at-arms sent by his serjeant from the camp – which was under attack from the Griffons on every side.

Richard thanked the soldier and ordered he be looked after. Scowling, he addressed the gathering, saying that time was of the essence. If they did not move fast – and here he glared at Del Pin and Margaritone – lives would be lost. Philippe made no comment.

The talks resumed, and progress was made. Del Pin admitted that fixing the prices of bread, wine and other staples was a good idea. He balked at the figure mentioned by Richard, however, and an argument began. Our time would have been far better served planning our campaign in the Holy Land, I decided, rather than bickering over money with these treacherous Griffons.

Into this heated atmosphere a second messenger arrived. The rioting had worsened, and incursions into the English camp had forced the king's men to give significant ground. Richard was only prevented from leaving the table by Archbishop Walter, who pleaded with him to find a peaceful way to end the violence. With clenched jaw, he sat down again. Again Philippe said and did nothing.

I was also restless. Over the hum of conversation, I could hear shouts and cries floating down the wind from our encampment. I motioned to Rhys, who padded to my side. 'Trouble is afoot,' I said in his ear. 'Ready my gear, and Pommers too. Direct Philip to do the same for the king. In fact, tell all the squires.'

Rhys gave me a grim nod and slipped away.

He had not been gone long when a third messenger came. This one was ashen-faced and had a fresh knife wound in his left arm. 'Hugh de Lusignan's lodgings are under attack, sire, but that is not the worst of it,' he said, dripping blood on the mosaic floor. 'We are being killed both within and without the city, sire.'

Richard was on his feet ere the messenger had been helped to a bench. 'You,' he said to Del Pin, his voice hard as granite, 'will go and try to stop this madness. Speak to your people. Issue orders to the city guard. Do whatever you have to!'

Del Pin's eyes went to Margaritone, who nodded, and then, nervously, back to the king. 'We will, sire. And you?'

'I shall do what I can,' said Richard. His gaze raked the watching knights. 'To arms, messires! Our men have need of us.' He looked then to Philippe. 'Will you aid us, my lord?'

'I will play no part in this violence,' said Philippe. 'My men and I have no quarrel with the people of Messina.'

Richard stared at him. A tic worked in his left cheek, a sign I knew to be unadulterated rage. He gave away nothing else, however, instead striding from the table without another word.

I glanced back. Philippe was watching, a calculating look on his face.

Once we had driven away the Griffons from the house where Hugh de Lusignan was quartered, we were joined by him and eight of his household. Rhys and the other squires had not come with us; their lack of armour made them easier prey. Now numbering twenty-one knights including the king, we made for the camp. Ours was not a large force, but fully armoured knights were a terrifying proposition to civilians using sticks and stones for weapons. The situation had eased by the time of our arrival; the officers had finally given orders to use as much force as was necessary. Not all the rioters had fled. A mob several hundred strong continued to attack the camp, which had only a shallow ditch around it. Numerous corpses could be seen inside, many of them by their garments our soldiers.

Cold rage swelled in me. Some men had behaved badly, it was true, but as far as I knew, no locals had been murdered.

Richard was in similar mood. 'See those bodies?' he cried. 'That is what the Griffons have done!'

An angry roar met his words; my voice was among them.

The king formed us into a line two deep and led a charge around the perimeter. I was in the front, near the king. It was exhilarating. Lance couched under my right arm and shield on my left, vision narrowed by my helmet slit, the great mass that was Pommers between my thighs, I felt invincible.

Our horses leaped to the full gallop. The earth shook. Inside the camp, men cheered.

We echoed Richard's cry, 'Dex aie!'

The Griffons broke and ran.

Like vengeful demons, we rode them down, our lances punching with the force of battering rams, our swords taking off heads and arms with ease.

When the ground outside the camp had been cleared of the enemy, Richard brought us to a halt. Not a knight had been slain, and only one injured, lightly. When he asked if we were ready to take the city, he was answered by a deep roar of assent.

We rested for a short time while he went to give orders to the captains of his foot soldiers. The main assault, he told us on his return, would be against the gate behind which FitzAldelm had been trapped the day before. We, on the other hand, were going to launch a surprise assault.

'Where, sire?' FitzAldelm asked, voicing the question in everyone's mind but mine and Rhys's. The previous day, the king had taken us on a surreptitious circuit of the city walls. We had spied a quiet tower with a postern gate at its base, a possible way in.

'Follow, and you shall see,' said Richard. A brief smile cracked his grim demeanour.

We went back to de Muhec's to abandon our horses and gather as many axes as could be found. Leaving the mounts in the squires' charge – Rhys was most unhappy at being left behind again – we followed the king out into the street. He took a circuitous route, weaving in and out of narrow alleys, avoiding the main avenues. Dogs barked furiously inside houses; an occasional scared face peered at us from a doorway, but no one barred our path. Our progress was good; no rioters were here, in the quarter closest to the walls.

Richard stopped in the shadow of a small church, beyond which lay the ditch that surrounded the city. Ordering us to peer around the corner one by one, that the defenders did not see us, he laid out his plan.

'Did you see the door at the base of the nearest tower?'

Everyone nodded. A natural outcrop had been incorporated into the defences, with the walls climbing its slope from our right to a strongly built tower, and then down the other side, where they ran off into the distance. The promontory was not all rock; at the structure's base, facing into the ditch, was a steep, stony gradient.

The postern door was proof, Richard told us, that men could make a safe descent. We were about to test the possibility of ascending it. His gaze, fierce and eager, roamed our faces. 'Are you with me?'

Telling myself that the sentries atop the tower would not see us, I muttered my assent with everyone else.

Richard wasted no time, leading us out into the open. We moved as fast as helmeted men in full mail, burdened with shields, axes and long-scabbarded swords can. Fortune was on our side at the ditch, which had part collapsed due to lack of care. Safely at its bottom, with no indication of being seen, we moved our shields around onto our backs, and began to clamber up the slope. It was precipitous, forcing us to use our hands and seek firm footholds at every step. Richard led, of course, and the four with axes came next. I was one; so too were de Chauvigny, de Béthune and FitzAldelm.

The effort soon had sweat pouring down from under my arming cap, stinging my eyes. Cursing under my breath, I tried to blink it away. I twisted my neck now and again to look upward. Mostly my view was of the soles of FitzAldelm's boots, and the torrent of pebbles and dust he sent my way, but sometimes I caught sight of the tower, now framed by blue sky. Still no alarm sounded, and I began to hope that we would reach the door unnoticed.

Perhaps thirty feet of the incline remained when a jutting rock gave way beneath the king's weight. God be thanked, he did not slide face first down into the ditch, but there was no concealing the thump of his landing nor the rattle of stones that had been dislodged.

We froze.

The clash of arms and men's cries reached us from the main gate.

Maybe they did not hear, I thought.

A head appeared at the top of the tower, that of a young man, barely old enough to shave. Shock filled his face, and he bellowed something in Latin.

'Quickly!' roared Richard, his voice muffled behind his helmet. 'Move!'

I did not dare to look up again. It was easy to imagine a crossbow bolt driving through the slit in my helmet. I went up the last section like a man possessed, overtaking FitzAldelm and reaching the base of the tower as the king did.

He pointed at the door. 'Smash it down!'

Laying my shield on the ground, I set to with a will. De Béthune joined me. A natural rhythm developed, each of us taking alternate swings. The door shook beneath our assault; splinters and small pieces of wood flew. It was solidly built, however, as might be expected from its dangerous position. We wielded our axes again and again. The effort required – we were both still in full mail and wearing helmets – was immense. After two score blows, my heart felt as if it was about to burst. Sensing us flag, Richard bellowed that we should stand back. For once, I was glad to let FitzAldelm take my place. De Chauvigny replaced de Béthune.

Chest heaving, I picked up my shield. Apart from our two axemen and Richard, everyone had his over his head. Crossbow bolts were raining down around us, fast as the men above could reload. A good number were hitting the ground near the king. I risked a glance up, and my hunch was proved correct. Four crossbowmen were visible, and two at least were aiming at Richard. His red crest, I thought. They might not realise exactly who he is, but it marks him out as a leader. I raced forward, angry that no one else had acted before me.

'Sire!' I shouted.

Richard's helmet turned. His blue eyes regarded me from the slit. 'Aye?'

'You must protect yourself, sire.' I scrabbled at his back, trying to pull around his shield, which still hung from its strap.

'Leave it, Rufus. We shall be in ere long,' he said.

He is cursedly stubborn, I thought, raising my own shield over his head.

Again he looked. 'Rufus! You will be hit.'

'Better I who is wounded than you, sire.' Despite my bravado, I could taste bile. A heartbeat before, I had felt the impact of a quarrel right at my feet. Hauberk or no, the distance from the tower's top was well within crossbow killing range.

'You are a bull-headed Irishman!' Richard cried, but he tugged off his shield, and lifted it up, allowing me to protect myself once more.

Thunk. A crossbow bolt struck the king's shield with enough force to drive the tip and half its own length through the planks.

He bellowed with amusement.

He fears nothing, I thought, and laughed too.

Under FitzAldelm's and de Chauvigny's assault, the door had splintered. A long, crooked opening now ran from its top down towards the lower hinge. They were tiring, however, so de Béthune and I took another turn. Concentrating on the bottom of the crack – reach the hinge and the door would fall inwards – we went at it with renewed energy. The planking creaked. Richard shouted encouragement.

A hammer blow struck my helmet from above. I staggered, and sparks flew as my axe hit the wall. Head ringing, stars spinning across my vision, I felt a strong hand seize my upper right arm. Thus supported, I regained my footing.

'Rufus?' The king's voice was concerned.

I sucked in a breath, and let it out. 'I am unhurt, sire.'

He pulled me aside, and let de Chauvigny in with his axe. Both of us partly under his shield, Richard stared at me. 'Truly?'

I had been lying before, unwilling to admit weakness, but I could now focus again. I no longer felt as if I were on the deck of a storm-wracked ship. 'My helmet took the worst of the blow, sire.'

He straightened, and peered at the top of my head. 'Christ, but you are right. I swear the gouge in it is half an inch deep.'

'Sire!' FitzAldelm's voice, excited. 'The door is about to give way.'

'We have work to do, Rufus,' said Richard, handing me my shield and telling the rest to be ready. 'Stand aside,' he ordered FitzAldelm and de Béthune.

The narrow doorway would only admit one man at a time. I took my place behind the king, peering around him at the splintered planking. A decent kick, I thought, and we will be in.

Sword ready in his fist, Richard raised his right foot.

A terrible premonition seized me. Dropping my blade, I seized the king by the shoulder and wrenched him backwards and to the side.

Click. A black blur shot through the space he had occupied, past us both. There was a soft, choking sound. Peter Tireproie, who by some madness had not fastened his aventail, dropped lifeless to the dirt with a quarrel in his throat.

Poor soul, I thought, wishing it could have been de Gunesse, the next in line.

Richard tensed, about to crash through into the tower again. We had a little time while the crossbowman reloaded.

'There may be two of them, sire!' I cried.

A nod – he had heard. Instead of his booted foot, he used his shield to punch through the ruined door.

Click. Crunch. A bolt passed through the king's shield and hit him in the ribs, but he was through, on top of the two men-at-arms on the other side. Both were frantically trying to load their weapons. A massive downward slash of Richard's sword clove the helm and skull of the first in twain, and I, who had come storming in behind him, buried my blade hilt deep in the chest of the other.

There was no one else in the small, dirt-floored chamber. We were in.

Richard clapped me on the arm, his way of thanking me for saving his life. I grinned behind my helmet, pleased as a dog with a meaty bone. I asked him if he was hurt, and he laughed again, telling me that the quarrel had not penetrated his hauberk. Wiping the worst of the gore from our swords, we sheathed them and slung our shields on our backs for a second time. To ascend the wooden ladder that led up into the tower, a man needed both hands. I stared at the square of daylight twenty feet above our heads with some trepidation. For all we knew, more crossbowmen were waiting up there. It was madness for the king to lead the way.

'I should go first, sire,' I said.

Richard chuckled. 'Trying to steal my glory, eh?'

'No, sire,' I replied, and I meant it.

'The danger is mine,' said Richard, and laid hand to the first rung.

I, who had neglected my prayers for months, threw up an urgent plea as up he went. Let not this be the hour of his death.

FitzAldelm, who had crowded into the room after us, made to follow, but I barged him out of the way. Such was the hatred in his eyes, he would have slain me as I climbed. But others were present, and he could do nothing save take his place on the ladder after me.

I forgot about FitzAldelm at once, so great was my fear that the king would be shot before he gained whatever chamber lay above. Christ be thanked, he made it unharmed. I reached the opening a few heartbeats later. Head and shoulders out, hands flat upon the planking to either side, about to heave myself up, I suddenly felt a hand on my helmet.

'Stay where you are!' Richard hissed.

I obeyed at once. The slit in my helmet was flush with the floor; all I could see were Richard's boots – he was crouching over me – and a few feet away, a bare stone wall. Nonetheless, my stomach heaved. Death was close by.

A crossbow clicked. There was a thunk as Richard's shield was hit.

A second quarrel buried itself in the planking beside his foot.

'Climb, while they reload!' ordered the king.

I scrambled up as fast as I could. Only when I had my shield over my head did I dare to look at Richard, who was protecting himself in the same way. 'Wait, Robert!' he shouted into the hole in the floor. To me, he said, 'Protect him.'

Loathsome though the order was, I could not refuse the king. Shield over my head, I crouched over FitzAldelm's helmet, which had just appeared.

'Two men stayed on the roof. It is they who are aiming at us,' the king explained. 'We cannot reach them, nor is that our purpose. Once they have shot again, you and I will leave by the door over there. It leads to the battlements, I wager. FitzAldelm can protect the next man, who can do the same for the one after him, and so on. It will not be long ere the whole group gains this floor, God willing, all unharmed.'

The crossbowmen loosed. One quarrel hit my shield and passed almost all the way through, bruising my fingers through the mail glove. The other bounced off the side of my helmet, struck my shoulder and dropped to the floor. Head ringing for the second time, I was glad to follow Richard and leave FitzAldelm at the mercy of the enemy crossbows. With luck, I thought, one would find a weakness in his hauberk.

The door opened onto a small, empty antechamber. It seemed to be a guardroom, with a fireplace, table and stools. Richard padded to another door on the far wall and opening it a crack, peered out.

'Good news, Rufus,' he said. 'There is a staircase down to the street not ten paces away.'

'Enemy soldiers, sire?'

'A few, but they are some distance off, and seem quite . . . occupied.' He chuckled.

This was what I wanted to hear. The assault on the main gate *was* diverting attention from us.

Before long, the rest of the party had joined us. Sadly, we had lost another man, Matthew de Sauley, to the crossbowmen on the roof. We were all angry. One of the other knights was for setting the wooden floor alight. It would turn the tower into a column of flame, he said, rightful punishment for the Griffons who had slain two of the king's mesnie. Richard missed FitzAldelm's nod of agreement – I did not – and cut him off savagely, saying that was a coward's way to kill.

'More important matters are at hand,' he said.

With a few brief words – we should stay close together, fighting only to clear the way in front of us, and at the main gate, spare no effort to open it – he led us through the door. Reaching the bottom of the stairs without incident, we found ourselves on a narrow, cobbled street. Not a soul was to be seen. Houses stood on one side, and on the other was the city wall with its walkway. Our greatest danger would come from there, I decided. Every crossbowman and archer would be able to shoot at us with impunity.

An astute commander, Richard noticed too. Hugging the base of the wall, he had us follow him in single file. In this manner, we passed unseen for perhaps a quarter of a mile. Nearing a junction with a thoroughfare that ran left, into the city proper, Richard stopped trying to hide. He gave the order to form a line across the street. The open area before us was crowded with civilians and soldiers of the garrison. Heads were turning in our direction. Arms were pointing. A challenge rang out.

Breaking into a run, Richard led us straight at them.

Showers of crossbow bolts and arrows landed among us – we had been spotted by the enemy on the ramparts. Rocks, bricks, and pieces of tile were being hurled from rooftops and windows. There was nothing to do but charge and hope not to be hit.

'De Roverei is down,' shouted someone behind me.

I checked my pace. De Roverei was a friend, an amiable type with a fine taste in wine.

'Keep going! He is dead,' said another voice.

These cursed Griffons, I thought, itching to wield my sword.

I got the chance soon enough. The mob swarmed forward to meet us in a great, chaotic wave. Richard did not slow even a fraction, and nor did we. Grieving for our dead companions, we carved a bloody path into the midst of them. I opened the arm of a man wielding a club, and as he screamed his dismay, I shoved him backwards with my shield, into his comrade behind. Stumbling, gaze fixed on me, he gawped as my sword tip took him through one eye. The Griffons who came after had seen enough. Turning their backs, they shoved a path through their fellows. This kindled fear, and some of the nearest men wavered.

A short distance away, Richard was reaping like Death himself. A Griffon's head leaped from his shoulders on a fountain of red. Another stared, dazed, at the place where his hand had been. The king slew a third man, and a fourth. Those facing him could take no more: around us it was the same. In no time, the street had emptied of the enemy, leaving us surrounded by the injured, dead and dying.

Now the crossbowmen renewed their attack, and the people in the nearest buildings. We hid behind our shields and continued on towards the main gate. The danger did not abate. Arrows and crossbow bolts hummed and whined, and thunked into shields or dashed sparks off the cobbles. Several of our number were hit, but our mail prevented serious injury. A table hurled from a second floor window landed with a mighty crash, narrowly missing FitzAldelm. Even as he shook his fist at the jeering culprit, a stool flew end over end towards him. It struck him a glancing blow, and he had to scurry out of the way not to be hit by another. The contents of a chamber pot – also thrown from a house – caused de Béthune to slip and fall on his arse. A liegeman to Richard's father Henry, and before that, his elder brother the Young King, he was a coolheaded man with a sardonic sense of humour. He was not laughing now, however.

I, on the other hand, was chortling so hard I could not help him up.

'You think it is funny?' he grated at me from behind his helmet.

'I am sorry—' I broke off again, choking with mirth. Regaining control, I stuck out a hand and said, 'My apologies.'

Growling an obscenity, he reached up to take my grip.

Next instant, standing on only God knew what vileness, one of my own feet went from under me. Down I went, landing like him, on my rear end in the mire.

De Béthune laughed harder than I had ever heard him.

I could do nothing but join in.

'When you are finished, we have a task to complete.' The king was amused, however, and took part in the inevitable jokes that were made at our expense.

A second encounter in the environs of the main gate with an even larger crowd also went our way. I have no doubt that the clamouring of our men on the other side of the gates helped our cause. The king himself, with me and FitzAldelm helping, lifted the massive locking bar and carried it to one side. Most of the yelling soldiers who rushed past did not even see Richard. Baying like hounds close on the heels of a stag, they charged into the city. The Griffons did not stand and fight. They fled, in their panic running into one another and even towards groups of our men. There was no mercy. Swords rose and fell. Griffons died.

'Like crops to the scythe,' said Richard, making no attempt to intervene.

The Griffons *had* brought this on their own heads, I thought. All the same, I turned my face away from the slaughter, and tried to imagine a similar victory over our real enemies, the mamluks of Saladin's army.

CHAPTER VII

Soon men were joking that the king had taken less time to seize control of Messina than a priest needed to say matins. Even if it was not quite true, the speed of the assault had been remarkable. Sieges could last for months, thanks to strong fortifications and insufficiently powerful artillery. Today resistance had ceased ere the afternoon had turned to evening.

The damage was not limited to the city. Some of Richard's troops rampaged down to the harbour and there set the Sicilian fleet alight. Messina itself might have burned too, had he not intervened. Not daring to disobey the king, a fearsome sight in his mail and crimson-stained surcoat, the soldiers withdrew to the army's camp. Barely a one was sober; most were laden down with booty. I saw men carrying barrels of wine, joints of meat, bulging flour sacks, bolts of cloth, silver plate. Hens squawked and flapped about in an alleyway, chased by a drunk man-at-arms. Two archers stumbled along, barely able to manage a rolled carpet twice the length of an oxcart.

As the sun dipped towards the western horizon, a flaming ball of orange, I stood on the battlements over the main gate with Richard and watched as banners bearing the royal colours and those of Aquitaine were fixed in place. Tancred's emblem had been thrown into the street below, where men-at-arms wiped their feet on it and laughed. Old anger stirred in me, and I wondered if the soldiers led by FitzAldelm's brother Guy had done similar things as my family's stronghold of Cairlinn burned. I did not let myself brood. Ireland was half the world away, and Jerusalem still had to be taken.

'A good day, Rufus,' said Richard, leaning his elbows on the parapet. 'Messina is mine.'

'As it should be, sire,' I said. The king had not started this fight, but he had finished it. He had also prevented a wholesale massacre.

'Look.' Richard jerked his chin.

A short distance from the gate, I spied two soldiers watching us. The fleur-de-lis marked both their shields. 'Frenchmen,' I said.

'Spying for Philippe,' said Richard. A wolfish grin followed. 'How will he like what I have done here, I wonder?'

An hour passed. Washed and changed, we were in the courtyard of de Muhec's house, our favoured gathering place. Men were comparing cuts and bruises from the day's fighting. Richard was combing his beard before a silver mirror. Wine was being drunk. There was joking and laughter, and to my annoyance, frequent mention of chamber pots. According to most, my hauberk and de Béthune's would never smell the same again.

Rhys was already hard at work, scouring it in a barrel of sand and water. He was not happy with me, and I could not blame him. Half a dozen silver pennies would see his mood change, I thought, in the same moment hoping that his efforts succeeded.

A fist hammered on the front door, loud and peremptory.

We watched the king, who had instructed that no one should be admitted save by his authority. Hearing that the messenger came from Philippe, Richard ordered him sent away.

Uneasy, I glanced at de Béthune, reading the same feeling in his eyes. Neither of us liked Philippe either, but he was our ally. Deliberately stoking bad feeling served no one, and would not aid our enterprise, to retake Jerusalem.

We did not say anything to Richard, however. He was still in combative mood.

Not long after, there came another pounding on the door.

A sentry rushed in. 'I am bid, sire, to tell you that Hugh, Duke of Burgundy, is outside. He says he will not leave until you speak together.'

The king gave me a conspiratorial 'What did I tell you?' smile. 'Bring him in,' he said.

Hugh was well-known to us all, and to Richard in particular. Prone to invade Aquitaine whenever opportunity allowed, the duke had also previously allied himself with the Young King and the irksome Raymond of Toulouse.

Jowly-faced and pompous, Hugh came huffing down the passage.

When the man-at-arms announced him, he pushed past, towards Richard. 'Sire.' He dipped his knee, but not to the floor.

'It is late to be paying house visits, Duke Hugh,' said Richard.

'Aye, well, the first messenger could not deliver his letter, sire.'

'As I say, it is late for such things,' Richard replied, his face bland. 'Is aught amiss?'

'I come from King Philippe, sire.'

'Do you indeed?' Richard sounded surprised. 'What is so important that it cannot wait until our meeting tomorrow?'

Hugh's complexion, already choleric, darkened. 'Y-your banners, sire,' he spluttered. 'They fly over the city's main gate, but of *my* lord's, there is no sign.'

Richard gave him a puzzled look. 'At the conference earlier, Philippe made much of his refusal to get involved. Not a single soldier of his helped to quell the unrest. Indeed, there were rumours that his men prevented my ships from entering the harbour today.'

'There is no truth in that, sire.'

'I have neither the time nor the inclination to argue the point. I also see no reason that Philippe's banners should hang there.'

'But he is your lord, sire, in the eyes of God and men.' Hugh was referring to the feudal agreement which saw Richard hold his continental territories – Normandy, Brittany, Aquitaine and the rest – of Philippe. It was a legal point only; Richard was far more powerful than the French king.

'He is, and I love and revere him for it.' Richard sounded genuine, but everyone present knew he was lying.

'If you respect the king's superior rank, sire, his banners should replace yours on the battlements.'

'He refused to take part in the fighting. Nor did he grant the Lombards his protection, although they begged for it. *Now* he stakes claim to the prize?'

Hugh said tonelessly, 'King Philippe requests that you see it done at once.'

'The mere suggestion is absurd.' Richard's tone was sharp. 'Messina is mine. Mine, do you hear?'

Hugh quailed before the bite in the king's voice, but he was not quite done. 'At Vézelay, sire, you and Philippe swore that all conquests should be shared equally.'

'Ones that we undertook together.'

'*All* conquests, sire.'

Richard pointed. 'You may as well bang your head off thon wall. My banners will stay where they are. On their own. Now, unless you have more to say . . .'

Unhappy but impotent, Hugh muttered a farewell and hurried away.

'Oh, to be a fly on the wall when Philippe hears,' said Richard, making no attempt to lower his voice.

I loved and revered the king, but at times like this, he was prone to overweening arrogance. I saw that de Béthune shared my reservations, and suspected by de Chauvigny's closed expression that he did too. The pair were better at hiding their emotions, however. The instant Richard looked my way, I was undone. He crooked a finger.

I crossed the mosaic with reluctance. 'Sire?'

'You think I am being unwise.' There was no mistaking his belligerent tone.

I seethed inside. Was I forever to be cursed by transparent emotions? I flailed for a convincing answer. 'It is not that, sire.'

He snorted. 'You looked most unhappy at the manner of Duke Hugh's departure.'

'He was discourteous towards you, sire,' I said, avoiding the issue. 'I did not like it.'

'Do you take me for a wet-behind-the-ears youth? There was more to it than that.'

'King Philippe is in the wrong, sire.'

'Indeed. My liege or no, he has *no* right to demand his banners are hoisted in place of mine.'

'He does not, sire,' I agreed.

'But?' Richard challenged.

'Philippe is your ally, sire.' My implication was clear.

'God's legs!' Still incensed, the king plunged into a tirade about the French king. His refusal to help put down the unrest. His long history of scheming against Richard. Like as not, he was conniving with Tancred here in Sicily. Philippe was a scoundrel and a deceiver, the king declared, who would broker a deal with the Devil himself if he thought it advantageous.

'He is all of the things you say, sire, but . . .' I stopped, leaving open the insinuation that Philippe and Richard remained sworn allies.

'The rogue has no right to any of the riches of Messina!' The king went off into a second tirade, but this one was not as long. His quick-to-flame fury was draining away, as was his wont – and as I had hoped.

From the minaret of a nearby mosque came the muezzin's haunting call to prayer. *'Hai ala-as-salah! Allahu-akbar! La ilaha illa'allah!'*

Richard's expression grew pensive. 'The men in Outremer who listen to that summons are our true enemies.'

'They are, sire,' I said, encouraged, 'and we will need all our strength to defeat them.'

A snort of amusement.

I glanced at him.

'The chance of victory over Saladin will be greater with Philippe's army alongside my own,' the king declared.

He was coming around at last, I thought with relief. Sure enough, his ill temper then vanished, and was replaced by a brighter mood.

'I was angry with Philippe – I still am – but that is no reason to treat him like a churl,' said Richard. 'He *is* within his rights to demand half of whatever we can prise from that monkey Tancred for Messina. I shall tell him that in the morning.'

'But I doubt Philippe will be satisfied with that – he is too proud and wilful. Appearance is everything to him.'

'He will continue to resent the fact that his standards are not atop the main gate, sire,' I agreed. 'If there was a way to assuage his pride without giving him the satisfaction of allowing his banners to stand alongside your own . . .'

After a moment's pause, delight sparked in Richard's eyes. 'I will send word to the Templars and Hospitallers. Until an agreement with Tancred is reached, the administration of Messina shall be theirs, and their banners alone shall fly from the walls. Philippe can have no quarrel with that.'

The French king accepted Richard's offer at a meeting the next day, although stuffily enough. Nonetheless, the deal was done, and they exchanged the kiss of peace. The military orders were more than happy to take charge of the city. 'They seize every opportunity to make money,' Richard said to me. 'Outremer places a constant, heavy drain on their resources. The population of Franks has been dwindling there for generations, you see, so the Templars and Hospitallers have had to play an ever-increasing role in the kingdom's defence.'

'Their soldiers will form an important part of the army, sire, will they not?' When the king nodded, I asked, 'Will de Nablus obey you in the field, sire?' De Sablé would, I knew, for he had reached his position thanks to Richard's influence and donations to his order. De Nablus was a different proposition, however, and no callow youth to be easily led.

Richard smiled. 'I believe he will.'

'You *wanted* the orders to have their standards on the walls, sire,' I said, grinning. 'So they would be in your debt.'

'You discern my purpose, Rufus,' he said slyly.

I glanced sidelong at the French king. I sensed a lingering resentment in him, for all that he had agreed terms. It was hard to see how he could be pleased with Richard's next intentions either. Firstly, hostages were to be taken from the most important families in Messina as a guarantee of good behaviour. They would be kept in our camp. Secondly, a massive tower was planned on a hill overlooking the city, a watch place for our soldiers. A more public statement of Richard's dominance was hard to imagine. I told myself that the riches promised to Philippe would satisfy him, that he would not care about such details, but my worries remained.

Ally he was in name, but he felt more like an enemy.

The following day, the sixth of October, Tancred's response to Richard's demands arrived. The king, delighted, made no attempt to inform Philippe of the letter's details, nor indeed any of us. Instead he set out for Bagnara, taking a few men and horses. I was one; so too were Rhys and Philip.

FitzAldelm was not, pleasingly. The cut on his cheek had festered, and he was confined to bed by order of the physician. Sad to say, his illness was not life-threatening. His terrier P'tit – Small – stayed by his bedside night and day, a trait I found endearing despite my hatred of its owner. Philip's guess had been correct: it was a sweet creature, although prone to yap incessantly when excited.

As we clattered through the archway and into the monastery at Bagnara, my excitement at the prospect of seeing Joanna grew wire taut. Rhys, Philip and the other squires were left in charge of the horses, while de Chauvigny, de Béthune and I followed Richard towards the abbot's quarters, the grandest rooms in the place.

Acknowledging the salutes of the amazed men-at-arms at the door, the king ordered that they should remain at their posts. 'I am here to surprise my sister,' he said to me with a grin.

'She will be delighted, sire.' I hoped Joanna would also be pleased to see me.

We crept in unnoticed, the creak of the door masked by the gentle music being played within. Two servants, waiting in attendance by the entrance, gaped at Richard, who raised a finger to his lips even as they knelt.

'Wait here,' he whispered to us.

Joanna was at the far end of the room with her ladies. Some were sitting in the window seats, others close to the harpist. Most were busy at needlework, although two were playing chess. Not hearing Richard until he was almost on top of her, she leaped up with a happy cry. Her embroidery dropped unnoticed to the rush-covered floor.

'Richard!' She flung her arms about him.

'Ah, but it is good to see you, lass,' he said, enveloping her in a hug.

'You sent no word of your coming.' Joanna stepped back, her expression anxious. 'You carry ill news, I guess. We saw the smoke yesterday – has Messina burned down? Were many people killed?'

'Worry not,' said Richard gently. 'I bring excellent tidings.'

Her face cleared. 'Did you come alone?' Seeing us then, she chided him. 'Do you think so little of your knights, to leave them stand like unwanted guests at the door?'

Richard beckoned, and we walked the length of the room to greet her. She was a vision, golden-haired, in a gown of sky blue, and soft leather shoes. The two of us knelt. 'Rise, rise. You must be thirsty after your journey,' Joanna said warmly.

Richard raised an eyebrow. 'Messina is but a short distance away.'

'Which makes your lack of visits all the worse!' She gave him a most unladylike dig in the ribs.

Discomfited, Richard said, 'I have been busy, lass.'

It was rare indeed to see the king so, and I exchanged an amused look with de Béthune. Her feisty spirit made her even more attractive.

Sweet wine was brought, and pastries. We partook, but Richard had no interest, so taken up was he with his news. Joanna would have none of it.

'First you will tell me what happened at Messina.' She listened, rapt, as her brother laid out the tale of the taking of the town. Richard made light of his own role – a habit of his – but mentioned how I had pulled him out of the way of a crossbow bolt.

'Must you take such risks?' Joanna asked. Richard shrugged, and she tsked in disapproval. Her blue eyes – the same intense colour as his – turned on me. 'It seems I am in your debt, Sir Rufus, for ensuring I still have a brother.'

Sweet Jesu, she was desirable. My colour rose. 'The king did the same for me not long after, madam.'

'You must tell me of it later.' A radiant smile.

My heart leaped. 'It would be an honour, madam.'

Richard finished, relating with delight how his tower overlooking Messina was called 'Mategriffon', meaning 'Kill the Greeks'.

'You cannot name it that, brother!' Joanna protested. 'Not all the people of Sicily are rebellious, or evil. Many are good folk – I have lived here for years, remember.'

'I know, lass, but the malcontents among them have done grievous harm to my men. A message needs to be delivered, and the tower does that in fine style. I have no intention of killing any more Griffons, save at need. If they rise up again, however, by God, I will take the whole island.'

It took a little more reassurance from Richard that peace had been restored, but at length Joanna seemed content. 'Now you can tell me what has you so excited,' she said, her cheeks dimpling.

Richard laughed, and dragging my eyes away from her, I exchanged another look with de Béthune. It was surprising, and amusing, to see the king submit so readily to command.

'I have made peace with Tancred,' said Richard.

'If he has any wit, the small dog relinquishes the bone to the larger.'

The king's lips twitched. 'There is more. When Tancred freed you, he did not send your dowry.'

'He is a miserly man.'

'I have no doubt. Since the happenings at Messina, however, he has seen fit to reconsider his position. Does twenty thousand ounces of gold please you?'

'Twenty thousand?' Joanna clapped her hands. 'Oh, happy day! That was well wrought, brother.'

'He is to pay it forthwith, but that is not all,' said Richard with relish. 'I extracted another twenty thousand ounces from him as well.'

'Not the legacy William left to our lord father?'

'Even so. I thought coin would suffice in place of a solid gold table and a two-hundred-man silk pavilion.'

Baffled, I looked at de Béthune, who explained quietly that Joanna's dead husband William had long intended to gift Richard's father Henry with a generous bequest, its purpose to help with his quest to free Jerusalem.

'Did Tancred not argue that the bequest was invalid because Papa died before William?' asked Joanna.

'He did,' said Richard.

'You forced him to agree regardless?'

'I did not. I suggested that if Tancred wanted to remain king of Sicily, he should pay.' Richard's smile was predatory.

Her tinkling laugh filled the room. 'That is no choice at all, brother.'

'I sweetened the agreement by making an ally of him. Like as not, we shall have to overwinter on Sicily – it seems unlikely that Berengaria will arrive before the New Year – and life will be considerably easier this way. If I had spurned Tancred, he would have climbed into bed with Philippe. The two of them had already been engaged in secret talks, if my spies are to be believed. That will continue no longer.'

'Tancred is giving you the gold. What does he receive in return?'

'One of his daughters is to marry my heir when she comes of age.'

'John is already married.'

'It is not he I speak of.'

'Who then?' she asked in confusion.

'Ah, lass, I forget how far from home you are here. John cannot be trusted.'

'I remember him as a sweet, chubby-cheeked boy,' said Joanna with a frown.

Even as I hid my own amusement, Richard snorted. 'Maybe he was, long ago, but he is far from that now, the whelp. For that reason and many others, he is not my heir – that falls to Arthur of Brittany.'

'Brother Geoffrey's son?' When Richard nodded, Joanna went on, 'He can only be two or three years old.'

'Three.'

'A babe. John will not be pleased by your decision, and he an adult man.'

'He was recompensed handsomely enough before I left. Four counties and more I gave him. But enough of John.'

She nodded. 'It is plain how Tancred benefits from a marriage alliance. With you as his shield, he will have little to fear from the Hohenstaufen family, and their designs on the island. What does the agreement bring you?'

'Apart from twenty thousand ounces of gold?'

She made a face. 'Forget not that the German emperor will be angered by your actions. Constance *is* the rightful heir to the throne.'

Odd though it seemed, Joanna had no legal claim to Sicily.

'I care little what Barbarossa thinks. I doubt he is much concerned with me either. If there are any issues between us, they can be dealt with in Outremer.' Frederick was already journeying to the Holy Land.

'Nevertheless, Tancred's daughter is not a fitting match for your heir, Richard.'

'These marriages rarely come to pass, and Arthur is only three. I am also to wed soon. Before next year is out, God willing, I will have a son of my own.'

'I look forward to that day.' Despite her words, there was a sadness in Joanna's expression.

Richard touched her arm. 'You would have wished for children.'

She nodded. 'William and I were happy. It is cruel that I have no sons or daughters to remember him by.'

'Cruel indeed, but there is still time for you.'

'Do not marry me off just yet!' For the first time, her air of confidence seemed fragile. 'We have not seen each other for fourteen years, Richard; I could not bear it if we were separated again so soon.'

'Worry not, lass,' said the king reassuringly. 'Berengaria is to travel with me, but I will often be taken up with the fight against Saladin. It was in my mind you and she would be good company for each other. That is, if you are agreeable?'

'I could not ask for more.' There were tears of joy in Joanna's eyes.

'Then we are agreed,' said Richard, satisfied.

The king did not notice my delight, but de Béthune did. 'Have a care, Rufus,' he whispered in my ear. 'She is sister to our king.'

I shot him a startled look. 'Is it that obvious?'

'The king has not seen only because all his attention is on Joanna. Much as he loves you, he would not be best pleased to know you have feelings for his sister.'

I nodded and smoothed my face into the best impression of a mask I could make. My intention to ignore her did not last long, alas. Soon after, Richard had to deal with an urgent message from Messina; begging his sister's pardon, he closeted himself in a side room with de Béthune. Almost alone with Joanna – her ladies were close by, worse luck – I found myself exhilarated, yet frustratingly lost for what to say.

She made it easy, requesting that I relate my account of the assault on the tower. Out we went to the garden, her ladies' eyes on our backs. One had offered to walk with us, but Joanna waved a dismissive hand. I exulted, de Béthune's warning already forgotten. A colonnaded walkway ran around the four sides of the garden, which was paved with herb beds and fruit trees, and had a well at its centre.

I began by mentioning Richard's foresight in spying out the tower before ever he had the need. 'He has been a tactician since childhood,' said Joanna. Not wanting to sound the braggart, I passed over the first moments of entering the stronghold. She halted me, smiling, and ordered that I tell the whole tale, not just part of it. A little embarrassed, I obeyed.

'You saved his life?'

'I would not say that, madam. I stopped the king from being struck by a crossbow bolt.'

'You are playing games! At that range, there is a good chance that Richard would have been slain.'

I admitted that she was right, and she chided me, but gently. 'Go on.'

My description of the king standing over me as I emerged through the trapdoor made her laugh. So did the episode when de Béthune and I ended up on our arses in piss and shit – although I did not use those words.

'You are a band of brothers,' she said when I was done. 'You, the king and the other mesnie knights.'

'We are, madam,' I said feelingly. Apart from FitzAldelm and de Gunesse, I thought.

'How long have you served my brother?'

'Eleven years, madam.'

'A long time. What age are you, can I ask?'

'Thirty, madam, in August.' I hesitated, then asked, 'And you?'

'Twenty-four.' She cast me a sidelong look. 'Are you married, Sir Rufus?'

'No, madam. I have not met the right lady yet.'

'And how will you know when that happens?' There was a challenging but playful look in her eyes.

I found it hard to meet her gaze. She was so close – only an arm's length away – and we were talking of love and desire. 'In truth, madam, I am not sure.'

'Inaction is a sure path to failure when it comes to women,' she said with a laugh.

'Maybe, madam, but it is the safer option.' I imagined my humiliation if I tried to hold her hand, and she rebuffed me.

'You take risks on the battlefield, Sir Rufus.'

I looked at her, confused. 'Of course, madam. In war, one has to.'

'It is the same with love.'

I told myself that I was imagining the trace of colour to her cheek.

Our talk was interrupted by Richard, his business dealt with. He loudly accused me of stealing his sister. It was a joke, of course, but I was grateful that his attention did not linger on me. De Béthune's advice rolled around my head, but I paid no heed. All I could think of was Joanna, and when I might next meet her.

CHAPTER VIII

Messina, December 1190

My mail shinked as I lifted my feet up and down, trying to get the blood flowing. It was early morning, and the stone-flagged corridor in de Muhec's house was chilly.

'Are your toes numb?' de Béthune whispered from the other side of the chapel entrance. 'Mine are.'

'The king must be half-frozen,' I replied.

'Probably, but he is closer to God.'

Our gaze moved to the door. Richard lay beyond it, in front of the altar, naked as the day he was born. He had entered a short time before, to pay penitence for his sins. We were standing guard to make sure only the religious could enter.

De Béthune had just told me of Richard's brother the Young King repenting in similar fashion, years before. It was an extreme way of seeking forgiveness, and one I would not have imagined for the king. Nor yet, I told myself, could I have envisaged the extent of his bawdy behaviour since the taking of Messina. Richard was fond of wine, and when the right one caught his eye, women. This was different. Night after night, he drank to excess. He had taken up with a beautiful half-Saracen serving girl, and spent days on end with her in his bedchamber.

Matters had come to a head the previous afternoon. Declaring he needed to clear his head, the king had ordered he and I ride out together. Delighted by this small move back to normality, and the chance perhaps to suggest a visit to Joanna – whom I had not seen for several weeks – I told Rhys and Philip to saddle the horses.

The Saracen girl was being shepherded out of the front door as we rode onto the street. Her face was tearstained, and when she saw Richard, she called out.

With a haunted look, he had let her approach. Even grief-stricken, she was stunning. They exchanged a few words; she reached out a hand, which he patted awkwardly, and then he muttered a farewell and urged his horse away. The girl took a step or two after him, and then stopped. Fresh tears ran down her face.

'Come, Rufus.' Richard's voice had been commanding.

I had obeyed. We rode side-by-side, the Griffons scrambling out of our path.

The king had said not a word.

Coming back to the present, I shot a look at de Béthune. 'Why do you think he got rid of the half-Saracen girl? Is it because he is to wed?'

'That would be my guess.'

'And yet it is normal enough for kings to have mistresses even when they are married.'

'Richard is not like that, Rufus. Think of how he is with regard to life, to leadership, to politics and war. He throws himself in headlong, and always seeks to be the first, the best.' De Béthune lowered his voice and added, 'Ploughing a serving wench is scarcely how a godly man, still less a king, is *supposed* to act.'

'We of the mesnie do not care,' I whispered fiercely. 'And I would wager a hundred silver pennies that his soldiers, if they knew, would not either.'

'Even so. Yesterday Richard stared into the mirror of his soul, and liked not what he saw.'

That was it, I thought, suddenly remembering the king's encounter with a Griffon woman the previous day. Spying Richard as we rode close to the city's main gate, she had run over and clung to one of his feet, crying and wailing in poor French. The king had not reviled her, but listened. Between us, we managed to understand that her only son was perilously ill.

'We went to see him,' I said to de Béthune. 'The wretch lay in her house, a rough bandage wrapped around his head, his eyes open but unseeing. He looked more a corpse than a boy, but he lived still. A neighbour woman with better French appeared; she was able to tell us that the boy – only thirteen years old – had been caught on the streets during our attack on the city, and been struck with a mace by one of our soldiers. Left for dead, he was found by his mother and carried home. There he had lain since, oblivious to all sight and sound, trapped somewhere between life and death.'

'Sweet Jesu,' said de Béthune, his face horrified. 'What did the king do?'

'He was distraught. He begged the woman's forgiveness, that an innocent child should suffer such grievous injury, and said that his physicians would visit to see what could be done. When we got back, he had a purse of gold sent as well, but all the wealth in Christendom could not cure the lad. The king must have known that.'

'Of course he did – and that the lad could not have been the only innocent casualty of the fighting.'

'I see now why he is within.' I should be in the chapel too, I thought, as the claws of my own black guilt tore at me. Richard had sinned by fornicating outside wedlock, but he had not ordered a soldier to break that boy's head. I, on the other hand, had murdered Henry in cold blood. My wickedness was greater.

Soft shoes at the other end of the corridor.

'The bishops are coming,' hissed de Béthune.

We straightened our backs and stared ahead, sentinels on watch.

They were all present, Walter of Rouen, Gerard of Auxienne, John of Evreux and half a dozen others. High men of God, come to witness the king confess his sins. With them was a mild-mannered but pleasant cleric, a man by the name of Ambroise. He worked as a clerk for Gerard, and was forever busy with quill and parchment.

I pulled wide the door, and in they filed. As I pushed it to, I caught a glimpse of the king, face down in front of the altar. Shame filled me to see him so, and I averted my gaze.

Time passed. I was aware of voices chanting in prayer, of Richard speaking, of the bishops' replies. I could not catch the words, for which I was glad. Whatever the king said was between him and God. The religious were merely a vehicle to the Divine. A path back to righteousness.

My conscience needled me. I should also have been in there, naked on the floor, and begging for forgiveness. Over and again I saw Henry's terrified face, heard his pleas for mercy. Nothing I did could stop my dagger opening his throat. I could almost feel his hot blood on my skin; I certainly heard the soft thump as his body landed on the floor.

Vaguely, I became aware of de Béthune opening the door, and the bishops emerging one by one. I blinked, and came back to the corridor. The king emerged, clothed again, walking with archbishop Gerard, and deep in private conversation. Richard's posture was confident, and his gestures were animated: he had been restored. I was glad for him.

'Are you well, Sir Rufus?' Archbishop Walter's voice was almost in my ear.

I jumped. Walter was peering at me with a kindly expression.

Nervous, I stammered, 'W-why, yes, my lord archbishop.'

'You are as pale as a winding sheet.' His eyes bored into mine, and in a low voice, he said, 'Does something weigh on your mind, perhaps?'

Disarmed by his acuity, I nodded.

'How long is it since your last confession?'

I had not the heart to lie. 'A year and a half, my lord archbishop, perhaps longer.'

A slight intake of breath. 'Step into the chapel, if you will.'

I could no more refuse an archbishop than the king himself.

The short walk to the altar seemed as doom laden as that to a scaffold. My mouth was dry; my heart pounded.

Walter faced me. 'Kneel.'

I obeyed. I bowed my head. 'Bless me, Father, for I have sinned,' I whispered, the words coming back unbidden. 'It has been many months since my last confession.'

'What sins would you repent of, my son?'

I stared into the abyss, but even now, I did not have to admit my crime.

Walter was a canny one. He said nothing, and the silence swelled.

'I have lied.' I reeled off a list of venial sins, the way youths do. I finished.

'Is there aught else?'

I wavered. 'No one else will know what I tell you, my lord archbishop?'

'Only God.'

I could bear the guilt no longer. 'I murdered a man,' I whispered.

'Murdered?' Walter could not quite conceal his shock. 'In a fight?'

'In cold blood.' I wanted to explain, but my tongue clove to the roof of my mouth. This was not about the *why* of my heinous actions, but the deed itself.

'And do you repent of this mortal sin?'

Aware that to hesitate would reveal lack of conviction, and unwilling to examine my own conscience further, I said firmly, 'With all my heart I repent.'

Silence.

He does not believe me, I thought in terror.

After what seemed an eternity, Walter spoke. 'Your penance shall be this. Once a year, for the rest of your life, you must pay for a mass to celebrate the soul of the dead man. You must *also* continue as a valiant soldier in the service of the cross. You must spare *no effort*, you must hold back *nothing* – even at the cost of your own life.'

'So I do swear,' I said, meaning every word.

Walter seemed satisfied. *'Dominus noster Jesus Christus te absolvat,'* he intoned. He continued for several sentences. At last the familiar phrase came, *'Ego te absolvo a peccatis tuis in nomine Patris, et Filii et Spiritus Sancti. Amen.'*

'Amen.' Although I understood only the ending – I absolve you from your sins in the name of the Father, and of the Son, and of the Holy Spirit – their effect was like balm to my tortured soul. I sagged down, my shoulders bowed. Tears of relief pricked my eyes.

'Rise, my son,' said Walter.

On shaky legs, I obeyed.

The archbishop gave me a tight-lipped smile. 'You have been forgiven, my son, but God is watching you.'

'My lord archbishop.' Uneasy, I waited.

'He will expect much of you in the Holy Land. Wherever the foe is thickest, wherever the danger greatest, He will want you to be.'

'Yes, my lord archbishop.' This I could live with, I decided. War and battle were what I knew. Through them, I could find Divine redemption. If death took me in the process, so be it.

Into my apparent good fortune, an unpleasant awareness came creeping. Try though I might to deny it, I was *not* wholly sorry. Letting Henry live would forever have threatened my place in the mesnie and my friendship with the king. Those were consequences I had not been – and was still not – willing to entertain.

I am sorry Henry is dead. I have confessed, I told myself, and been forgiven. I will pay my penance in Outremer, in blood. That will be enough.

So I hoped.

Two months passed. The year of our Lord 1190 became 1191. My guilt did not vanish altogether, but it eased. Life became liveable again, and at night, I slept. Guilt niggled me now and again, but when it did, I told myself that my sins would be washed away by Saracen blood. I would pray to God in the Holy Sepulchre in Jerusalem, the holiest site on earth, and there be forgiven once more.

The situation in England continued to fluctuate. In December, Richard had sent word to Longchamp that Arthur was to be his heir. His brother John reacted by crossing the Narrow Sea in contravention of his oath. Longchamp quailed before this royal challenge and made no attempt to force John back to Normandy. With the guile of a fox, John had used Longchamp's silence to claim that this amounted to a rescindment of the order barring him from England. As Richard said furiously, his brother was probably now whispering in the ear of every noble and prelate who would listen to his smooth words. Powerless to return himself, the king was planning to send Archbishop Walter of Rouen back as a justiciar. He was to have the power to overrule Longchamp, and if necessary, dismiss him. 'More than that I cannot do,' Richard said to me in frustration.

On the morning of Candlemas, the second of February, I crossed the courtyard of de Muhec's house, glancing at the sky. It was a brilliant blue, as it always seemed to be here. The temperature was pleasant; I had no need of my cloak. It was a much different world to Aquitaine at this time of year, or Ireland for that matter. I was much taken with the climate, and often said so. De Muhec laughed to hear me say it on the first occasion, and declared that I had not yet seen a summer on Sicily. By the time that season arrived, I had replied without thinking, I would be in Outremer. It was an even hotter place, de Muhec had said, laughing, and full of Saracens who would want to kill me.

The same might have been said of the Griffons, but happily, peace had reigned since the riots in October. Matters had been helped by the fixing of prices for the two staples, bread and wine. The king's order that the goods and property stolen by his men should be returned had also been well received. Profiteering and speculation were banned, and Richard's soldiers and sailors ordered to follow a strict code of conduct. As for the Griffons, well, they had learned to keep their heads down and live with the armed foreigners in their midst.

The locals would still be glad to see the back of us, I thought, as we would of them. After almost half a year on Sicily, I chafed to leave.

Every man in the army was the same. Such had been the discontent in the camp at Christmastide that the king had seen fit to distribute rich gifts not just to his knights, but to the ordinary troops as well. This sensible move had seen the discontent reduced to a manageable level, a situation that would, with luck, continue until Alienor arrived with Berengaria.

My breakfast eaten, I was looking for Rhys. It was time, I decided, to buy the new sword belt I had promised myself, and he had mentioned an excellent leather worker in some backstreet. Making for the stables and workshops, the most likely places to find him, I was called back to the courtyard by Richard. Behind me, I heard a dog yapping. It sounded like P'tit, but I paid it no heed.

The king was pacing to and fro, hands clasped behind his back. A messenger stood, waiting for further instruction. I spied a document tight in Richard's grip.

'Sire?'

'Good news, Rufus. My mother and Berengaria have landed safely at Naples, God be praised. They should be here within the month.'

'Fine tidings, sire.' I grinned, imagining the wedding celebrations, and Joanna, radiant. A chance might come my way to talk with her. My spirits lifted further; the women's arrival brought our departure for Outremer one step nearer.

'I need to talk to Philippe, and soon. He must hear of Berengaria's coming from my lips, else I risk him finding out from someone else.'

The French king was still unaware of the impending wedding. Richard had talked much of breaking off his betrothal to the French king's sister Alys, but had not done so. I suspected he had been avoiding the issue.

'If half the stories about Tancred are true, sire, I would not put it beyond him to tell Philippe.'

'By happy chance,' said Richard, 'Philippe invited me to ride out this afternoon, together with a few companions. I will need some privacy – you can see to that, Rufus.'

'Of course, sire.'

A sentry announced the army quartermasters. 'Duty calls,' said the king. 'See that Philip knows we are to ride out. Tell him to saddle the bay rouncy, not the black.'

'Sire.' Again I made for the stables. There was time, I decided, for a trip to the leather worker's before we set out.

P'tit was still barking, which was odd. She did not usually stray far from FitzAldelm. Curiosity pricked me. Emerging from the passage between the main building and the stables, I realised the barking was coming from the haybarn. Mixed with it was the sound of voices. She is chasing vermin, I thought, and FitzAldelm is with her. With luck, he will get bitten on the ankle by a rat.

I spied Usama, the groom with whom Rhys was friendly, lurking by the stables. The instant he saw me, he came hurrying over, his normally jovial face pinched with worry.

'What is it, Usama?'

He pointed to the barn. 'Rhys is in there, sir, with de Drune,' he said in his heavily accented French. 'They were playing dice.'

'And FitzAldelm went in there with his dog?'

His head bobbed up and down. 'She chased a rat across the yard, sir, and he went after her.'

Concern pricked me. 'And de Gunesse?'

An unhappy nod. 'He is in there too.'

I cursed, and began to run. Rhys and de Drune betting on dice was of little import. Not a soul in the royal household paid any heed to the royal decree prohibiting gambling unless an officer were present. FitzAldelm and de Gunesse would take a more jaundiced view, however.

There was no sign of P'tit inside, although I could hear muffled barking. She will have gone around the back of the hay, I thought.

FitzAldelm and de Gunesse were facing away from me. Rhys and de Drune knelt before them at the foot of a ladder which led up into the loft. The pair had been dicing up there, I decided, and were seen before they could hide. Black amusement tickled me. This was not the first time that my enemy, Rhys and I had been in a haybarn, even if my enemy did not know it.

FitzAldelm stepped forward, and I saw with horror that he carried a short horse whip. His right arm went back, and I shouted, 'Hold!'

The blow did not fall. He turned. Scorn twisted his narrow mouth. 'Ah, Rufus. I wondered when you would appear.'

'What in God's name do you think you are doing?' I cried, advancing until there was only a short distance between us. Behind FitzAldelm,

I could see Rhys burning with fury. De Drune wore a stoic expression, that of a man who is enduring what he can do nothing about. Both had their hands bound in front of them.

'Administering an initial portion of the punishment due them, nothing more,' FitzAldelm gloated. 'I caught the churls dicing, you see. Tomorrow will be the first of three consecutive days that they are stripped naked and whipped through the ranks of the army. What a sight it will be.'

I shoved past without a word, and using my dagger, slit Rhys's bonds.

'Those men are my prisoners,' snarled FitzAldelm.

I paid no heed. I was reaching out to free de Drune, when with a flick of his eyes, he warned me.

Quickly, I swapped the knife to my left hand. When de Gunesse seized my shoulder on the same side, I twisted around violently, breaking free of his grip. Air whooshed from his mouth as my right fist drove into his midriff. He dropped like an ox with a butcher-hammered spike in its brain. I stared over his prone shape at FitzAldelm, daring him to come at me. I sensed Rhys at my side, bristling like a dog in a fighting pit. For the first time since Vézelay, I cared nothing about the consequences. I will gut him, I thought. Gut him and then let the bastard die of the festering belly rot that follows.

FitzAldelm saw my intention, and did not move an inch. 'The king will hear of this!' His voice was almost as high as a woman's, a querulous mix of outrage and fear.

'I shall also tell Richard,' I said in an even tone, 'how my squire and this loyal man-at-arms were enjoying a quiet game of dice, which I sanctioned. I had been watching, but a call of nature forced me to step outside. Upon my return, I found you and de Gunesse beating them both.'

'Liar! We have been in here some little time, and not a sign of you anywhere.'

'I spoke the truth,' I lied blithely, 'and so I will swear to the king.'

'It shall be the word of two belted knights against one,' FitzAldelm spat. He glanced at his crony, who was beginning to stir. 'De Gunesse here will verify every word of my account.'

'And Rhys and de Drune will confirm mine. That makes three against two.'

FitzAldelm made a little sound of contempt. 'The word of ordinary soldiers counts for nothing against that of a nobleman. These two will be punished, and so will you, for assaulting another knight.'

'We shall see whom Richard believes.' I hoped that I sounded more confident than I felt.

'Two against one,' repeated FitzAldelm, his expression exultant.

'What is that I hear? Two against one?' called a voice.

In walked André de Chauvigny, the king's cousin. His gaze ran over us: de Gunesse half-comatose on the floor, de Drune still kneeling with his wrists bound, Rhys standing beside me, and I with a naked blade in my fist, confronting FitzAldelm. P'tit's muffled yapping continued unabated.

'This is an odd scene, and no mistake,' said de Chauvigny. 'Is all well, Rufus?'

'FitzAldelm here has accused me of lying. He claims I did not give permission to my squire Rhys and this man-at-arms to play dice in the hay loft.'

De Chauvigny's face grew perplexed. 'Yet I heard you say just that not long since.'

FitzAldelm caught the surprise in my eyes – I knew it, because pure rage filled his own. He looked at de Chauvigny, who stared back with a bland expression, and then returned his gaze to me.

'Well?' I asked FitzAldelm. 'Can this sorry little episode be forgotten, or shall we take it to the king?'

'Let us say no more about it,' he replied, each word sounding as if it was being dragged from him with pliers.

With a polite nod to FitzAldelm, and a promise to me that we should talk later, de Chauvigny left us.

'Good.' I pointed behind my enemy. 'You had best attend to P'tit. She is limping.'

His terrier had finally emerged from the gloom at the back of the barn. Her muzzle bloodied, with bite marks visible on her forelegs, she still wagged her tail at the sight of her master. FitzAldelm picked her up gentle as a babe, and walked out, talking quietly in her ear. De Gunesse he left still sprawled at my feet.

'P'tit goes from a dead rat to a living,' Rhys muttered.

'Keep those thoughts to yourself,' I warned.

He mouthed the words, 'One day I will kill him.'

De Drune had seen. 'I will help you,' he said, holding out his wrists so I could cut him free.

'No,' I said in a firm voice, adding in a whisper in case de Gunesse somehow heard, 'that task is mine. Rhys?'

He met my gaze unwillingly. 'I understand.'

'See that you do.'

Our ride that afternoon proved memorable for more reasons than one. At its heart, oddly, was not Richard's betrothal to Alys, nor his intended marriage to Berengaria, but an impromptu tourney between us and the French. It came about thanks to Guillaume des Barres, one of the most famous knights in France. Barrel-chested, with an unfashionably long beard, I had found him to be a courteous, amusing character. Spying a local farmer on the road, his cart full of sugar canes, des Barres laughingly suggested we use them as lances in a contest against one another.

Months of inaction meant the notion was seized upon, and before Richard or Philippe could protest, the two groups, French and English, had armed themselves and prepared to set to.

It is worth explaining that Richard and des Barres had history. The Frenchman had got the better of the king at Châteauroux, the dread place where I lost Liath Macha, my valiant horse. He had also once been captured by Richard and given his word not to escape. When the opportunity had come his way, though, des Barres fled on a stolen horse. The king had borne a grudge against him ever since, and so when the Frenchman took his place among his comrades, Richard had been quick to join our number.

To our astonishment, not only did the king repeatedly fail to unhorse des Barres, he almost lost his own seat thanks to a loose cinch. Apoplectic with fury, he had cursed the Frenchman and ordered him from the field, telling Philippe afterwards in no uncertain tones that des Barres would have to be sent back to France.

After this public disagreement, it seemed impossible that Philippe should grant approval for Richard to end his betrothal to Alys – a topic which had not even had the chance to be aired. And if this problem could not be resolved, we knights said to each other, Berengaria's arrival and the royal wedding would cause the situation to unravel further. Philippe would not travel to Outremer in the company of a man who had slighted his sister so; Richard could not stay away on his own. With Philippe back in France, his territories in Gisors and the Vexin, to name but two, would be at major risk of invasion.

Unless an agreement was reached, our chances of ever reaching the Holy Land, still less taking Jerusalem, were slim indeed.

CHAPTER IX

Almost a month passed, and *still* we had not left Sicily. I had seen little of Joanna either, and for reasons that remained unclear, the arrival of Queen Alienor and Berengaria had been delayed. The king and Philippe had met several times, most often parting in acrimony. The entire future of our bold enterprise remained in doubt.

Rioting broke out at the harbour one evening between gangs of Pisan and Genoese sailors and crewmen from English ships. It was widely acknowledged that the Italians initiated the trouble. So widespread was the unrest that Richard failed to put it down until the following morning, with a strong force of mounted knights. Scores of men were slain on both sides, a complete waste, the king thundered to the Pisan and Genoan captains. Imposing heavy fines on the chastened captains, and a demand that a dozen ringleaders among the sailors be tried and hanged, Richard dismissed them.

'God's legs,' he growled, banging a fist on the table. 'I did not take the cross to fight Christians!'

'We all feel the same, sire,' I said. There had been no pleasure in charging the poorly armed Pisans and Genoans.

'It would be better to leave for the Holy Land at once, but I have to wait for my mother and the princess Berengaria. I do not know what Tancred is playing at, to delay them as he is. Curse him!'

He was referring to the news that had come earlier, carried by another Philippe, the count of Flanders. We had met him before, at Châteauroux, when the French king and Richard's father had so nearly gone to war.

According to Count Philippe, Alienor and Berengaria had reached Naples, only a short voyage from Messina. Told by Tancred's officials that there was insufficient room aboard the ships sent to fetch them, they had continued overland to Brindisi, where they had remained since. Not wanting to delay his own departure for the Holy Land, Philippe had come straight to Sicily and approached Richard first because of his poor relationship with his namesake King Philippe of France.

'What will you do, sire?' I asked.

'Meet Tancred, and if necessary, wring the truth from his scrawny neck. It would not surprise me if Philippe has a hand in this. He is never content unless he is stirring the pot. But two can play at that game. I can yet turn the matter of Alys to my advantage.'

How that could be achieved, I had no idea.

To me, the king's betrothal was yet another reason why the French contingent would never sail for the Holy Land.

Yet another reason why the taking of Jerusalem would prove impossible.

A sennight later, Richard took me to Catania, a town south of Messina where he met with Tancred. Our party included Archbishop Walter, de Béthune, de Chauvigny and Philippe, the Count of Flanders. The king of Sicily was as ill-formed as the stories had it. Short, stumpy-legged and with features that might have been moulded from clay by a drunk, he nonetheless had a confident manner. Welcoming Richard with great courtesy, he bent a knee as well. So too did his nervous-faced advisers, del Pin, Margaritone and various bishops. The calculated move by Tancred yielded instant results. Richard gave a deep bow in return. He had approached the meeting as if it were a battle, but now his demeanour was calmer, and his face once more unreadable, a diplomatic mask.

Courtesies paid, Richard demanded an explanation. 'My mother should have been allowed to sail to Messina. Her entourage is not large; the ships I sent were more than capacious enough.' There was no mention of Berengaria, in case, no doubt, Tancred informed Philippe of her impending arrival.

'Queen Alienor is a venerable age,' said Tancred, being evasive. 'Her motives for coming to meet you must be pressing indeed.'

'All the more reason for her to come direct,' said the king sharply. 'Why did you prevent her from doing so?'

'I am told that she broke her journey at Lodi,' said Tancred, paying no heed to Richard's question. 'And there she met Heinrich of Hohenstaufen.'

'A chance encounter. Heinrich was on his way to Rome, where he is to be crowned as Holy Roman Emperor.'

His accession to the throne had come about because of the death of his father Frederick Barbarossa, who had drowned in Asia Minor while travelling to Outremer.

'You make no mention of Constance, Heinrich's wife. She is with him,' said Tancred slyly.

'What has she to do with anything?'

Tancred made a little noise of surprise. 'She is, or was, William's aunt, as well you know.' This was the dead King William, Joanna's husband. 'Some say that she and Heinrich, not I, should rule Sicily. It is not all that far from Rome to Naples, and thence to Messina.'

'I have no wish to ally myself with Heinrich,' said Richard, waving a hand. 'Besides, you and I already have an agreement.'

Tancred was like a dog with a bone. 'Which makes me even more curious as to why your lady mother would meet Heinrich. He is no friend of mine, but the same cannot be said of you. Were you not once to marry one of his daughters?'

'Half a lifetime ago. There is an odd logic to your suspicion, but no truth.'

'So you say. For all I know, Heinrich intends to march south and cross to Sicily. His forces and yours would have little problem in deposing me.'

'I need no help to do that, should I wish to.' Despite the threat, Richard's tone remained even.

'I suppose that is true,' Tancred admitted.

'Since we made our agreement—'

'An arrangement we came to after you had taken Messina by assault and extracted forty thousand ounces of gold from me?'

'Those monies were rightfully mine and my sister's!'

Tancred's lips twitched, but he made no denial.

'Since that time, have I done anything to make you think that our alliance was not genuine? My soldiers have returned the riches they stole; they are not allowed to gamble, or to drink to excess. Prices have been fixed for wine and bread. When the Pisans and Genoans rioted, I was quick to quell the unrest. Messina has for the most part been at peace.'

A short silence, and then, 'You speak true.'

'Arranging a mid-winter meeting between my mother and Heinrich in a remote location such as Lodi is nigh on impossible. Their encounter was caused by nothing more than chance.' Richard went on, challengingly, 'My guess is that Philippe Capet has been sowing the seeds of your concern.'

I saw del Pin glance at Margaritone, and thought, the king has put his finger on it.

'Well?' asked Richard.

Tancred coughed. 'Philippe says that your word cannot be trusted. He believes that you and Heinrich are in league.'

'Philippe is a losenger, a deceiver of the first order. I, on the other hand, am a simple and straightforward man.'

'You are also a fighter, and have good reason to look favourably on Heinrich and Constance's claim to the throne.'

It was a gamble to be so forthright, I thought, but Tancred's ploy worked.

Richard chuckled. 'True enough, but you and I made peace. We swore oaths of friendship. Know that once given, my word *is* my bond.'

They stared at one another. It seemed to me that Tancred's expression softened, but I could not be sure.

Richard made the first move. 'Would you like to know the real reason for my mother's journey?'

'I had heard more than one rumour . . .'

'You shall have the truth.' The king rose from his stool. 'Let us walk together, you and I.'

'He is going to tell him about Berengaria,' I whispered to de Béthune. 'That should convince him there is nothing more to what happened at Lodi.'

So it proved. Tancred believed Richard, whose account of events was backed up by the credible Philippe of Flanders. Witnessed by the bishops on both sides, they renewed their oaths of alliance. Queen Alienor and Berengaria could leave Brindisi for Messina at once. The king gifted Tancred with a priceless sword reputed to have belonged to the legendary Arthur. In response, the Sicilian monarch gave Richard fifteen galleys and four large transport ships. A curious friendship then sprang up between the two, the small, brutish Tancred and the long-limbed, warriorlike Richard, and we spent five days at Catania instead of the intended two.

The king's excellent mood was improved further by Tancred's parting gift, a letter sent by Philippe the previous October. In it the French king had spoken much of Richard's guile, and offered to fight with Tancred against him.

'I have the French dog now, Rufus,' said Richard, his eyes dancing. 'I have him in a corner.'

We left Catania before Philippe arrived, a deliberate snub designed to anger the French king before their next encounter. That took place at Messina several days later, when Philippe had had, in Richard's words, 'plenty of time to stew in his own juice.'

Even though he urgently needed to talk with Philippe, he let the French king make the first move. When a letter arrived requesting a meeting, Richard did not reply. Not until a second, more carping message came did he agree to a meeting.

In the end, it was quite simple. Philippe blustered and threatened, accusing Richard of shunning him like a leper. Word of Berengaria's imminent arrival had reached him at last, and he accused the king of wanting to break off his arranged marriage to Alys.

Calm as a mill pond on a windless day, Richard proffered the parchment given him by Tancred.

There were plenty of witnesses: me, de Béthune, de Chauvigny, Philippe of Flanders, and on Philippe's side, Duke Hugh of Burgundy and several others, nobles and bishops. All the same, you could have heard a needle drop as the French king read the letter.

When he was done, his colour was noticeably paler. His eyes rose to meet Richard's.

'Well?' demanded the king.

'This is a forgery, clearly.'

'Tancred says otherwise.'

'He would.'

'What reason could he have for trying to drive a wedge between us?'

'He is a misbegotten creature, driven by base emotions. No doubt he thought to strengthen his own position.'

Richard snorted. 'The letter does nothing of the sort for him. It merely exposes you as a double-dealing losenger.'

Hisses of disapproval from Philippe's followers.

The French king drew himself up to his full height, which was not that impressive. 'If Tancred did not pen this, mayhap you had someone write it – to provide the excuse you have desired these many years.'

'What could that be?' Butter would not have melted in Richard's mouth.

'You know full well,' said Philippe, his voice rising. 'To break off your betrothal to my beloved sister Alys.'

Beloved sister, I thought. You hypocrite. How many times have you bothered to see her when you were visiting Richard's court?

'Tancred swore before God that the letter was genuine, and I believed him.' Richard glanced at Philippe of Flanders. 'What say you, sir?'

The French king and his count stared at each other. Dislike sparked between them – a blind man could have sensed it.

'How came you to be there?' snapped Philippe Capet.

'I broke my journey to Sicily in Rome, sire. After meeting Queen Alienor by chance, I travelled with her for a time, for our paths were the same. When Tancred's officials diverted her to Brindisi, I chose to sail direct to Messina. There I met King Richard, who asked me to accompany him to the meeting with Tancred.'

'Better it would have been to pay loyalty to your own king, rather than the English one,' said Philippe caustically.

'Be that as it may, sire, I went to Catania. I witnessed Tancred give the parchment to Richard, and explain how it came to be in his possession. I will swear the same on a holy reliquary.'

'This is still no proof that the letter is genuine,' said Philippe. 'I say it is a ruse to give you, Richard, just cause to call off your betrothal.'

'You are correct in one thing at least,' said the king. 'I have no intention of marrying Alys.'

'I knew it!' cried Philippe.

'It is not because of your attempt at treachery with Tancred.'

Philippe's eyes filled with suspicion. 'How can you justify yourself then?'

'I will not marry another man's whore.'

There was a stunned silence, and then everyone began to speak at once. Everyone French, that is. Richard stood with folded arms, his face impassive, his gaze heavy on Philippe.

'You dare to insult my sister so?' Spittle flecked Philippe's lips.

'I speak nothing more than the truth. Every man in this room knows it.' Richard barked a laugh. 'Every man in Aquitaine, Normandy, Brittany, Anjou and France knows it too! First to my lord father's bed was Rosamund de Clifford, and then Alys. Some say that she even bore him a child, although I have no proof of that. Perhaps you can enlighten me.'

More shocked mutters from the French.

'These are monstrous falsehoods!' said Philippe, crossing the room to confront Richard. 'You lie!'

'Say that again,' grated the king, 'and you will regret it.'

'Messires, please.' Philippe of Flanders raced over, gently separating the two men. 'This must not come to violence.'

Richard's smile was evil. 'For we know what way that would end.'

Philippe Capet sniffed. 'My sister's honour is beyond reproach.'

'There are numerous men who will bear witness to my accusation,' Richard declared loudly. 'One of them stands before me.'

The French king looked at Philippe of Flanders in shock. 'You?'

'Yes, sire. I cannot lie about this. What Richard says about his father and Alys is true.'

'He is but one,' said Richard. 'There are plenty more.'

Utter silence fell.

To my surprise, the French king recovered his composure first. 'Very well. You and my sister will not be wed.'

Richard was a little taken aback. 'You agree?'

'I do. She must be well-compensated, however.'

'Naturally. Had you a price in mind?'

'Ten thousand marks.'

Richard did not bat an eyelid. 'That is fair.'

Like that, the tension in the room began to dissipate. It was incredible, I thought, how a problem that had festered for years like an unlanced boil could be settled with relative ease. The French king had ever trumpeted about his sister's honour, but in the end, it too had had a price.

As if relieved by the ease with which the impasse had been brought to an end, Philippe's manner became positively effusive. He suggested that a fresh treaty of friendship be drawn up, in order to publicly avow their alliance, and to make clear that Richard would have the freedom to marry whoever he wished. In this apparent spirit of amity, the two monarchs also resolved their territorial differences over the ever-troublesome Gisors and the Vexin, as well as other areas. When Philippe boldly suggested that des Barres should rejoin the rest of the French, and travel with them to Outremer, Richard agreed on the condition that the renowned knight was never to come near him.

'Better to let Philippe think he has won something,' I whispered to de Béthune.

'Aye, but the Frenchie is not happy,' came the reply. 'Mark his face when he thinks no one is looking.'

The meeting was drawing to a close. Richard and Philippe had exchanged the kiss of peace. The king was talking to Archbishop Walter, while Philippe had retreated into a huddle with his party. I kept a surreptitious eye on him, and it was not long before he shot a look at Richard.

I saw no goodwill, only rage and humiliation.

Philippe, I decided, could never be trusted, which brought me back to my sober realisation.

Despite the newly agreed truce, the future of the two kings' joint venture to the Holy Land remained balanced on a knife edge.

CHAPTER X

My suspicions were borne out a few days later, on the thirtieth of March. Hours before Queen Alienor and Berengaria were to reach the town of Reggio, Philippe set sail. Richard, unconcerned, made no attempt to stop him. Standing on the deck of his galley – we had travelled the first few leagues with Philippe – and watching the French fleet move slowly off to the south, he said to me, 'I would have done the same.'

Remembering Philippe's malevolent look, I replied, 'He will not forget, sire, despite what he may have said.'

My comment was batted away with a laugh, and a declaration that Philippe could do what he wanted.

The king had every right to be confident, but I thought it unwise to discount Philippe entirely. His attempted alliance with Tancred was merely the latest in a long history of deviousness, and Richard knew it. He was in ebullient mood, however, all talk of his mother and Berengaria, and so I stitched my lip.

To Reggio we went next, and a meeting with Alienor and Berengaria. I was as excited as any to see the king's bride-to-be. She was to accompany us to the Holy Land, and, Richard said, so was Joanna. This last was even better news, and when I confided in de Béthune, he ribbed me mercilessly about it.

Alienor and Berengaria were waiting in the citadel at Reggio, where they had been made welcome by the local lord. Excited as a small boy, Richard went haring down the gangplank the instant it was in place. He was richly dressed in purple tunic and brown hose, with an ornate dagger at his belt. Standing half a head taller than almost everyone else, with his red-gold mane of hair marking him out among the black-haired Italians, he cut a fine figure.

Received by the steward at the citadel's gate, the king moved so fast that the plump little fellow had almost to run to keep up. Wheezing our arrival in the doorway of the great hall, he stood back and watched Richard advance towards the women who sat in the window seats at the far end.

I picked out his mother, and my gaze roved over the rest, eager to spy out Berengaria. The slim young woman with sallow skin and long black braids who was looking at the king had to be her, I decided. Clad in a blue wool dress, she was comely enough. Not a patch on Joanna, I caught myself thinking.

Alienor rose to her feet, the picture of poise and regal beauty. Joy suffused her face, but it could not completely erase the tiredness. 'Richard, you are come.'

'Mama!' Richard knelt, and seizing both her hands, kissed them. 'What a joy to see you.'

'Stand. You are the king,' Alienor said, but she was beaming.

Richard kissed her hands again, and got to his feet. His gaze moved to the slim girl with the long braids. Up and down it went, appraising, until most women would have blushed and looked away. Berengaria, however, met his stare with her own.

'Richard,' said Alienor tartly. 'She is not a horse.'

'Nor is she, Mama,' said the king, grinning. 'Forgive me, my lady.'

'There is nothing to excuse, sire,' Berengaria replied in accented French. 'You were curious – as was I to see you for the first time.'

'So, what think you?' asked Richard, his face mischievous.

'You are as handsome as they say.'

He laughed with delight, and stooping, took her beringed hand and kissed the back of it. 'And you, my lady, are as fair a lass as I have seen in an age.'

The comment made Berengaria blossom. As I would learn, she had a tendency to be serious, but her smile could light up a room.

We did not linger at Reggio, but took ship at once for Bagnara, where Joanna still resided. I watched another joyous reunion there, that of mother and daughter. Tears were shed; I even noted Richard dabbing at the corner of his eyes. While Alienor and Joanna caught up on the last fourteen years, he and Berengaria went for a walk in the same garden that I had strolled through with his sister. Those of the mesnie who were there, de Béthune, de Chauvigny, FitzAldelm and I, retreated to the front courtyard where our horses were in the care of Rhys, Philip and the other squires.

'She is feisty, which is good,' I said.

'Aye,' said de Chauvigny. 'Richard is a force of nature. He needs a strong woman.'

'He seems taken with her, and she with him,' de Béthune added. 'It is an auspicious start.'

'Let her provide the king with a son, and all will be well,' said FitzAldelm.

We fell to talking about the preparations for departure, which were moving apace. Richard and Berengaria's long-awaited wedding could not yet proceed, because Lent was not over, and so we were to leave as soon as the ships had been loaded and the captains deemed the weather suitable.

After so long, Outremer seemed almost within reach.

It was the tenth of April, Wednesday in Holy Week, before everything was ready. Queen Alienor had left a sennight earlier, remaining only three days in the company of Richard and Joanna. The parting of mother and son had been even more emotional than that at Nonancourt the previous year, for neither knew if they would ever see the other again. Archbishop Walter was gone with Alienor, but he had taken me aside on the final morning and warned that I should not forget my penance. Dreams of Henry plagued me for several nights after.

The king oversaw the last of the embarking himself. The knights' mounts, rouncys and destriers both, had been left until the end. Despite their training, confinement and voyaging by sea was not something they liked. Once the horses had been coaxed on board, they were each placed in a stall and tied by the head. A canvas sling under the belly would prevent them from falling when the sea got rough. Richard personally loaded Tempest, which gave me the opportunity to take Pommers up the gangplank myself. I hated leaving him, but Rhys had volunteered to stay on board and care for all my horses, so I did not worry overmuch.

I witnessed the loading of the last dromonds as well. They were full to bursting with supplies: barrels of water, and of salted beef and pork, sacks of flour, salt, nuts, dried fruit. There were tuns of wine, jars of honey and medicines, blankets and tents. Sails, oars, ropes and spare rudders had been bought. Thousands of crossbow bolts and arrows went in, and extra bowstaves and crossbows. Stones for siege engines served as ballast, while the great weapons themselves, disassembled, were stored below decks. Even the tower of Mategriffon had been taken down in sections to be transported.

The citizens of Messina cheered to see us go. Not a few probably cursed as well, but we could not hear. Not that we cared. Good riddance to bad cess, my father had been fond of saying. South from the city we sailed, with the wind at our backs and Richard's red-and-gold banners snapping at the masthead. The channel began to widen on either side as Sicily and Italy moved further apart.

'A grand sight,' said Richard, looking back from our galley when we had reached open water.

The entire horizon was covered with ships, more than two hundred of them in the fleet. Three quarters were dromonds and large transports, fat-bellied beasts that wallowed in the water, and the rest fast-moving galleys with bright-painted shields adorning their sides and pennants at the masts. These were the guard dogs that would protect the rest from any enemies.

'Truly it is, sire.' I tried and failed to spy the dromond that carried Berengaria and Joanna. To my disappointment, Richard had deemed it safer for them to travel aboard a slower, steadier craft than our low-slung galley.

'The biggest army ever assembled by an English king. Seventeen thousand soldiers and sailors. I swear the sun has never risen on such a rich fleet.'

The figure was staggering. I thought of Cairlinn, and the sixty warriors my father had been able to muster.

'God willing, it will be enough.'

The way Richard said it made me look at him. The most decisive person I had met, he was also quick to act. Now, however, he seemed quiet and pensive. 'Does something worry you, sire?' A messenger had arrived from Outremer just before our departure, carrying word of the desperate straits in which those besieging Acre found themselves.

He glanced at me. 'It is scarcely believable, eh? Men fighting to get meat from dying horses, eating them right down to the intestines.'

I shook my head, trying to imagine being hungry enough to eat grass.

'We can do nothing for the poor wretches, save get there as fast as we may. I would that we had left earlier, but there is nothing to be done about that.'

'And Philippe, sire, does he concern you?'

A smile. 'No, not that losenger.'

'Saladin and his mamluks?'

'I am respectful of them, aye, but it is also the land that I am wary of.'

'The sun and the heat, sire?' I was dreading the burning temperatures.

'Those, yes, and the lack of water. Marching along the coast will be trying, but to reach Jerusalem will be our hardest task.' He fell into a thoughtful silence, which I, also worried, chose not to break.

Our hope that the voyage should be swift and without incident proved a vain one. Becalmed on the second day and struck by a storm on the third, Good Friday, the formation of the fleet was broken up and the ships separated. Great rollers battered us, and the never-ending creaks of the hull timbers were terrifying. I had never vomited so much in my life. Later I heard that at various times the sailors had had to leave us at the mercy of the waves. God and all His saints be praised that we did not founder. Richard's placing of an enormous candle in a lantern at the prow of his galley, a beacon to keep his vessels together at night, was a masterstroke. Each time the waves abated, we heaved to, allowing those who had fallen behind to catch up.

A spell of fine weather finally saw us anchor off Crete on the evening of the seventeenth of April. Darkness made it impossible to know how much of the fleet had limped in to the sheltered bay. Our biggest concern was the dromond carrying Berengaria and Joanna, which had last been seen three days prior. Richard was beside himself, although he hid it well, and declared that the morrow was a new day. I too was consumed by worry, and slept badly, despite being bone weary.

Rising at dawn, I paced the deck, my stomach still uneasy, and counted the ships which had stayed with us. Twenty-something, there were, and not a dromond among them.

The unease that had plagued me all night returned with a vengeance. When a grinning Rhys appeared, brandishing a no-doubt-stolen loaf of almost-fresh bread, I waved him away, my stomach turning. I stayed by the rail, counting the vessels at anchor over and over, and telling myself that Berengaria and Joanna's ship had either been carried far beyond Crete, or blown off course altogether. They would appear if not with the two galleys I spied on the horizon, then with other stragglers who would reach us as the day wound on.

That did not happen, and my worries increased. Richard too was concerned, but decided that we could not linger, nor search for the missing ships. 'We could beat about the sea for weeks, and not find them,' he said to me, frowning. 'They will meet us at Rhodes, and if not, at Cyprus.' He ordered a message sent to Outremer, to let the Christians at Acre know that we were delayed. This done, the king sank into a grim silence that few dared break; he answered questions with only a 'yes' or a 'no', and men began calling him by his old name, 'Oc e non', in private.

We spent a difficult day of heavy waves and strong winds reaching Rhodes. In the brief moments of calm, I prayed for Joanna, and after, Berengaria. Rhys, unaffected by the turbulent sea, and knowing how anxious I was, spent his time on the lookout for their dromond.

It was not with the ships that had reached the agreed anchorage before us, however, a good-sized squadron, forty-odd strong.

Uncaring of the mirror-bright, flat sea, and the glorious sunshine, I battled a deep gloom. The dark possibility that I had refused to countenance throughout the voyage forced its way to the forefront of my mind. Berengaria and Joanna's ship might have sunk, giving them a terrible, watery death. I told myself that God could not be so cruel to take Richard's betrothed from him before they were wed, still less his beloved sister.

I had my own reason for wanting Joanna to be alive, of course, a selfish but precious one. The details of our conversation in the monastery at Bagnara lived on in my memory; I could picture the colour in her cheeks when she had made gentle fun of me about women, and love. Although I had not spent much time in her company before or since, my feelings for her had grown strong indeed.

That she might well be dead seemed too harsh a fate for such a golden one.

Hope came from an unexpected quarter when Rhys returned from shore, part of a party sent to replenish our water. Sharp-eyed locals had seen a number of ships blown past the isle some days before. There was no way of knowing if Berengaria and Joanna's dromond was among them, but as Richard said, it was entirely possible.

I wanted to set sail at once, and I suspected the king felt the same way. Alert, however, to the care of his men – the sailors were exhausted from the brutal voyage – he ordered a rest of several days at anchor. Ill fortune struck the following night when he was again laid low by quartan fever, causing a further delay of ten days. My worries about Joanna buried by my concern for Richard, I barely moved from his bedside for the duration. Worryingly, the surgeon's medicines, vile-smelling and foul-tasting, seemed to make no difference to his condition. He was a strong man, though. The illness subsided, and he began to recover.

The first of May saw us sail eastward to Cyprus at last. Still sunken-cheeked, Richard was like a small boy travelling to the fair, so excited was he. 'We shall find Berengaria and Joanna tapping their feet, and asking what has taken us so long,' he declared.

I laughed, and told myself that they had indeed survived unscathed.

Not long after dawn on the sixth of May, the hawk-eyed lookout spied Cyprus. His cry brought Richard up to the platform at the prow, where I was already standing, hopeful, eager to spy out Joanna and Berengaria's dromond. The king was in a fine mood and no less keen. We fell to talking, and he mentioned the transport we had met the day before, come with news from the Holy Land. Philippe Capet had reached Acre on the twentieth of April; since then his troops had constructed siege engines and filled the ditches outside the walls with earth. Although there had been setbacks, his attacks continued.

'Saladin is being kept on his toes,' said Richard, laughing. 'And God willing, we shall be detained in Cyprus long enough only for a wedding.' He winked.

His confidence that Berengaria and Joanna were unharmed was infectious, and I grinned back at him, a glorious vision of his stunningly attractive sister filling my head.

'Would that our business in Outremer were about the Saracens, and nothing else' said Richard.

'It is galling how Philippe has thrown his support behind Conrad of Montferrat, sire.' This news had also come to us on the transport.

Conrad was an Italian noble with intentions on the throne of Jerusalem. He controlled the coastal city of Tyre – the only one left in

Christian hands – and had approached Philippe to improve his position with regard to the throne of the kingdom of Jerusalem.

'What do you make of Conrad, sire?'

'He is the stronger candidate, there is no denying it.' Guy de Lusignan, the current king – ruler of nothing, thanks to Saladin – had lost his only real claim to the throne, his wife Sibylla and two little children. They had been carried off by disease the previous autumn. Richard fell silent, obviously warring with himself, because Guy was his vassal.

Like Sicily, I thought, politics might concern us as much in Outremer as our fight with the Saracens. It was not just there, however.

'More troubles await us,' said Richard ruefully, with a nod at the mountainous coast of Cyprus, which now filled the horizon. 'If even a fraction of the rumours about the self-styled emperor, Isaac Ducas Comnenus, are true, he is a most unwholesome character. And if Berengaria and Joanna have reached its coast . . .' He paused before adding, 'God help him if he has harmed a single hair on their heads.'

I muttered my agreement, my fears about his sister resurging. I was grateful to be distracted by Richard's loud cry.

'See there! Ships at anchor!'

As my gaze followed his outstretched arm, the lookout roared the same thing. 'Are they ours, sire?' I asked. They were too far away for me to be sure of their identity.

'God willing, they are.'

Plagued by a fitful wind, we did not near the group of vessels for more than an hour. In that dragging time, our excitement, tinged with nerves, I have to admit, reached new heights. Richard paced the deck like a man possessed, promising celebratory masses and golden chalices to the church in thanks for the lives of his bride and sister. I tried to hide my own eagerness by playing dice with de Drune and Philip, and lost ten silver pennies to the former. I did not care, because my hope that the ships were ours became reality. Among the dromonds, five of them, was the vessel that carried Berengaria and Joanna. Whether they were on it was as yet uncertain, but after the weeks of not knowing their fate, its presence seemed an auspicious sign.

The moment our anchor struck the seabed, Richard had us rowed over. Spying the women on deck, watching, he roared a loud, joyous greeting. I raised a hand, all a mere knight would do, and grinned until my face hurt. They waved and called back, and the king gripped my shoulder. His face was bright with happiness. 'They are alive, Rufus! Alive!'

I nodded, thanking God in my head, and praying that Joanna noticed me. That my hope to win her affections was not complete tomfoolery.

To my joy, our eyes met as I came up the rope and over the side-rail, after the king. A spark leaped between us, or so I thought, and my heart sang. An instant later, she had thrown herself into Richard's arms, burying her head in his shoulder.

'You are unhurt,' she said, her voice catching.

'I am.' He squeezed her tight. 'Sweet Jesu, lass, but I am right glad to see you.'

'And I you, brother,' she said, laughing and crying at the same time. 'Your ship came to no harm, praise God.'

'Nor did yours,' he said fervently.

He set her back on her feet, and kissed her cheek. Turning his attention to Berengaria, waiting a few paces away, he bowed. 'My lady. All the saints be thanked that you are unharmed.'

Berengaria took a step towards him. 'I can say the same about you, sire. After the severe weather we endured, we have been very worried. But you do not seem quite yourself – have you been ill?'

'It was a bout of quartan fever, nothing more. I am well on the road to recovery, thanks to the surgeon, and Rufus here, who sat by my side night and day.'

Berengaria gave me a grateful look; so too did Joanna, and I flushed crimson with embarrassment and delight.

She reached out her hands, and he kissed them. They moved closer.

I, meanwhile, was trying not to gawk at Joanna, and failing miserably.

She saw me looking. 'Sir Rufus!'

'Madam,' I said, bending a knee.

'Ah, but this is a good day.' She beckoned.

With pounding heart, I crossed to stand before her. 'I have been praying for your safety, madam.'

'And that of the princess Berengaria, I hope?'

Mortified, I stammered, 'O-of course, madam.'

One of her eyebrows went up, a wickedly attractive gesture.

I cursed my colouring as my face flamed again. Tongue-tied as I had never been, I gazed at her. Jesu, but she was a goddess. Wisps of hair had escaped her golden hair net; they floated on either side of her face. She had been caught by the sun on the voyage too; her skin was an alluring gold. I could see the curve of her bosom beneath her dress.

'Sir Rufus, you are staring.'

I ripped my tongue into movement. 'Your pardon, madam. I cannot help myself.'

Again her eyebrow arched. 'Why might that be?'

I would rather have faced a hundred enemies than answer that question, but skewered by her blue eyes, I could not lie. 'Because you are the most beautiful woman I have ever seen.'

'I could swear, Sir Rufus, that you were trying to cozen me.'

I drank in her warm smile, and said hoarsely, 'I speak only the truth, madam.'

Her lips twitched; she was pleased. 'Come, tell me of your voyage.'

'There is not much to it, madam, save a couple of storms and a lot of feeling ill. I am no sailor.'

'Nor am I.' Her attention moved to the shore, where in the distance, the buildings and harbour of Limassol were visible. 'It has been hard being so close, and unable to leave the ship.'

'Because of Emperor Isaac?' I cried.

'Even so, the evil creature.'

She laid out their tale. Three ships had sunk upon their arrival, broken up on the rocks by vicious waves. A number of sailors and passengers had drowned, among them the king's vice-chancellor Henry Malchiel, but the majority had made it to shore, where they were promptly taken prisoner by Isaac's soldiery.

'With my blessing, the captains sent a strong sortie ashore two days hence. They stormed the citadel and freed our men from captivity. There was fierce fighting – they were greatly outnumbered by the Griffons – but they reached the ships without many casualties, God be thanked. Since then, Isaac has been trying to lure me and Berengaria ashore. He sends us bread and fine meats, and the best Cypriot wine, and promises that we will be treated as befits our status.'

'You did not believe him, I hope?'

A firm shake of her head. 'Not a word.'

'That is well, madam,' I said, deciding that my concerns about Cyprus had been justified. 'In Crete we were told much of Isaac's misdoings. It seems he managed to seize the throne by pretending to be an appointee of Byzantium. He is a fork-tongued liar who hates Christians. Some say also he is in league with Saladin, and that their alliance was sealed with a blood pact.' I grimaced. 'My heart is gladdened that you resisted his approaches.'

'As is mine, to have my brother here.' A look at me from under her lashes, and she added, 'And you.'

I swear I grew a foot taller.

Our tryst was brought to an end by Richard. After listening to Berengaria's version of events, he wanted to hear his sister's. Next he took counsel with the ship's captain and the knight in charge of the royal party's protection.

'Isaac has behaved like a churl, for certes,' the king declared after. 'Yet he is the ruler of Cyprus. Courtesy is still demanded.' He ordered de Chauvigny ashore to find the emperor. 'Pay him every respect. Ask politely that any of our men yet held as prisoners are released, and that the goods and chattels taken by his people from the wrecked ships are returned, or coin to the same value.'

Richard also had a message sent to the entire fleet. Every knight, man-at-arms and crossbowman was to prepare for battle. All ships' boats were to be readied.

I caught the king's eye. 'You think Isaac will refuse, sire?'

'Look at the beach.'

I squinted past the five Cypriot galleys that lay between us and the land, and saw what looked to be a makeshift barrier running along the sand. Understanding dawned. 'He has already decided to fight.'

'Even so.' Despite the danger of an amphibious assault on a defended position, Richard sounded pleased.

I have to confess, my own blood thrilled.

CHAPTER XI

De Chauvigny was not gone long. His grim demeanour as he reached the top of the rope ladder spoke volumes.

Richard strode forward. 'Isaac said no?'

'Worse than that, sire. He swore at me in Greek – I did not understand, and the interpreter would not translate. Then he said, "The king of England is nothing to me," and told me to go.'

A pulse throbbed in the king's neck.

I waited for him to erupt.

Instead, he bellowed, 'To arms!'

Trumpets were sounded. Men scrambled to put on their hauberks. Rhys was on the transport ship, so I was slower doing this than normal. The leather thongs at the knee which distributed the weight of the mail stockings were simple enough, but the thongs which did the same at my wrists required two hands. I cast about, looking for someone who could help.

Richard noticed. 'Robert, aid Rufus, will you?' He could not have been unaware of the rancour between me and FitzAldelm; mostly, he ignored it, but on occasion, like this, tried to push us together.

FitzAldelm could not refuse the king. Sullenly, he indicated I should hold out my arm. Richard was watching, so I obeyed. FitzAldelm took the strip of leather from my other hand and tied it around the wrist, but tighter than was normal.

I made a fist, moved my hand left and right. 'Loosen it.'

With a sneer, he did so, and did the same with my other wrist.

I offered no thanks.

His gaze met mine. There was no friendliness in it. 'They are rickety boats we are getting into. Have a care you do not fall in. That amount of mail would drown even a strong swimmer like you.'

A white-hot fury exploded in my chest. 'Try it, FitzAldelm, and I swear before God and all His saints, I will take you to the bottom with me.'

He flinched a little, and although he muttered a rejoinder, we both knew that the victory was mine. He made no attempt to get in the king's boat, which I sat in with Richard, de Béthune, de Chauvigny and half a dozen crossbowmen, but instead clambered aboard the second craft.

Our plan was simple, the king shouted. We would make for the Cypriot ships first, raining down crossbow volleys. Then we would do the same on the beach. The word was passed along from crew to crew. A nervous but excited air hung over us.

It was mad, I thought. A motley force in a fleet of rowboats we were, attacking an overwhelming enemy force. Buoyed up by Richard's confidence, however, I set my concerns aside.

Only two crossbowmen could stand in the bow at a time, so they would shoot while the other four reloaded. In this way, they explained to the king, they should be able to keep a continuous barrage on the Griffons. He responded with encouraging words, and said he was relying on them to get us ashore. The crossbowmen grinned and bobbed their heads. The king said much the same to the oarsmen, who reacted with similar enthusiasm. His ability to inspire ordinary men when their world is about to descend into bloody chaos was nothing short of remarkable.

By rights, our assault should have been easily repulsed, and yet we overwhelmed the Griffons on the enemy craft with volleys of crossbow bolts. Inside a hundred heartbeats, most had deserted their positions. Next we heard shouts and cries, followed by splashes. They were leaping into the sea, simply abandoning the galleys.

At that juncture, Richard split our force, ordering some men to take the enemy ships while he with the rest made for the shore. What faced us there was truly intimidating. Limassol had been emptied, it seemed, to build the haphazard, ramshackle barricade that straggled along the beach for half a mile. Barrels and casks had been stacked in lines, and doors propped up against them. Windows, frames, shutters and all, had been ripped out of house walls and put to use. Upturned galleys, benches, chests and planks had been cobbled together, and shields used to plug gaps. It was a bizarre-looking thing.

Scores of riders rode up and down in front of the barrier, pennoncels and banners flying from their spear tips. They were richly dressed, and their mounts fine, and when I spied one with a golden circlet about his helmet, I suggested to the king that it might be Isaac. Richard agreed. 'I pray he has the courage to stand and fight,' he cried. 'I will soon hew him down to size!'

It was almost as if Isaac had heard. As we drew near, and our crossbowmen began to shoot, the horsemen cantered away, out of range, and withdrew behind the barrier. The fight would be left to the hundreds of Griffons who manned the strange barricade. Armed with spears, axes, and hammers, they bayed at us like dogs as our boats entered the shallows.

Richard barked an order, and our crossbowmen leaped into the water. The command was passed on to left and right, and soon the beach was swarming with groups advancing in twos and threes. They shot and handed their weapons to the men behind, accepted a freshly loaded crossbow, took aim and shot – and did the same again. By the time we knights had waded ashore, the top of the barricade had been cleared. Quarrel-ridden bodies lay slumped over barrels and planking; the air was filled with screams and terrified shouts. Our men howled in response, scenting victory.

'Forward!' Distinguishable by his red-crested helmet and his massive stature, Richard led the way.

Slow and awkward, we climbed the barricade. If there had been Griffons to meet us, we would have been butchered. Most were already running, however, as we saw at the top. Hundreds of others milled about, helping the wounded, pointing in terror at us, shouting in dismay.

Richard leaped to the sand, a drop taller than a man. Lucky for him, he landed on his feet. One Griffon stood his ground, a huge man in a leather apron with a smith's hammer. Such were his muscles that a single blow would have burst Richard's skull inside his helmet.

The smith swung sideways, his hammer a lethal iron-headed blur.

I was momentarily paralysed, terrified he would kill the king.

Richard ducked down lower than he should have been able.

The hammer whistled by overhead.

Richard rose, fast as a lion, spitting the smith like a capon on a roasting prong. His sword tip burst out of the man's back in a spray of scarlet. Up came Richard's booted foot, and he shoved his dying enemy back off the steel. He fell, limbs floppy, mouth gaping.

I could scarcely believe my eyes. God loves those who dare, I thought, and He also loves those who lead from the front, on His business.

The king raised his leopard-emblazoned shield and crimson-daubed sword high, and yelled, 'Dex aie!'

It was like a summons to the wolf pack. Down we jumped, knights, men-at-arms, crossbowmen, screaming our lungs out at the men who had dared to oppose us.

The Griffons turned and ran for their lives.

And we, like a pack of ravening beasts, chased after.

Scores of Griffons fell to our blades and crossbows. Consumed by panic, they fled into the fields and the wooded countryside around Limassol, leaving the city to us. Before we reached the walls, Richard found an old nag with a worn-out saddle and a bag strapped behind, and thin cords for stirrups. Leaping on its back, he charged alone – ignoring my shouts – after a group of horsemen he had spied. He came back soon after, laughing so hard he was having difficulty retaining his seat.

'What is it, sire?'

'I caught up to Isaac!'

'On his own, sire?'

'No, he was with his household.'

I closed my eyes, trying not to imagine what might have happened, with the king on his own against God knew how many of the enemy. 'Did you speak to him, sire?'

'Aye! "Emperor, come joust!" I cried, but he made no answer, only fled as fast as he could.' Richard waved at the hills to the north. 'That way he went, on the fairest steed I have seen in many a year. Swift as the wind, it was. This broken-down creature had no chance of catching him.'

I shook my head, amused and frustrated. 'Sire, it was not wise to ride off on your own, without any protection. You might have been killed.'

A booming laugh came from inside his great helmet. 'But I was not, Rufus. I was not! God was smiling on me.'

What could I do but nod and agree. Truly, it seemed that the king's life was protected by the Divine.

*

I had cause to think the same the very next day. Expecting further trouble, we had unloaded our horses in the night. The poor beasts were stiff and lame and dazed from a month at sea, but the squires walked them up and down on the beach for hours, and fed them the best of hay and a little grain. By dawn the next day, they were much recovered. Although they could have done with more rest, Richard was in no mood for delay. A party of Griffons had been spotted in an olive grove nearby.

Fifty of us including the king rode to the attack. I say attack, but the enemy riders made no attempt to stand their ground, instead retreating pell-mell to the north. We gave gentle chase, still treating our destriers easily. Within a mile it was plain that the Griffons were heading for a large encampment spied out by de Drune and a number of other scouts. A chaotic, sprawling arrangement of tents and wagons, it had no defences, not even a ditch. Richard reined us in a few hundred paces away.

The riders we had pursued reached their own lines. They too slowed up. Men twisted in the saddle to hurl taunts at us. Sunlight flashed off helmets and spear tips to either side of them – plenty of soldiers were armed, and watching. They rattled their shields, and shouted, but made no sign of attacking.

'Shall I send a messenger to bring up the men-at-arms, sire?' I asked.

'No need.'

Confused, I asked, 'Are we just to leave them be, sire?'

'Far from it.' A wicked grin. 'We will charge the camp.'

He was not joking. A glance at de Béthune and de Chauvigny revealed they were as surprised as I. De Béthune shrugged, as if to say, *who are we to argue?* and I chuckled. We had done much the same the day before.

Ambroise the scribe was with us – he often followed the king about – and so too was a companion of his, a thin-faced armed clerk by the name of Hugh de la Mare. Clearly nervous, he chose this moment to make an impression. 'It would be wise to come away, my lord king. Their numbers are too great.'

Richard, much amused, gave him a broad wink. 'You stick to your scriptures, lord clerk, and leave the fighting to us.'

As de la Mare, puce with embarrassment, withdrew, the king had us form a line.

There must have been two thousand Griffons in that camp, the majority infantry, but several hundred were horsemen. Although we were more heavily armoured, in our helmets, hauberks and mail stockings, we numbered fifty. Fifty.

The Griffons watching us had no idea what was about to happen. Confident among their fellows, they continued to clatter weapons off shields, and to shout insults.

Lances couched, our destriers stamping their feet, we readied ourselves. The king was in the centre.

'All winter we caroused. Drank too much. Gambled,' said Richard.

'Made the beast with two backs,' quipped a voice from the end of the line.

This was a barb directed at Richard – referring to the half-Saracen wench he had bedded – but the king just laughed. 'Now it is time to blow out the cobwebs. Dex aie!' He pricked spurs to his horse's flanks, and shot forward, ahead of us all.

A heartbeat's delay, and then we were after him. Knee-to-knee almost, our lances out before us in a jagged-tipped line, our destriers' hooves pounding the soft earth.

The Griffons did not react immediately.

A quarter of the ground we covered.

A cry of alarm. A man pointed at us. His companion gaped, and shouted something in reply. A few heads turned.

We had gone a third of the distance.

I was beginning to make out faces. They were stunned, terrified, or a mixture of both. Men afoot were shuffling backwards, staring, as a mob retreats from a burning building. Those on horses were still uncommitted, perhaps wondering whether to launch a counter charge.

A hundred and fifty paces remained.

We were at the full gallop. The ground beneath was a blur. Pommers and I were one, a solid fighting unit that could be stopped by nothing. My world had shrunk. Everything sprang into sharp focus. My breath, panting hot against the inside of my helmet. The lance wedged under my right arm. The shield heavy on my left, and my grip on the reins. My thighs gripping tight, and heels, pushing down into the stirrups.

My vision, framed by the narrow slit, and the Griffon in the gilded helm I had picked as my target.

The enemy broke and fled long before we reached them. We crashed into the rest with the power of a massive landslide. Horses went down kicking. Men died. Any remnant of their formation was shattered into little pieces. Into the Griffons' tent lines we rode, armoured demons who sliced flesh and guy ropes with equal abandon. Only a short distance into their encampment, and a wholescale rout was in full flow.

It was an incredible victory, won against overwhelming odds.

All of it thanks to Richard.

I had heard the name Lionheart used before, but not often. From that day at Limassol, however, it was what the ordinary soldiers called out any time they saw him.

There were no more battles in the several days that followed. Richard had Berengaria and Joanna brought ashore and installed in the finest building in Limassol, a palace that had belonged to Isaac. With the emperor fled, and his army scattered to the four winds, opportunity allowed the king to take his ease with his betrothed and his sister. I was also quartered in the palace, which meant that when the king was visiting Berengaria, I could try to see Joanna. The first time, I was as skittish as a yearling colt. The warm smile she gave me by way of greeting was greatly encouraging, but did little for my nerves.

My excuse for seeing her – a lie – was that I carried a message from the king.

I admitted the falsehood as soon as her ladies were out of earshot.

She pursed her lips, which only made me want to kiss her more. 'Fie on you, Sir Rufus. That is no behaviour for a knight.'

Worried that her chiding was real, I blurted the truth. 'I could think of nothing else, madam. Subterfuge does not come naturally to me.'

'Come now.' Her tone was sceptical, even a little mocking. 'A man of your fame and stature must have had lady loves before, and needed to prise them away from their chaperones.'

'Far fewer than you might think, madam,' I said with feeling.

'In that case, you shall have to learn the skill.'

I prayed that her meaning was what I thought. 'Madam?'

She looked at me from under her lashes. 'Even a loyal knight of the king's mesnie needs good reason to be in my company alone.'

My heart leaped. She *did* want to see me. 'I shall do my best, madam.'

Again the smile that turned my legs to jelly. 'Tell me of Richard's recent exploits. He made little of what happened when you landed. When I asked him how he had put Isaac and his Griffons to flight twice, despite being heavily outnumbered, he laughed and said something about setting a nag against a racehorse.'

I happily obliged. The tale of the smith and his hammer made Joanna's eyes open wide – I had to look away briefly not to lose the thread of my story – and she laughed to hear about Richard chasing Isaac on a broken-down mare with stirrups of cord.

'Jesu, but it would have been good to see him do that. "Emperor, come joust!" Is that truly what he said?'

'The king told me himself, madam.'

Her expression grew fond. 'He was like that even as a boy, making light of the serious. It was one of the things that made me love him so. When Mama and Papa argued, which was often, he would make up the most fantastical reasons that they were fighting: ridiculous, funny things that made me giggle and forget our problems. Only when older did I realise that he had fabricated it all to distract me from the disharmony and strife.'

'He was protecting you, madam.'

'The only one of my brothers who did,' she said quietly. 'In fairness, Johnny was too small, but Hal and Geoffrey never had any time for me. Hal was obsessed with tourneys, and Geoff had no interest in anything not of direct benefit to him.' She made a visible effort to dampen her emotions, and then asked, 'What of your family, Sir Rufus?'

'Call me Rufus, madam, I beg, or Ferdia if you wish.'

She cocked her head appealingly. 'Ferdia?'

'Yes, madam. It is an ancient Irish name.'

'Forgive me, I should have remembered. Richard told me you were from Ireland.'

I wove the tale of my childhood, of sunny afternoons climbing Sliabh Feá – I laughed at her first attempt to pronounce it, and finally succeeded in getting her to say, 'Shlee-uv Fay' and 'Care-lynn' for my birthplace – and stormy nights by the fire, listening to the legends of old. 'According to my father, my brothers and I were like three wolf cubs, forever playing, or nipping or causing trouble.'

'Are they still in Ireland?'

'In a manner of speaking, madam.' Seeing her questioning look, I added, 'They are dead. And my parents.'

'All of them?'

I nodded.

Her hand went to her mouth. 'Rufus, I am sorry.'

'God giveth and he taketh away.' I hated how trite the words sounded. My brothers were given no quarter, I wanted to add, and my mother and father were murdered. FitzAldelm's brother was responsible.

'I will not pry – I can see you still grieve for them.'

'Aye. Let us talk of happier things,' I said, relieved not to have to explain more, or worse, lie about my family.

'If you are Irish, how came you to serve my brother? To my knowledge, he has never been to Ireland.'

I willingly recounted the story of my journey with Rhys from Striguil to Southampton, although I gave a different reason, wanting to join Richard's service. Not wanting to seem boastful, I skimmed over the detail of the brigands' ambush on me and Rhys, and made much of Richard's intervention. 'He saved our lives, madam,' I said. 'I will always remember that.'

'He made you his squire after that?'

'Yes, madam. We crossed the Narrow Sea soon after—'

'Wait.'

'Madam?'

A tiny frown marked her brow. 'My brother would not take you into his service lightly. He did not do it because of saving your life.'

My eyes flickered away from hers.

'Rufus? Ferdia?'

I dragged my gaze back up. 'Madam?'

'Do not be coy! Why did Richard act so? Tell me.'

I could not refuse. Out it came. The figure aiming an arrow at Richard's back. How I had thrown him to the ground. The stone thrown by Rhys, and my frantic bowshot that had flown truer than any I had ever made.

'You saved *his* life,' she murmured.

'I did, madam,' I admitted reluctantly.

'You and he seem to make a habit of this, if recent events at Messina are anything to go by. Do you take turns?'

My lips twitched.

She smiled.

I cannot remember who started to laugh first, but the next instant, we were both giggling like little children.

Looks, both curious and disapproving, came from her ladies. Joanna paid them no heed, so I did not either.

When we had calmed, Joanna said warmly, 'Thank you.'

'For what, madam?'

'I worry about the king. He seems to throw himself into every perilous situation. When we reach Outremer, he will risk injury or death every day, or I am not his sister. Knowing that he has you by his side—' Her voice caught.

It was all I could do not to reach out and touch her.

She stared into my face. 'I am glad you will be with him.'

'I am his man until my dying breath,' I swore.

A tear rolled down her cheek. She reached out and taking my hand, squeezed it.

I could have died then, so happy was I.

'It will not come to that, madam. All will be well,' I said confidently. 'The Saracens may be a doughty race, but they will not stand before our army. It would not surprise me if we celebrate Christmastide in Jerusalem.'

Her face lit up. She began to wax lyrical about walking in the Garden of Gethsemane and worshipping in the Church of the Holy Sepulchre.

Delighting in our closeness – we were scarce two feet apart – I drank her in.

Finishing, her attention came back to me. 'Ferdia, you are staring again!'

'I cannot help it,' I said thickly.

A little sigh. 'What am I to do with you?'

Kiss me, I thought.

Escaping my grip, her hand came up to touch my cheek. My skin tingled at the brief touch. 'We can never be married, you know,' she said. 'Richard will find me another husband eventually.'

My heart sank, and I blurted, 'That does not change how I feel.'

Her lips parted. There was a softness in her expression I had not seen before, and more colour in her cheeks. 'You said you had no way with women, Ferdia. I call you a liar.'

In that moment, only the knowledge that her women were watching stopped me from wrapping her in my arms.

'You had best go. Richard is to visit after he has seen Berengaria. Much as he loves you, he might not be pleased to find you here, especially as you came under false pretences.'

Her smile showed she did not mind, but dread filled me at the thought of the king's reaction. Bowing deep, and managing to plant a swift kiss on the back of her hand – she was still smiling as I rose – I bade her farewell.

'I shall arrange to ride out and see the countryside,' she said. 'Richard will provide some of his knights as protection. See that you are among them.'

'Madam.' I was grinning like a fool.

CHAPTER XII

Much to my frustration, events overtook us before Joanna managed to organise her excursion. The very next day, I was sparring with Richard in the paved courtyard of the palace when a messenger arrived. Spying him, the king stopped, and we moved to the side. Oblivious, the other knights continued to swing and batter at each other.

The messenger, a man-at-arms who had been part of the guard set on the harbour, delivered his news. Three ships had just sailed into the harbour, and aboard one was no less than Guy de Lusignan, the king of Jerusalem.

At that, a ripple of excitement went around the courtyard.

'It will be to do with Conrad of Montferrat,' said Richard, and indicated that I should come at him again. He did not discuss the matter further.

We were still training when Guy arrived, trading blows, shuffling around one another, seeking a chink in the other's defences. As men noticed the group standing at the courtyard's entrance, they stopped fighting. 'He is here, sire,' I said, dodging a side swing.

Richard lowered his arm. Tall and broad, with sweat-draggled hair and a jutting beard, he had rippling muscles under shining mail, a razor-edged sword and a red-painted heater shield emblazoned with a golden lion. He was a magnificent sight, every inch the warrior king. This was why he had not stopped to change out of his armour, I realised.

He wanted Guy to see him thus.

The king beckoned to de Drune, one of the sentries, who had brought in our visitors.

'Three of them look like brothers, sire,' I said quietly as the party approached.

'They are. Guy, Geoffrey and Amaury.' His lips twitched. 'Ironic, is it not?'

I nodded.

The de Lusignans were vassals of Richard as duke of Aquitaine, and had been a thorn in his family's side for more than twenty years. The brothers had rebelled against Henry on a number of occasions. All were men not to be trusted, and yet here they were, humble expression on their faces, walking towards us. There were others with them, but I recognised none.

Richard's mask, the face he used during serious discussion, slipped into place. He watched as de Drune, a few paces in front, bent his knee.

'King Guy of Jerusalem is come, sire, and with him, his brothers Geoffrey and Amaury de Lusignan, the nobles Humphrey de Toron, Raymond of Tripoli and Bohemond of Antioch, and Leon, brother of the prince of Armenia.' De Drune bowed and stepped aside.

The newcomers all took a knee – even Guy. A handsome man with thick fair hair and a confident air, he was like a pea in a pod with Geoffrey – but for the age separating them, the pair could almost have been twins. Their shared blood was less obvious with Amaury, but still undeniable. Humphrey was a thin, sallow-faced youth, whose sad gaze was locked on Richard. Like the rest, Raymond and Bohemond were clean-shaven after the fashion of Outremer. So too was Leon, a sharp-faced individual with a sword so ornate, I judged it never to have been used.

'I bid you welcome, messires. I had not thought to meet you until Acre,' said Richard.

'Necessity drives us, sire,' said Guy. He gestured at Richard's sword and shield. 'You have been at training?'

'Aye. Preparing for the fight against Saladin. Your arrival makes me wonder if there are other battles in the offing, and not with the Turks.'

'I – we – are here to pledge our fealty, sire,' said Guy. His brothers and companions made loud agreement.

'You could have done it when I reached Acre, surely? Saved yourselves a voyage.'

Guy glanced at Geoffrey, who nodded. His gaze returned to Richard. 'I am come to beg for your support, sire.'

'Against Conrad?' Guy's face showed surprise, and Richard continued, 'Some news has been reaching us from Outremer. Your lady wife

Sibylla died last autumn, God rest her soul, and since then Conrad has been seeking to take the throne. He has married Sibylla's sister Isabella, which gives him some claim, I suppose.'

'It was against her will, sire,' Humphrey de Toron interjected, emotion raw in his voice. 'She is still my wife, for we were never divorced. The marriage is a sham. It is also bigamous, for Conrad is already wed, twice, and incestuously, because his brother was once married to Isabella's sister.'

Richard gave Humphrey a sympathetic look, but under his breath, he murmured, 'Possession is nine-tenths of the law.' He continued, 'Since his arrival at Acre, I am given to understand that Philippe Capet has allied himself with Conrad, which leaves you in a perilous situation.'

'You are all-seeing, sire,' said Guy, dipping his chin.

'And your brothers, are they also willing to swear to serve me?' Richard did not look at Amaury or Geoffrey, who nonetheless, both shifted their feet uncomfortably.

'They are, sire.' Guy shot a sideways glance at the pair.

'I would swear undying loyalty to you, sire, if you are willing to accept it,' said Geoffrey. Amaury echoed his words. To their credit, they did sound genuine.

'Given our previous family history, most would advise me to take any such promises with a large grain of salt,' said the king.

I watched with amusement as Guy and Geoffrey, with help from Amaury and the others, promised and cajoled the king. They did not know as I did, that he was playing with them. Despite their unreliability, Richard felt the bonds of lord and vassal keenly. In addition, given the volatility of his relationship with Philippe, it was inconceivable that he would also back Conrad.

It was soon resolved. On bended knees, Guy, Geoffrey, Amaury and the others swore their fealty to the king. One hundred and sixty knights who had come with them would do the same. In return, Richard promised to do everything in his power to see Guy recognised again as king of Jerusalem.

Formalities concluded, a smiling Richard gave the destitute Guy two thousand marks, and twenty drinking cups from his treasury, two of which were gold.

Then he invited them all to his wedding, the very next day.

*

Richard married Berengaria on a Sunday, the twelfth of May in the year of our Lord 1191. The ceremony took place in the grandest church in Limassol. A mouse could barely have squeezed into that place, so crowded was it. My position in the mesnie meant that I was close to the front, however, with a view of the king and his bride, who were married by Nicholas, the bishop of Le Mans.

I, however, had eyes only for Joanna, who was quite close to me. I caught her glancing in my direction once or twice. She made no sign of recognition, but my heart soared.

De Béthune gave me a dig in the ribs.

I glared at him.

'Do not stare so,' he hissed. 'Do you want someone to see – FitzAldelm, maybe?'

Brought to my senses – my enemy was a short distance behind me – I nodded my thanks.

'If you must proceed, be careful. It would be too easy for a little bird to whisper in Richard's ear.'

Again I nodded, grateful to have such a friend.

With the marriage completed, a second ceremony took place. Berengaria was crowned Queen of England by John, the bishop of Evreux. Richard gifted her with a generous dowry, including full rights in all territory in Gascony south of the River Garonne. These lands, which ran down to the border with her father's kingdom, had been agreed on when the king had met with Sancho.

After that, the celebrations began. Every cook for fifty miles had been brought in to prepare the lavish feast which awaited us in the great hall of the palace. It was a long night, full of music and laughter, and capped by a stolen moment with Joanna. When she went to answer a call of nature, I made my move. The garderobe was gained by a short corridor that led from the end of the hall. Arriving casually a short time after she had passed through, I found one of her ladies on guard at the entrance. Although we knew each other to see, she stiffened at my approach.

I hesitated. The sensible thing was to walk away. I risked all by proceeding.

I thought of the ride into the countryside that Joanna had mentioned. Pleasant though it would be, I would have no chance whatsoever of talking to her alone.

Plunging forward, I said to the lady, 'I am Rufus, one of the king's knights. The queen has asked to see me.'

Her normally pleasant face was pinched with disapproval. 'Here?'

'Yes. By your leave.' Firmly, I moved her to one side and entered the corridor. Ignoring the lady's strangled demand that I stop at once, I walked the ten paces to the garderobe door. Now my courage deserted me, for there was no polite way of interrupting Joanna's toilet. Fortune intervened. The latch lifted, the hinges creaked, and my heart rose into my mouth.

Joanna's lady was at my back, demanding in a furious whisper that I leave.

Joanna opened the door and saw me. Her face was a picture of surprise. 'Rufus?'

'Forgive me, madam. I needed to speak with you.'

My words hung in the air. Our gaze locked. I could no longer hear the lady behind me.

'Wait down there.' Joanna pointed along the corridor. 'Do not let anyone in.'

With a startled and not entirely approving bob of her head, the lady obeyed.

Joanna took my hand, and leading me into the candlelit garderobe, shut the door. 'This is no place to speak to a queen,' she said, but she was smiling.

I said nothing, but just stared.

'What is it?' Her voice was husky.

'You are an angel come to Earth, I swear it.'

As she opened her mouth to answer, I stepped forward and kissed her. She met my passion with a fierce one of her own, and I enfolded her in my arms.

All too soon, she pulled back. 'I must get back to the hall.'

I kissed her again, and her fingers entwined themselves in my hair, holding me to her. I could have stayed that way forever.

Again she pulled away. 'Rufus.' Her voice was a little breathless.

I stared into her eyes, grazed my lips off hers. I risked saying, 'Joanna?'

'Someone will notice how long I have been gone. We cannot be discovered, especially in here.'

Cold reason sank in. 'Of course.'

She rearranged the neck of her dress, and laid a hand to the latch. 'Count to a hundred before you follow.'

'I will.' I darted in for another kiss, which she gave me.

'I am leaving now, Ferdia.' She gave me a languorous look that set my knees to trembling, and opened the door.

'When can I see you again?'

'I know not.' She stepped into the corridor.

My heart sank. I peered around the timbers, desperate that this meeting should not end like this.

She glanced back. 'I will find a way.'

Christ Jesus, I could have fought every man in Saladin's army in that moment and expected to win.

It seemed as if the conflict with Isaac was over. Soon after the days-long wedding celebrations, the emperor asked to see Richard, and with Garnier de Nablus, the Grand Master of the Hospitallers mediating, they met in a garden of fig trees between the shore and the Limassol road. No demand of the king's was too much for Isaac. He pledged to voyage to Outremer with the king, bringing with him five hundred knights. The castles of Cyprus were to be held by English troops as a sign of his sincerity. Three thousand five hundred marks would also be paid into Richard's coffers. He was even to marry his daughter Beatrice to whomsoever the king deemed fitting. Despite this high price, Isaac, a thin-faced man with a long nose, seemed cheerful and content. He exchanged the kiss of peace with the king, and accepted an offer to dine together. Tents were set up; wagons arrived, bearing cooks and all the necessaries to lay on a banquet.

It was all a ruse, however. In the depths of night, Isaac and his retinue took to their horses and fled. The deception was only revealed in the morning. Far from being annoyed, Richard was positively buoyant.

'By breaking his oath, the fool has played into my hands,' he declared over a rich breakfast of leftovers. 'Now I have the justification to take the whole island.'

We seized the town of Famagusta, eighty miles along the winding coastline, some days later. In fact, there was no resistance: the place was deserted but for a few ancients and those too frail or unwilling to flee. Isaac was long gone on his fleet horse Fauvel. Nicosia, deep inland, would be our next objective; we halted long enough to buy enough supplies for the hot, dusty march.

In the welcome cool of early evening on the second day, Rhys suggested we try our luck at fishing from the harbour wall, as we had done in Messina. Unable to see Joanna – she was often secreted with Berengaria – I readily agreed. De Drune came along also. We had landed perhaps half a dozen fish, and were enjoying a costrel of wine, when a brace of ships came tacking in from the east. Rhys, blessed with hawk-like vision, was first to spot the fleur-de-lis pennants atop their masts.

'They will be from Philippe,' I said, pulling in my line. 'Let us to the dock and meet them.'

My hunch proved correct. Aboard the lead vessel were representatives sent by Philippe Capet: the bishop of Beauvais and a bullnecked nobleman by the name of Drogo de Merlo. They were nonplussed to be greeted off the gangplank by a trio of fishermen, albeit French-speaking ones. I had heard of the bishop; a corrupt individual and a cousin of Philippe Capet, it was he who had conducted the recent illegal marriage between Conrad of Montferrat and the unfortunate Isabella, wife of Humphrey of Toron. The bishop was portly and round-faced, and eyed Rhys, bare-chested in the warm sunshine, with overfriendly eyes. Rhys, blind to that kind of attention, did not even notice. I sent him to run and fetch horses for the French emissaries, and de Drune to advise the king of his unexpected visitors.

I had no desire to speak to the arse-loving, lawbreaking bishop, but I was keen to know how things were at Acre. I had little joy. Either de Merlo had not heard that I was a knight of Richard's mesnie, or thought himself better than me. Perhaps it was both, I thought, as a second attempt to draw him into conversation met with abject failure. Rude French prick, I decided, and diverted myself by thinking of Joanna and whistling a love song.

Rhys came back with Philip, leading two extra horses each. The finest of the four was my rouncy; de Merlo made straight for it. I took enormous pleasure in telling him it was mine, and that he could ride whichever of the others he pleased. His face was as sour as curdled milk the whole way to the fortress where the king was quartered, but I did not care. They carried news that would anger Richard, I was sure of it, and thus felt no need for courtesy.

When we arrived in the great hall, the steward told us to wait. This was quite deliberate; the king had never taken long to get dressed. When he appeared, however, it was plain that he had made an effort to impress. Over a tunic of rose samite, he wore a cloak decorated with little half-moons, glowing white in solid silver, with shining orbs like golden suns scattered densely among them. From a silken cross belt hung a fine sword with a gold hilt, sheathed in a silver-indented scabbard. His mane of hair was covered by a scarlet cap embroidered in gold thread with the shapes of birds and beasts, and he carried an ivory baton as a symbol of his office. The sight of him was a pleasure to the eyes, and quite magnificent.

I introduced the French emissaries, and stood aside. Richard gave me a nod of thanks; seeing it, FitzAldelm scowled. I winked at him, which blackened his expression further.

Both men knelt, the bishop with a great deal of wheezing, and then introduced themselves.

'Philippe has sent you,' said Richard.

'Indeed, sire. He bids you fond greeting,' said the bishop with an oily smile.

I liked him even less.

'As I do to him,' said Richard, sounding sincere. 'What message has he given you?'

'He has built numerous siege engines, sire, and bombarded the defences of Acre for days, causing much damage.'

'And a breach – has he made one?' Richard's expression was bright with interest. 'What of his assaults?'

'There are several places along the walls where an attack might be essayed, sire, but the king has not yet ordered his troops forward. He is waiting for you.'

'Still?' cried Richard. 'I heard that news weeks ago! What does Philippe do from dawn to dusk – sit on his hands?'

The bishop pursed his lips; de Merlo's face suffused with colour. They glanced at each other, and the bishop said, 'The king demands that you cross the Greek Sea to Acre as fast as you may, sire, so that you might both press home a decisive assault.'

'*Demands?*' Richard's voice was low, but it cut through the room like a blade.

The bishop pulled at the neck of his tunic, as if it had, of a moment, grown too tight. 'Yes, sire, that is what he said. He wants you to make ready your fleet and sail within the week.'

'Sooner, if possible, sire,' added de Merlo, nervously.

'The barefaced cheek of him,' said Richard, adding in an acid tone, 'is there anything else?'

The bishop coughed, and looked anywhere but at the king. De Merlo had more courage. He took a breath, and said, 'The king says that you are ignoring the essential business of defeating Saladin and recovering Jerusalem, sire. You are persecuting innocent Christians here, when you should be attacking the thousands of Saracens in Outremer.'

A shocked silence fell.

The vein that signified Richard's purest rage pulsed in his neck. He stared at de Merlo, and raised an eyebrow as if to ask, *Are you finished?*

'You seem so valiant, the king says, sire, but when it comes to engaging the Saracens, you are a coward,' de Merlo finished in a virtual whisper.

I was not alone in gasping with surprise and anger.

Richard erupted. The oaths he hurled at the bishop and de Merlo would have turned a saint's hair white. He roared and threatened them with his baton until I thought the whey-faced bishop would faint. De Merlo took it a little better, but even he looked frankly terrified.

At last the king drew breath. He gazed, flint-eyed, at the emissaries, who took great interest in the patterned floor.

'Tell your master, *Philippe*, that not for half the wealth of Russia would I leave Cyprus until I am ready! When I have conquered the island, and secured both its harbours, and gathered all the corn and wine I need for the taking of the Holy Land, then and only then will I come to Acre,' said the king. 'Do I make myself clear?'

The bishop and de Merlo muttered fervent agreement.

'Then begone, lest I forget that you are emissaries.' Richard's hand dropped to the golden hilt.

Never has a fat man moved as fast as the bishop of Beauvais that day. De Merlo was only a step behind.

'It is well that Philippe is not here,' growled the king. 'I would not be responsible for my own actions.'

It was natural Richard felt that way, I thought, but his fury increased my concern that our war against Saladin was doomed ere it even began.

CHAPTER XIII

Fifteen days later, the entire island of Cyprus was in Richard's hands. The short, sharp campaign would have ended faster but for a bout of illness – the cursed quartan fever again – which had struck the king down at Nicosia. He had divided his forces into three, leading one himself, with Guy de Lusignan and a senior knight called Robert de Turnham the others. The coastal towns had capitulated without a fight, and despite the inaccessibility of Isaac's various mountain fastnesses, they too had yielded to Richard. Isaac himself had proved to be no valiant leader, fleeing eastward on Fauvel after just one failed ambush, and at the last skulking in a monastery. After his surrender, he had been treated with courtesy, but Richard's sardonic humour saw him grant Isaac's plea not to be fettered in iron shackles, ordering that manacles of silver and gold should be made for the former emperor. Isaac's daughter Beatrice, a girl of thirteen years, had also been taken captive, and passed into the care of Berengaria and Joanna.

Hostilities ceased, the king had inventories made in every town and castle on the island. Everything that was of worth was to be seized as funds for his venture to the Holy Land. As the wealth flowed in, it seemed to us that Cyprus was as rich a place as the lands ruled by the legendary king Croesus.

Strong rooms in the towns of Candaira and Cherinas yielded gold cups and plate, salvers and silver pots, cauldrons and great casks. In the fortresses of Dieu d'Amour and Buffavento there were golden saddles, bridles and spurs, all with precious stones of great virtue. There were valuable clothes made from scarlet fabric and silk from the Orient, and more treasure besides. Granaries bulged with wheat and barley; merchants' warehouses were filled with tuns upon tuns of wine. The Griffons were also taxed personally, each man forced to pay over half their wealth.

The vast quantities of gold and silver held little interest for the king, other than to pay for the war in Outremer. A far greater pleasure to him was Fauvel, Isaac's fleet-footed stallion; he soon became Richard's favourite mount. At times, he seemed to have more time for Fauvel than Berengaria. I confess to feeling jealous that the king, free to do so, did not spend time with his lady love, while I, burning to see Joanna, managed only an occasional moment in her company.

Powerless to change the situation, I threw myself into the preparations for our voyage.

The morning of the sixth of June saw cause for great rejoicing. We had sailed from Cyprus only the day before, and already the coast of Outremer was in sight. Rhys stood beside me on the deck, his lean face taut with excitement. Twenty-four ships were with us, but fine weather meant the rest of the fleet would not be far behind. We made landfall at the Hospitaller castle of Margat, some hundred and fifty miles north of Acre. There the king delivered a cowed Isaac, still in his chains of gold and silver, into the care of the commander of the garrison, with orders that he was never to be set free.

After a quiet night at anchor, we sailed south the next morning, passing small towns, various strongholds, and a great tower at Gibelet. It was sobering to know that barely a one remained in Christian hands. It made our reception that afternoon sting all the more. The great island fortress of Tyre, loyal to Conrad of Montferrat, refused to admit us, nor even to replenish our water.

Richard showed no emotion to the men standing atop the walls, but when we reached the open sea once more, his temper burst free. Pacing about the deck, he cursed Conrad and Philippe – for the French king's hand had to be in this too, he shouted – as faithless curs. They were treacherous hellspawn, the pair of them, that could have been whelped from the same bitch mother.

Everyone gave him a wide berth. Better it was to stay clear of the thunderstorm and lightning, and wait for the better weather that generally followed.

Today, however, Richard's foul mood showed no sign of lifting. He snapped at Philip when offered a cup of wine; he cuffed a broken-nosed sailor around the head when he came too close; the captain received a dressing down for what seemed no reason at all. My attempt to draw him into conversation saw me dismissed with a curt wave of the hand. FitzAldelm brought P'tit to the prow where the king stood, but even that ploy did not work. Richard stroked her once, and resumed his staring out to sea.

It was getting on for midday – the sun was high in the sky, and the sea a beaten sheet of silver – when the king gave a shout. 'A ship!'

I came haring up from the deck with half a dozen others; we had been sheltering from the roasting heat under a sail canopy. I reached the king first. 'Where, sire?'

He pointed off to our left, closer to the forested coastline.

I saw it. Perhaps a mile off, the vessel was large, and had three masts. 'Is it crewed by Christians or heathens, sire?' I asked eagerly.

'We shall soon see.' Richard shouted for the captain, and ordered a change of course. It was sailing in the same direction as we were, and under normal circumstances could have used its great expanse of sail to outdistance us with ease, but the wind was limp and half-hearted, allowing us soon to draw near. It was a magnificent vessel, with a red-painted hull. To prevent fire arrows setting its planking alight, green felt had been hung down the side nearest us. The decks were packed with armed men: this was no simple merchantman.

A faster craft than ours was deputised to approach the ship and demand to know their allegiance, and whither were they bound.

The message came back to us that they were Genoese, bound for Acre.

Richard looked disappointed. 'I had hoped for some action this day,' he said.

I noticed the broken-nosed sailor he had struck creeping up the ladder from the deck. I jerked my chin to tell him to begone, but he paid no heed. On your own head be it, I thought.

'Sire,' whispered the sailor.

Richard did not hear.

'Sire,' said the sailor, louder.

The king looked around. Glowered.

Remarkably, the sailor was undeterred. 'My lord, may I be killed or hanged if that is not a Turkish vessel.'

Richard's eyes went from the sailor to the three-masted ship, which was tacking out to sea, and back again. 'Are you sure?'

'Yes, sire. I have seen it being loaded before, in Beirut. They are already going away fast. Perhaps send another galley after them, whose rowers do not offer them a word of greeting. Then we shall see what their intention and faith really are.'

The king seemed convinced by the sailor's earnestness, and gave the order.

We watched with rising anticipation as one of the swift-moving galleys pulled ahead, its oars rising and falling in smooth unison. No sooner had it drawn within range of the strange ship than arrows arced towards it in dense volleys. Cries of pain carried over the waves. More arrows flew. On the enemy's deck, I saw figures manhandling a long tube towards the stern. I had no idea what it was, but the king swore.

'That is for directing Greek fire – they are Saracens, for certes,' cried Richard.

He had already commanded every fighting man to arm himself; now he had the trumpeters sound the attack. The rowers bent their backs as they had not done since leaving Messina. On either side, the other galleys kept pace. Everyone wanted to be first to the fight. The captain prowled up and down, roaring encouragement. Our prow knifed through the water; spray flew high into the air. Glittering droplets of seawater fell on us as invigorating rain.

Our assault did not prove easy. The Saracens were numerous, and so powerful were their bows that our ships suffered many casualties. Gouts of blueish-grey Greek fire – which made a hideous, thunderous noise – threatened to incinerate any vessel that came within range. This did not stop the king from making several attempts, but our efforts also failed. We lost ten men and suffered twice that number injured, and if Philip and I had not been close to Richard with our shields, the tale might have been altogether more tragic. Again and again, I plucked arrows from mine; Philip had to do the same.

Richard laughed when we showed him our peppered shields. His earlier temper was gone; he was in bright, combative mood. The broken-nosed sailor had been rewarded with the promise of a gold coin, and sent away grinning. 'God's legs, but I would like to close with the heathens,' said the king. 'But I will not throw away the lives of my men. We needs must ram the devils.'

The order was shouted from galley to galley, and following a trumpet blast from our ship, four of us rowed in from different angles. Close to, we could see the decks were loaded with barrels and sacks of goods, supplies, no doubt, for the wretched defenders of Acre. Defiant to the last, the Saracen archers shot and shot; their crew blasted the deck of one galley with Greek fire, but they could not stop the inevitable.

The impact as we struck was massive, terrifying. Timbers screeched. Cracked, split. The air filled with yells. Screams. The harmless-sounding but deadly click, click of crossbow triggers. Arrows whizzed past, driving into our deck, shields, men's flesh. The noxious stench of Greek fire choked my throat. Gaping holes in the enemy ship's side became visible as our rowers backed water, allowing the greedy sea to pour in. Before we were a hundred paces away, our victim was listing badly. Some men ran hither and thither in blind panic; others leaped overboard. The firing tube had been discarded; around it, blobs of Greek fire burned on the deck. A few archers, mad with battle lust or uncaring that their deaths would soon be on them, were still shooting at us. Their aim, so accurate before, was off. Arrows plunked into the waves, or banged into the hull.

Scarce thirty-five survivors – many of them high-ranking officers – were plucked from the water by Richard's orders. He interrogated them, and to my surprise, gave orders that they were to be well-treated.

Exhilarated by our first victory against the Saracens, we sailed for Acre.

As the afternoon drew on, a welcome north wind filled our sails and hurried us down the coast. The king, who had not stirred from his vantage point on the prow platform, was one of the first to spot our destination.

I also drank in the sight. Acre was not big, but its defences were impressive, and its very solidity made our great enterprise seem real for the first time. The Christian encampment was visible also. It looked magnificent, and absurdly courageous, perched as it was on the landward side of the walls with the Muslim defenders on one side and Saladin's army on the other. Beyond our people's camp, up into the nearby hills, the land was covered by the enemy's tents.

'Now I can make sense of the geography and the siege,' said the king. 'Acre is built on a promontory that juts into the sea, and is triangular in shape. All along its landward side, see there the beginning of it, runs a double wall and a deep fosse. It is against those that most of the attacks have been made. As we sail south, the city's two other sides, the sea defences, will be revealed. High walls and the water itself guard against assault there.'

We sailed on, and the harbour entrance came into sight. Masts were visible by the score within. A walled mole served as its protection, and at the rocky end of that stood a squat tower, a stronghold with the hideous name of the Tower of the Flies. From the structure's base, a massively thick chain ran underwater to the other side of the harbour mouth, barring the passage to ships.

I was glad we would not have to try and take the tower. Richard had told us of the disastrous attempt to capture it the previous September.

Our coming had been noticed. Heads were dotted all along the rampart. A few overconfident bowmen shot at us, but their arrows fell far short of our ships. More nerve-wracking were the efforts of the artillerymen within the city; they lobbed several stones in our direction. Thankfully, these too landed nowhere near us.

The sandy beach to the south of Acre was thronged with people as our ships entered the shallows and the anchors were dropped. Standards flew, trumpets sounded. Bells rang, and pipes were played. Horsemen rode up and down, waving. There were figures dancing and singing with excitement.

Richard seemed well-pleased, although his expression darkened when I pointed out the fleur-de-lis of Philippe Capet. 'I shall have to smile and make pleasant,' said the king.

'As shall he, sire,' I retorted.

That got a laugh. 'True enough! He will hate it as much as I. Still, it must be done for the sake of unity. The poulains have enough to quarrel about with Conrad and Guy. I do not want to add to the discontent.'

Richard was as good as his word, greeting Philippe like a long-lost brother. The French king also played his part well. Kiss of peace exchanged, a short parade along the beach so the assembled crowds of foot soldiers, men-at-arms, knights and raggletaggle of civilians could cheer, the two monarchs rode side-by-side to the main encampment, which lay on Le Toron, a low hill to the east of the city.

I stayed behind to oversee the unloading of our ship, and to ensure that our equipment, weapons and supplies were not plundered. Loudly they had applauded our arrival, but the gaunt-faced civilians in ragged clothing who lingered near our landing spot would steal anything that was not tied down *and* guarded.

Although evening was nigh, and I had nothing to do but stand in one place, the brutal climate was impossible to ignore. The air was close and humid, and thick to breathe. The sea, as we waded ashore, had been blood warm, and the sand underfoot was painfully hot to the touch. Flies swarmed about us in clouds, landing on eyes, lips, cheeks, any exposed flesh. A fearful reek hung in the air; in it, I discerned both urine and faeces – animal and human – the distinctive odour of horses and mules, and the unmistakeable whiff of rotting flesh.

Rhys seemed not to care. Delighted as a child with a plate of marchpane fancies, he stared about him in wonder. When the wailing call to prayer carried from the mosques inside Acre, he exclaimed, 'We are in Outremer, finally!'

I smiled. It did feel like an historic moment in our lives.

God willing, I prayed, our time here would prove fruitful.

PART THREE

JUNE 1191–AUGUST 1191

CHAPTER XIV

The next morning, I awoke overhot, and with a slight headache. I gave silent thanks that I had not drunk myself into a stupor as de Drune and Richard Thorne had done. Peeling my eyes open, I stared at the canvas above me, through which an intense heat already radiated. My straw-filled palliasse was stuck to me with sweat. I leaned up on an elbow, reaching for my leather water bag. The previous night's revelries came back to me, a riot of music and dance and drinking, lit by bonfires and torches, that had gone on until late in the night.

I had not spent long in the main body of the encampment – the poor souls there were packed like rats in a drain, with sewage running in channels between their wretched tents – but instead watched the celebrations from where the king's pavilion and those we were to stay in had been erected. Close to Philippe Capet's camp, and surrounded by its own swiftly erected palisade, it was near to the double ditch that protected us from Saladin's army.

'Rufus?' The king's voice had me off my palliasse in a heartbeat. Rhys, who had been sleeping on a blanket at my feet, also woke.

'Sire?' I unlaced the flap and peered out to find the king there with Philip. Both were dressed in tunics and hose, and carrying crossbows. Each also had a sword strapped to his belt, and on the opposite hip, a quiver full of bolts. There was an excited cast to Richard's face.

'Get your weapon, Rufus. You too,' he said to Rhys. 'Let us see if my aim has improved since Nonancourt.'

We went scrambling back inside. Emerging a short time later, I found the sun had not yet cleared the hills to the east, where Saladin's camp lay at a place with the unpronounceable name of Tell al-'Ayyādiyya.

'What is your plan, sire?'

'I mean to spy out the defences.'

Unsurprised, I was nonetheless a little concerned. 'Is it just we four, sire?'

He grinned a yes, and then, before I could protest, said, 'The Saracens are sleeping like everyone else, Rufus. We will be back ere the first muezzin calls.'

I might as well bang my head off the Tower of the Flies as argue further, I thought, so I nodded my assent. Before we had gone ten feet, however, I sent Rhys hurrying back for a brace of heater shields; we slung them from our backs. Whatever about us, the king had to be protected. I chided Philip for not having brought one at least, but he replied that Richard had forbade him.

'All his bear the Angevin lion,' he said. 'I cannot think of a better target for a Saracen archer.'

I cursed my own stupidity. Without asking the king, I sent Rhys on another swift mission. De Drune and Richard Thorne, their faces puffy from too much wine and not enough sleep, caught up with us before we had gone far. As well as their crossbows, they had shields. I hoped that four between six men would prove enough.

We passed the surprised-looking guards at the compound entrance – Richard told them to mention our passage to no one – and entered the camp proper. Padding between the tents, we avoided the foul matter that caked much of the ground. Evidence of the night's celebrations was everywhere. Sleeping bodies lay half-in, half-out of tents, on the bare earth, blocking the very avenues we trod. Men lay on their backs, snoring, many still gripping a wine sack or a cup. Scrawny mongrels and pigs searched for scraps. A lonely hen pecked in the dirt.

Richard aimed southeast. Reaching the edge of the encampment closest to the sea, where not a soul was stirring, he had us load our weapons. We passed a number of flame-blackened catapults and reached the end of the city wall, which ran right to the water's edge. Off to the left, we could see ships' masts in the harbour. The king halted fifty paces from the imposing stone ramparts, and a mighty gated bastion that projected forward from the wall. Although there were no enemy sentries in view, I did not like it. We were completely out in the open, and well inside the range of a crossbowman or archer.

Richard seemed oblivious. 'See there?' he pointed. 'The fosse is deeper than I am tall.'

We walked north, the king in front. The towers were frequent, sometimes as close as a hundred paces from each other, and the ditch steep-sided. The charred remains of timbers marked the places where attempts had been made to level the ground and allow attackers to reach the wall, only for the Saracens to pour Greek fire down and burn the lot. Frequent pock marks in the stone, and an occasional partially collapsed section marked the efforts of the Christians' siege engines.

'Hold!' The king froze. We stopped.

A head – helmetless – appeared in a crenellation opposite us. It was side on – the man had paused to do something, and was not looking in our direction. All he had to do, however, was turn his face, and he would see us.

Richard raised his crossbow and took aim.

I held my breath, and prepared to unsling my shield and move in front of him. The risk to us was slight, but if he missed, every sentry for a hundred paces would be shooting at us. If he did not, there was still a chance that his falling body would raise the alarm.

Click.

A black blur, the king's quarrel flew straight and true.

The sentry's head was punched sideways by the impact, and he dropped from sight.

'A fine shot, sire,' whispered Rhys.

'The praise of the praiseworthy is high praise indeed,' Richard answered, reloading.

Rhys bobbed his head, delighted.

Crossbows at the ready, we watched the battlements intently for any sign of the enemy. After a time, it was evident that the fate of the king's victim had gone unnoticed, and we resumed our patrol along the wall. The ground beneath our feet must once have been farmland, I judged, but it had long since been torn up by the vicious struggles that had swayed to and fro across it. We picked a path over broken weapons and discarded pieces of equipment, and around burnt siege engines. I saw the butchered skeleton of a horse, and remembered the dreadful tales of the previous autumn's famine.

'There is the Accursed Tower,' said the king quietly.

We were approaching a high bastion on a salient at the northeastern corner of the defences. Considerable damage had been done to its walls and roof, but it had not collapsed. The artillery – French for the most part – that had battered it so often stood a couple of hundred paces back, close to the Christian ditches. Any guards must have been drowsing, because no shout or call to arms met our arrival.

'It is said that in ancient times, the thirty silver coins paid to Judas the Traitor were minted in the tower,' said Richard. 'Probably another old wives' tale.'

We crossed ourselves just the same, and then studied the Accursed Tower. Built on a right angle in the wall, it was regarded as the weakest point of the defences, and had been the focus of numerous attacks by Guy de Lusignan and more recently, by Philippe. Although some had come close to succeeding, none had, in the main due to the Saracen's ferocious tenacity. Another reason, as Richard explained with pleasure, was that the French trebuchets were operated by traction. His used counterweights.

'Mine are twice as powerful as any of the Frenchies' ones, even the *Malvoisin*, the Evil Neighbour.' He pointed at the most famous weapon, a mighty contraption the size of four ox carts. 'Once my artillery arrives, we will soon reduce the walls to rubble.'

We continued our reconnaissance. The detritus left by Philippe's failed assaults was most obvious in the fosse, which he had had filled so his men could cross to the base of the defences. For scores of paces in either direction, it was full of charred and blackened timbers, and uneven piles of stone. It looked lethally dangerous to try and cross, and that was without Saracens shooting at me.

The city's main gate lay in the section of wall that ran west from the Accursed Tower to the sea. Strong towers and a honeycomb of ditches around it meant the entire section was invulnerable; Richard abandoned our walk in that direction inside two hundred paces.

The ease with which we had completed our mission saw a more relaxed mood settle on the group. De Drune and Thorne began talking quietly to Rhys and Philip about their exploits the previous night. Richard was deep in thought, no doubt planning his tactics over the coming days. I was dreaming pleasantly about Joanna. All of us were giving less attention to the rampart than was wise.

The crossbow bolt came out of nowhere. God be thanked, it thumped into the ground, although it almost skewered one of Richard's feet. Frantic, in case there was more than one crossbowman, I dropped my weapon and ran towards him, grabbing for my shield. ''Ware, sire!'

To my relief, it was only one sentry who had spotted us, and he had to reload. We were in great danger, however. He was shouting out for his comrades. The four of us with shields protected the king as we shuffled backwards in an undignified scramble, away from our assailant. We could see him, a dark-skinned man with a pointed beard. His second shot glanced off my shield. We kept retreating, and were soon at the limits of crossbow range. Guts churning still, I darted back and retrieved my crossbow. The Turk shot at me and missed. Clearly annoyed, he called out insults in his own language, and then, to my surprise, in bad French.

'Cowards! Come back and fight!'

Rhys raised his weapon, loosed and shot, all in one smooth movement. The bolt hummed a few inches over the Turk's head. Then, indicating that Philip should pick up his shield, Rhys paced back towards the wall, spanning his crossbow again.

'Rhys!' I hissed.

He paid no heed.

You fool, I thought. The Turk was staring down his crossbow at him, and Rhys, wearing only a tunic, had no shield.

The king held his peace; this was the kind of mad bravery he liked.

The Turk loosed at Rhys, and overshot by a short distance.

Rhys, who had reloaded, pulled his own trigger. The quarrel knocked splinters off the stone by the Turk's left hand, which he had just placed on the parapet.

'You shoot well,' called the Turk in accented French, climbing up on something so that his entire torso was visible. 'Let us play a game. I will shoot and you will stand still, not turning in any direction. If I miss, I will remain still for you, and not move. This I swear by Allah, the great and merciful.'

'The sun has cooked his wits,' I said. 'Rhys!'

Again my squire ignored me.

'Very well,' he answered, walking ten steps closer.

De Drune muttered a vile, blasphemous oath. Thorne began to pray.

Heads were appearing in other crenellations; the noise had brought further defenders to the scene. I was concerned that the Devil's mob would loose at Rhys, but the Turk cried out in his own tongue, which seemed for the moment to stay their hands.

I held my breath as the Turk shot, and gave thanks to God when his quarrel tugged at the shoulder of Rhys's tunic, but caused no further damage.

Rhys lifted his crossbow, stared down its length, and pulled the trigger.

It was hard to judge, but I decided that no more than a fingers-breadth had separated the bolt and the Turk's left ear as it flew by.

Rhys glanced back at us, scowling.

'This a game for lackwits. Get back here,' growled de Drune.

Rhys ignored him.

Richard said nothing.

I wanted to speak, to urge Rhys again to retreat, but I held back. This was his fate.

'My turn again,' said Rhys's enemy with a grin.

'It is.'

The Turk was in no hurry. 'What is your name? What land are you from?'

'Rhys, they call me. I am from Wales.'

'I have never heard of this *Wales*. Does it rain there much of the time, as they say it does in France?'

Rhys chuckled. 'Every day it rains almost. What is your name?'

'Grair.'

'Do your best, Grair,' said Rhys stoutly, but there was a slight quaver in his voice. Nonetheless, he stood up straight.

The Turk took aim.

Fear knotted my belly. I could not bear to watch any longer, so I closed my eyes.

Click.

There was no rush of air, no impact with either flesh or soil.

I looked up to see the Turk cursing and struggling with his crossbow. 'His string came off the latch prematurely, sire,' I said with delight to the king. Sometimes this happened.

'God is watching.' Richard was gleeful.

'Now I will shoot. Stand still for me,' called Rhys.

'My string slipped,' replied Grair. 'Let me draw again, and I will let you draw twice.'

No, I wanted to scream. Richard looked unhappy, but said nothing. De Drune and Philip were white-faced.

'Certainly,' said Rhys.

He is a dead man, I thought. The Turk will not miss again.

Grair tugged and pulled at his weapon, adjusting the string.

Calm and measured, Rhys aimed and shot.

The bolt punched deep into the Turk's chest. He tumbled backwards without even a cry, and a heartbeat later, I heard his body hit the ground.

'You did not keep your agreement with me, Grair,' Rhys cried, as screams of outrage rose from the battlements. 'Nor shall I with you, in the name of Saint Denis.' Then he turned and ran.

Arrows and quarrels filled the air as Grair's comrades sought vengeance.

Jesu be thanked, they all missed.

When Rhys reached us, I squeezed his shoulder, hard.

He merely nodded, but a world of emotion passed between us.

'That was a contest and a half and no mistake,' said Richard, looking mightily pleased.

'You are not angry with me, sire, for shooting rather than letting him loose again at me first?' Rhys seemed a little worried.

'Hellfire, no! His string slipping was not your fault. It was your turn.'

Rhys's beam grew even broader when the king promised him a purse of silver by way of reward.

In high spirits, careful to keep out of range of the plentiful enemy archers and crossbowmen who were now watching us, we made for our camp on Le Toron.

The first opportunity that came my way, I hissed in Rhys's ear, 'What possessed you?'

A sheepish expression. 'I wanted to show the king I could still shoot as well as he, or better. To refuse Grair's challenge would have looked yellow-livered. I had to accept. I tell you, though, I was as close to shitting myself as I have ever been.'

'You were not the only one,' I replied.

A little manic, we both laughed.

Our arrival had filled Philippe with newfound courage. Despite our siege weapons not having reached us yet – lack of wind had delayed the ships carrying them at Tyre – he insisted on an all-out attack that morning, the ninth of June. Richard was furious, but he could not stop the French king. Rather than join the assault, which was to take place at the Accursed Tower after a mighty pounding by the siege engines, we divided our forces to cover the French flanks and to protect the ditches that faced towards the hills where Saladin's camp lay, three miles away.

To acquaint himself with the previous battles, Richard spent an hour in consultation with Philippe, Guy de Lusignan and a host of other veterans of the siege. He refused to speak to Conrad of Montferrat, whose men had denied us entrance to Tyre. Afterwards, the king related what he had learned. Each time the Christians launched an assault, the garrison inside Acre lit fires and banged drums, tambourines and even copper basins to alert Saladin. It meant that every attack had to be fought on two fronts – at the city walls, and at the edge of our encampment.

We took up our positions, and when the Saracens answered the summons from within Acre, sweeping towards us in a great tide of horsemen, we held our own. Lethal volleys from our crossbowmen scythed down the hated race in droves. I wish I could have said the same for the Frenchies' efforts. During a lull in the fighting, Richard went to see how they were getting on. He returned, grim-faced, with tales of chaos. Black clouds of arrows were killing Frenchmen by the dozen, and Greek fire burning men and siege engines alike. Only the heroism of those such as Guy de Lusignan's brother Geoffrey were preventing our erstwhile allies from being routed.

The battle ended soon after when the battered French could take no more. We, however, had forced Saladin's troops to withdraw from the flanks and the ditches some time before. They did not seem keen to launch a counterattack. Our morale was high that night. Although the walls of Acre had not been breached, our losses had been light, and the enemy had failed against us.

The following day, Richard received deputations from both the Pisan and Genoese contingents in the camp. He spent a short time with each group, and sent them away with kind words. 'How quickly they desert Philippe,' he said to me. 'But in good faith I could only accept the service of the Pisans.'

'The Genoese can hardly serve Philippe and Conrad *and* you, sire.'

He snorted. 'It was typical of the grasping-fingered Genoese to try anyway. They profess to love our cause, but merchants' minds are always on coin. The Pisans are no different, save they had the wit to wait and pledge allegiance to me.'

The day after that, Philippe's petulance reached new heights. Furious with his artillerymen – they had asked for better wages, despite failing to batter down the city walls – he dismissed most of them from his service. Seeing the French siege engines unguarded, the Saracens sortied out and destroyed them. Even the wonderfully named *Malvoisin* did not survive.

Richard meanwhile took the French artillerymen into his employ, and compounded Philippe's humiliation by offering four bezants a month to any knight in the camp – there were many without a lord – who entered his service. Philippe had only been paying three.

On the same day, the tenth of June, our tower of Mategriffon was unloaded from the ships, and assembled not far from the Accursed Tower. The dromonds were arriving offshore, God be thanked, and soon our catapults and trebuchets were being erected, and great numbers of the flint boulders quarried in Sicily piled beside them.

Talking with the chiefs among his new artillerymen, Richard oversaw the placing of his siege engines near Mategriffon. I was there too, with Rhys and Philip. The instant a new weapon was in place, the king had it loose a test shot. It was exhilarating to watch, even when they flew too high, into the town itself, or too low, and smacked into the massively thick, invulnerable base of the fortifications. Adjustments were made to the angle of throw, or the distance the weapon was from the walls, and another shot released.

When the stones hit true, smashing down sections of rampart or obliterating Turks from this world, a great cheer would go up from the watching crowd. Hundreds of Christians, civilians, soldiers and religious, had come from the camp. Richard's presence and the power of his artillery saw a general air of merriment descend, despite the scorching golden orb that beat down, relentless, from the cloudless sky. A battered catapult named 'God's Own Sling', and built with monies raised from among the ordinary soldiers, was hauled by thirty or more men into a position beside one of the king's weapons. A smiling Richard consented to a display of its shooting, and was enthusiastically cheered when he loosed a stone himself.

He showed no sign of leaving even when a messenger came with news that the ships carrying Berengaria and Joanna had been spotted.

Isaac Comnenus' daughter Beatrice was with them. Anxious to see the king's sister but unable to protest, I chafed even more as the sun fell toward the westering sea, bathing the land in an orange-red glow that could not but remind me of blood. On and on the artillery barrage went. The Accursed Tower had lost its roof, and a decent section of wall had collapsed nearby. Our efforts were to be concentrated there, Richard ordered. 'Let another ten feet fall, and we can attack,' he declared excitedly.

Weighed down by my mail, I was cursedly hot, and my mouth was as dry as cold fire ashes. I had thought for some time that the king could be no better, but he batted away my every suggestion that we should leave the artillerymen to their work. Philip had a hard time getting him to drink water as well, because Richard kept sharing his skin with the ordinary soldiers.

As we walked between two catapults, briefly alone, I at last persuaded him to have some of my supply. Raising the bag high, he drank like a man possessed.

Finishing, he smacked his lips. 'Hot, reeking of grease and leather – and yet it tasted like nectar. Thank you, Rufus.'

I took it back, much lighter. 'What is mine is yours, sire.'

He smiled. 'Ever loyal Rufus.'

My heart swelled.

Abruptly, he swayed and almost fell.

I grabbed his arm, steadying him. 'Are you well, sire?'

He wiped his brow, and his palm came away slick with sweat. 'I am burning up,' he said.

No, please, no, I thought. Not the quartan fever again.

CHAPTER XV

The heat woke me, as usual. Head muzzy with sleep, parched with thirst, I rolled over and opened my eyes. It was dim inside the tent; the sun had not yet risen. I was on a blanket a short distance from Richard's bed. I spied Philip, faithful heart that he was, asleep at its foot. I had no memory of retiring, only of watching and worrying over the king until late in the night. Philip and the other squires must have laid me down, although I had no recollection of it.

I had been really tired. Twelve days had passed since Richard had been taken ill, and I had been awake for much of that time. There had been brief periods of lucidity, but his condition had deteriorated rapidly, worrying everyone. Even more troubling – something I had dared only whisper to Rhys and Philip – was the shocking mortality rate among the Christians here. Scores of high-ranking nobles had perished from disease during the siege, including our own Archbishop Baldwin of Canterbury. Since our arrival, the Count of Flanders, who had supported Richard against Philippe Capet at Messina, had also succumbed. I was no physician, no leech, but I determined not to leave the king until he recovered.

I tiptoed to Richard's side. He was asleep, his mouth slightly open. I noted the strands of hair lying on his pillow, and the portions of scalp I could see. His face and lips were pale too, despite the warmth in the tent. Arnaldia, the medical cleric Ralph Besace called his illness. Similar to the quartan fever, it had wracked the king's body with high temperatures, and was causing his hair to fall out. Some of his fingernails were loose as well. My heart ached to see the great warrior brought so low, and I wished I could exchange places with him.

My foot knocked against one of the vessels by the side of the bed, bottles containing the ubiquitous oxymel, as well as galingale, black hellebore and columbine.

The king stirred.

I froze, cursing my clumsiness.

Richard's gaze came into focus. 'Rufus?'

'I am here, sire.' Relief filled me that he had not woken with a fever. Let him be turning the corner, I prayed.

'What day is it?'

'The twenty-second of June, sire, I think.'

'Christ Jesu. The last time I remember was the eighteenth. Four days more I have lost. But you look exhausted, Rufus. I told you to seek your own bed at night.'

'I did, sire, some of the time.'

Richard gave a knowing but grateful look.

Philip stirred, and clambered to his feet. He gave me a quick smile, and asked the king if he needed anything. Richard waved him away. 'See to yourself, Philip. Rufus is looking after me.'

Philip vanished, no doubt to empty his bladder.

Richard pushed himself up into a sitting position. 'You must rest, Rufus. I do not want you also to become unwell.'

'I care nothing for myself, sire.'

His blue eyes, sharper than ever in his pale face, pinioned me. 'You may not, but *I* do, and I am your king.'

Emotion choked me, and I bowed my head. 'Sire.'

'Before you go, have you energy enough to relate what has happened since I have lain abed?'

I grinned. 'Of course, sire.' Seizing a stool, I perched by the king's side. 'Philippe is also ill with arnaldia.'

A throaty chuckle. 'How badly?'

'His condition is not as severe as yours was, sire, I regret to say.'

'He was taken unwell since the eighteenth, I take it, when his army last assaulted the city?' Richard had been furious to hear of Philippe's efforts, even though they had been miserable failures.

'Indeed, sire.'

'Has he sent any more letters about the division of spoil?'

This was another quarrel. From his sickbed, Philippe had sent a letter demanding half the wealth that Richard had seized in Cyprus. The king had replied that their arrangement concerned Outremer only, and if it did not, Philippe should cede half of Artois, the lands that had fallen to him with the sudden death of Philip, Count of Flanders.

'He has not, sire.'

A snort.

'He has another attack planned, however, sire.'

'Enough of Capet. Has my tower been built? How fare the new mangonels?' More questions tumbled from his lips.

Delighted by his strength, which seemed much renewed, and the colour that had come into his cheeks, I answered as fast I could. 'The tower is ready, sire, and covered from top to bottom in vinegar-soaked leather, the better to resist the Turks' fire arrows. It but awaits your order to be used. The mangonels have kept up a steady attack these past days. The larger of the pair is so powerful that it can hurl a stone into Butcher's Row, which lies on the seaward side of the city.'

''Twould be better employed against the walls. Godless heathen the people inside the walls may be, but they are civilians, nonetheless.'

'Indeed, sire. That shot was unintentional. The artillerymen have rained down an intense barrage near the Accursed Tower, and done a goodly amount of damage. One shot yesterday killed a dozen men, they say, and took down two perches of the walkway. Other parts of the walls in that section have been weakened also. Philippe is right in one respect at least: the time is ripe for another assault.'

'I must get out of this cursed bed,' said Richard, grimacing.

'A few days' rest might be wise, sire,' I said gently. 'You must not overtax yourself, the surgeon says, lest you suffer a relapse.'

An impatient click of his tongue. 'Then I shall have myself carried to the Accursed Tower in a litter.'

I considered trying to dissuade him from this idea, then gave it up as futile.

'And the Saracens, have they counterattacked?'

'Aye, sire, but with little success, thank God.' I related the tale of the sortie the previous day that had been repulsed except for its leader, an emir by his rich armour. Bravely he had carried on alone, his purpose to incinerate one of our catapults with a clay bottle of Greek fire. 'FitzAldelm cut him down, sire.'

'That was well done! Did the emir live to be taken prisoner?'

'No, sire. FitzAldelm snatched the bottle, and emptied it onto his groin.'

Shock filled the king's face. 'He did what?'

'He set his privates aflame, sire.' My ears rang with the emir's piteous shrieks, and his men's cries of outrage as they tried unsuccessfully to reach their leader.

A frown. 'That is most unchivalrous. Even Saracens deserve better than that.'

I nodded, sorry for the unfortunate Turk, but glad that FitzAldelm's malign nature had at last been revealed to the king. Let him continue to act so, I prayed.

Voices came from outside the tent, and Richard sighed. 'That is Ralph Besace, or I am no judge. He is here to poke and prod, and to dose me with whatever new concoction he has made. Go, Rufus, and get some rest. We shall speak again later.'

Tossing Rhys the double fist-sized pomegranate I had taken from the basket in Richard's tent – like as not, sent by Saladin, who had heard of Richard's illness – I asked him to prepare it. He rolled his eyes; separating the juicy seeds from the white flesh was hard work, but he cheered up when I said he could have half. The red fruit had become a favourite of ours in Sicily, and to find them here also was a pleasant surprise.

'How is the king?' Rhys asked.

'Better. He wants to lead an attack.'

'Is he well enough?'

'Not yet, but he is talking of surveying our positions from a litter.'

Rhys smiled. 'Imagine Philippe doing the same.'

'He barely stirs from his bed,' I said contemptuously, walking away.

'Where are you going?' Rhys asked, working his knife into the pomegranate.

I held up a bundle of rags. 'To do what every man has to do.'

'Be careful.'

I nodded. Currently, only the king had a private latrine pit. One *was* being dug for the knights of the mesnie, but had not yet been finished. Until then, we were in the same boat as everyone in the army and indeed the camp. More consequential calls of nature had to be answered just beyond the defensive ditch that lay between us and Saladin's army. Of course plenty of men had no wish to go so far, or to endanger themselves; the spaces between ordinary soldiers' tents were a patchwork of turds. It was impossible to find a clean patch of earth outside the ditch, and there was no dignity baring one's arse with others around. I had discovered that the earlier I went, the fewer people were around. Logic also dictated that Saracens were unlikely to be in the vicinity so early.

I worked my way through the disorder that was the Christian camp. Tents bleached by the sun, ramshackle huts built with broken pieces of timber, washing lines hung with clothing. A mongrel curled its lip at me – many of the strays were wild – and I stooped as if to pick up a stone. It scuttled off, tail between its legs. Reaching the last tents, I crossed the open space before the ditch. Supposed to be fifty paces in width, to allow troops to assemble in the event of an attack, it was often half that. Two years of siege had seen the build-up of a huge profusion of discarded equipment and detritus, not to mention excreta of every kind.

Pleased to see no one close by, and that the ground on the other side of the ditch was also empty, I edged my way down the earthen slope. It was shallow enough, just, that a man could make his way to the bottom standing. Then he had to watch the placing of his feet. Some soldiers emptied their bowels here, and the carcasses of animals were common too. Going up the other side was more of a scramble, and needed both hands. Rags tucked into my belt, urged on by my twingeing guts, I clambered up with all speed.

At the top, there was no sign of even a single enemy rider. I cast about for a clean patch of ground. It was easier said than done. Close to the ditch, closest to safety, the earth was littered with little mounds of human shit. Gingerly, I picked a path eastward, gaze always on the earth. Almost a hundred paces I had to go, the furthest yet. Our soldiers had more than quadrupled the size of the camp, and this was one of the results.

Loosening my belt, I tugged down my hose and braies, and squatted. I faced not towards Saladin's army, but our encampment. The Turks, three miles off, could not perceive what came out of my rear end. Position myself the other way, however, and anyone in the vicinity would see.

Things began to happen. All was not well with my insides. I did not have dysentery, thank God, but something in the water or food since our arrival was playing havoc with my intestines. I closed my eyes, and hoped more visits here would not be necessary today.

Voices carried from the other side of the ditch. I paid them no heed. Guts churning, farts bubbling free, I wished to be left alone, undisturbed.

The conversation opposite my position fell silent. 'Look!' cried a man.

Do not let him be pointing at me, I thought. It was commonplace for ordinary soldiers to poke fun at comrades who were about their toilet. Rhys had already had de Drune shouting abuse at him, and planned to get his revenge at the first opportunity.

'That Saracen has come from nowhere,' said the man.

I scarcely heard. A bout of cramp had seized the lower half of my belly, and I had to lay a hand flat on the ground not to fall over. More liquid spattered out of me. I groaned.

'Jesu, he has seen that knight.'

'Even a Saracen would not attack someone having a shit,' said a second voice.

'No? See how he pricks spurs to his horse's flanks! You, sir!'

Somehow I knew he meant me. I stared over the ditch. Four men-at-arms I did not recognise were waving. 'A Turk is coming for you, sir,' shouted one. 'Look behind you!'

My head twisted, and fear exploded within me. Perhaps a quarter of a mile away, and closing at the full gallop, was a Saracen rider. Sunlight bounced off the metal spike atop his cloth-wrapped helmet, and he had a spear couched in his right armpit. Where he had come from, I had no idea, but he was aimed at me for certes. There was no one else on this side of the ditch.

My toilet was not over, but to linger risked death. I was already unsure if I had time to reach safety. Cursing ill-fortune, my lack of weapons, the diarrhoea, I pulled up braies and hose, tied my belt, and took to my heels. The pile of precious rags, still unused, I left behind.

'Run, sir, run, run!' called the men-at-arms, beckoning as if they could increase my speed.

Hooves pounded the earth to my rear. How distant, I could not tell, but they did not sound far off.

My guts roiled. I desperately needed to squat again, but that was an impossibility. I clenched everything tight as I could, and ran.

The men-at-arms' cries grew more urgent. 'Run, sir!'

An ululating cry shredded the air. I did not understand the Arabic, but its intent was clear.

Sweet Jesu, I thought. If I am to die in the Holy Land, let it be with a sword in my hand and at the king's side, not running, shitty-arsed, like a coward.

I felt reverberations in the earth beneath my feet.

'He is almost upon you, sir!'

The ditch was still thirty paces away. I glanced over one shoulder. The Saracen was close enough to see his fist gripped on his spear shaft, and the pink inside of his horse's flaring nostrils. Panic threatened to overcome me. There was no chance of reaching safety before I was skewered like a rabbit on a spit.

I skidded to a halt.

Again the ululation came, twisting my already liquid guts into fresh, painful knots.

I turned.

The Turk's lips peeled back from his teeth in triumph. The spear tip was a silver blur, aimed at my heart.

Limbs atremble, I waited. Waited until he was so near I could count the beads of sweat on his cheeks, and then I threw myself to the side.

The horse and rider galloped by; the death-giving blow met only thin air.

The men-at-arms cheered.

I landed hard, one hand in a lump of human shit. The other, praise God, touched a stone. It was not large, but it filled my palm, and there was another beside it. Gripping one in each fist, I scrambled to my feet even as the Saracen hauled on his reins. His horse spun as if on a silver penny – even in the depths of my fear, I marvelled at how the enemy could ride – and they charged again.

I had no time to think, or to aim. I simply cocked my right arm and hurled one of the stones. It smacked into the Turk's forehead, just below the rim of his helmet. His eyes rolled up, exposing the whites, and the spear that had been about to send me to the next world slipped from his nerveless fingers. Back he went in the saddle, lolling like a drunken man, and losing control of his mount. An instant later, he fell off. The horse slowed, and I was able to snatch the hanging-loose reins as it came alongside.

'Easy there,' I said, hoping my gentle tone would make up for my lack of Arabic commands. 'Easy.'

Snorting, skittish, the horse pulled me along for a short distance before I managed to calm it down. 'Twas a beautiful creature, a fine-boned grey Arab with a long, flowing mane and well-muscled hindquarters.

Remembering its master, my gaze shot to where he had landed. To my delight, he still lay there, unmoving. Wary, in case he was playing dead, I picked up another stone and led the horse towards him. The Turk did not stir, not even when I kicked him. I went and picked up his spear, and saluted the men-at-arms, who were leaping about with glee and cheering.

Armed, I felt confident enough to approach my enemy again, but my wariness proved to be unfounded. He was as dead as dead, the only mark on him a neat indentation in his forehead. I decided that either my stone had cracked his skull, or the fall had snapped his neck. Not only had I survived, but I had slain the Turk who would have murdered me as I shat.

I stood, an unpleasant stickiness between my buttocks, holding the reins of a magnificent horse that was now mine, and my ears ringing with acclamation, and concluded that this was without doubt *the* most bizarre event of my life.

My story made Rhys laugh so hard I thought he would burst. De Drune actually cried with laughter. Thorne, come to break his fast with us, almost choked on a hunk of bread so amused was he.

The depth of their hilarity rankled a little. 'I could have died,' I complained.

That caused them to laugh even harder.

I gave up, and joined in.

By the time I returned to Richard's tent, I had endured so much ribbing that I decided to tell the king what had befallen me. Laughter was good for the soul, it was said; it could only help his recovery.

Panels of canvas had been lifted along the royal pavilion's sides, but with no wind, it made little difference. Going within felt like clambering inside a baker's oven. I picked my way towards his sickbed, thanking God for the servants who stood over Richard, fanning him with long-fronded date branches.

He was not alone. Ralph Besace was putting away his instruments, and Philip explained that the physician had delayed the bloodletting procedure from the morning. 'Something to do with a better time to drain the noxious humours,' he whispered. I nodded, although I had no understanding of medicine.

Richard, even paler than before, lay with his left arm still resting on a pillow. A squire knelt by the bed, holding a linen compress to the spot where Besace had sliced into the king's basilica vein.

I padded closer, concern nipping at my guts.

Richard's eyelids fluttered open, and he saw me. I got a weak smile. 'Rufus.'

'Sire,' I said, dipping a knee, and deciding that now was not the time for my story.

The king soon rallied, however. Declaring himself hungry – a first since his illness had struck – he allowed me to feed him a couple of plums. Then, asking me if I had seen how the day's assault was going, he frowned when I admitted I had not yet been to the walls. Inevitably, I had to relate what *had* happened. Richard listened, agog, his face fixed on mine. Chortles kept escaping him throughout my tale, and by the end, he was giggling helplessly.

My cheeks were red with happy embarrassment, and I delighted in the king's pleasure. It was good that Ralph Besace had gone, I decided; no doubt he would have deemed the king too frail to be stirred so. In my opinion, however, this was good for Richard.

'God's legs,' said the king, wiping away tears of mirth. 'I would pay a hundred bezants to have seen you in that state *and* fighting a Turk. Nay, five hundred! What a sight it must have been.'

I was about to say that my dignity would not have survived the king witnessing me in straits so dire, when a familiar voice said, 'What sight do you talk of, husband, that is worth such a fortune?'

My heart thumped. With Berengaria were Beatrice and Joanna; the latter had seen me too. As a pleased Richard beckoned to his wife, I stood and then at once took a knee. 'Madam, madam.' Rising, I moved aside, that they might approach the king, but did not go as far as probably I ought. Standing close to Joanna was not the same as enfolding her in my arms, but was better than nothing.

Berengaria gave me a friendly nod; we had not interacted much, but I had the feeling that because I was one of the king's favourites, she approved of me.

'Sir Rufus.' Joanna bestowed a wondrous smile on me, and her eyes danced. As ever, she was a vision of loveliness, a rose to Berengaria's daisy, and she made me tremble with desire.

As the two women talked to Richard, I resolved to see Joanna again. Caught up with first the disembarkation and organisation of the army, after that the attacks on Acre and then the king's illness, I had seen her only here in the royal pavilion, and been able to talk with her not at all.

'My heart is gladdened to see you in fine spirits, Richard,' said Berengaria, her voice husky with emotion.

'You are on the road to recovery, God be thanked,' added Joanna no less fervently.

'I have Him to thank,' agreed the king. 'But I also owe much to the care of Ralph Besace, and Philip there, and Rufus.'

The recognition made Philip beam, and when the women's gaze fell on me once more, I grinned – at Joanna, really, not Berengaria.

To my mortification, the queen then asked again what Richard had been offering five hundred bezants to see. The king chuckled, and made no answer.

Women's curiosity knows no bounds. She pouted, and stroked his arm, and repeated her question.

Yielding, Richard said, 'Rufus was caught in the open this morn by a Saracen. By rights, he should be dead now, for the Turk was armed and on horseback while he was not. By some miracle Rufus not only survived, but slew the Saracen and took his steed as a prize.'

'It sounds an incredible tale. What were you doing, Sir Rufus?' asked Joanna.

Horrified, I glanced first at Richard, whose face wore a *don't-blame-me* expression, and then at Joanna. Her lips were twitching, and I realised she had guessed the reason.

Berengaria, a more innocent type, had not. 'Well, Sir Rufus?'

I wager my face turned the dark red of my hair. I coughed. 'I was answering a call of nature, madam.'

Bless her, Berengaria's cheeks went pink.

'You may spare us the details,' said Joanna mischievously.

Richard laughed, and pulling Berengaria close, whispered in her ear. Understanding filled her eyes, and she nodded.

I spun the story as best I could, avoiding details such as having to haul up my braies and hose. The two women hung off every word. Not wanting to seem arrogant, I made light of my stone throw, saying that the fall from his horse must have killed the Saracen rider.

'Do not listen to him,' said Richard. 'Rufus is a crack shot with a crossbow. He is as good with a stone, I have no doubt. The Turk never had a chance.'

I muttered that it had been a far closer-run affair than the king suggested.

'A remarkable story,' said the queen.

My cheeks still warm, I bowed my thanks.

Joanna's approving gaze lay heavy on me; I basked in it. It would have been obvious to a blind man, but, deprived of each other's company for so long, we were in that moment unable to conceal our desire for one another.

I was grateful that the king had not seen. Luckily, his attention had been taken up by Berengaria, who was perching on his mattress and talking to him in a low voice. Their heads bent close together; they kissed.

My mind filled with images of doing the same with Joanna; I blinked, and looked at her. It seemed she was thinking the same thing, because she mouthed, *Come to my tent tonight.*

When? I silently replied.

As near to matins as you can.

I nodded, my blood pulsing with excitement, lust, and nerves.

I did not notice FitzAldelm, come to speak with the king, watching me.

CHAPTER XVI

With no church bells to rely on, I had judged the time as best I might by the setting of the sun and the cries of the muezzins inside Acre. Impatient, I wanted to move the instant complete darkness had fallen, but I forced myself to wait until after the evening meal and a period spent at dice with de Drune, Rhys and Thorne. I drank a cup of wine, but when they ploughed ahead with more, I refrained, complaining of a slight headache.

'This is not like you.' His blue-grey eyes concerned, Thorne asked if I was coming down with a fever. 'I hope it is not arnaldia,' he said.

I batted away his concern, saying it was likely to be a touch of sunstroke, nothing more. I lay down on my palliasse and pretended to doze.

Dice clicked as they landed on the gaming board. My friends talked in low voices, laughing now and again. Wine was poured, quiet toasts made.

Despite my best efforts, sleep enfolded me in its comforting embrace.

I jerked awake some while later. Sweat bathed my forehead, and every other part of me. I sat up, rubbing at my eyes, wondering what hour it was. All the torches had been extinguished; the tent was black as pitch. De Drune and Thorne were snoring on the floor beside the dice table. Rhys was in his usual spot at the foot of my bed.

I fumbled about for my clothes, somehow not waking either him or the others. At the door, I realised my dagger was still lying by my palliasse. Indecision battered me; venturing abroad unarmed was akin to walking about naked. Going back risked waking Rhys, a light sleeper. I had no need of a weapon, I told myself, and slipped into the night.

A sliver of moon rode high in the sky, telling me that matins had possibly been and gone. Maybe it was too late, I thought with a lurch of dread. Feeling slighted, Joanna would be furious with me. I steeled my nerve. I had to try.

Not a soul was stirring. An owl screeched in the distance. Instinctively, I froze. No alarm followed. I could hear no movement close by. The bird was just calling, I told myself. Light-footed, borne up by worry at having missed our assignation, I sped onwards, aiming for the tent that Joanna was sharing with Beatrice and the queen; the latter had moved out of the royal pavilion when the king had been taken unwell.

The sentries who had been set to guard the royal ladies were dozing by the tent's entrance. I gave them a wide berth, making my way without challenge down the long structure's side. Fresh concern nipped at me. I had never been inside; I had no idea where Joanna slept, and stupidly had not asked her. The last thing I wanted was to enter the queen's sleeping area by mistake. Do that, and I risked Richard taking my head.

A yellow glow through a section of canvas gave me sudden hope. I stopped, and pressing my ear to the fabric, listened. I heard nothing. No murmur of voices, snoring, not even the sound of a person's breath. I hesitated. A burning torch did not mean that Joanna's quarters lay on the other side of the canvas. The light could instead be burning in a servant's antechamber, a servant who might scream if woken by a midnight intruder.

Ours was a mad plan, I thought, laden with risk. We had been foolish even to consider it. The wisest thing to do was go back whence I had come.

A woman such as Joanna was not to be spurned, however. The next time we spoke, she would probably order me never to come near her again. I took a deep breath and scratched on the canvas. 'Joanna?' I whispered.

Silence.

My heart sank.

I tried again. 'Joanna?'

A short delay, and then the sound of a person stirring.

My heart gave a painful jolt. Had I just woken Berengaria, or perhaps the young Beatrice, or a servant? Any of them might scream. I agonised, fearful, and unsure whether I should try again.

'Rufus?'

'Joanna!' I replied joyfully.

With a last glance around for sentries, I scrambled under the canvas panel and into her presence.

She was clad in a blue gown, no jewellery, her hair down. From the mark on one cheek, she had been asleep, lying on that side. I had never seen her more beautiful, and told her so.

'It would be unladylike to tell you off after such a fine compliment, Rufus, but what hour do you call this?' In spite of her words, she rose and came to meet me, hands outstretched.

'I cannot apologise enough, madam,' I said, reaching out. 'Despite my best efforts, sleep took me.'

She came into the circle of my arms. Looking into my eyes, she said huskily, 'You will have to make it up to me.'

I stared at her. Her beauty was overwhelming. I had never been happier in my life. Nothing, no one could have moved me from where I stood. Not Richard. Not even God Himself.

'I will do my best,' I whispered, and bent to touch my lips against hers.

In the cool before dawn, her soft kisses woke me. 'My heart would have you stay, Rufus,' she whispered in my ear, 'but you cannot.'

I pulled her close, and she responded with the same passion that had met mine earlier. I cupped one of her breasts with my hand, and threw a leg over hers. She pulled away, smiling. 'Nay, Rufus. Time is not on our side. My ladies will be stirring soon. The opportunity to bring them into my confidence will come, but it is not now.'

'Wise words,' I admitted reluctantly. We had kept silent during our lovemaking, but to have any chance of keeping our liaison secret, we would need help. Allowing her ladies to see us dawn-risen from the same bed was not the place to start from.

For answer, she kissed me again.

Jesu, but it was difficult to tear myself away. I did it, though, with many a sweet word whispered, and a promise extracted from her that we would meet at the earliest opportunity.

Safely out of Joanna's tent, I stole in the direction of my own. I was horrified to see the terrier P'tit before I had gone a hundred paces, and a moment later, her master FitzAldelm. He gave me a knowing look. 'Slept well?'

His barbed comment set my heart racing like a mouse trapped by a cat. He had not seen me emerging from under the canvas of the queen's chamber – I would have wagered my life on it. He was suspicious only because of my proximity to her tent. Richard's pavilion also lay behind me, I told myself. I could have been there also. 'No, sadly,' I lied. 'I have been walking the camp for hours.'

'I see.' His look was disbelieving. 'Mayhap you went to keep the king company.'

Glad to have this lifeline thrown to me, I said without thinking, 'I did.' Horror filled me even as the words left my lips.

'It is a noble thing. I should do the same. When I see him, I will ask if he would like me to sit with him at night, as you have.'

Too late, I saw the trap I had walked into. Flailing, I said, 'I stayed but a short time. The king did not know I was there; he was sleeping.'

Irritation sparked in his eyes before FitzAldelm could conceal it. My suspicion was correct: he had been hoping to have the king unknowingly expose my deception.

Muttering something about my duties, I gave P'tit a pat and took my leave. When I glanced over my shoulder, he was staring after me. Determined to leave nothing to chance, I doubled back on myself at the first opportunity, and came to the royal pavilion by a different way. To my immense relief, there was no sign of FitzAldelm. The king was still asleep, so I cornered Philip and made him swear that if my enemy asked, he was to say that I had spent time by the king's side in the few hours just past. He agreed without question, although I could see he was curious. I would tell him, I thought, but not yet.

Next my mind turned to the four sentries – if FitzAldelm talked to them, I was also undone. I emerged to find their replacements had arrived; the men-at-arms who had come off duty were already walking away, yawning. A quick question asked of the new sentries established that the two lots were from different troops. My good humour was restored. Even if my enemy had been suspicious enough to question the first set of men-at-arms, he had missed his chance.

Belly rumbling, I went in search of Rhys, who was likely to be up and about, preparing breakfast. What I would tell him if he asked about my whereabouts, I was still unsure. Although he too needed to be brought into my confidence, I wanted to keep my tryst with Joanna secret – to treasure it – for as long as possible. A bout of insomnia resulting in a midnight walk would suffice for my story, I decided. Rhys had no reason to think otherwise. I decided also to ask him to watch FitzAldelm when he could.

Three days later, Guy de Lusignan was proclaimed King of Jerusalem by his brother Geoffrey. Conrad of Montferrat, whose position had been uncertain since the incident over the allegiance of the Pisans and Genoese, promptly fled to his stronghold of Tyre. 'Good riddance,' said Richard when he heard. A sennight and more passed, and the king's strength returned day by day. I had masses said in thanks, eager to let the Almighty know that I was grateful for this latest reprieve.

Our artillery continued to pound the walls of Acre, and there were occasional clashes with the Turks, but no full-scale attack was made. Patrols rode out every day, but so many knights wanted to go, I only managed to ride out now and again. The mesnie trained; so too did Rhys, de Drune and Thorne. Philip joined us when he could. We jousted on the open ground between our camp and Saladin's, ofttimes watched by groups of the enemy. On occasion, they cheered our efforts, and we waved acknowledgement. It felt odd, to be recognised so by sworn enemies, but I sensed a curious respect there too.

When not at training, we played dice and chess, but there were only so many games of those a man could play before interest palled. The daily masses held in the tent that served as a makeshift church grew interminable too. I hoped with all my heart to liberate Jerusalem, and be forgiven for Henry's murder, but an hour of Latin on Sundays – of which I understood barely a word – was enough for me.

The main purpose of each day was my visit to the king. Thanks to the constant stream of visitors, however, we rarely had a moment alone. I learned to be content with that. The rest of each baking-hot day tended to drag; I would lie sweltering in my tent, longing for the sun to go down. Richard retired early, which meant that my evenings were free. I would bathe, and change my tunic and hose, and share a meal with Thorne, de Béthune and de Chauvigny, and then, making my excuses, retire. Another impatient wait followed, until it was late enough for my nightly encounter with Joanna. Not since the blonde beauty Alienor had I fallen so for a woman. I thought of Joanna every waking moment of every day, and dreamed of her too.

It seemed blasphemous to use the muezzins' late-night call as a way to mark the time, but it was the most practical thing to do. As soon as the wailing cry came from Acre, I set out. Reaching her tent was easier now, since her complaint that the patrolling sentries kept her awake. Once an hour only they came past, affording us far greater privacy.

There was little preamble once I entered. We would all but tear each other's clothes off – in that regard, she was truly commanding – and tumble onto her bed. It was not just about coupling. Hours were also spent locked in passionate embrace, talking, and laughing quietly. We had much in common: a love of family, of animals, a similar sense of humour, enjoyment of good food and wine. Our feelings for each other deepened fast; we called each other 'my heart', and pined when not together.

Rhys soon grew suspicious of my nocturnal absences; on the third night, he threatened to follow me and make sure I was safe. A little relieved, I let him in on the secret. He was at first incredulous, and then delighted. I swore him to silence, and told him about my unhappy encounter with FitzAldelm close to Joanna's tent. Seeing the murder rise in Rhys's eyes, I swiftly reminded him of his vow to leave my enemy be. I wanted nothing to upset my arrangement with Joanna. My own hatred of FitzAldelm was still there, of course, but much dampened by my ardour. To act against him, I reminded myself, I would risk all: punishment from the king for harming a fellow knight, and eternal damnation for another murder. I therefore took the easy path, and buried my feud for the time being.

I even began to dream of wooing Joanna, of becoming man and wife. I was rash enough to bring it up one night. Her face had filled with sadness, and touching a finger to my lips, silencing me, she whispered not to ruin the beautiful thing we had. Crushed, I nodded and managed a smile, and buried my heart's wish in a dark corner of my mind. Siren that she was, Joanna had then taken me to Heaven and back, and by the time she was done, I had almost forgotten what I had asked of her.

Almost.

My absence might have been noticed on the night of the third of July, had I not been late departing to see Joanna. Saladin, the wily fox, launched a surprise attack on our camp. Instead of going in secret to my lover, I had to arm myself and join the fighting. The Turks' attempt was half-hearted, however, almost as if they were only there because of orders from their general. We drove them in the direction of their encampment with heavy losses.

Exhausted, stopping only to strip off my armour, I went to see Joanna upon my return, to apologise for breaking the tryst. She was charmed by my devotion, and sweat-drenched though I was, had kissed me tenderly and told me to seek my own bed and get the sleep I deserved. The following night, worried the Saracens might attack again, I did not visit her either. I managed to warn her of my intention beforehand – I had seen her in Richard's tent – which was a relief. So too was the fact that we saw neither hide nor hair of Saladin's men. They had learned their lesson.

What did happen that evening was the unexpected arrival of an embassy from Acre. No less than the garrison commanders, Mestoc and Karakush – as we pronounced their impossible-to-say names – came to plead with the two kings. They offered to surrender, as long as they could leave the city with all their weapons and apparel. Philippe was content with this request, but Richard dismissed it out-of-hand, declaring that the Turks would strip the city barer than a pauper's house. The disappointed Saracen leaders went back to Acre empty-handed; the two kings parted on bad terms.

Richard was beyond caring. 'Philippe is a fool. The garrison is on its knees,' he declared. 'We have no need to grant their requests. Another day or two, and the city will be ours. Philippe will do anything to avoid fighting, however – even when he is winning!' Declaring that if he continued to feel well in the morning, we would attack the city, the king retired.

Early on the fifth of July, I was munching bread and honey by my tent. The latter was a wonder that Rhys bought from an audacious Turkish trader who ventured inside our camp with fresh produce; I ate it every day. Onto my third slice, I spied a page running towards me. As I hoped, he carried orders to attend Richard at once. 'The king is up,' the fresh-cheeked lad said happily. 'He is to order an assault.'

Delighted, I kicked de Drune awake and told him to stick his head in a basin of water and get ready, before girding myself for battle. Crossbows in our arms, the three of us – Rhys would not be left behind, so happy was he to hear of the king's recovery – made our way to the royal pavilion. My gaze lingered on Joanna's tent as we passed, but my hopes of seeing her were in vain. She was not with Richard either. The king's tent was full to bursting, however, and humming with excited conversation. I saw de Chauvigny, de Béthune, the grand masters of the Orders, Guy de Lusignan and his brothers, the usual gaggle of bishops, and a dozen other captains and officials. Of FitzAldelm there was no sign. I supposed he was hunting for supplies; this was his speciality.

The king was dressed, and sitting up in bed. Despite the thinning of his hair, there was more colour to his cheeks than the previous day, and his eyes had recovered their customary gleam. Seeing me, he beckoned.

'You look well, sire. I hear rumour of a fresh attack,' I said.

'Thine ears have not betrayed you, Rufus.' He grinned. 'God willing, a tower or two will fall today, and maybe Acre as well.' He saw my look – it was nigh on half a mile to the section of the defences where our catapults were – and said, 'Fear not. I have had a litter fashioned from a silken quilt. Unkinglike as it is to be carried to battle, I desire only to take the field.'

My heart swelled with pride.

The soldiers were overjoyed to see him too. Applause broke out when he left his tent. Men rushed to line the sides of the track as he was borne past, I and a dozen others of the mesnie marching on either side. Roars of 'The king, the king is here!' and 'Richard, Coeur de Lion!' rang out.

A loud voice in the crowd declared, 'Now the most valiant of kings has arrived, the best warrior in all of Christendom. Now let God's will be done!'

I cheered myself to hear those words.

'Rufus.'

I moved closer to the litter, so I could hear the king above the din. 'Sire?'

'I am going to send fresh messengers to Saladin. Acre will soon fall, and he knows it. A treaty with him could be of much benefit. It was in my mind that André and Baldwin should go again. Will you also?'

'I would be honoured, sire,' I said. Excitement ran through me at the prospect of meeting the legendary general who had defeated Guy de Lusignan at Hattin.

There had been desultory contact during the king's illness, in the main conducted by de Chauvigny and de Béthune, but not much had come of it. After initial courtesies, which included the sending by Saladin of fresh fruit and even bowls of snow from the high mountains to the northeast, and the gift in return of a Saracen prisoner, he had refused a face-to-face encounter with Richard. Kings who had met each other, he had written, could not then fight. Richard had cursed at this, and relapsed into a fever.

'I shall decide later when you will go,' said the king. 'Let us see how we fare against the Turks today first.'

I liked the sound of that.

Our passage did not go unnoticed. Someone must have spied the Angevin lion on a shield too, or perhaps even the king in his silken quilt. We were sensibly beyond the limits of crossbow range, but that did not stop Turks from taking potshots at our part of the column all the way to our destination. As they dinked off rocks and thumped harmlessly into the earth, Richard laughed. 'Ah, but it is good to be back in the thick of it!'

His men were attacking a section of the ramparts close to where the Accursed Tower had stood until its destruction by the French a few days before. By his order, a cercleia had been built, a richly wrought construction of wood and metal that afforded protection to those who wished to approach the walls. It was a copy of that used by Philippe, but larger and more stoutly built. The French king's cercleia had been burned to a crisp with Greek fire by the Turks soon after their successful attack on the Accursed Tower, but this did not stop Richard having his one dragged to within a hundred paces of the fortifications, far closer than I was happy with. I had seen Greek fire leap the same distance more than once. I whispered a quick prayer, and told myself that I would have time to carry Richard clear if clay pots were lobbed from the battlements, and that no enemy crossbowmen would hit the king with a lucky shot.

The various captains made their reports. First were the serjeants in charge of the sappers. Tunnels had been dug right under the tower, they explained, further than those attempted by the French. When the order was given, the timber props holding them up would be fired, bringing down the shafts and with it, we all hoped, the tower. This pleasing news was followed with more of the same from the artillery captains. A large section of wall adjacent to the same tower was about to collapse. 'But say the word, sire,' they promised, 'and we will unleash the final barrage.'

In high spirits, Richard commanded both groups to go to.

The artillery began shooting at once. Their first effort broke off chunks of the top of the rampart, and sent at least one Turk to Hell. Spurred on, the crews redoubled their efforts.

Seizing his crossbow, the king called out to the entire mesnie, 'A competition, messires. Ten gold bezants to the man who brings down the most Turks while we are here. Every hit does not need to be a kill, but it must be witnessed by a comrade. Shall we play?'

An eager growl of assent followed, and we looked to our weapons.

Rhys, to his delight, was the first to hit one of the enemy. It was as true a shot as I had ever seen him make. The quarrel punched through a Turk's spiked helmet, killing the man before he even knew it.

'I have a contest on my hands, I see,' said the king, telling Rhys in the same breath he would have a bezant as reward.

I delayed loading my weapon, wanting the king to hit a Saracen next. I suspected others were doing the same; rather a lot of quarrels were going nowhere near the enemy. Fortunately, the king was so focused on his task that he did not notice. Moments after Rhys's success, he winged a Saracen in the shoulder.

'A hit, sire!' I shouted, and shot at a man peeping through an embrasure. Stone chips flew in every direction, exploded by the quarrel, and my victim screamed as they tore into his face.

'That does not count,' said the king, wagging a finger. 'He was wounded, but not by your bolt.'

'As you say, sire.' I did not care, so happy was I to see Richard's vitality and competitiveness return.

Rhys slew another Turk; de Béthune and de Drune killed their first each. Richard Thorne, who had joined us, sent a bolt through a man's hand and stuck it to his crossbow.

Thunderous crashes from the tower interrupted our contest. We all stared as dust rose in vast clouds, and stone screeched, a horrible noise that hurt my ears. Those Turks who were in the structure cried out as it wobbled, swayed and then tumbled block upon block into the fosse.

Our soldiers whooped and roared like madmen.

Richard frowned as the dust began to settle. 'Curse it, look. The tower is half-fallen, but the wall yet stands.'

He was right. Of the tower, only the lower part remained. Never again would it be used as a place of great height and strength, but it might still be used as a fighting platform. The wall to its right, which ran west to the ruins of the Accursed Tower, and after, the main gate, seemed entirely undamaged. That did not matter so much, for it was not the focus of our attention, but the defences to its left, the same which had been battered by the catapults, had not collapsed the way we had hoped.

'All is not lost, sire,' I said, pointing. A great diagonal crack ran right to left from the level of the walkway, down almost to the ditch. It was at least fifty paces in length. 'Let the catapults shoot at that, and a breach will soon be made.'

He growled acknowledgement, and sent Philip running to the artillery captains with fresh orders. During the wait, we supped wine and shot at the Turks. I hit an officer of some kind, clad in burnished scale mail, and the king knocked down a Turk bowman. Men came to the aid of the officer I had shot, in their haste not ducking down low enough behind the embrasures. Richard killed two of them, and Rhys and Thorne another each.

Slam. Crash. Our catapults rained down balls of Sicilian flint on the damaged section of wall. Nine strikes, and it came tumbling into the fosse.

Richard gave a shout of frustration. 'It is as if the wall is protected by an evil spell!'

Again, not enough of the fortifications had come down. Although a breach had been made, the slope men would have to climb to get inside the defences was steep and dangerous, formed by a mass of rubble and broken rocks.

Richard called to one of his trumpeters.

The musician clambered atop the remnants of a siege tower burned by the Turks, a position which took him up the height of a two-storey house. A short blast of his instrument got everyone's attention. The catapults ceased shooting. For a hundred and more paces to our left and right, men were staring. Listening.

'Hear ye! For every large stone carried away from the wall, King Richard will pay one gold bezant. The wall, mind, not the ditch. A bezant for every large stone. Go to!'

An air of disbelief hung briefly over the soldiery, and then a Welsh man-at-arms laid down his crossbow. With a loud request of Christ to protect him, he ran towards the fosse. The Turks manning the rampart did not react at first. They probably thought he had gone mad,

I decided. Reaching the bottom, the man-at-arms clambered up to the wall's base, and seized hold of a loose block. Horrendous creaks accompanied his every heave. Dust puffed into the hot air. He swore and cursed, but after a moment, wrenched the stone free. His head turned, seeking approval.

Richard clapped, and nodded his head.

Like a stream unleashed when the mill race is opened, his soldiers flooded towards the ditch, shields at the ready. Thanks to the artillery barrage, the Turks were still at sixes and sevens. The few left on the rampart began to shoot, but they could not stop the tide of men throwing themselves into the fosse and clambering up to pull at the stones in the great crack. To judge by their frantic shouts, however, it would not be long before reinforcements arrived.

Richard smiled and congratulated the beaming man-at-arms who had begun the quest. He ordered the clerk Hugh de la Mare to keep a tally of names and the numbers of stones they had brought back. Delighted, the man-at-arms rushed off in search of a second.

The pile of rocks in front of the cercleia did not grow fast enough for the king. Soon he had the trumpeter announce that each stone carried a reward of three bezants. His soldiers cheered, and some of the civilians who came to watch every attack joined in, despite their lack of shields. The task was becoming more dangerous. The battlements were lined with Turkish archers and crossbowmen, shooting as fast as they could reload. Rocks and pieces of pottery were being dropped; I even saw an old table thrown over the wall. This barrage did not stop, or even slow, our soldiers' efforts. Men banded together, some standing with upheld shields, protecting those who were removing stones from the wall. The civilians scrabbled about, and got in the way; many were brought down by the Turks. The king and we in the mesnie did our best to help, killing and wounding a steady number of Turks with our quarrels.

Our casualties began to mount, inevitably, and not just among the gold-crazed, unarmed civilians. Richard increased his reward to four bezants, which rallied his men for a time, but then a powerful Turkish sortie over the breach and down the slope forced every soldier there to fight for his life. The civilians were either butchered or fled, some still carrying rocks.

'Who is that Turk?' Richard was spanning his crossbow, but he inclined his head towards the battlements. 'Yon figure in a hauberk with a red-and-blue surcoat. That is a Christian's armour he wears, as God is my witness.'

'It belonged to Aubery Clément, sire, a valiant French knight,' said Philip. Seeing the king's enquiring look, he explained, 'I was talking to one of King Philippe's squires last evening. Clément fought in the last French attack; so sure was his purpose that he told his comrades he would die that day, or enter Acre. In the event, sire, he did both. He was first to scale the defences and take a section of rampart. All might have been well, but so many men began to climb his ladder that it broke beneath their weight, throwing them into the ditch.'

Richard's face grew serious. 'Clément was left alone atop the wall?'

'Even so, sire. The Turks mocked and jeered the injured and dead in the fosse, and threw themselves against him. He killed or wounded a goodly number, but in the end, he was slain. Philippe had the attack called off immediately, so that his men might mourn the fallen.'

'And there stands the dog who stripped Clément's corpse,' said Richard. 'Listen. He taunts us.'

Through the clamour, I heard the Turk shout and point at the men retreating from the wall.

Rhys made to aim his crossbow, but I shook my head, no. Understanding, he stepped back.

Richard lifted his weapon and took sight down its length. Click went the trigger.

I held my breath.

The king's bolt hummed as it flew, driving through surcoat and mail, silencing the mocking Turk forever.

Our soldiers cheered, but the enemy was enraged by the dramatic loss of their fellow. They poured forth from the breach in even greater numbers. The king, who had only brought about five hundred troops, was forced to order almost every man forward, including the squires. Only the crossbowmen, whose bolts were so vital to our part, and we knights, protection for the king, were held back. The fighting grew savage, moving now up the rocky ruin of the wall, and then down again. Little by little, however, our soldiers formed a solid wall of shields and pushed the Turks back. The battle drew near to the breach.

Worried for Philip and my other friends, eager to be involved in a great victory, I chafed with impatience, but the king's safety was paramount. I had to be content with my crossbow. Twice I shot down men who were attacking Philip – I would remind him of that, I decided with glee.

Everything went to Hell when a frame-mounted catapult appeared in an embrasure directly above the thickest of the fighting. A moment later, a second poked into sight.

'They are about to use Greek fire, sire!' I shouted.

'Damn it all,' he cried. 'The Turks were about to break. Had I but fifty score more men here, Acre would fall!'

He ordered the retreat sounded at once. Fortunately, Richard's soldiers had also seen the catapults, and knew their significance. Not all could retreat in time, however. Up soared the familiar clay pots, their fiery tails and roaring noise clear warning of what they contained. Down they came, exploding in massive fireballs. A dozen men were turned into living torches and twice that number severely burned in the pell-mell withdrawal. The reek of burning flesh filled the air. The Turks screamed fierce war cries, and beat drums and cymbals. More clay pots were launched, and soon the bottom of the ditch was a sea of flame. It was a terrifying sight.

I thanked God to see Philip, de Drune and Thorne come back unscathed.

Nonetheless, it was a frustrating end to what had promised to be a pivotal point in the siege. Acre remained untaken, which meant another delay to our main purpose, that of marching on Jerusalem and delivering it from the unbelievers.

CHAPTER XVII

The following morning, I told Rhys and de Drune that I was to be in the embassy sent to Saladin's camp. They both demanded to come, and were most indignant that the party's size was to be only three. 'The king decreed it be so,' I said, hating how pompous I sounded. 'De Chauvigny will lead, and de Béthune and I shall serve as his protection.'

'Much protection two of you will be against thousands of Turks,' said de Drune sourly.

'Would it be any different if you and Rhys were there?' I shot back.

He lapsed into a surly silence. Rhys muttered that it was not fair, that he could tag along and the king would never know.

He was probably right. I vacillated, deciding that I could win over de Béthune and probably de Chauvigny. I looked at de Drune, whose face had lit up. That made up my mind. If I allowed Rhys to be part of it, de Drune would have to come as well. 'I will tell you everything I saw,' I promised.

Rhys shot me a glower, which I pretended to ignore.

'If my squire addressed me so, I would whip him until his back bled,' said a familiar voice.

'No doubt you would, FitzAldelm. Certain it is also that your squire hates you,' I said. 'Whereas mine, despite his sulky mood, would do anything for me. I know which of the two relationships I prefer.'

FitzAldelm sneered, but for once he had no quick riposte.

'Have you come to play dice with my men?' I asked, needling him further. 'I will make de Drune here go easy on you.'

His lip curled. 'That is not why I am here.'

A devil took me. 'Is it to congratulate me then on my being chosen by the king to speak with Saladin?'

'Richard appointed de Chauvigny to do that, not you!'

'Maybe so, but I shall be present. I will contribute if needs be, whereas you . . .' I paused for effect, and added, 'what will you be doing? Buying wain-loads of grain?'

FitzAldelm's lips pinched white.

We glared at each other, our enmity scraped fresh.

'While you are gone, perhaps I shall visit Joanna.'

His dart slid inside my guard with the ease of an assassin's knife. I could not stop a little gasp of anger escaping me. As casually as I could, I said, 'The king's sister?'

'There is only one Joanna in this camp.'

'I cannot think why you would call on her, FitzAldelm. It is unlikely she is fond of snakes.'

Again he sneered. 'Art grown high and mighty, you Irish cur. Would Joanna think so much of you, I wonder, if she knew of the thatched hovel you were reared in. Your brigand father was drunk from one end of the day to the next, while you and your brothers rolled about in the reek with the dogs.'

Managing to control my fury, I dismissed Rhys and de Drune. The moment we were alone, I said, 'Speak your piece and leave.'

'I know what you have been up to.' His tone was gloating.

I kept my face granite hard. 'Visiting the king, participating in the assaults, and training?'

A nasty laugh. 'Of course not. I mean your assignations with Joanna. Almost every night they have been. You are quite the pair of lovers.'

'They say the sun can boil a man's wits here.' I pointed skyward. 'You are the living proof.'

'What will Richard say when he finds out you have been ploughing his sister?'

I had prepared myself against this insult, but it still sank deep. I managed a scornful laugh. 'Piss off with your lies and deceit. I have better things to do.'

'So you deny repeatedly creeping into Joanna's tent like a thief? Only you were not looking for coin, but cunny.' He sniggered.

The red mist descended. My vision blurred, yet my hand had no trouble finding my sword hilt. I will kill him, I thought. Slit open his belly, and let his guts flop out. Then, while he is dribbling and weeping, I will whisper in his ear that I murdered his brother in Southampton. Only then will I cut his throat from ear to ear. I could see his terrified expression, could smell the coppery tang of blood, feel his flesh part beneath my blade.

A hand grasped my shoulder. 'Sir.'

My head twisted. 'Rhys,' I croaked.

'He is not worth it, sir.' He had seen my loss of control from afar, and stepped in. In my ear, he said, 'FitzAldelm cannot have seen you, because I was watching his tent most nights, and he never stepped outside.'

I gave him a wooden nod, and with a supreme effort, reined myself in. To FitzAldelm, I said coldly, 'These are baseless lies. You have no proof of your allegations.'

A smirk. 'That is where you are wrong. One of my followers will swear under oath that he saw you enter her pavilion late on a number of occasions.'

'One of your followers?' I asked.

'Aye, a man-at-arms,' he said, stepping right into my trap.

Like a drowning soul, I lunged for the spar that floats within reach. 'You are willing to go to the king with such portentous news, FitzAldelm, with only the word of an ordinary soldier? I will swear blind that he lies. I have no doubt that Joanna will bear the same witness. Let us see what Richard says, shall we?'

He made no reply, and I leaped to the attack again. 'Think well before you act. Imagine how angry Richard would be to have the reputation of his sister – the Queen of Sicily – besmirched so!'

FitzAldelm hesitated. He had acted prematurely, and he knew it. The man who made a baseless accusation of this gravity would bring down Richard's wrath as surely as the perpetrator of any dishonour to his sister.

He stalked away, stiff-backed with rage and frustration.

'Did you hear any of that?' I was mortified if Rhys should have heard the filth FitzAldelm had said about Joanna.

'Enough to know what it was about and little more.' Rhys could be as diplomatic as a royal ambassador when he chose.

I stared after my enemy. Despite my apparent victory, FitzAldelm had dealt a lethal blow. He had friends and cronies who were knights. From now on, men like de Gunesse would stand nightly watch over Joanna's tent. To continue visiting my lover risked everything. The word of two or three knights, say, against mine, would cause irreparable damage to the queen's reputation, even if their accusations were never wholly proven. That was something I could not countenance. As for myself, I dreaded to think of what might happen to my friendship with Richard, let alone my position in his household. Even if I escaped execution for what I had done, I risked disgrace at the least. Driven out of the mesnie, I would lose all that I had built up over a decade. Never would I be lord of Cairlinn.

'Say the word, and I will kill him. It would be a pleasure,' Rhys muttered. 'De Drune will help.'

God forgive me, I was tempted. If the pair did their work well, my enemy's killing might never be solved. Even if they were caught, it was not certain that I would be blamed. Compared to the horrors of what might unfold if my relationship with the king's sister was exposed, either of these outcomes seemed far preferable.

'Well?' asked Rhys.

Stupid and stubborn though it was, as well as risking my affair with Joanna, I decided that I did not want to delegate the killing of my oldest enemy, even if the man who did it was Rhys. 'There must be another way,' I said.

'We have been at this crossroads many times, and never seen it.'

He was right, but I decided that was no reason to rush into something from which there was no return. For the moment, painful as it was, I had to stop seeing Joanna. FitzAldelm would thus be prevented from gaining further evidence, while I secured a breathing space.

I pictured de Gunesse lurking near Joanna's tent, and Rhys, who had done the same outside FitzAldelm's. There it was, I thought, staring me in the face – a possible solution to my quandary. 'I have an idea,' I said to Rhys. 'Your efforts must be redoubled; de Drune will help. FitzAldelm must be watched day and night. He will not be so quick to run to the king if I can prove he has had dealings with Philippe Capet.'

'But what if he has not?'

'Then,' I replied with grim intention, 'we shall talk again about your offer just now.'

Three of us prepared to ride for the enemy camp in the early morning cool, de Chauvigny, de Béthune and I. We also had with us a high-ranking Saracen prisoner who would serve as a gift for Saladin. It was tempting fate perhaps, but I chose to saddle my new Arab, the one that had belonged to the Turk who had tried to kill me as I emptied my bowels. Recognising it, de Béthune shook his head and told me I was a fool.

'It will be all right,' I said bluffly and hoped that was true.

He shook his head and muttered something about pig-headed Irishmen.

I gave back in similar vein, and was glad when he responded. Such banter helped to put the threat posed by FitzAldelm from my mind.

Riding a mile and a half from our lines, the midpoint between the two armies' positions and the furthest I had come when jousting, my stomach tightened. We were bearing the white staff and standard of heralds, but that did not mean we were safe.

Parties of Saracen horsemen came to shadow us. There were heavy cavalry with mail-clad riders, and armed with long spears similar to ours, and also mamluks, the mounted archers about which we had heard so much. The latter did not look especially fearsome, but I knew better than to distrust their reputation. These were possibly some of the very men who had slaughtered Guy de Lusignan's men at Hattin, the ones Richard had talked about a lifetime ago at Chinon.

No one attacked or even gave challenge; instead, the Saracens accompanied us on either side, towards their lines. 'An honour guard,' declared de Chauvigny. 'This is quite usual.'

A vast, well-laid-out affair, the enemy encampment was truly impressive. There were at least as many men here as in our entire army, I decided, if not more. Hundreds of leather tents stretched off into the distance, pitched in neat ranks. Soldiers lounged about, much as our men did, repairing kit, gossiping and talking. A notable difference between our camp and theirs was the lack of whores. I spied numerous cookshops, places for the soldiery to eat – far more than we had – and rows of clay-lined holes that, de Béthune told me, could be filled with hot water to bathe in. These had never been heard of at Le Toron.

De Chauvigny reined in. Seeing my curious glance, he said that someone would soon arrive to greet us.

'To take us to Saladin?' I asked eagerly.

'He does not always deign to meet us. Ofttimes that falls to his brother, al-'Ādil, Saif al-Dīn.' The foreign words sounded odd falling from de Chauvigny's lips. 'Al-'Ādil – we call him Saphadin – is a most interesting character.'

I curbed my disappointment, and hoped that today would be different.

De Chauvigny's prediction was correct, however. Saphadin it was who arrived with an interpreter and a score of tall, richly dressed spearmen. A hook-nosed, bearded man with dark skin and a friendly expression, he clasped the hands of de Chauvigny and de Béthune, and greeted the prisoner with evident happiness. After being introduced to me, he spoke in accented but clear French. 'Rufus, you are called?'

'Yes, although my birth name was Ferdia.'

His French was not good enough to conduct a conversation. The interpreter translated, listened to Saphadin's response, and said, 'Ferdia. That does not sound English, or even French.'

'I am Irish.' When the interpreter explained, Saphadin's brow wrinkled, and I explained in brief where Ireland was, and its troubled relationship with England.

The next question had an inevitability to it. 'How comes an Irishman to fight for Malik Rik?' This was the name given to Richard by the Saracens.

A good question, I thought. My service to the king felt so normal to me that I rarely gave it any mind, but when it was questioned, I could still feel discomfited. 'Ask the same of the Sudanese I see here,' I said, indicating a group of black-as-soot men in red headgear who were watching us.

Saphadin seemed mightily amused by my answer. He spoke to the interpreter, who said, 'They serve because their master, who rules Egypt, forces them to. Is it the same for you?'

I bridled. 'It is not. I serve the king freely.'

Saphadin's bird-bright eyes stayed on me as the interpreter did his work. His reply was a simple question, one my own family would have asked had they been there. Had they been alive. 'Why?'

'We are brothers-in-arms,' I said curtly. 'Do you understand?'

The interpreter did his work. Saphadin's answer came back at once. 'I do. Malik Rik is a born warrior. You also have that look. If God grants us the time, I would hear the tale of your friendship.'

Mollified, I nodded. 'It would be my pleasure to relate it.'

Saphadin now cast a look at de Chauvigny, and asked, via the interpreter, 'Have you come to ask for more fowl, to feed your poorly hawks?'

De Chauvigny laughed. 'Not today.'

I had heard the tale. During the first attempts at negotiation, Richard, keen to make a good impression, had asked for some poultry to feed up his falcons, weakened by our travels. Once his birds were recovered, the king said, he would gift them to Saladin. Cunningly, Saladin had replied that fowl were good nourishment for those who were ill; this was Richard's real reason for wanting them.

More banter ensued as we were led deep into the camp.

Riding with de Béthune behind the rest, I was free to study the enemy in his own environment. To my amusement, I was the subject of similar interest from the Turks. There were no insults or jeers, but men were talking and pointing. 'I wonder what they say about us,' I said to de Béthune.

He chuckled. 'We are badly barbered, unbearded devils who never wash, apparently.'

I saw he was not joking. 'Really?'

'So Saphadin says. Some of us know a bar of soap from a stone, he maintains, but it is not many.'

'It is hard to argue with that,' I said, thinking of the ripe odour inside de Drune's tent – or anyone else's – whenever I had had to stick my head into it. 'What else do the accursed race say of us?'

'We are foul and dirty because we eat pork—' de Béthune lowered his voice and added, 'and because we are uncircumcised, and do not wash after intercourse.'

I yelped with surprise, amusement and not a little embarrassment. 'He told you that?'

'He did.'

''Tis a wonder he condescends to speak with us.'

'He can see past our differences, he says. Saphadin is a well-educated man, and no diehard fanatic. He likes a drop of wine, for example, which is prohibited to Saracens.' De Béthune winked, and slapped the costrel hanging from his saddle. 'This is for him.'

'And what of Saladin? Is he also fond of wine?'

De Béthune shook his head. 'A more sober type you could not meet, or ruthless. He is courteous, and a gentleman, however – you will see.'

Saladin's pavilion was far larger than Richard's. Protected by massive, spear-armed warriors in polished helmets, it was a virtual palace made of woven cloth. We were not disarmed, but ten guards flanked us as we were taken to a large, rectangular reception area. My excitement rose.

Although I knew from de Chauvigny and de Béthune that Saladin was not a big man like Richard, I was nonetheless surprised by how short and unimpressive he was. Rather stout, red-faced with a close-cut, greying beard, he appeared blind in one eye. The other watched us upon our entrance; it stayed on us as we were walked to within a dozen paces of him and Saphadin made loud introductions. Saladin was clad in a white full-sleeved gown, belted at the waist, such as the Saracens wore, except that his was embroidered with gold. By his side hung a curved sword in a plain leather scabbard. A turban of fine white wool sat on his head, and he was shod in soft leather boots.

Unsurprisingly, our host had his own interpreter, a jovial-faced man of middling years. We were bid welcome by Saladin; during this fulsome monologue, the interpreter called his lord by every title and honour he had, which dizzied my head. Al-Malik al-Nasir Salah al-Dīn, Abu' al-Muzaffar Yusuf ibn Ayyūb – no wonder we Christians just called him Saladin, I thought.

Saladin dipped his head in recognition of our own bows to him. After a short conversation with our host, the prisoner was escorted from the room. Cups of a delightful, fizzing sweet drink were given to us by servants. I had had sherbet before, in Sicily, and sipped it appreciatively. Saphadin, who had moved to his brother's side, murmured in his ear. Saladin's eye rested on me next. He spoke.

'You are another of Malik Rik's household knights?' asked the interpreter.

'I have that honour,' I answered proudly.

Saladin's attention returned to de Chauvigny, who, smooth as a honey-tongued lawyer, gave thanks for our warm welcome, and offered Richard's compliments. Saladin asked after the king's health, and seemed genuinely happy to hear of his recovery. A click of his fingers saw buckets of ice and platters of fruit – pomegranates, figs and plums – borne from the depths of the pavilion. These, we were told, were for Richard, to ensure that his illness did not recur.

More thanks and compliments were exchanged. It was true what they said about the Saracens, I thought. Diplomacy was a dance, with its own cadence and music. I was grateful that de Chauvigny was the leader of our embassy and not I. Before long, however, he steered the conversation around to Acre.

'The garrison is valiant – never have there been braver soldiers than these, the honour of their nation – but they are hungry and exhausted. The city will fall. It remains to be seen when, but it cannot be more than a matter of days.' De Chauvigny paused, and then added, 'All of this is known to you, of course. Some of the messengers who swim from the city walls or take small craft out into the bay we capture, but not all. We see the pigeons fly too.'

When this had been translated, Saphadin spoke to his interpreter. 'You take more care with your hawks than King Philippe,' the man said. 'That is good.'

'We do our best.' De Chauvigny smiled and bowed.

De Béthune and I were also amused. Before our arrival, Philippe's prize white falcon had been set to hunt near the walls of Acre. Instead of returning to the falconer, it had flown off and landed on the roof of a building in the city, and from there retrieved by the enemy. Philippe had yet to secure the bird's release, and was said to be most unhappy about it.

Saladin's expression had not changed as the interpreter did his work, but for certes his attention now seemed more focused as de Chauvigny spoke again.

'Mestoc and Karakush are seeking peace terms. They are worried that if the city is taken by storm, everyone within the walls will be slaughtered,' said de Chauvigny.

Again the slight delay while his words were translated. It was fascinating to hear the garrison commanders' names correctly pronounced. I tried to say them in my head, and failed again. Mestoc and Karakush came more easily to my tongue.

The interpreter listened to Saladin, and then replied, 'Perhaps the commanders are right to be scared.'

The words hung in the air. De Chauvigny muttered something to de Béthune.

Saladin was a sharp negotiator, I decided. Twice had Jerusalem fallen in the previous hundred years. The first had been to the Frankish armies led by Godfrey de Bouillon, and the second, just four years before, to Saladin's own host. A starker difference between the two battles could not be made; while the Christians had engaged in an orgy of violence, killing Muslim, Christian and Jew without discrimination, Saladin had taken the city peacefully, and allowed thousands of its inhabitants to ransom themselves to freedom.

'My king and the French have no desire for such carnage,' said de Chauvigny. 'And this despite the treatment meted out after Hattin.' He was referring to the hundreds of Templars and Hospitallers who had been executed, and obliquely to Saladin, who had personally beheaded Reynald de Châtillon.

Another silence followed; the cordial air faded.

At length, Saladin gestured at his gifts, and spoke.

'It grows hotter. The snow will melt if it is not soon taken to Malik Rik.'

'That is true,' said de Chauvigny, 'and it would be unchivalrous to let my tardiness be the cause of it. Would you hear our terms?'

The jovial-faced interpreter translated. Saladin nodded.

Again the tension eased. Sometimes, I decided, the easier path was to step around an obstacle rather than attempt to remove it.

'They are these,' said de Chauvigny. 'The life of every Saracen within Acre shall be guaranteed upon the release of fifteen hundred Christian prisoners and an additional ten score named ones. The sum of two hundred thousand dinars will be paid over to the kings, and the remnant of the True Cross returned also. In addition, the men of the city shall be baptised as Christians. A period of forty days shall be granted for these terms to be met. Until then, the inhabitants of Acre shall remain in our custody.'

I did not take my eyes off Saladin as the conditions were laid out to him by the interpreter. He was as much the politician as Richard, because not a muscle of his face moved, but I thought I detected a slight stiffening of his posture.

'Have Saif al-Dī 'Alī ibn Aḥmad al-Mashṭūb and Bahā' al-Dīn al Asadī Qara-Qūsh agreed to these conditions?' came his question. These were Mestoc and Karakush.

'They have,' answered de Chauvigny.

Saladin made no immediate response, which was understandable. Although the fate of Acre was sealed, the terms were exorbitant.

He will not reject them, surely, I thought. So humane a man cannot condemn thousands of his own kind to certain death.

At length Saladin spoke again. 'Malik Rik's words must be given the consideration they deserve,' said the interpreter. 'My lord's answer will be sent to your king.'

De Chauvigny seemed a little annoyed. 'When?'

'In due time,' came the enigmatic reply.

De Chauvigny exchanged a look with de Béthune; he made to speak again, but Saladin, with a flick of his hand at the guards, indicated that our audience was over. He turned and was gone. Smiling his effort to keep relations friendly, Saphadin bustled over. 'I shall accompany you to the edge of the camp,' he said via his interpreter.

'Is Saladin going to refuse Richard's terms?' I quietly asked the others.

'I do not see how in all faith he can,' replied de Chauvigny, but he looked worried.

'Would you put a wager on it?' asked de Béthune.

CHAPTER XVIII

Richard was quite pragmatic when we told him of Saladin's non-committal answer. It changed the fate of Acre not an inch, he declared. Saladin would come around – what other choice did he have? In the event, he delayed for a full sennight. During this time, the defenders heroically managed to throw back another assault not just by Philippe, but also Richard. By the eleventh of July, however, Mestoc and Karakush were asking to surrender; Conrad, brought hurrying back from Tyre by the news, had managed to secure the promise of a large sum from the defenders for his late involvement in the negotiations. By the twelfth, Richard and Philippe's pennants were flying from the battlements of Acre. Backed into a corner, Saladin acceded to the terms agreed by his followers inside the city. The future of our enterprise seemed bright.

The siege was over, but I was caught up in a tumult of my own. FitzAldelm had made no move that I knew about, a relief, but since taking part in the embassy I had had no chance to speak with Joanna in private. Perhaps I should have asked de Béthune to carry a message to her. With his courtly manner, he might have made things clearer, but pig-headed to the last, I did not want to bring him into it. Instead Rhys had carried my short note the same day I met Saladin; in it, I explained our secret was in danger of being exposed, and that until things changed, we needed to wait. I did not mention meeting. I was aware that this brevity and lack of clarity – not to say emotion – might hurt and anger Joanna, but felt compelled to be as opaque as I could.

I was desperate to talk to her, but was thwarted at every pass. Berengaria was always with her, and often Beatrice, Isaac's daughter, as well. It appeared the queen had become very homesick – I heard this in confidence one day from Richard – and requested Joanna's company morning, noon and night. Beatrice often needed comforting too. 'I am to be deprived of mine own wife, like it or no,' he had mock-grumbled. In truth, I thought he seemed not to care that much.

As I said to Rhys, the king had been wedded to war for long years before his marriage to Berengaria. He was content with the gargantuan task of dealing with Acre, and the march south afterwards. It was not, however, enough for me, longing as I did to see Joanna.

A chance finally came my way on the twenty-first of July, and in the most unexpected fashion. Richard, finally content that all was as he wished it within Acre, arranged for Berengaria, Joanna and Beatrice to move into the citadel. Those knights and soldiers who were to be quartered within the walls were also to leave our camp. As the king dressed before we accompanied the royal ladies from Le Toron to the city, he joked that Philippe had had the best quarters at Messina. Now he must needs be content with the Templars' building.

'It is not as if he will be here for long anyway,' said Richard.

'So you think the rumour that Philippe will soon leave is true, sire?' I asked.

'There is no smoke without fire, Rufus. Philippe's heart has never been in this enterprise – he said as much three days ago. When the justification to extricate himself becomes clear, he will seize it with both hands.' Richard began to pace up and down, forcing Philip, who had been belting on his sword, to scurry after him.

'And the risk to your lands, sire, such as Gisors and the Vexin?'

'Hast put thy finger on the heart of it.' The king sounded exasperated. 'I *will not* leave Outremer with my task here less than half-achieved, yet Philippe returning to France is a real concern. I can demand little more of him than an oath of friendship, however. I will also send word to Normandy, Gisors and the Vexin, that my vassals be on constant guard against French trickery.'

A commotion outside the tent turned our heads. A man shouted, demanding to be let in; the guards remonstrated with him.

'What needs my attention now?' cried the king. 'Berengaria is waiting.'

'I will go and see, sire.' I hurried away.

Close to the entrance, I met one of the sentries, heading in the king's direction. He quickly explained what was going on, and I followed him outside. There I found a short, florid-faced man in a plum tunic, his waist circled by an ornate jewelled belt, jabbing a forefinger into the chest of the senior sentry, and repeating in German-accented French, 'I want to see Richard! Now!'

'Duke Leopold,' I said loudly, and bowed. 'What a pleasure.'

'You are?' He stared at me with no sign of recognition.

'Rufus O'Kane, a knight of King Richard's mesnie,' I said, hiding my anger. Although we had not been formally introduced, he and I had been in each other's presence a number of times. I made a spur-of-the-moment decision. 'Allow me to accompany you to the king.' I gave the sentry a tiny nod, and he stood aside.

Leopold stamped past without as much as a thank you.

I increased my pace so that I remained ahead of him. 'Can I ask why you wish to see the king?'

A scowl. 'You cannot.'

My annoyance and curiosity deepened. Leopold of Austria had arrived in Acre with his small retinue some months before us. Because both Frederick Barbarossa and his son Duke Frederick had died, he was the de facto leader of the German contingent in the Christian army. This sounded grander than it was, for the splintering of Barbarossa's host had seen precious few Germans reach Acre. More than once I had heard the joke that despite his family connections – Leopold was related to both the Hohenstaufens and Comneni of Constantinople – he was ruler of a sandcastle and little more. Richard, however, had shown great courtesy by receiving him and even, it was rumoured, loaning funds to pay his followers. In return Leopold had done nothing but act in high-handed fashion, such as complaining when he was not invited to meetings between Richard and Philippe.

Close to the king's private quarters, I said, 'If you would wait here, please.'

Leopold's colour rose. He seemed about to speak.

'The king is dressing, Duke Leopold,' I said. *'You will wait here.'*

He gave me an annoyed nod.

I went within. Philip was brushing motes of imaginary dust off Richard's tunic of rose samite, the same he had worn in Sicily. Next Philip picked up the royal cloak that was decorated with little half-moons and golden suns, and placed it around the king's shoulders.

'You look magnificent, sire,' I said.

Richard gave me a pleased look. 'Who was it?'

I stepped closer, and said in a low voice, 'Duke Leopold of Austria, sire. He is just without, and insistent he speaks with you, but would not tell me why.'

'I know his reasons.' The king's expression was amused, but fierce. 'Duke Leopold,' he called. 'Enter!'

In stamped the duke, chest out like a fighting cock. He bent a perfunctory knee, which increased my antipathy towards him even more. 'Sire.'

'To what do I owe the pleasure?' asked Richard.

'My banners, sire . . .' Briefly, Leopold's indignation rendered him lost for words. Regaining control, he cried, 'They have been tossed into the ditch by your soldiers, and worse, trampled into the dust!'

I glanced from one to the other, thinking, the fool did not have his put up alongside the king's and Philippe's, surely?

'I know,' said Richard.

Leopold purpled further. 'I am leader of the Germans here, sire. My standards should be displayed for all to see. This must be a mistake!'

'No mistake. I gave the order to take them down.'

Leopold's eyes bulged with disbelief. 'You, sire? Why? I have a right to a share of the plunder.'

'No. The spoils of the city are to be divided between me and Philippe Capet.'

'But I arrived here in the spring, sire.' Leopold's tone had grown high-pitched and strident. 'Am I, and those who have been here longer, years in some cases, to receive nothing for the battles we have fought and the hardships suffered? Hardships suffered, need I remind you, in the name of Mother Church?'

'It was my catapults and those of the French king which battered the Turks into submission, not yours!' shouted Richard. 'Do you have even a single artillery piece to your name?'

Leopold, dumbfounded, shook his head.

'I will take what is mine, and Philippe what is his. Be content with that, or begone.' Richard, towering over Leopold, gave him his most glacial stare.

'This is not right!' protested the duke. 'I am minded of the way you treated my cousin Isaac Comnenus of recent months.'

'That treacherous serpent deserved everything he got,' said Richard, genuinely angry. 'Now curb your tongue, lest you also be placed in fetters of silver.'

'You would not dare.'

'Do not test me!'

I moved to stand by Leopold's side. 'By your leave,' I said firmly.

Incandescent with rage, yet wise enough to say no more, he suffered me to accompany him from the king's presence. All the while, he muttered to himself in German. I understood not a word, but it was clear that Richard had made a lifelong enemy. He stamped off, with many a furious glance over his shoulder.

As I made my way back to the king, I found it hard not to feel some sympathy for the duke, arrogant and pompous though he was, and for the hundreds of nobles, knights and ordinary people who had fought and bled here long before Richard's galleys ever appeared on the horizon. They had come from all over Europe to answer the Church's call to arms, and deserved some recompense, I thought. I said as much to the king, but he was in fey mood, belligerent and spoiling for an argument.

'Do you take his side now, Rufus?' he roared. 'The part of a self-important Austrian nobody?'

'I stand with you, sire, always,' I said calmly. 'Leopold was wrong to erect his standard—'

Richard cut me off, crying, 'Was he now, by God? How good of you to say so!'

He will hear reason, I told myself. 'Forget Leopold, sire. Imagine yourself an Italian knight, say, who has been fighting valiantly here for two years. Now that the city has fallen, should you not receive something by way of reward?'

Richard breathed in and out through his nose, the way a man does to calm himself. 'I see where you are taking this, Rufus, but if every empty-pursed soldier of fortune dipped his hand into the pot, there would be nothing left for me and Philippe. I cannot show favouritism either, by giving a share to a puffed-up bladder like Leopold and not to others. They must all go without.'

I could see Richard's point, although he was being monstrously unfair. If I, one of his most loyal men, thought that, those who were being denied recompense would think far worse. The king was alienating a decent section of the soldiery he wanted to lead to Jerusalem, and Duke Leopold most of all. I sighed. Self-important Austrian nobody and puffed-up bladder he was, but he might also prove a dangerous enemy. I could not change Richard's mind, however, and it would be foolish to try any further.

Bristling, the king ignored me as we went to fetch Berengaria and Joanna, but his good humour was soon restored. Like thunderclouds scoured from the sky by a brisk wind, his scowling expression transformed into one of happiness and contentment. When next he spoke to me, our disagreement would have been forgotten; thus it ever was with Richard.

Berengaria was in high spirits. She made much of seeing the king, and of moving into the city. She billed and cooed, as I had rarely seen her do, and twined herself about Richard. Seeming to enjoy her attention, he was much distracted, which allowed me to ease my horse closer to Joanna's. Her ladies, walking behind, were busy pretending not to notice the attention of the men-at-arms bringing up the rear.

She gave me a reproving look as I drew close. 'Rufus.' Her tone was cool.

My heart ached. 'Madam.'

'Art well?'

I was about to reply that I was, but instead blurted, 'I am not, madam, in truth.'

One eyebrow rose, that beguiling mannerism that turned my muscles to jelly. 'Did you take a hurt in the last of the fighting? I would not know, for I have scarce seen you.'

A short distance in front, Richard was still bent towards Berengaria, who was whispering in his ear. I shot a look behind me to ensure that none of her ladies could hear. 'Madam, every hour of every day since our last night together has pained me more than an arrow wound.'

Her eyes bore down on me, but she said nothing.

Desperate to be believed, I quickly laid out what had happened with FitzAldelm. I ended by saying, 'You do not know him as I do, madam. Long has he been my enemy. He is a man without conscience, and would happily drag your good name into the mud in order to harm me. I could not risk that, nor could I endanger you by explaining more in my letter. Try as I might in the days since, I have been unable to snatch even a moment in your presence, to explain. I apologise profusely for the hurt I may have caused you. I acted in good faith, meaning only to protect you and us. Being able to talk with you now . . .' I paused, my throat closing with emotion, and added, 'it means everything to me.'

'Rufus.' She reached out to touch my arm, a brief gesture that said more than a thousand words.

'Madam,' I said thickly.

'I knew that something serious must have happened. You did the right thing.'

'Do you forgive me?'

'There is nothing to forgive, Rufus.'

My heart swelled with delight.

'This FitzAldelm – Robert, I think he is called?'

I nodded.

'Is there nothing that can be done about him?' She sounded angry.

'He sits high in the king's regard, madam.' I wanted to mention how he had tried to kill me at Chinon and Châteauroux as well as my long-held suspicions about his loyalty, but I did not. If Joanna, outraged on my behalf, were to say something to Richard, it would come back on me. I *had* to have proof. 'I have racked my brains these past years with little success.'

'We shall seek opportunities together, you and I.'

'There is one solution,' I said, feeling as wary as a man with lake ice creaking beneath his weight.

'Tell me.'

I wavered, wary of vocalising such a ruthless option to her.

'Rufus?'

There was no mistaking the command in her voice.

'He could be removed,' I muttered, telling myself – but not believing – that I would feel no guilt killing FitzAldelm in cold blood.

'By removed, you mean *slain*?'

I made no answer.

'Speak.' Now iron had entered her tone.

She was Richard's sister, for certes, I thought. Unwilling to damn myself further aloud, I nodded.

Her gaze grew condemnatory. 'I am surprised, not to say disappointed, to hear you speak thus. To act so is beneath you, Rufus. It would be unknightly, cowardly even.'

Stung, I almost blurted that FitzAldelm had already tried to kill me, twice, but terrified she might think I had invented it to excuse my evil intention, I swallowed the words down. 'He is not such a fine example of knighthood himself.'

'His intentions are base and unkind, but cannot be compared to foul murder.'

If only you knew, I thought. Had I not taken that pace towards Rhys in Chinon, FitzAldelm's bolt would have smashed apart my skull.

'Promise me, Rufus, that you will not harm him.'

'Madam, he is a vile creature,' I protested. 'There are things you do not know about him—'

'Rufus, please.' She took my hand. 'I would not have you dishonour yourself so. We shall find a way to deal with him.'

I could not resist the appeal in her eyes, the mere proximity of her, whom I loved and desired so much. 'Very well.'

'Promise,' she said softly.

At war with myself, for revealing too little, or maybe too much, still concerned about the harm FitzAldelm might wreak, but relieved to have the guilt for his murder taken from my grasp, I did as she asked.

She dazzled me with her smile. 'In the meantime, an obstacle that cannot be removed should be circumvented.'

I looked at her in confusion. 'Madam?'

'The city, Rufus,' she said, indicating the narrow street that led on from the great arched gateway through which we were about to ride. 'If meeting in safety in my quarters or yours is impossible, then we needs must find another location.'

Understanding blossomed; joy filled my heart.

Acre was the first city or town in Outremer that I had seen. With its flat-roofed buildings entirely built of stone, it was reminiscent of Messina, but altogether more compact. Its bustling network of streets and alleys were filled with markets, cookshops, and businesses of every shade and hue. Bath houses were numerous. The flesh shops, or brothels, for which it was famous, had already re-opened, and from the numbers of soldiers outside the busiest, were doing a roaring trade.

It was impossible to ignore them, so as we passed a particularly long queue, and a window in which stood a golden-earringed, silver-ankleted young woman in a diaphanous, filmy garment, I aped the king. He had just said something humorous to Berengaria because she was tittering behind her hand. I joked to Joanna that the troops' long-standing celibacy had been involuntary, and the queue was the result.

Rather than smile politely, she replied in a quiet voice that her own recent celibacy had also been involuntary.

How my cheeks flamed. How my ardour grew.

'I see you shifting in the saddle, Rufus,' she said to me in a throaty voice.

'What I would give to have you to myself, alone,' I muttered.

'That idea fills me with pleasure. Let us see it happens ere too long.'

My mind spun with pleasant fantasies as we rode towards the citadel, which was incorporated into Acre's northern wall.

To reach it, we passed through a gated entrance and into a magnificent open space, a marble-paved courtyard bordered by fruit trees. There we dismounted; our rouncys were taken to the nearby stables by Rhys and Philip, with the help of local grooms. I cast my gaze around, drinking in the stone benches to take one's ease, the caged songbirds, the pattering fountains. Berengaria and Joanna were both entranced; so too was Beatrice. After weeks spent under canvas in primitive conditions, it was no wonder.

The great square citadel stood at one end of the courtyard, its iron-strengthened door reached by a set of stairs. Another open square lay a short distance off to the left; it was for the use of the garrison's knights, to train on their horses. They even rode up the ramp to the next level, Richard told us with delight.

'Care to try that, Rufus?' he asked, all trace of his ill-temper vanished.

'I will if you will, sire,' I replied, grinning.

As a smiling Berengaria and Joanna watched, we shook on it.

I would have stayed with them, but with the escort over, my presence was no longer required. Richard took Berengaria and Joanna off in search of their quarters, and a servant accompanied Beatrice to hers. Promising Joanna with a look that we would soon meet again, I took my leave and went in search of Rhys. The stables were as grand as the rest of the citadel. I noted with approval the pipe-fed water trough in the yard.

I met Philip, who had left the king's horse in the charge of a groom, and was hurrying to the citadel. We promised to share a cup of wine at the first opportunity. Rhys was grooming Pommers, whom he had ridden into the city. I took over, telling him to take his ease for a moment. He needed no encouragement, producing from nowhere a small bunch of the greenish-yellow fruit known locally as 'apples of paradise'. He offered me one; I shook my head, no.

'However did they get their name?' I asked, tugging free a knot in the rouncy's tail. 'Yellow, soft-fleshed, and curved – they look like no apple I have ever seen.'

Rhys made an obscene gesture. 'You know what the men call them?'

'Saracens' cocks,' I said, chuckling. 'That is more apt.'

We were still joking and laughing a while later when a woman in a hooded mantle approached us. By her dark blue dress and simple leather shoes, and the wicker basket on her arm, I judged her to be one of the queen's or Joanna's servants, although with her face obscured, I could not be sure.

I gave her courteous greeting. 'May I be of service, my lady?'

She came much closer. 'Queen Joanna has bid me go out into the city. She has need of various items. Will you accompany me, good sir?'

For an instant, I must have looked like a stunned fish. I saw the same amazement in Rhys's face, for the voice was Joanna's own. I recovered myself as best I could, and said, 'It would be my honour, my lady. Rhys shall accompany us; he already has a good knowledge of Acre.'

Joanna thanked us, and without a soul giving us a second look, we walked through to the treelined courtyard towards the front gate. Rhys went a little way ahead, discreetly giving us privacy.

'This is most risky, madam,' I said in a whisper. 'The king—'

'Richard is abed with the queen. We need have no concern in that quarter for some hours.'

'Your ladies . . .?'

'They are faithful. Not a one will say a word.'

Although I exulted to have her by my side, concern still nipped at me. 'Madam, FitzAldelm might see us.'

'I enquired of Richard. He and his men are at the harbour, overseeing the delivery of a shipment of grain from Sicily that docked this morning. That too will take some hours. Your protests, Sir Rufus, begin to make me think you do not want my company.'

'Nothing could be further from the truth, madam,' I protested. Seeing then the look in her eyes, I said, 'You are playing with me.'

A butterflies-in-the-stomach-inducing smile. 'We need only get past the sentries at the gate, and no one will know us.'

She had thought of it all, I realised with amazement. Well is it said that women have more guile than men. I was helpless before her. Well, not quite. Whistling to Rhys, I told him to distract the men-at-arms at the entrance. This he did with aplomb, allowing us to stroll past undetected. Happily, there was no sign of FitzAldelm, de Gunesse or any more of his cronies.

A short distance down the street, Joanna steered us into an alleyway. There she switched her hooded mantle for a veil, such as the local women wore, Saracen or Christian. 'I will fit in better now,' she said.

I lifted the veil and, cupping her face in my hands, kissed her.

We embraced, and long would have stood there, if I had had my way.

She pushed me away, gently. 'Fie on you, sir. Do you always treat serving women in this bold fashion?'

'Only ones I love,' I said, and drew her back into my arms.

Much sooner than I would have wished, she pulled away again. 'I would have more privacy, Rufus. Do you know a place we can be alone?'

I did not, but calling an embarrassed Rhys into the alley, I explained that he had been into Acre many times since the city's fall. I did not elaborate, that he had been carousing with de Drune and Philip, when he could get away from his duties. 'Do you know a good inn?' I asked. 'A clean one, mind.'

'Follow me, sir. Madam,' he added, with a quick, respectful bob of his head.

A short time later, having guided us to the Genoese quarter with its covered main street, Rhys left us examining the wares on display at a perfume-maker's while he darted inside an inn. It was past noon, but the vaulted roof that crossed from one side of the thoroughfare to the other kept off the worst of the sun's heat. A gentle sea breeze came in from the shafts high above, diluting the scent of perfume and soap, baking bread, herbs and spices, from the many shops.

Rhys returned, and beckoned. Taking us past the quarter's main square, with its palaces, fortified tower and the Church of Saint Lawrence, he entered a side alley, and indicated we should follow him up a wooden stair. This granted private entrance to the rooms above the inn proper. Inside was a short passage with two doors on each side. He stopped by the second on the right. 'Here, sir.' With another respectful bob of his head, he made his exit. At the top of the staircase, he said, 'I shall be on watch outside.'

To my relief, Joanna gave no sign of embarrassment at Rhys's involvement.

I opened the door; we entered. The chamber was simple, but clean. Fresh rushes and herbs had been scattered on the floor. The only furniture was a timber-framed bed, and a chest at its end. Shuttered windows allowed in light and fresh air, but afforded us privacy.

'I have never stayed at an inn before,' said Joanna.

'Is it to your liking, madam?' I asked, suddenly nervous about the humble surroundings.

She slipped her arms around my waist and looked up into my face. 'It is perfect, Ferdia. Stop wasting time, and take me to bed.'

I obeyed.

CHAPTER XIX

Two days passed, my abiding memory of which was the afternoon assignation on the twenty-second with Joanna. Her ruse of leaving the citadel dressed as a serving woman was perhaps a little demeaning, but faultless. Nobody apart from her women realised; Berengaria had accepted Joanna's plea for an afternoon nap, and the king was busier than ever, organising the army for our planned march south. FitzAldelm, assuming that Joanna was beyond my reach, unable to monitor what was going on in the citadel, seemed to have abandoned his spying attempts.

The hours I spent with her felt like Heaven, God forgive me for the blasphemy. I could think of little but our reunion the following day, the twenty-third.

Early that morning, before the heat grew too much, I was with the king in the knights' courtyard, as we called it, and a dozen others of the mesnie, including de Chauvigny, de Béthune, FitzAldelm and de Gunesse. Guy de Lusignan was there too, with his brothers Geoffrey and Amaury. Berengaria was watching with Joanna and Beatrice from a balcony; I cast frequent furtive looks in their direction, and hoped that my enemies did not notice.

We were fully armoured, and astride our destriers, taking turns to clatter up and down the staircase I had seen on the day of our entry. It felt bizarre at first. Pommers had balked initially, as had the other steeds, but took to it with coaxing. My own confidence growing, I soon had him cantering up to the next level. The king thought nothing of charging Fauvel at the stairs. Even though I wished to impress Joanna, I was not that much of a daredevil. I hoped she did not think less of me for it.

As the king rode down for a second time at speed, my heart was in my mouth, but I cheered with everyone else. I say everyone else, but

Berengaria had not joined in the applause. Her face tight with fear, she was talking to Joanna. I wondered what she would say to Richard afterwards. It would make little difference, of course. He was ever his own master, and as he climbed down from his destrier and took off his helmet, he was beaming from ear to ear.

'God's legs, but that felt good!' he said to me. 'Would that there had been a line of Saracens at the bottom. They would have scattered like sparrows before a cat.'

'I have no doubt, sire. Do you not think it was a little dangerous to come down so fast? If Tempest slipped—'

His hand waved dismissively. 'But he did not. Away with your coddling, Rufus! Philip, some wine.'

As Philip proffered a brimming cup, I refused one for myself. I wanted a completely clear head when I met Joanna.

A moment later, our attention was drawn by a man-at-arms – de Drune, no less – who announced Henri of Blois, the Count of Champagne. I had met him at Nonancourt in March of the previous year. The affable young man, of whom Richard was very fond, was honour-bound to spend much of his time in Philippe's court since the French king's arrival, but he made frequent visits to ours. A valiant man, he had been at Acre for a twelvemonth, and directed numerous assaults on the city.

Richard, smiling, beckoned to Henri as he entered the courtyard. 'Have you seen the staircase, nephew? It was especially built for the knights to train their horses on. Would you like to try it? You can use my destrier.'

'I would greatly like to essay the attempt, but another time, uncle,' replied Henri, bowing. 'I bring grave news.'

'Speak,' ordered the king, his humorous expression slipping away.

'Philippe has decided to return to France.'

Uproar. Swords were waved in the air. Knights cried out. Sparks flew as the disquieted horses stamped on the flagstones. Above us, Berengaria's hand had gone to her mouth. Beatrice seemed to asking Joanna to explain what was going on.

Richard was calmer than most. 'It is unwelcome news, but not altogether a surprise. Continue, I pray you.'

'The king says that the vow he made when taking the cross has been fulfilled by the taking of Acre, sire.'

'Has he forgotten Jerusalem, the Holiest city, which continues to be held by the Saracens?'

'He said nothing of Jerusalem to his lords and vassals, sire.'

'Because it did not serve his purpose,' said the king acidly. 'Did he say aught else?'

'His surgeons have advised he leave Outremer for the good of his health. He has been ill once already, Philippe says, and the maladies which stalk our camp care not whom they strike down.'

'Yet here I stand, the one who was far nearer to death than he, while he prepares to skulk away like a whipped cur in fear of its life,' Richard snapped. 'I am also suspicious of his surgeons' recommendation. A hundred bezants that they say whatever he tells them.'

Henri shifted about, uncomfortable.

Seeing this, the king said, 'Forgive me, nephew. You are merely the messenger. I am grateful to you. Tell me, what of your own vow? Will you also abandon the hope of taking Jerusalem?'

'No, sire,' said Henri, straightening. 'When Philippe sails away, I will not be with him.'

Richard nodded, satisfied. 'Speak to me of Hugh of Burgundy, that rogue des Barres, and the rest – will they also hold true?'

'Count Peter of Nevers is the only great lord to say he will accompany Philippe. Everyone else plans to remain with the army, which will be led by Duke Hugh.' Henri's pride in his countrymen was evident.

'Ha!' cried Richard. 'A more damning indictment of Capet's actions a man could not ask for.'

I wholeheartedly agreed. Glancing at de Béthune, who was standing close by, I saw he was of the same mind. FitzAldelm's expression was calculating, and I wondered what scheme he was up to.

'Did Philippe not waver when this became clear?' asked the king.

'He was not happy, sire – indeed I would say he was furious – but they were resolute. He could do nothing.'

'Like as not, my opinion will make no difference either, but I cannot let this pass.' Richard kissed his palm and blew it at Berengaria. 'I will be back before long.'

I shot a look at Joanna, and prayed that the king was correct. Important though our mission was, my assignation with her mattered more.

'Ready to beard the lion in his den, Rufus?' His mailed fist bashed me on the shoulder. Despite the protection of my own armour, it hurt.

There was no point trying to change the king's mind – memories of his previous clashes with Philippe, and more recently, Leopold of Austria were bright in my mind, and so I nodded and smiled.

On the short ride to the Templars' building, Richard told me of its underground stables. 'Today will not be the time to ask to see them, more's the pity,' he said drolly, 'nor the tunnel that leads from their complex to the harbour.' The subterranean passage allowed the Templars to come and go as they pleased, avoiding the frequent disputes between the Pisans and Genoese.

The serjeants outside the Templars' headquarters were not alone. French men-at-arms stood there too. All looked surprised to see the English king arrive in full war gear with Count Henri and a dozen knights at their backs. None refused us entry, however. One scurried ahead of us to bring word to Philippe, for Richard refused to wait at the door.

The king led. The clash of our mail-shod feet on the floor and the jingle of our hauberks echoed off the walls. Torchlight reflected from the burnished surfaces of our helmets, borne under our arms. More combative an arrival I could not imagine, short of storming in with naked blades. I wondered again if we were being a little rash, but by Christ and all His saints, it felt exciting. I glanced back at the rest, and amid the eager expressions, noticed unhappiness clouding FitzAldelm's face. Sensing my attention, his mask slipped into place. I had no time to give this odd reaction more thought, for we were nearing the refectory.

Philippe and his followers were at dinner. A shocked silence fell as our entrance was noted – the man-at-arms who had run ahead had arrived just a moment before us. Two of the soldiers at the door obeyed Richard's barked order to take him to the king. The sound of our heavy tread rose to the refectory's vaulted roof. All attention focused on us. With the guards hurrying to keep in front, Richard marched straight towards the French king. I recognised Conrad of Montferrat close by him, and the portly bishop of Beauvais who had ogled Rhys at Famagusta, and Drogo de Merlo, his companion on their ill-fated embassy.

Philippe was reclining on a couch as the poulains did; a leg of roasted fowl was gripped in his pasty white hand. Grease shone on his cheeks; there were crumbs on his dark blue tunic. Hair as dishevelled as ever, he was the furthest thing from a monarch one could imagine. That was, until you looked at his eyes, which were cold and shrewd.

Carefully laying down the piece of meat, he said nothing as Richard approached.

'Taking your ease, I see,' said the king.

'It *is* the usual hour for dinner,' Philippe replied. 'Have you been fighting? I thought the Saracens had surrendered the city.' His lips twitched, and a few titters followed.

'I and my knights like to train, to prepare for the battles to come. The gates of Jerusalem will not open themselves, not that you will be there to see it. My nephew Henri—' the king gestured at the count of Champagne, beside him '—tells me that you are to return to your lands with all haste because your surgeons are concerned for your health. And here I find you, gorging on rich food and drink – quite the invalid.'

His bold, discourteous assertion elicited gasps from the other diners. Conrad's expression grew sharp. Of all those present, I thought, he would be one of the most affected by the French king's decision. Robbed of his main supporter, he would have little chance of taking the throne from Guy de Lusignan, not least because *he* was supported by Richard.

Philippe dabbed his lips with a napkin. 'Art ever the boor. A man could be forgiven for thinking you were born in a stable, not a palace.'

'Hear the pot call the kettle black! I could compare you to a slovenly peasant at table. I am not here to name call, however, but to hear from your own lips that you intend to break the solemn vow you took, to recover Jerusalem from Saladin's grasping hands.'

'Acre has fallen to our armies – my work here is done,' said Philippe. His gaze flickered past Richard, and I wondered if it was possible that he was looking at FitzAldelm.

'That was not the oath you swore! Not until the Holy City itself is again in the hands of Christians will it be fulfilled.'

'My doctors insist.' Seeming to realise how weak this sounded, Philippe continued, 'My heir is a sickly four-year-old child. If anything were to happen to me here, I need not say what might happen to France.'

'I know only too well your plight. A small child is also my potential successor. That does not weaken my purpose here. I ask you again, what of your vow, sworn to God Himself, that you will retake Jerusalem from the Saracens?'

'Speak not to me of sacred oaths.' Philippe was furious now.

'Why should I not?'

'You were the one to plight troth to my sister Alys, and then leave her dangling for twenty years. Nor did you make good at the end. Instead you swore yourself to the daughter of a jumped up little Spanish "monarch" – this, when you could have wedded the sister of the King of France!'

'We came to cordial agreement over this months ago; you were well-satisfied with the compensation I paid, as I recall.' Richard's tone had grown icy cold. 'But if you wish to dredge it up, we could—' he gestured at the rapt, watching faces '—hear once more my reason for refusing to marry your sister. Shall I continue?'

The tension was sharp as a knife blade. Every man in the refectory knew of Alys's liaison with King Henry, Richard's father, but to air the details in public again would be deeply humiliating for Philippe – not least because the great majority of those present planned to reject his lead, and stay behind to continue the war.

Philippe's expression was murderous. 'I see no need to talk about it.'

Richard's mouth crooked.

If this had been a fight, I thought, he had just knocked the French king's sword from his hand. But Philippe was not done yet.

'I will remain in Outremer on one condition,' he said.

'What is that?'

'Before leaving France, both of us swore an oath to share equally all the spoils taken during this enterprise. We pledged to do so for a second time at Messina. Render to me half the riches from Cyprus, and I will stay.'

'This argument is not new. You wrote to me of it from your sickbed. My answer to you is the same now as it was then. I *will* cede half of the proceeds from Cyprus to you, but in return I will have half of Philip of Flanders' domain, Artois.' Since the count's recent death, his lands had reverted to the French crown. 'What say you? Cyprus divided in twain between us, and Artois also cut in two?'

Utter silence reigned. The refectory felt like a battlefield upon which the opponents had paused to draw breath before they fell on one another for the last time.

My gaze moved from a stony-faced Richard to Philippe, whose flabby cheeks were marked by red pinpricks, and back again.

Richard went for the kill. 'No doubt your lords and knights here watching would prefer you to remain in Outremer. Their hearts' desire would have you lead them onwards, to victory over the Saracen. Will you not do so, and win everlasting fame?'

Backed into a corner, with every eye on him, Philippe could not remain silent. Through gritted teeth, he said, 'You will *not* have half of Artois.'

'That is a small price to pay, surely, for the glory of riding through the gates of Jerusalem, and giving thanks and praise to God Almighty in the Church of the Holy Sepulchre!'

'Get out!' cried Philippe.

The coup de grâce, the killing blow, had fallen, I thought, and he had had nothing to prevent it.

Richard faced the other diners, the great and good of France. 'I understand most of you wish to fulfil the holy vows you made when taking the cross.' He waited.

'I am staying,' said Count Henri loudly. A head nodded in agreement. So did another. A voice said quietly, 'Aye.' A second man, and a third, spoke up. More heads nodded.

Philippe's mouth worked. He was furious, and powerless.

'To Jerusalem!' cried Richard.

Again the silence fell, and my heart jumped nervously.

'JERUSALEM!' The cry soared to the stone-vaulted ceiling.

I breathed again, exhilarated. Richard had not just won. In battle terms, he had annihilated Philippe, and by the look in the French king's eyes, he would never forget – or forgive – this moment.

Even as we walked from the refectory, I felt a sneaking concern that Richard had made another lifelong enemy. I glanced at his relaxed, smiling expression. He was joking and laughing with de Chauvigny and de Béthune.

If my lord knew it, I decided, he did not care.

It remained to be seen if the humiliation he had inflicted on Philippe returned to haunt him in the future.

Intrigued to know of the confrontation with Philippe, Joanna rebuffed my kisses until I had recounted every detail.

'Why can Richard not control his arrogance?' she cried at the end. 'There was no need to demean Philippe so. Loathe him he might, but

Philippe is also a king. It is also he, like Leopold, who is to return home. My brother might rue this yet.'

'Leopold is a bladder filled with hot air,' I said, unhappy with the concern that her remark had reawakened.

'Maybe, but Philippe is a different creature altogether. Why make a greater enemy of him when there is no need to do so?'

It was hard to disagree. A thought came. 'He will not listen to me, but you would have more of a chance. Can you talk to him?'

A most unladylike snort. 'He will not take my counsel, Ferdia. I am but a woman.'

'You are far more than just a woman,' I growled, and pulled her, unresisting, to me.

We wasted no more time with talk.

It was early evening when Rhys appeared in my room in the citadel. I was not long come back from the inn, and Joanna. In languorous mood, my head full of the things I had done to her and she to me, I was unprepared for his urgency. Without as much as a knock, he barged inside.

'I have news.'

I stared at him in confusion. 'About the king and Philippe?'

A withering look, such as he would not have dared to give any other knight. 'I speak of FitzAldelm.'

Some understanding returned to my love-sated mind. Although my enemy had given up trying to monitor my comings and goings, I had tasked Rhys with watching him whenever his duties allowed. Reluctantly, I shoved away thoughts of Joanna. 'Tell me.'

'I was just down by the harbour, talking to some locals as best as I could, about the richest places to fish, when I heard a familiar voice. Luckily, I was facing the water, not the city. I took a careful look over one shoulder, and spied FitzAldelm and de Gunesse.'

Rhys had my full attention now.

'Cloaked and hooded they were, despite the heat, but I would know FitzAldelm anywhere by his walk, and de Gunesse by his nasal tone.'

'Where did they go?' I asked eagerly. 'Not the Templar tunnel?'

'Aye. First a handful of silver dropped into the palm of one of the Templar sentries, then FitzAldelm had a quick word with a Frenchie who had appeared. The three of them vanished into it quicker than you could say the Lord's prayer.'

Was it possible, I wondered, that Richard could have sent my old enemy to talk with Philippe? I immediately discounted the notion. The king *might* entrust FitzAldelm with such a duty, but highly improbable that he would seek peace with the French king so soon after the day's events. Another possibility, that they wanted to speak with Robert de Sablé, Grand Master of the Templars, seemed just as unlikely. De Sablé owed his position to Richard; he was fiercely loyal.

'They were going to talk with Philippe,' I declared. 'I can think of no other reason for using the tunnel.'

Rhys nodded grimly. 'Do you regret now my offer to slip a knife between his ribs?'

'A little,' I said with a rueful chuckle.

Rhys gave me what passed for his smile when his temper was up. It would have greyed the hair of a saint. 'Until he is dead, you will know no peace. Given that we know he is a traitor now, why do we not act? De Gunesse can die with him, for what he did in Messina.'

De Gunesse would be no loss either, I thought. With the next heartbeat, I wished I had not promised Joanna to leave FitzAldelm unharmed.

''Twill be done easily enough, with de Drune's aid.' Rhys's voice was hopeful.

I was sorely tempted, more than I had been since confessing to Archbishop Walter in Messina. There was no need to involve myself. Rhys and de Drune could dispose of FitzAldelm and de Gunesse, if they tackled them one at a time.

He saw me wavering. 'But say the word . . .'

I thought of Joanna, and imagined her asking about FitzAldelm after he had disappeared. I was not a good liar at the best of times, and she, who could see through my every fibre, would soon winkle the truth out of me. Having the blade wielded by someone else – Rhys – would be no excuse. I sighed. 'No.'

'Why not?'

I wavered, but not for long. Rhys deserved my honesty. 'I admitted to Joanna that I had thought of killing him. She made me promise to leave him alone.' Rhys tried to speak, but I cut him off. 'I know what you want to say, but you and de Drune finishing him amounts to the same thing.'

'Did you not tell her what he did at Châteauroux? About Chinon, and the crossbow?' Rhys's voice was strident with anger.

I explained how I had left it too late. 'She might have thought I made it up, to excuse planning to kill him.'

Rhys swore. 'You have made a fine mess of it, Rufus.'

Ignoring his disrespect – in a way, I deserved it – I tried another tack. 'Enough talk of murder. We need to find out if FitzAldelm really is in league with Philippe, and to bring it before the king, we need proof. Seeing him enter the Templars' tunnel is not enough.'

'How shall we find this proof?' Rhys cried. 'I am not a spider, to clamber inside the very room where he meets Philippe, and listen to their talk! Nor are you.'

'That is true, unfortunately, but it is our duty to find out what we can, and set aside our feud with FitzAldelm.'

Rhys clearly disagreed, but he nodded his acceptance, and promised not to take matters into his own hands. Instead, he would enlist de Drune's help and redouble his efforts to find out what FitzAldelm was up to.

There seemed little hope of success in this regard, but my mind was made up. Better to try and fail at this than be exposed to Joanna as a red-handed murderer.

CHAPTER XX

Three days later, the twenty-sixth of July, I found myself in the great hall of the citadel. The chamber was packed. No one wanted to miss out; more than one man had come from his sickbed to witness the dramatic conference, which was being held at Richard's insistence. Its purpose was to ascertain if Guy de Lusignan should continue as king of Jerusalem, or be replaced by the scheming, urbane Conrad of Montferrat.

Since the confrontation with Philippe, Richard had been courted by both Conrad and Guy. I had been present at both meetings. Loath though I had been to admit it, Conrad, a short, compact man with long hair and a neat-trimmed beard, had by far the stronger case. The ruler of Tyre, he was more charismatic than the well-meaning, likeable but ineffective Guy. Most importantly of all perhaps, it was not he who had commanded the Christian army butchered at Hattin four years before, but Guy. No man in his right mind wanted to follow such a leader, as Conrad had eloquently put it. With Guy in charge, he had continued, the poulains would continue to operate in factions, rather than uniting to fight their common enemy, the Saracens.

Richard had been swayed by Conrad's argument. For hours after their meeting, he warred with himself as I had rarely seen him do, torn by his desire to choose the best option for the Holy Land's future and his loyalty to a sworn vassal. In the end, he *had* chosen Guy, but eager that all should have a say, had called this gathering so that the matter could be settled.

The different blocs mixed a little as they entered, but then separated, like oil from water, taking different sections of the neatly rowed feasting benches. An open area had been left at the hall's end, from where the audience could be addressed.

Philippe Capet was there, tousle-headed and dishevelled-looking;

with him were Duke Hugh of Burgundy, Count Peter of Nevers, the bishop of Beauvais, Drogo de Merlo and a score of others whose faces I knew. Humphrey de Toron sat with his fellow poulains, including Balian d'Ibelin and Joscius, archbishop of Tyre. Conrad of Montferrat was muttering in the ears of the latter two, who were chief among his allies.

I noted Humphrey's mournful expression, and decided its cause was not just the presence of Conrad, the man who had stolen his wife, but the likely knowledge that beside the very future of the kingdom of Jerusalem, an illegal marriage could be ignored. In short, Humphrey's and Isabella's happiness counted for naught. 'Twas no wonder he was miserable.

Richard's entire court was also present, the barons, the bishops, and the mesnie, FitzAldelm and I among their number. The grand masters Robert de Sablé and Garnier de Nablus sat side-by-side in tunics bearing the insignia of their orders, and a score of their marshals too. They were the picture of grim readiness. Lesser men, soldiers and servants, packed the back of the hall, where there was standing room only. I fancied I spied Joanna and one of her ladies, mantles covering their heads, lurking behind a pillar, which made me smile. I had been told in no uncertain terms the previous day what she thought of not being invited.

With Joscius presiding, the meeting began. Guy de Lusignan was allowed to speak first. Although he had not Conrad's persuasiveness, he was a passionate speaker. With raw emotion, he described his marriage to Sibylla, accession to the throne, and the births of their daughters. Passing over the details of Hattin, he spoke of his release by Saladin, and even the pledge he himself had made not to fight the Saracens again. 'An oath made to the unbelieving, black-faced brood is no oath at all,' he said, to loud cries of agreement. Continuing, he detailed how he had received no succour at Tyre – here Guy threw a hard look at Conrad, who blithely ignored it – and had marched south to invest Acre, where, against the odds, he had prosecuted the siege for more than two years.

'My wife and daughters are dead, God rest their souls, but I have done nothing to deserve losing my throne,' Guy cried, his voice full of raw emotion. 'Recognise me as monarch, and I will dedicate my life to serving the kingdom.'

His words had gone down well, I thought, studying the audience. Men's expressions were favourable. Nods were being exchanged. I knew already that Richard planned to back Guy; now it seemed others would too.

Conrad of Montferrat was already on his feet, waiting. Dressed in reds and yellows, wearing eastern-style shoes with upturned toes, and reeking of scent, he was more poulain than Frank. The instant Archbishop Joscius had thanked Guy and introduced Conrad, he began to speak. 'You have already heard Guy condemn himself, messires.' As the room filled with exclamations of surprise – and Guy's shouted denial – Conrad raised his hands for calm, and said, 'King Guy, he was then, commanded the army lost at the Horns of Hattin. Under his charge, the flower of Outremer's manhood was either killed or taken prisoner. I wish that the cruelty of the accursed race had ended there. After the battle, the lord of Kerak Reynald de Chatillon was foully murdered by Saladin himself; hundreds of Templars and Hospitallers were also butchered.'

The angry shouts that had accompanied his words reached a crescendo, and Conrad smiled. When it died down, he went on, 'But for Guy's disastrous leadership, the tragedy of Hattin would never have happened. Jerusalem would still be in Christian hands! Small wonder, therefore, that he forbade from mentioning Hattin during his address.'

Guy, furious but powerless to stop his rival, listened with the rest of us as Conrad described his seizure of Tyre just as it was about to fall to the Turks, and how he had valiantly kept it safe since. Married now to Isabella, sister to the deceased Queen Sibylla, he was the clear and obvious heir to the throne. Master of the stage, Conrad all but bowed to the audience as he concluded.

Joscius then requested both candidates to swear that they would abide by the ruling of the kings and nobles. Guy and Conrad duly did so.

It was time for the kings, lords and prelates to make their decision. Everyone else had to leave the great hall. Remembering Joanna, mischief took me. De Béthune, de Chauvigny and Thorne were in such animated conversation as they walked, my leaving went unnoticed. Finding no one where I thought I had spied Joanna, I paced through the crowd, my gaze seeking anyone in headgear. My luck was in.

Noticing two mantles, a brown one and a blue, passing through the doors, I chased after, pushing past men with many a muttered 'by your leave'.

Sure enough, the women wearing the mantles went left, towards the stairs that led to the royal quarters. I cursed, thinking I would not catch them, but then a gaggle of priests blocked their path, and I managed to get ahead. At the foot of the stairs, I stopped, as if to tie a boot lace, standing just as they walked up.

Joanna's beautiful face was a picture. Her mouth opened and shut. 'Sir Rufus,' she managed.

Her lady, one of those I knew well to see, pursed her lips in disapproval of this public meeting.

I bent my knee. 'What a surprise and a pleasure to see you here, madam. I thought only men were to attend the debate. Did the king . . .?'

Colour suffused her cheeks. 'Richard would be happy to know I was there.'

'I have no doubt, madam,' I said, although I was not sure she was speaking the truth. 'Will you return for the judgement?'

She shot me a challenging look. 'I had intended to, yes.'

I smiled. 'Mayhap we can talk again then, madam.'

As Joanna passed, I whispered into her ear, 'Can we meet later?'

She flashed me a hungry look, one I knew, and mouthed the words, 'I would have it no other way.'

Already imagining our tryst, I watched her go. Thinking then to rejoin de Béthune and the others, I turned – and almost walked into FitzAldelm.

His high-cheekboned face was triumphant. 'Cozening your lady love?'

'I have not the slightest idea what you are talking about,' I said, making to push past.

He blocked my way. 'I think you do.'

Fear bubbled up inside me, fierce and undeniable.

'I am going to speak to the king,' said FitzAldelm with vicious delight. 'I imagine he will summon you soon after, and that the meeting will not be pleasant.'

I threw caution to the wind. 'I shall tell him directly afterwards of your secret meetings with Philippe.'

He jerked back, like a hound pulled by a leash. '*What?*'

'You heard me,' I snarled. 'Creeping in by the Templars' tunnel, you and de Gunesse, like two spies. What treachery are you planning?'

'You could not have seen me go through that tunnel!'

'I have a man-at-arms who did. The king will take a dim view of hearing that you went in secret to the king of France's lodgings. What possible motive could you have, other than betrayal?'

'The testimony of a man-at-arms counts for nothing against mine,' he spat.

He was right. I knew it. He knew it.

Desperate to preserve my relationship with Joanna, I could think of only one solution. I fixed FitzAldelm with my eyes. 'We are in the same position, you and I.'

He sneered. 'How might that be?'

'Neither of us wishes the king to know something. In my case, it is my dealings with Queen Joanna; in yours, the sneaking to and fro to treat with Philippe Capet. Swear on a holy reliquary that you will keep silent – the same applies to de Gunesse and your man-at-arms – and I will do the same.'

'Done.' His reply was instant, proving his guilt.

Hoping against hope that I had not betrayed Richard, I shook FitzAldelm's hand. We agreed to meet later in a nearby church to make our oaths on the leg bone of a local saint, and went our separate ways.

I found a quiet spot in the tree-shady courtyard, and there considered what I had done. Waves of emotion battered me: relief, that my affair with Joanna would remain secret from the king, and utter fear, that FitzAldelm's murky dealings with Philippe might harm Richard in some way. Guilt soon crept in. What was my reputation compared – potentially – to the king's life? Nothing. I wrestled with the problem, wishing I had not been so quick to strike a deal with FitzAldelm, before resolving that Rhys should continue to shadow him. If hard evidence came our way and drew matters to a head, I would go to Richard; if that meant my affair with Joanna was exposed, so be it. I continued to feel uneasy, however, and for the first time since entering the king's service, disloyal. A dark mood took me.

De Béthune found me not long after.

'There you are, Rufus. Have you been hiding?'

I pleaded a headache, the result of too much wine the night before. We had not been together, so my lie went unchallenged. 'Any word of the debate ending?' I asked.

'They have come to a decision – that is why I came searching for you. Hurry, lest we miss the announcement.'

My excitement rising despite myself, I followed him. We met de Chauvigny by the entrance to the great hall, and went in together. The crowd had swelled further; men were packed as tightly as salted fish in a barrel. It took repeated use of our sharp elbows and de Chauvigny's mention that he was cousin to the king to see us reach the benched area, and a better chance of witnessing history unfold.

Archbishop Joscius was talking to Richard; I saw the king nodding, his face satisfied. 'Guy is still to be king,' I said to de Béthune.

He peered. 'I think you are right.'

Total quiet fell as Joscius stood forth. I glanced at Guy, whose face was twisted with anxiety. Conrad, on the other hand, had a serene confidence to him. I wondered what his reaction would be if my gut instinct was right.

'Know that the kings, nobles and prelates have reached a decision.' Joscius paused, and the expectancy in the air swelled even more.

'Conrad of Montferrat!' shouted a voice.

Joscius glared, and waited again until silence fell. 'We have decided that Guy de Lusignan shall be King of Jerusalem to the end of his days, on the understanding that if he takes a wife and has sons or daughters, they shall have no right to claim succession to the kingdom. If Conrad and his wife Isabella should survive Guy, they will succeed him in the kingdom, and their heirs will also wield the sceptre and possess the same hereditary rights.'

'This is no justice,' cried Guy.

Conrad was just as unhappy. 'I am the older; it is monstrously unfair that I should succeed Guy only when he dies. By then there will be no kingdom left!'

Both sides descended into bickering and name-calling. Order was restored after a time when Joscius had the guards hammer their spear butts off the floor. Sour-faced and still muttering, Guy, Conrad and their supporters subsided.

'This is the ruling of both kings, as well as the nobles and prelates here gathered. I remind you, my lords—' Joscius aimed a pointed look at Guy and Conrad '—that not an hour since, you both took a solemn oath to abide by the court's ruling.'

Slowly, the arguing and indignation died away.

Joscius laid out further details. The revenue of the kingdom was henceforth to be divided equally between Guy and Conrad. In recognition of his defence of Tyre, Conrad was confirmed as its ruler; he was also granted the cities of Sidon and Baruth; all three were to be held in the service of the King of Jerusalem. Guy's brother Geoffrey, whose valour in the attacks on Acre was acknowledged by all, was rewarded with the towns of Joppa and Caesarea, under the same terms as Conrad.

Patting his sweaty brow with a cloth, Joscius stepped away from the speaking area. An excited hum of conversation sprang up as the audience was released from the solemnity of the occasion. Guy and Conrad withdrew at once, the former with his brothers, and the latter with Balian d'Ibelin. A dejected-looking Humphrey de Toron was left on his own, a lonely figure whose rightful grievance had not even been considered.

The court's ruling was not unexpected, but I had an uncomfortable feeling in my gut. I said as much to de Béthune.

His response was succinct. 'Guy is king; there is no going back on that after so public an announcement.'

I thought of Conrad's eloquence, and the tenacity he had shown in taking and holding Tyre, and of Guy, whose raison d'être, the siege of Acre, had now ended. 'I would be amazed if Conrad does not seek to have the ruling changed,' I said.

'He is not one to take defeat lying down,' said Richard, materialising at my shoulder.

'If Conrad lays fresh claim to the throne, sire, will you continue to support Guy?' I asked.

'The poulains have accepted him as their king, but Conrad may change their minds. If that happens . . .' the king's mouth worked. 'Then the fate of the Holy Land is of greater import than the bond between liege lord and vassal.'

It *was* the most practical option, I thought.

After a short but unpleasant meeting with FitzAldelm in the church where we had agreed to take our oaths, I waited for Joanna at the inn until the sun was low in a red-pink sky. She did not come. At the evening meal in the citadel, she threw me a regretful look, from which I took to mean that something had prevented her from leaving the citadel. To my relief, this was later confirmed by one of her ladies, who waylaid me in the passageway to the garderobe. Berengaria had insisted on the queen's company, she said, and might well do on the morrow. I was not to worry.

I could have kissed the lady, plain as an old maid though she was, so happy was I. Asking her to tell Joanna that I would wait until she again sent word, I spent the rest of the evening in excellent humour.

The following day, Richard requested a meeting with the French king. Ostensibly, his purpose was the division between them of the Saracen prisoners taken after the fall of Acre, but as he told me, his real motive was demanding a fresh oath that Philippe would allow no harm to come to Richard's lands while he was in Outremer.

'Will he give it, sire?' I asked. 'Surely half the reason he wants to leave is to be a gall under your saddle blanket, and to threaten your realm?'

'Do I not know it?' Richard agreed. 'God's legs, I will wring a promise from him one way or another.'

His temper unleashed, the king declared that the entire mesnie had to train in the knights' yard. Ignoring the grumbles – from men like FitzAldelm and de Gunesse – that it was over hot, that the high walls made it an oven, Richard cried that on the road to Jerusalem we might have to fight in the sun every day. He was right, but even I was none too pleased. I had taken to wearing tunic and hose made of cotton, a fabric used by Saracen and poulain alike, and wonderfully cool. I had no desire to pull on my usual thick woollen garments.

Helping me into my gear, Rhys was most amused by my grumbling. 'You are getting soft,' he declared.

I punched him, not gently, and ordered him to put on his own armour. I added, 'Fetch de Drune from over there in the shade where he stands, idling. 'Tis only fair that the pair of you also work up a sweat.'

Muttering under his breath, he got some revenge by leaving me to don my hauberk, a beast of a job without help.

Richard, still annoyed by FitzAldelm's complaints, selected him to be his sparring partner. Fascinated, I delayed starting my bout against

Thorne, who had come to join us. FitzAldelm, although a skilled swordsman, had never been one to give his all when facing the king. This approach always angered Richard, who demanded we spare no effort against him. Twice he disarmed FitzAldelm, and twice declared that he was not fighting a stripling youth, before starting another bout. 'Pretend I am Saladin, or one of his emirs!' said the king.

My enemy made more of an effort this time, driving Richard back several steps, and raining down blows on his heater shield. He did not strike the king's armour, however, or disarm him, and it was not long before Richard was on the counterattack. A flurry of powerful strikes culminated in a mighty downward cut on FitzAldelm's shield, exposing his chest and belly, and an up-sweeping slash that would have seen his hauberk there rent in two had the king landed the blow.

'I yield,' cried FitzAldelm from behind his helmet.

'So easily?' bellowed Richard. 'Sweet Jesu, where is your spirit, Robert?'

I did not hear FitzAldelm's answer, so muffled was it, but Richard did. Angry, he shouted that he had need only of men who *wanted* to be here, who *wanted* to fight the Saracen and take Jerusalem back for all Christians. He dismissed FitzAldelm and called for a new training partner.

When my enemy took his helmet off at the side of the courtyard, his face was scarlet with humiliation. My delight at seeing FitzAldelm cut down to size was such that I did not pause to consider the full effect on him. It was only afterwards that the possible ramifications sank in. FitzAldelm's grievance towards Richard would just have increased tenfold. I told Rhys and de Drune we would have to keep our eyes on him even more than before. Rhys again mentioned a dark alleyway. Again I refused.

More surprises unfolded later. As the mesnie took their ease in the shade, drinking cups of fizzing sherbet, the king revealed that he was to send a party of trusted men to carry word of Philippe's return to his own realm. He could not sit by and do nothing. Richard then told a shocked FitzAldelm that he was to lead the group.

I could scarcely believe my ears, nor conceal my delight. Soon Joanna and I would be able to meet without hindrance or fear. In my selfishness, I did not consider the harm FitzAldelm might cause.

'It is an important mission,' said Richard. 'Every lord in Normandy,

Brittany, Anjou and Aquitaine must be on the alert from the moment that Capetian dog reaches Paris. Whatever he may swear on the morrow, he *cannot* be trusted. You are cut from different cloth, Robert. I can think of few other men worthy of this task.'

I would have paid a fortune in that moment to have had the scales fall from the king's eyes.

'Do not send me from your side, sire,' FitzAldelm protested, but when Richard shook his head, no, he made little complaint.

The bastard was glad, I thought. The order served his purpose, and if it went as Richard intended, FitzAldelm and the rest of the party would join Philippe on their journey back to France. The two men could spend the entire journey plotting against the king. I imagined FitzAldelm also revealing to Philippe his links to the malevolent John.

Fearing the consequences, I wondered again about going to the king and telling all. To do so before FitzAldelm left, however, risked his exposing my night-time meetings with Joanna. I would deny the allegations of course, but Richard's reaction would be volcanic regardless. He would interrogate me and Joanna, and one of us might inadvertently expose the truth.

I decided I could not tell the king now. Nor, thanks to the promise extracted from me by Joanna, could I murder FitzAldelm and have done. Which meant he could be free to spin webs and work deceits all the way back to England.

When I retired that night, unhappy and worried, my mind spun with endless dark possibilities. One thing only was crystal clear. I could tell the king about FitzAldelm's dealings with the French *after* he had left.

The option was not without risk. Richard would want to know why I had not spoken when FitzAldelm was there to be questioned. He would accuse me, correctly, of seeking to wreck the reputation of a man who was not there to defend himself. To act so therefore risked losing the king's trust. My enemy's dealings with Philippe might never be proven, moreover, and when Richard saw FitzAldelm again, *he* would expose my affair with Joanna.

There was another choice, a tempting one. I denied it for as long as I could, but as the night dragged by, marked every three hours by chiming church bells, I decided that I could also pretend to know nothing about my enemy's involvement with Philippe. Even Joanna did not need to be let in on this detail.

FitzAldelm is not Philippe Capet, I told myself, nor Richard's brother John. One mid-ranking knight he is, soon to be far away, and not to return for the foreseeable future. He poses *no* danger to the king.

It felt traitorous even to have the thought, and I thrust it away. Again and again, however, it came creeping back, enticing, easy, safe. I rolled about on my palliasse, sweating, desperate for a way out of my predicament.

In the end, exhausted, bleary-eyed, I took the coward's choice.

I would remain silent, and FitzAldelm would do no harm to the king.

So I told myself, even as guilt flayed me.

CHAPTER XXI

Richard got his promise in public from Philippe three days later, on the thirtieth of July, but the French king's insincerity as he uttered the words was plain. There was little Richard could say; to accuse his fellow monarch of lying after taking a holy oath on a reliquary would shatter any chances of peace. Wary, however, Richard increased the size of the party who would travel to his realm from six men to a dozen. The faster his warning spread, the king's reasoning went, the less damage Philippe could do.

De Gunesse was one of the additions, which was more good news for me. So too was the fact that Rhys had not seen FitzAldelm anywhere near the French king. I told myself that my choice not to tell Richard had been a good one.

It eased my guilt and shame not a whit.

The two kings divided the Saracen prisoners, each taking half of the more important individuals. Karakush was given to Philippe, and Mestoc to Richard. The French king then made the grandiose gesture of granting Conrad his share of Acre's riches, including the prisoners. As a smug Conrad bowed and offered his thanks, Richard muttered to me that he had best not get any ideas about sending the Saracens to Tyre.

Which is precisely what the wily Italian did. Embarking with Philippe on the third of August, he took every last man of them – without having said a word to Richard. FitzAldelm, de Gunesse and the others followed in their own ship, and I exulted to see them go.

The king was incensed by Conrad's underhand behaviour. In the negotiations with Saphadin, restarted just the day before, frequent mention had been made of the captives taken during the fall of Acre. With Turkish spies everywhere in the city, Richard shouted, it was probable that Saladin now knew half the prisoners were in Tyre, not Acre.

'Their freedom will become his leading demand,' said the king, pacing about the citadel courtyard. 'A demand I cannot grant, even if I wished to. Damn Conrad to Hell!' He summoned Bishop Hubert of Salisbury and Count Robert de Dreux, and sent them to Tyre. There they were to order Conrad to return the Saracens at once.

To Richard's good fortune, however, Saladin accepted his terms without mention of the captives. By the eleventh of August, thirty-one days after the fall of Acre, the Holy Cross would be delivered up, together with Saladin's Christian prisoners, and half of the agreed ransom, a sum of one hundred thousand dinars.

All seemed well. The king had his suspicions about Saladin's intentions – the more protracted the negotiations, the longer the delay to our departure – but as he remarked, the enemy leader was a man of honour. 'He shall have until the eleventh,' said Richard, in the same breath giving orders for the dismantled siege engines to be loaded into the ships waiting in the harbour. Other preparations for the forthcoming campaign continued apace, and I played my part, curbing my impatience to march south.

Every smithy in the city was commissioned to make quarrels for the soldiers' crossbows. Hay and grain for the horses and foodstuffs for the soldiers – biscuits and flour, wine and meat – were sourced in great quantities. Maps detailing roads, wells and settlements along the coast were replicated by clerks, so that every captain had one. Units of troops were drilled in the early mornings, when the temperature was bearable. We knights practised also, riding in formation and charging en masse, and retreating together, without breaking ranks. Over and over we did it, with Richard leading as often as he could. Discipline was everything, he would say. Discipline.

The king's workload would have seen him work every hour from sunrise to nightfall and still not be finished, but even he conceded that the hottest part of the day was too much for any man. We were to make the most of Acre, he declared, because on the march south, the conditions would be brutal. Each afternoon therefore, everyone was to have a rest, just as the locals did. The practice was instituted at once, and proved massively popular with everyone from the men-at-arms to we knights.

I was most amused to find out that it was Berengaria who had suggested the break in duties, and at Joanna's suggestion. If the queen was to get with child, Joanna explained, she needed to lie with Richard at every opportunity. Rather than rest each afternoon, I quipped back at her, he was taking exercise of an entirely different kind. Just as we do, she retorted, smiling. I was pleased for the king, and grateful, for his 'rests' allowed Joanna and I to meet at the inn.

I was woken on the eleventh of August, the year of our Lord 1191, by the muezzin's ululating call. Despite its ungodly origins, it was a sound I had come to like. Rising from my palliasse, I stepped over Rhys, still asleep at its foot, and reached up to open the wooden grille that covered the window. A square of blue sky was revealed; bright sunlight shafted in. The muezzin's voice was perfectly audible now, and I stood, transfixed, able now to make out the words as I had not been before. 'Hai ala-as-salah! Allahu-akbar! La ilaha illa'alah!'

'Cursed heathens.' Rhys's voice was yet thick with sleep.

I smiled; he did not share my appreciation of the Muslim summons to prayer. 'It is a timely call, nonetheless. Get up. Need I remind you, we go to meet Saphadin this morn.'

Grumbling to himself, Rhys dragged on his tunic and hose.

Once I was also dressed, we went to a bathhouse just outside the citadel, the complex inside having been commandeered for the king's use. Our morning bathe had become a daily ritual; even Rhys admitted it was a civilised thing. Sweating naked in a heated room and then plunging into a cold pool were still novel to me, but hugely refreshing. The massages offered afterwards by callus-handed, beefy Saracens were also less intimidating than they had been, but this morning I had no time for that. Rosy-cheeked, skin scrubbed clean, we headed for the refectory in search of breakfast. There, as ever, Rhys ate twice the amount I did. It was a standing joke of mine that he was still but a growing youth, whose growling stomach could never be filled. That, de Drune would add coarsely, or he had a tapeworm, like the one they had both seen writhing at the bottom of a latrine trench.

Joined at table by de Béthune and de Chauvigny, and a short while after by Thorne, we devoured fresh-baked bread, sliced and spread with honey, and a delicious selection of fruit: figs, pomegranates, carobs, and apples of paradise.

'Today is the day,' said de Chauvigny.

'Do you think Saladin will meet our demands?' I asked.

'The True Cross, fifteen hundred of our men, and a hundred thousand dinars,' said de Béthune.

'I will be pleasantly surprised if he does.' De Chauvigny peeled an apple of paradise, and popped a chunk in his mouth. Chewing, he said, 'Where will he have got the money from, though? Think on it. Our scouts have seen no camel trains arriving from north or south, from Baghdad, Damascus or Egypt.'

'No Saracen ships have landed since the siege ended either,' I said.

'Just so. Unless Saladin has a vast hoard hidden in his camp, which is improbable, he does not have the coin.'

It was hard to argue with his logic, I decided unhappily. 'Which means he will play for time.'

'As he did nine days ago when you met Saphadin,' said Thorne, who had heard every detail from us.

'Aye,' replied de Chauvigny.

'He might demand all of the captives taken during the fall of the city, knowing half of them are in Tyre with Conrad,' I said.

Bishop Hubert and Count de Dreux had returned empty-handed a few days before. Conrad's absurd counterdemand to Richard's had been to split the True Cross between them. The last of the king's patience had vanished; he had sent Duke Hugh of Burgundy to Tyre with strict instructions not to come back without the prisoners.

'They will arrive within a day or two,' said de Chauvigny. 'If Saladin is not playing tricks, he can wait until then. If he is up to something, however . . .'

'Richard will not stand for trickery much longer,' I declared. 'He knows the camp gossip: that the French are unhappy he has not given the order to march yet, that Guy has been complaining to his followers.'

'Our men do not care,' said Thorne. 'They are too busy drinking and whoring.'

We chuckled, for he was right. Acre had long been famous as a den of iniquity, full of inns and brothels. With the siege ended, the wine had flowed again, and prostitutes flocked to the city in large numbers, from God only knew where. Both types of business now did a roaring trade all hours of the day and night.

De Chauvigny clapped his hands. 'Enough talk of wine and painted women. More important matters await our attention. Let us to the meeting place.'

Everyone rose from the table, eager to hear Saphadin's words.

We returned to Acre hot, dusty and sweaty, but most of all, angry and frustrated. Previously friendly and welcoming, Saphadin had been aloof and distant. He had brought with him, moreover, neither the True Cross, nor the agreed sixteen hundred Christian prisoners and initial payment of one hundred thousand dinars. He had offered a new proposal from Saladin, that those terms would be met if all our captives were freed first. There were more complicated variations too, the most outrageous of which involved Christians being offered to Saladin as hostages in surety for the lives of the Saracens in our custody.

Our news sent Richard into a towering rage. Picking up a great ornamental vase that served as decoration, he smashed it on the floor, scattering chips of glazed pottery everywhere. He soon calmed down, however, and cold reason replaced his fury. He would not agree to Saladin's terms, the king said, but nor could he force our enemy to honour his side of the agreement. We would wait until the duke of Burgundy came back with Conrad's prisoners – intelligence known to Saladin, and used to challenge us during the meeting – and see then what he had to say.

Duke Hugh reached Acre the following day; he had the Saracen captives with him, but the devious Conrad had opted to stay in Tyre. It was as well for him, Richard said with a dangerous laugh. A message was sent to Saladin at once, and negotiations reopened the following morning.

They came to naught, because Saladin, through his brother Saphadin, continued to ask for the release of all our prisoners before he parted with as much as a single Christian or dinar. De Chauvigny rejected these terms utterly, and demanded that Saladin honour the agreement he had made more than a month before. Politely, Saphadin said that this was not possible.

During the sennight that followed, we met him twice more. Although our relations had regained much of their previous warmth – we brought wine for Saphadin, and he gifted us with more buckets of snow and platters of fresh fruit – neither side would give way. The gap between our positions remained a deep, bridgeless chasm, and as I said to Joanna, there was only so long we could continue to pretend that it did not exist.

With the summer's heat growing more intense each day, the situation beyond our truce-honoured meetings unravelled further. Rumour spread in Acre and through the camp that Saladin had poisoned his Christian prisoners. Angry mobs of drunk French soldiers ran amok in the city, beating Saracens; several houses were burned to the ground. Our men-at-arms took to marauding close to the enemy camp, and were waylaid by the mamluks. Inevitably, fighting broke out. On the first occasion, our men fought their way free, leaving a dozen dead behind; on the second, a hundred knights had to be dispatched to see that they were not annihilated.

Something had to be done, and Richard knew it. ''Twill be unpleasant, Rufus,' he said to me as we supped a cup of wine late one night. 'But the army has to march south. Delay much longer, and the autumn rains will turn every road into a quagmire.'

He laid out his plan, and I quailed inside.

But I did not speak against it.

I arose on the eighteenth of August, irritable and overhot. My sleep had been fitful, and plagued by dreams of slaughter. I got dressed in silence.

Rhys sensed my dark mood, and said nothing. He had voiced his agreement with Richard's announcement to the army. De Drune was of the same mind, as were de Chauvigny, de Béthune and Thorne. Some were more in favour – Rhys being one example – while others appeared to feel the same reticence as I. Tellingly, not a single man had objected to the king's ruthless but practical suggestion.

Rhys was waiting for me.

I broke the silence. 'Are you still of a mind to volunteer?'

'Aye.'

'Why?' I asked. Rhys had not been here at Acre through the long, brutal months of the siege.

A shrug. 'It is a job that needs doing. I will do it well.'

I could not argue with those reasons.

'What about you?'

'I will also take part.'

It was his turn to look nonplussed. 'Why?'

'It would feel wrong if you and de Drune were there, and I was not.' I concealed my real motivation. Even to Rhys I did not want to mention my confession to Walter, or the penance he had given. 'You must hold back *nothing* in the battle to defeat the Saracens.'

After our visit to the baths, I let Rhys go the refectory alone. I had no appetite. I returned to our room, and sharpened my sword until it took hair off the back of my arm. That done, I tried to sleep. A short time passed, and still I lay on the palliasse, unhappy, staring at the ceiling. The task that lay before us was repulsive, and despite the blessings of the religious, did not sit well with me. At length, I abandoned all hope of rest and focused on the sounds coming through the open window.

Women's voices carried from the treelined courtyard, where Berengaria liked to breakfast with Joanna, Beatrice and her ladies. Wishing I could have been there, innocent as they, I cast my hearing further. Wagon wheels creaked in a lane outside the citadel, a donkey brayed unhappily as it was beaten by its cursing owner. Then, the happy shrieks of children at play. Nearer again, hoofbeats in the knights' yard as one of my comrades put his destrier through its paces. From a church tower, the bells sounding terce. An innkeeper's employee, walking the streets, calling that his master had just opened a cask of Rhenish wine. Anyone who wanted to try it should go to . . . and directions to the inn followed.

Relaxed by the ordinariness of the day-to-day goings-on, I fell into a deep, dreamless slumber.

A hand shook my shoulder. 'It is time.' Rhys's voice.

I came up to consciousness slowly, as if rising from the bottom of a deep black pool. My eyes opened, focused. Rhys was standing over me, already dressed in gambeson and hauberk. I heard the familiar yet alien call of the muezzin, noticed how fuggy and hot the room was. Reality crashed in. Sext, midday, had been and gone.

'The messenger from Saladin?' I asked, hoping against hope.

'He did not arrive. The king has ordered the prisoners be taken from their holding places, and the men to assemble. We leave as soon as everyone is ready.'

Hardening my heart, I rose and armed myself.

The afternoon was roasting, hot as it had ever been during our time in Outremer. The sun dominated the sky, a ball of incandescent malevolence, its blinding light hurting my eyes. Thick and soupy with warmth, the air was uncomfortable to breathe. Moments after emerging from the citadel, my entire body was coated in sweat. I clambered abroad Pommers, realising that to ride in this infernal heat *and* fight the Saracens would be monumentally difficult, and far worse than I had imagined.

Two-thirds of the army marched and rode out onto the baking, bone-dry plain east of Acre; the rest waited in readiness a short distance from the walls. Saladin always had scouts in the field, so our movements would not long escape his notice. Thinking that the king was deploying for battle, he might mobilise his host. If such an opportunity presented itself, said the king, he would seize it with both hands: hence our display of strength.

Guy de Lusignan's Turcopole cavalry, several hundred light-armed skirmishers, led the way. The rest of us followed in blocks, mounted knights flanked by units of men-at-arms. I was with Richard and the rest of the mesnie, near the column's centre. Behind us in long lines, roped by their necks to each other, and with their wrists bound, came our Saracen prisoners. Two thousand six hundred men, they walked with heads downcast, miserable, speaking little.

I wondered, with a sick feeling, if they had any idea of what was about to unfold.

Richard halted us in the middle of the plain. The choice of location, close to the enemy camp, near where we had met Saphadin so many times, was quite deliberate. Saladin could no more ignore what happened here than deny the nose on the end of his face.

He was probably aware of our presence already. Less than a quarter of a mile away, visible through the shimmering waves of heat, I could see mamluks watching.

Calmly, Richard ordered a battle line deployed. Everything had to be in place for a possible Saracen response. Messengers rode hither and thither, relaying his command. Squadrons of knights eased their horses behind the men-at-arms, who spanned their crossbows. It was all matter-of-fact, normal. If I did not look at the prisoners, there was no indication of the horror to come. Inexorably, however, my gaze was pulled in that direction. I wished that I was at the inn with Joanna, that the day was over, that I had not volunteered.

'Ready?'

Rhys had ridden out with the other squires. He looked staunch, and I told myself it would be yellow-livered not to join him. Another reason was that if God saw my cowardice, my confession and forgiveness for Henry's murder would count for naught. The thought of that pricked my tongue.

'Aye,' I said.

I got down from Pommers, and gave the reins to Philip, who was not to take part. My shield and helmet, neither of which I would need, I stacked with the rest. We gathered with the others who had volunteered. De Drune was more bleary-eyed than usual, and half-drunk with it. I said nothing; many of the men-at-arms were in similar shape. This, I decided, was how men numbed themselves from the horror. It appealed, but I had not taken even a drop. I wanted my right arm steady and sure.

Fifteen hundred, we numbered. Fully half had been at the siege of Acre under Guy's command, men who had fought and bled, suffered, seen innumerable comrades and loved ones die from disease or at the enemy's hands. Another quarter were knights of the military orders, Templars and Hospitallers eager to avenge their fellows murdered by Saladin after Hattin. The remainder were Richard's soldiers, mostly men-at-arms, but a score or more of knights like myself.

We formed a loose circle around the prisoners, who stared at us, terrified. They had bunched up in groups, realising something odd was going on.

I looked away from the fear-pinched faces, and licked moisture onto my dry lips, and told myself this was the only practical solution. We waited for the king. The sun beat down on my head. Under my mail and gambeson, I was sweating like a man who has spent too long in a Turkish bathhouse. I thought with longing of my waterskin, hanging from my saddle.

At length, Richard, content that his army was ready, rode his destrier into position before us.

I locked eyes with him.

He beckoned.

Aware that everyone was watching, I walked to him, and turned side on, so I did not have to stare at the prisoners. 'Sire?'

'This will be bloody work.'

I nodded. 'Yes, sire.'

'I can see in your face that you do not wish to be involved, Ferdia.' Even as I cursed the transparency of my emotions, which had betrayed me again, he went on, 'There will be no dishonour if you withdraw. You have my word.'

I was sorely tempted, but even as I wavered, Walter's words came back to haunt me. I pictured Henry's terror-filled expression as I slit his throat. I hardened my jaw, and said, 'I will play my role, sire.'

He held my gaze for a moment, and then nodded. 'So be it.'

There was no more timewasting. 'Let it be done,' the king cried. 'Go to, with God's blessing.'

Shouts filled the air, encouraging, and fearful, ours and theirs. I drew my blade, heard Rhys do the same with his. We exchanged an odd look. It was similar to that we had shared in Henry's house, as Rhys held him, struggling, and I hesitated, briefly. Then we faced the prisoners, and closed in.

The Saracens milled about like frightened cattle in a slaughterhouse yard. They wailed their terror at the sky, a heartrending sound that was impossible to block out, try though I might. Retreating from our advance, they pressed tight against one another, as if that could prevent the inevitable. With steady pace, we drew nearer. Jeers and insults rained down, as men who had fought at Acre for long months enjoyed their power, while others stoked their bloodlust.

I tried to stare only at the Turks' legs and feet, but I could not stop my gaze lifting. Every face was contorted in fear and horror, and my stomach threatened to empty itself. Walter's words, thoughts of penance, meant nothing to me now. If Rhys and de Drune had not been to either side of me, I would have turned on my heel. Unwilling to abandon my comrades, however, I kept pace. The Turks were crowded together like caught fish in a bulging net. Weaker ones were being trampled underfoot. No one tried to help them up.

A spear length from the mass of tethered prisoners, we halted. At such short distance, the momentousness and sheer barbarity of our task could no longer be denied. From the corner of my eye, I sensed a man twist around and walk away. Another followed. I did not look to see who they were. Although I wavered again, I could not retreat. Rhys and de Drune stood steady. Prepared. Resolute.

Five heartbeats dragged out to ten. Prayers to the unbelievers' god rose, louder and louder. La ilaha illa'llah. There is no god but God. La ilaha illa'llah.

I had begun to wonder if no one had the stomach for cold-blooded murder, when from the far side of the mass of Saracens, I heard a loud cry. There were no discernible words, but the sound was familiar, one I had emitted myself before. It was the roar of a man charging to the attack, a primeval sound from deep within the soul, a mixture of fear and courage combined.

The shout was the winter flood that, raging between narrow banks, smashes aside the dam.

I sensed movement on both sides of me. Men were stepping forward, swords ready. Rhys was advancing, so was de Drune. Gritting my teeth, I joined them.

Placing my boot on the middle-aged Saracen's chest, I pulled at my blade, which had caught between two ribs. It came free with a wet, soughing sound. The man flopped back to regard the sky, the light already gone from his brown eyes. I began searching for another victim. There could not be many; the last time I had checked, our enclosing circle had shrunk to perhaps a fifth of its original size. A carpet of gashed, hacked, mutilated corpses lay at our backs. A vile soup of blood and bodily fluids soaked the earth underfoot. Those who yet lived trembled before us.

I had not counted the Turks who went down under my blade, but my heart was heavy with the knowledge it had been many. Rhys, de Drune and I had scythed a path of destruction through the defenceless prisoners. My hands and face were scarlet-spattered, and the white cross on my surcoat was no longer discernible. My blade was sticky with ichor. I had long since given up trying to keep my boots clean.

Weary as if I had been fighting all day, my throat lined with dust, I let my sword tip rest on the bloody ground. The nearest living Saracen took this to be a sign. A narrow-faced man of perhaps my own age, he raised his clasped hands towards me in a beseeching gesture, and spoke in Arabic. I did not understand, nor did I care. In a moment, I thought, I will kill you.

'Spare me, I beg you!'

It was not my next victim who had spoken in French, but someone to his right. I looked. Rhys, right arm frozen in the very motion of thrusting his sword, had a smooth-cheeked youth directly in front of him. His arm wavered, and then steadied.

'Rhys, hold!' I do not know why I shouted.

His sword arm did not move. His gaze, cold as a wolf's, found mine.

'He speaks French,' I said.

'I do! I do!' cried the youth. 'Do not kill me, sir, please! I am not a warrior, but a humble clerk.'

Strange it is how a shared tongue can, in an instant, change a man's purpose. His words had the ring of truth, and pity stirred my heart. 'Rhys, stay your hand.' He made no reply, and I added, 'He is a boy, and no soldier.'

A trace of reason returned; Rhys's feral expression eased. He nodded when I told him to cut the Saracen's bonds. The youth fell to his knees, babbling thanks, and scrambled over on all fours to wrap his arms around my legs.

Dazed still, I stared about me. Swords continued to rise and fall, voices were being cut off mid-shriek, but the killing was almost over. Humming, de Drune was wiping his sword clean on a corpse's tunic. Rhys was already rifling through a purse he had cut from another's belt.

'Thank you, sir,' cried the Saracen youth, squeezing my legs.

Awkwardly patting his shoulder, I noticed that my fingernails were rimed with blood. Instead of feeling elation, that I had done God's work, and completed part of my penance, I was consumed by revulsion. Mastering it by force of will, I told the youth to get up. He obeyed, teeth chattering with terror, his gaze fixed on the ground.

'How came you to speak French?' I asked.

It emerged haltingly at first, but as he realised I was not about to murder him where he stood, the youth's voice strengthened. His father had been in service to a poulain lord as an estate manager. He had grown up friends with the lord's son; the one learned French, the other Arabic. By the time his voice had broken, it had been agreed he was to follow in his father's footsteps, taking over as estate manager when he grew too old. All four men had been in Acre when it fell to Saladin. The poulain and his son were killed in the fighting; being Muslims, the youth and his father survived.

Conscience pricked, I cast about for someone with similar features. 'Is he here?'

'By God's mercy, he is not, sir.' A shadow passed over his face. 'Disease took my father a year since. He died in my arms.'

'That is something,' I said, thinking of my own parents, who had departed this world without any family near. 'What is your name?'

'Abu al-Majd, sir. Are you going to kill me now?'

Again I patted his shoulder. 'Not if you will swear one thing.'

'To be become a Christian?'

'No,' I said with a smile. There was little point making him take such an oath, for Saracens who escaped captivity reverted to their own religion as a matter of course. 'You will pledge allegiance to me, to serve faithfully, and never to run away.'

'I will gladly swear such a promise.'

Pleased, I nodded.

With a little movement of his chin, Abu indicated several men-at-arms who were staring malevolently at him, and said, 'They want to slay me, sir.'

'No one will lay a hand on you. You are under my protection.'

'And Malik Rik?' His voice shook to say the name.

My gaze followed his across the mounds of dead to where Richard sat on Fauvel, watching. In my haste to be merciful, I had forgotten him. 'I will talk to the king,' I said with more confidence than I felt.

I did not have a chance to plead my case that day. Alerted by a messenger to the arrival of Saladin and his army, Richard galloped off to direct his troops. Fierce fighting had broken out as the Saracens, desperate to save their fellows, battered our lines again and again. Soon all the knights were deployed into the front ranks. I left a terrified Abu in the care of a bemused Philip. Before long, I rode in two charges, both led by the king. We smashed the mamluks asunder. Had Richard not roared and shouted until his voice went, we would have chased pell-mell after them, and this after what he had told us a score of times.

'That is what they want,' the king said as we rode our exhausted destriers towards our own lines. 'Look. They have regrouped already.'

I turned in the saddle, first one way and then the other. Vision narrowed by the slit in my helmet, it was the only way to see much of what was behind me. Scores of mamluks had gathered together and were riding after us. I was reminded of Richard's description of a cloud of gadflies parted by a flailing arm. Separating, it soon reforms its shape and resumes the attack. The king had been wrong in one respect, I decided. Mamluks were a great deal more lethal than gadflies.

Waves of them galloped after us, loosing arrows high into the air in the hope of bringing down our destriers. Thankfully, we had forced them far enough back that most knights had time enough to reach our own lines. A handful of horses were slain, but their riders were rescued by comrades. Wary of the men-at-arms' crossbows, the mamluks reined in as we came within range. As we loathed their arrows, they respected our steel-tipped quarrels.

Safe behind the men-at-arms, I took a long pull from my waterskin. It wet my mouth only, but still left me with a raging thirst. I held back from drinking more. We might be hours yet in the field. I jerked my chin at the lines of watching mamluks. 'Will they charge again, sire?'

'I would wager so, aye. Saladin probably still hopes that some of the prisoners remain alive. With the task done, however, there is no need for us to remain. We shall retreat towards the city in good order, and leave the Turks to discover the carrion we have left them.'

The king was underestimating Saladin's wrath, as we were to discover in the hours that followed. Wave after wave of mamluks rode to the attack, showering dense clouds of arrows on the men-at-arms, and preventing an easy retreat. Soon an angry Richard was forced to give the order to stand our ground. The mamluks' assaults were followed by heavy cavalry, which often threatened to break our lines. They were prevented every time by we knights, who galloped forward in an armoured mass and drove the horsemen back.

Because the Saracens knew better than to stand and fight, each charge saw only a small number of enemy dead and the temporary removal of the threat to our men-at-arms. It was massively frustrating. Over and again, the Saracens reformed by the time we reached our positions again. When they were ready, fired up by their infernal drums and cymbals, the mamluks or heavy cavalry launched another attack. This would be driven back by the knights, who then had to withdraw or risk envelopment and annihilation.

Flow and counterflow, back and forth the battle raged, both sides fighting tooth and nail, neither willing to give an inch. Not until the sun had sunk below the western horizon and the light was fast-leaching from the sky did the attacks and counterattacks come to an end.

The king stayed on the field until only the rearguard, a combination of men-at-arms and knights whose destriers had not foundered, was left. I was there also, with Rhys and de Drune. Thorne, who had had a narrow miss from a Saracen arrow when he briefly took off his helmet, stayed as well.

It was pitch black by the time we reached the torchlit ramparts of Acre, and the sentries waiting for our approach. I was grateful for the shadowing darkness, which had aided our withdrawal from the battlefield and concealed the dreadful charnel house left behind. A fatigued silence blanketed us. Heads were bowed, shoulders slumped. Snores rose from those asleep in the saddle. Many destriers were so exhausted that their riders had to walk alongside them, but Richard was astride one of his rouncys. Pommers, brave heart that he was, still bore me on his back. I let him amble as slow as he wished.

Deep in thought, I told myself that my penance had now surely been paid. I had been absolved of Henry's murder. To my horror, my long-held hope that this juncture would bring me complete relief proved false. I had cut down at least six unarmed Saracen prisoners today, men whose wrists and necks had been bound with ropes. The fact that they were infidels, bound for Hell, would not stop their faces from living long in my memory.

It was not possible to visit Joanna so late, and forget my worries that way. After washing off the worst of the blood, therefore, I went with Rhys, de Drune and Thorne to a nearby inn and there drank far more wine than was good for me.

CHAPTER XXII

I awoke early the next morning with a foul taste in my mouth and a thumping head, and was bemused to find Abu regarding me. I had been vaguely aware of movement and a figure kneeling as the predawn call to prayer had floated in the window, but full realisation only sank in as I sat up.

'You did not run away,' I croaked.

'I gave you my oath, sir. I am bound to you now.' He bobbed his head. 'I must thank you again, for sparing me.'

I nodded, aware that I needed to bring him before the king without delay.

Rhys was still dead to the world, no surprise given that he had drunk twice what I had. That did not stop Abu from glancing at him. He was still worried my squire might do him harm, I thought. It was something that would need to be addressed.

I poked Rhys with a foot. He grunted, but did not wake. I tried again, harder. 'Up, man. The sun is high in the sky.'

He groaned, and pulled his tunic-pillow over his head.

I saw Abu staring, and remembered that the Saracens did not drink. 'He is "hungover". Feeling bad because of the wine he consumed last night.'

Abu looked mystified.

It was too hard to explain. 'I am for the bathhouse,' I said. 'Do you wish to come?'

'Yes,' he replied, his surprise replaced by clear puzzlement.

Amused, I asked, 'You think we Christians never wash.'

'By the smell, many do not.'

His accusation was impossible to deny, and I chuckled. 'Well, this one does, and so does Rhys.' I kicked him this time. 'Up, you lazy dog!'

*

Washed and clean, my hair pleasantly damp, and feeling human again, I walked back to the citadel with Rhys and Abu. The pair were ignoring each other completely, a status quo that suited me. There had been many a strange look as we had left the main gate; it happened again upon our return. The sentries let us pass without challenge, but their gaze, which I could not command, laid long on Abu as we passed by.

He felt it; terror was writ large on his brown face. In his mind, I thought, he would be beaten, or even slain out-of-hand if he were alone.

'Fear not,' I said. 'We go now to the king.'

Abu gave me a terrified glance.

I pretended not to notice, and hoped that I was not making a serious mistake.

Rhys, red-eyed and morose, nursing a bad head, did not seem to care one way or another. I dismissed him. 'Go and line your belly with some food.'

He shambled off, clearly relieved not to have to present himself to Richard.

The guards outside the royal quarters were as unimpressed to see a Saracen as their fellows at the main gate had been. I had to remind them with raised voice who I was and how high I sat in the king's regard before we were admitted. Even so, their trust did not go far: despite my protestations, two accompanied us.

We found the king at breakfast with Berengaria, Beatrice and Joanna. Happiness filled me; it was not only because my heart leaped at the sight of the latter. The three women's presence meant I had a chance of escaping Richard's wrath for leaving Abu alive.

The king saw us coming. He leaned back from the table, and ran his fingers through his beard. His face was expressionless, but his eyes resembled those of a hawk, keen and fierce, and cruel.

Now Berengaria noticed us too.

Joanna, who had her back to the door, was last to see. Delight bathed me at the pleasure that rose in her face. She gave me a little smile, which only I could see.

'Rufus. It is early to come calling, and with a strange companion.' The king's tone was not warm, but nor was it glacial.

'Your pardon, sire.' I knelt, and to my relief, Abu did the same. I had told him to copy me.

'Rise.'

I did so, meeting his daunting gaze as I did.

'Who is this Saracen, and why is he here?' Richard bit off a chunk of fig and began to chew.

I seized the bull by the horns. 'He is one of the prisoners, sire.'

A royal eyebrow cocked. 'One of the noblemen kept to ransom?'

'No, sire.'

'*No?*'

My nerves as taut as a cocked crossbow string, I said, 'I spared him, sire. He is young, and no warrior. He is also fluent in French. I thought he might be useful as an interpreter.'

Richard stared at Abu, who quailed. 'Is this true?' he demanded. 'You speak French?'

'Yes, sire,' said Abu. 'I grew up with the son of a poulain lord. French is as natural to me as my own tongue.'

Joanna smiled to hear him, and said something to Berengaria, who looked intrigued. My love, I knew, had come to womanhood in Sicily. She had had Saracen servants, many of whom were dear to her. Some remained with her still, although two had fled to Saladin's camp at Tell al-'Ayyādiyya, thereby revealing their true natures. Despite this, it was plain to me at least that she regarded Abu as a human being, not an unbeliever who deserved to die.

I could not be so sure of Richard, whose expression was inscrutable. I gave Abu a reassuring look, and said, 'If I did wrong, sire, I apologise.'

'*If* you did wrong?' Richard barked with laughter. 'God's legs! You *did*, Rufus. I ordered that every last Saracen we brought out from Acre should die, and yet here this one stands.' The last six words came out hard and flat.

Abu's face went a pasty shade of grey.

My own pulse beat faster, but the king's tone was not bubbling with fury, I decided. I even thought there had been a hint of amusement in it. Again I gambled. 'Scores of the wealthier Turks remain in captivity, sire, useful because of the ransoms that will be extracted from their families. This man – Abu al-Majd – is not rich, but his worth as an interpreter is greater, I wager, than many of those still in the citadel gaol.'

The king made no reply, his face still unreadable. My hopes plummeted. One command, and the guards would drag Abu out and kill him on the spot.

'Was not enough blood shed yesterday, Richard?' pleaded Joanna. 'This Saracen is a well-spoken lad, and you have few men who speak Arabic.'

I felt fresh hope. The queen began whispering to Richard, distracting him, and I mouthed a *thank you* to Joanna.

The king's attention came back to me. 'Who is to say that the boy will not run off at the first opportunity?'

'He has sworn before his god that he will not, sire.'

'And you believe him?'

'I do, sire. If you grant clemency, I shall be responsible for him.'

Richard snorted, but it was not an angry sound. 'Very well. Keep him. Ensure he is close by when I have need of an interpreter.'

'Yes, sire. Thank you.' I shot Abu a look, eager that my trust would not be broken, and was moved by his tears of gratitude. I bowed deeply to the king, and to the queen and Joanna. Again Abu imitated me. I said, 'By your leave, sire.'

Richard waved a hand. 'Attend me within the hour. We leave tomorrow. The journey to Jerusalem can wait no longer.'

'Yes, sire!' Excited – this was what we had been waiting so long for – I could not help my eyes from going to Joanna again. For reasons of safety, she was to remain in Acre with Berengaria. I risked all. *This afternoon?* I mouthed.

Her tiny nod filled me with joy, and by God's grace, the king and his wife, talking together, did not see.

'Why did he order us all killed yesterday?' Abu asked in a low voice as we made our way out.

'Time and again, Saladin reneged on the terms of the treaty agreed when Acre fell. He delayed our march south by weeks, and would have continued to do so had the king not acted.'

'Did the prisoners have to be slain?' He gave me a reproachful look.

Defensive, I said, 'They could not be left, even if there had been supplies enough. The garrison must needs be small, and the two queens are to remain in the city also. The king had little choice but to act as he did.'

'A Muslim leader would have made slaves of us.'

'How barbaric!'

'And to slaughter thousands of unarmed men is not?'

I stared at him, nonplussed to be wrongfooted by a youth who owed me his life. 'Slavery would have been a better fate, I admit, but it is not practised in England or France. It is unlikely that the idea even occurred to the king.'

'That is a great pity,' said Abu, his voice laden with sorrow.

'It is,' I found myself admitting, my mind bright with images of the men I had slain.

'It was bravely done this morning, Ferdia.' Joanna was nestled close. It was late in the afternoon, and we lay entwined, naked on the bed in our room at the inn. 'Challenging him on his own ground! Did you know the queen and I would be there?'

I kissed her forehead. 'I hoped so.'

'And if we had not been?'

'It *might* have proved more difficult to persuade him.'

'You would have had no chance, you rogue.' She pushed herself up on an elbow, and gave me a mock-angry look. 'Admit it.'

'If you had not been there, my heart, I would have failed,' I said, content not to disagree.

Pleased as a cat with a bowl of cream, she straddled me. Her hair fell on both sides of my face, and she bent closer, creating the most intimate of spaces. 'You are a good man, Ferdia,' she whispered, 'with a kind heart.'

I tried not to think of what I had done the previous afternoon, and smiled my thanks.

She read my pain. 'Was it terrible?'

'Horrific.'

Tenderly, she kissed one of my cheeks, and then the other. 'I tried to dissuade Richard yesterday morning. I told him my husband William would have enslaved the prisoners, that the resulting coin would raise the hundred thousand dinars Saladin should have paid. Richard would not listen.'

It was disquieting to hear that the king *had* known of another possibility to the bloodshed. 'Did he refuse because of the delay – how long it would have taken to sell them?' I asked.

A sad nod.

'It was a brutal choice, but a practical one.' Trying to convince myself, I added, 'If the army's departure is delayed much further, it risks being stranded in Acre for the winter.'

'A time we could be together.'

I reached up and caressed her face. 'I have thought of that much.'

Again she read my emotions. 'But . . .'

'Half a year's delay would see the army crippled by debauchery, illness and desertions, my love. It could deliver a fatal blow to the king's campaign. Imagine if he failed to recapture Jerusalem because of it.'

She made no argument, instead doing things to me that drove almost everything from my mind.

Afterwards, however, my guilt was swift to return. I shoved it away as best I could, telling myself over and over that I had been doing God's work.

It helped – a little.

Thursday the twenty-second of August dawned clear and fair, like all the summer days before it. My heart was sorrowful on rising, for I had said farewell to Joanna the previous evening. God only knew when our next meeting would be, if indeed there was to be one. The road south would see fighting against the Saracens on a daily basis, and my chances of emerging unscathed were uncertain. I had no time to be lovesick now, however, so I gently placed my thoughts of Joanna at the back of my mind, and shut the door on them.

From this juncture, war would be my mistress, and heat, dust and thirst its dread companions.

If I had wished for a swift start to the campaign, and victory over Saladin fiercely won, I was to be disappointed. The army, not yet fully formed, moved a miserable two miles from the city on the first day. Of all the contingents, only the military orders had marched forth with their complete strength. The reason was not difficult terrain or Saracen attacks, but the sloth of the troops. After nigh-on six weeks of abandonment to pleasure, the fleshpots and taverns within the walls held far greater appeal than the burning, waterless road south.

Richard was not pleased, but nor did he fly into one of his thundering rages. He had expected this reluctance, he told me, and planned for it. Groups of men-at-arms, each led by a knight, scoured every quarter of Acre from top to bottom. Officers were dressed down in front of their men, and the order given that everyone had to join the army by the next day. No women apart from laundresses were to be allowed to accompany us. If these directives were not complied with, severe punishments would follow.

It was a duty I fast grew to hate, sitting on my rouncy beneath the scorching sun as men-at-arms barged and pushed drunken soldiers out of brothels and drinking dens. I harangued them, sullen-faced, red-eyed, resentful. If they were Welsh, Rhys spoke for me. Occasionally I ordered a recalcitrant or mouthy individual beaten. And all the while, Joanna was but a few streets away, as far beyond my reach as the baleful sun in the sky.

The second day was no better. We forded the River Belus, but hundreds and hundreds of men remained in Acre. Patient, calm and measured, the king ordered camp be set up just two miles from where we had slept the previous night. Again we rode back to the city, and forced grumbling soldiers out of the gates. At one point, close to the citadel, I could have sworn I heard Joanna's tinkling laugh. My heart ached to hear it, and a foul mood seized me. When a French man-at-arms threw a muttered insult soon after, I punched him in the stomach so hard that he collapsed to the ground and there lay, unmoving, for the entire time it took to empty a couple of taverns and a whorehouse. Finally, with many a hate-filled glance, his companions dragged him away, still comatose. Furious that I could not see Joanna, angry at my loss of self-control and the snail's pace of our mission, I paid them no heed.

By nightfall of the twenty-fourth of August, Richard was content that enough men had joined the army. Almost twenty thousand we numbered, when every grouping and nationality was included. The laggards who yet remained, he declared, were the dregs of the barrel. There was no current need among our ranks for such cowards.

Late in the evening, as the ferocious temperature dipped a little, he called a meeting of every noble and officer of consequence. It was held in the open air, under a wondrous sky lit by a myriad glittering stars. A light breeze from the close by sea caressed our faces and kept away the mosquitoes, and the king waxed lyrical. Rarely had I seen him so enthused and passionate. This was his moment, his hour, I thought, my own eagerness fanned hot. Almost three years had passed since we had taken the cross together at Tours. The delays and pitfalls in his path since had often seemed God-sent, so difficult were they to traverse.

Conflict and then open war with his father. A tangled web of alliance and mistrust with Philippe Capet. His coronation, and the attendant problems that came with setting his kingdom in order. Sicily, Messina, Tancred and again, Philippe. The island of Cyprus, the treachery of Isaac Comnenus. The king's multiple bouts of illness. And then, at last, Acre and the siege. The prolonged negotiations with Saladin, the double dealing, and the massacre of the prisoners. A long and winding road, it had been, I thought, and the end was not even close to being in sight. But here, now, with the full army encamped around us, and a ring of fierce, expectant faces watching Richard's every move, it felt at last as if our war was truly underway.

'In the morn, we march south and for Jerusalem,' said Richard, his eyes shining in the torchlight. 'Jerusalem!'

'Jerusalem!' we cried.

Smiling, Richard explained that there were two possible routes. The first, one hundred and fifty miles long, went inland to Nazareth, then south to Mount Tabor, the Pools of Jacob and Ramallah. 'That is not the way we shall choose, my lords. I have taken counsel with those who know the land.' He nodded in the direction of Garnier de Nablus, Grand Master of the Knights Hospitaller, Guy de Lusignan and Humphrey de Toron. Abu was given no acknowledgement, although the king had listened to his description as well. Richard continued, 'On the inland route we would be forced to travel much of the time through valleys with the Saracens on the heights above. Constantly exposed to attack, our supply lines stretched thin and also susceptible, the journey could take months – if we completed it at all.'

No one disputed this decision. The parallels with Hattin were obvious. Rapt, we listened as the king laid out his proposal.

'The coastal road is by far our best option, messires. It is eighty miles from here to Joppa, give or take. With the sea on our right flank, we shall have welcome protection from the Saracens. The fleet can sail alongside, moreover, carrying excess food and water, supplies and heavy equipment such as the siege engines. Saladin will be worried, for it will not be clear if we intend to strike for Jerusalem or Egypt. Not until Joppa when we cut inland will he realise that taking the Holy City is our aim.'

'What is the distance from Joppa to Jerusalem, sire?' asked Henri of Blois.

'Some thirty-five miles,' answered Richard. 'Not far, and not all sand, as I once believed, but make no mistake: it will be the most arduous section of the march. With the wells poisoned, like as not, the enemy lurking behind every hill and area of woodland, the heat even more extreme than it is here, we will be tested as never before.'

Far from daunted, he appeared positively exuberant. His burning passion, his sheer force of personality, were infectious. I could feel the sun burning my skin as I rode with him, see the Saracens breaking before our charge, could imagine my joy as the lofty walls of Jerusalem came into sight for the first time, and my awe as I fell on my knees in the Church of the Holy Sepulchre. Glancing at the nearby faces, I saw that they too were being carried along.

'In my keenness, I have neglected to mention what must come first. Eighty miles lie between us and Joppa. It will not just be a hot, dusty and difficult journey.' Richard waved a hand at the eastern hills. 'Saladin and his army are out there, patient as cats by a mousehole. His mamluks have been watching over the last two days. He knows our exact location and the route we will take come the morning. It is not a question of *if* the accursed race attack, but *when*.'

An expectant hush followed. It was broken by a jackal's bark, the high-pitched tone of which brought up the hairs on my arms.

'What is your plan, sire?' I asked.

His eyes glinting in the starlight, Richard began to explain.

PART FOUR

AUGUST 1191–OCTOBER 1192

CHAPTER XXIII

Not long after dawn on the twenty-fifth of August, we moved off southwards. First went a protective screen of several hundred men-at-arms. Richard was next, leading the vanguard with his mesnie around him, and another five score knights as well. How proud we were setting out, and high-spirited. How quickly our conversations died away as the temperature soared, and sweat drenched each man's body beneath the great load of hauberk and mail hose. If it had not been for our surcoats, I said half-jokingly to the king, we would be cooked alive in our shells of steel.

A short distance behind us, guarded by Norman knights, was the wagon bearing the king's standard. A great four-wheeled thing pulled by a dozen horses, it consisted of an iron-clad wooden platform upon which a tall beam like a ship's mast was affixed. Also shod in iron, the vertical beam had at its top the royal standard, a single gold Angevin lion on a crimson background. It was lofty enough to be seen from a long way off, and dust permitting, for a sizeable chunk of the army to be sure that Richard was alive and in command.

The host was formed into three columns. On our left flank, the men-at-arms marched in tight formation. Their spears and crossbows would be our defence against the Saracens. In the middle were the knights, stirrup-to-stirrup, our horses nose-to-tail. Closest to the shore, with the fleet on their right and safe from attack, marched a second column of infantry. During the day the men-at-arms in this line were to take turn and turn about with those on the left flank, to ensure that every soldier was exposed to danger no longer than necessary. The rearguard, tasked with protecting the at-risk wagon train, was today commanded by the duke of Burgundy. Richard had granted the honour to the prickly Duke Hugh in the hope it would improve relations between them.

By his own request, Rhys was with de Drune in the left-hand column, nearest the enemy. I knew he was in one of the first units and therefore slightly ahead to us, but between the dust and the close-marching ranks of the men-at-arms, he was impossible to see.

Perhaps an hour had passed since our departure, and the Saracens had not yet attacked. Hundreds of them, mamluks and heavy cavalry, were already in view beyond the men-at-arms. They rode through the scrubby bushes and low trees, on a course roughly parallel to our own. From further off, came the ominous sound of drums, and cymbals, and other instruments, an infernal racket that made me think of demons and eternal Hellfire.

'It will not be long,' said Richard, as if reading my mind.

We were both right and wrong. The Turks attacked, not with the intent we had expected. Bands of mamluks cantered towards the section of column to our left, loosing showers of arrows at the men-at-arms, but retreating without pressing home their attack. Nonetheless, I could not look away from the unfolding drama. Beyond reach of the enemy bows, raised up on our destriers, we knights had a good view of what was going on – that was, when dust clouds did not obscure everything from sight.

First would come the pounding of hooves, closely accompanied by the noise of drums and cymbals, and then came the mamluks, line after loosely-linked line. Arrows would arc up the moment they came within range of our men-at-arms, and continue as they rode along the column and then broke away into the safety of the treeline. The mamluks were every bit as skilful and dextrous as we had been told, able to ride and shoot at the same time; their well-trained mounts obeyed commands without use of the reins. It was an awe-inspiring display, but it was not relentless as we had expected. Periods of time would pass when the mamluks vanished from sight, allowing the men-at-arms to march unhindered.

Perhaps the enemy was assessing their resolve, Richard said, or softening them up for a major attack. He sent messengers down the line, but all returned with the same news, that no serious assaults were being made. His orders, that no one was to retaliate unless and until he gave permission, were also holding.

A second baking hour went by; we had now covered about two and a half miles, and still the enemy harassed rather than went for the kill.

There had been casualties among the infantry, but not many. The men-at-arms' thick gambesons, a weighty burden in the heat, afforded good protection against arrows.

Richard, who had been riding deep in thought, eventually opined that the hammer would not fall on us, in the vanguard. This was something I too had wondered, and yet the enemy did not appear to be assailing other sections of the column either. Even at the rear, where Duke Hugh and his knights protected the wagons, the Saracens' efforts had been moderate.

'What is Saladin playing at, sire?' I asked, irritable, every part of me burning up.

'Endeavouring to tire us out. To wear us down, sap our strength. A heavy attack *will* come – it is inconceivable that he will hold back on this, the first day of our march.'

'He is a wily devil, sire,' I said, thinking with longing of the grey, rain-laden skies of Ireland that I had so loathed as a boy.

'That he is, Rufus.' Richard palmed away sweat from his face. 'Which is why we must be patient, as the spider on its web waits for a fly.'

The task of a spider was a great deal easier than the ordeals faced by our army, I thought darkly. Arrow storms from the enemy. Unbearable heat. Crushing thirst.

The exhausting conditions made it hard to judge the passage of time. With no church bells to guide us, we relied on the angle of the sun in the sky. Another hour dragged past, slow as setting mortar. We rode on, our destriers trudging steadily over the bone-dry earth. Dust clouds surrounded us, covered us from head to toe, caked our throats. The mamluks came and went, just like gadflies. Their musicians, never visible, kept up their relentless assault on our ears with a cacophony of noise. Unit by unit, the men-at-arms close to the shoreline changed places with those who had been suffering the Saracens' attention.

During a lull in the fighting, we stopped to give our destriers water, and a brief respite from carrying us. It had been Rhys's brilliant idea to have a cobbler stitch a double-skinned, oiled leather trough; when the king saw it, neat and half the size of a typical stone trough, he had ordered one made for every two knights. I shared mine with Richard, and carried it strapped to the back of my saddle, along with the thin lengths of wood that fitted ingeniously inside. Swiftly I erected it, pouring half the contents of a spare waterskin into the rectangular, boxlike shape. Poor Pommers was so thirsty that if Richard had not been holding his reins, he would have barged me over to get to the blood-warm liquid.

'Fauvel should have gone first, sire,' I said, staring over Pommers' neck at the king.

He chuckled. 'You filled the trough, not I.'

Truly we were in this hell together, I thought.

Philip, who was riding at the back of our group with the other squires, came hurrying up to see if the king needed anything. He had bread, cheese, olives and wine, but Richard refused it all. Philip, caring as a mother hen, pressed him, even producing nut-covered pastries from the best bakery in Acre. They were past their best, a little crushed, and the honey within oozing out the sides.

'It is too hot to eat,' said the king, waving a hand.

Philip glanced at me. 'Rufus?'

I shook my head. Food was the furthest thing from my mind. I pointed to the column of men-at-arms, which had also halted. 'See if you can find Rhys over there. Tell him the pastries are from the king. He will eat every last one, or I am a Saracen.'

Tickled, Richard ordered Philip to do just that, and to distribute the rest of the food among the soldiers. 'The wine at least will get drunk,' he said.

We were about to clamber back onto our destriers when I spied a rider approaching. He was coming hard, bent low over his mount's neck, and spurring it every few strides. Whatever news he carried was important.

'Sire,' I said.

He looked. Smiled grimly. 'Saladin has made his move.'

John FitzLucas was the name of the knight. Young, eager, his face badly sunburned, he was one of the king's messengers. He had been sent to the very rear of the column, a thankless task, constantly riding through the dust thrown up by our passage. FitzLucas had already done it twice without complaint, on each occasion bringing us no news of import.

This time was different, I decided. The king had been right about Saladin.

'Sire!' FitzLucas called from fifty paces out. 'Sire!'

Richard sprang into the saddle before he even reached us, at the same time issuing orders for the mesnie to prepare to ride. Collapsing the now-empty leather trough and reattaching it behind my saddle, I retrieved my lance. Long, iron-tipped, awkward, it had thus far been nothing but deadweight to carry. Now I might get to use it at last.

'What news, John?' called the king.

FitzLucas eased his mount to a trot, then a walk. He was coated in dust from head to toe, and when he tried to speak, only a croak came out.

The king urged his destrier forward and after FitzLucas had pulled off his helm, offered him his own waterskin. Not until FitzLucas had swallowed several mouthfuls would he permit him to speak.

'My thanks, sire,' said FitzLucas, bobbing his head. 'The Saracens have fallen on the wagon train at a section of narrow path where the wains have to go in single file. They are wreaking fearful slaughter.'

'Where is the duke of Burgundy?' demanded Richard.

'He and his knights have lagged behind, sire. They were nowhere to be seen when I rode to bring you this counsel.'

'God's legs, I knew that fool would not listen to me!' Richard bellowed. 'Art ready, Rufus?'

'Yes, sire.' I was already fumbling with the strap that held my helmet to my saddle horn.

The king signalled to his trumpeter, and as the notes died away, shouted, 'Saladin has struck. We ride for the wagon train!'

We formed up, with Richard in the front rank, and I beside him. On his other side were de Chauvigny and de Béthune. To my right, I had FitzLucas, Thorne and several others. A dozen wide, our formation was. However hot, tired and sweat-covered we were, nothing could conceal the eagerness in our posture, nor the tightness with which we gripped our skyward-pointing lances. Sensing our excitement, the destriers stepped from side to side, barging into one another.

'With me!' Richard pricked spurs and led off.

I followed. Helmet on, the clamour around me reduced to a more pleasant level. That was the only good thing I could say. The weight was brutal, and my head, squeezed tight, felt as if it had been shoved into a Turkish bathhouse. I could see only what lay straight in front of Pommers. I sensed Richard close on my left hand, however, and heard his Fauvel's pounding hooves. I had the same awareness of FitzLucas on my right.

I felt no fear at how close the two were, but rather a mad exhilaration. This was what we had trained for. This was what our destriers knew. God help the Saracens when we arrived, I thought.

Through all-enveloping dust we trotted, men-at-arms now on our right, cheering us as we passed, and rank after rank of knights on our left. Many a solemn salute we received from them, but we gave no acknowledgement, so intent was our purpose. The royal standard was left behind, and then the Templars, and after them the knights and nobles from Anjou and Poitou, and the Hospitallers.

Richard reined his destrier to a walk, and we did the same. Desperate the situation might be at the wagons, but if our mounts arrived exhausted, we would be of no use. I looked left; we were alongside the knights from Brittany. The wagon train was not far.

'Do you hear it?' asked the king.

Pricking my ears, I thought I made out the ring of arms, and the shrieking of wounded men. 'Yes, sire,' I answered.

'Curse the faithless ones. Curse Hugh for being a stiff-necked, arrogant fool!'

Despite Richard's anger and obvious impatience, we continued to walk our destriers for another while. Only when their breathing was even, their nostrils no longer flared, did he give the order to trot once more. Again we rode, and soon the noise of battle was loud in our ears. I heard a captain shout to his men to stay where they were, to hold positions unless told otherwise. I tried to see, but the dust had been replaced by a swirling sea mist.

'With me!' Richard cried all at once.

We eased straight into a canter. Tendrils of grey obscured my vision; the drumming of hooves filled my ears. Pommers thundered beneath me, his movement shivering the lance in my right fist. Despite the mist and the breeze, I was hot, so hot, but I did not care. Excitement gripped every part of my being. More than three years since I had taken the cross, I was riding to battle with the king. My lord. My brother-in-arms.

The murk eased, licked away by air currents off the sea, and opening up the view to our left. Trees pressed in close towards the shore, narrowing the path as FitzLucas had said. Of the column of men-at-arms that should have been on our right, there was no sign. The middle column, here made up of wagons and non-combatants on foot, had disintegrated. Carts lay on their sides, uppermost wheels turning idly, or at a standstill, their mules slaughtered in the traces. Still more were pointed seaward, or indeed moving in that direction, urged on by their frantic drivers, and harassed by score upon score of Saracen horsemen: mamluks and heavy cavalry. Bodies lay everywhere in pools of tell-tale crimson: carters, townsmen, laundrywomen, fortune-seekers, an occasional man-at-arms or Turk. The wounded, of which there were also many, wailed and screamed at the sky, and called on God for help.

He was nowhere to be seen.

But Richard had arrived.

The enemy, whooping and slaying, had no idea.

The king issued no command; he couched his lance and charged. Fauvel shot forward like a lightning bolt. I followed, desperate not to be left behind. The thunder of noise, of galloping hooves, told me that every man in the mesnie was with us.

We fell on the unsuspecting Turks with cold, controlled fury. I saw Richard slay the first. His lance struck with such force that his target was ripped from the saddle, impaled through and through. The king dropped the now-useless lance, and drew his sword. He bellowed a war cry, and galloped on.

A short distance behind – Richard had outstripped me in his eagerness – I picked my own enemy, a Saracen cavalryman in a spiked helmet. He was still gazing in horror at his comrade killed by the king when my lance hit. God forgive me, but it was a sweet strike. He rose into the air, like a piece of meat on a skewer, and then I released my grip and let lance and corpse tumble to the dirt.

Right hand tugging free my sword, I searched for Richard. Utterly possessed by battle rage, he was wait for no one. Fear pricked me. The advantage was with us, but that did not mean a lone knight was invulnerable. I spurred Pommers forward, eager to find him. Then a mamluk on my right took aim with his bow, and my belly twisted. I was an easy target, and he was too far to reach before he loosed.

I sawed on the reins. Pommers, great heart that he was, twisted in the tightest of circles, and charged the mamluk. Fear took him, and he loosed, too early. The arrow shot past me, close, but it missed. I roared with delight and relief, and hewed the man's arm off at the shoulder. A look of stunned disbelief twisted his brown face; an instant later, the pain hit. I wheeled Pommers, uncaring of his screams and the spraying blood, and chased in the direction I had seen Richard go.

I cut down a Turkish cavalryman, and rode around a wagon that had rolled over entirely. Of its four mules, two were standing, another was dead, and the last had a broken foreleg. The lifeless body of its driver lay half-free, half-trapped under one of its timber sides. Arrows hummed and whizzed through the air around me, but they were badly aimed, and the frightened mamluks loosing them unprepared to stand their ground. Everywhere I stared, the Saracens were already trying to flee.

Thorne appeared, his sword red down its entire length. We saluted one another. I shouted had he seen the king, and he pointed his weapon at the sea. In unspoken agreement, we both rode that way.

A trio of Turkish cavalrymen came at us. We charged them stirrup to stirrup. Cut from better cloth than most, they did not falter. Two had spears, and one a curved sword. The gap closed; I picked my man, the-left-hand most of the three. We hit, and at once our destriers' great weight made a difference. My opponent's horse was driven back, staggering; he was still essaying not to lose his seat when my blade took off half his head. I looked right; Thorne had hacked away the spear tip of his enemy and was now driving at him while the man, helpless but for the ruined wooden shaft, tried desperately to draw his sword. He failed. Thorne ran him through.

The third mamluk wheeled his mount and rode off like the Devil himself was in pursuit.

A laugh rumbled in my dry throat.

'See, the king!' cried Thorne. 'On the beach.'

Again we made in Richard's direction. He was still on his own, but thank Christ, no harm had come to him. Bodies were scattered in his wake; riderless horses trotted hither and thither. In the time it took us to arrive, which was not long, he killed another Saracen, and drove off a party of four who had been attacking a large, high-sided wagon.

We had reached the shoreline. The ships in the lead flotilla were visible, but too far out to be able to help. Plenty of wains had actually been driven into the water by their terrified drivers, although it had not saved them from the vengeful Saracens. Not all had been attacked, however. A short distance to our left, a number of knights had formed a defensive line in front of some wagons. I could not make out the insignia on their shields.

Richard had seen us. He rode closer, and indicated the knights I had seen. 'Some of the French did what I asked at least. A mark of silver says that Duke Hugh is not one of them.'

'I will not take that wager, sire.'

Thorne had a hand raised against the sun. He peered. 'I think des Barres is there, sire.'

Richard said nothing. The ill feeling he bore against des Barres continued; the two had not spoken since Sicily. It was a sorry state of affairs, for the knight was a likeable type, and twice the man most of his fellows were.

I counted the wagons behind the French knights; there were more than a dozen, and they were the big, heavy-axled ones that carried flour or grain. 'See how many wains they have saved, sire.' Mischief took me, and I added, 'If it is indeed des Barres there, he has done valiant work.'

'It *is* des Barres, I am sure of it,' said Thorne confidently.

I noted the insignia on the shield of the group's leader, two black horizontal bars separated by a white, and said, 'Thorne has the right of it, sire.'

'Curse you for a pair of nagging women,' said Richard, but there was a note of amusement in his voice. 'If it is indeed des Barres, I shall make things right with him later. There are still Saracens to harry.' He pointed to a pair of our knights who had somehow got separated from the rest. A band of mamluks were circling them, and raining down arrows. Struck twice, the nearest destrier stumbled.

Again Richard took off.

It was as well that he had seen the two, for one proved to be de Chauvigny and the other de Béthune. The mamluks fled long before we reached them. Richard stayed long enough to ensure that neither man was unhurt, and to see de Béthune onto the destrier of a slain knight. Then he rallied together a score or so of the mesnie, and ordered us to the chase again. This time, we would be riding inland.

The Saracens, who had suffered heavy casualties, fled before us as doves scatter upward, wings clattering, when a cat pounces among them.

So exhilarating was the pursuit – off the beach, past the wreckage of the wagon train, into the broken ground – hacking and killing, many of our number would have kept riding. As I said to Thorne when we paused to wet our parched throats, they would have hunted the accursed race to their very camp and there tried to capture Saladin himself. Which would not have been a good idea, we both agreed, for the number of Saracens there would have seen us slain to a man.

Nonetheless, it took several commands from Richard, passed on by myself and those around him, for all of our fellows to rein in. By now, we had almost reached the hills in which the bulk of the enemy army had to be. Content that his order was being obeyed, the king turned his horse and rode back to the beach alone. He did not want an escort.

Thorne and I were too busy riding to and fro, gathering together the mesnie once more, to give it much consideration. To anyone who complained at the order to cease the pursuit, I declared that only part of the enemy's host had attacked. A complete victory could not be won here, and our destriers' energy had to be preserved against the time when that opportunity *did* present itself.

No one questioned my authority.

When an amused de Béthune congratulated me about this soon after, I was quite surprised.

'Truly, Rufus, art a leader now,' said de Béthune. Helmet off, he was using his arming cap to wipe his purple, streaming-with-sweat face. 'Cometh the hour, cometh the man.'

A little embarrassed, I said, 'I was only following the king's command.'

'That you were, but your tone brooked no refusal. It was well done.'

Delighted, for I held de Béthune in high regard, I muttered my thanks.

We made camp by the River Kishon, and there, thanks to Abu, found large cisterns that proved to be full of good water. The grass and earth close by had been flattened over a large area, telling us that Saladin's army had rested at least one night in the same location. Rhys, who like de Drune, had come through the fighting unscathed, declared that it was strange to be setting up our tents where our enemies had, and resting our heads where theirs had lain perhaps just the night before. I felt the same way.

Before Richard had even taken off his armour, he sent for the duke of Burgundy. Hugh arrived, also still clad in his battle gear, and clearly annoyed by the summons. With no attempt to find privacy, the king sharply reprimanded him for his failure to protect the wagon train. Scores of men had been slain, and many wagons destroyed. Never again would Hugh be entrusted with its care. Richard gave the duke no opportunity to answer, but dismissed him from his presence.

Hugh's face was a picture of outraged pride. Although he had merited the dressing down, his expression boded ill for any future cooperation. What a pity it was, I thought, that Henri of Champagne was not the leader of the French contingent.

My hunch about where Richard had gone on his own was proved correct later, when des Barres came to the royal pavilion. The only French knight among us at dinner, his presence was even more noticeable because of the treatment meted out to Hugh of Burgundy. The king greeted des Barres warmly, and they exchanged the kiss of peace. He was invited to sit by Richard's right hand, and the two talked much as we ate a light meal of bread, cheese and olives. The unrelenting heat meant that few men were truly hungry, despite the exertions of the day. The same could not be said of our thirst. Exhilarated by the manner in which the Saracens had been driven off, we drank wine as if it were nectar, the fabled drink of the gods worshipped by the pagan Greeks. Lucky for us, the king ordered it well-diluted, else we would all have been in a terrible state the next day.

If darkness took away the threat of the Turks, we were not to be left unassailed. Never have I seen so many massive spiders – tarantulas, Abu called them. Swarms of the hairy-legged creatures appeared as the night drew on, creeping into tents, under blankets, into empty boots and shoes. Their bite was terribly painful, judging by the cries and curses of the afflicted. These were not the only devilish creatures we saw. There were numerous poignanz too, fierce eight-legged creatures with a long, curved-over tail at the end of which was a barbed stinger. These scorpions, as they were known, varied in size, some scarcely the length of a child's finger, others that would fill a man's palm. Their sting injected an agonising poison. According to Abu, it could kill children and those who were sick or debilitated.

Abu's knowledge extended a great deal further than the fauna of Outremer. He seemed happy to answer my endless questions as we searched the tent. He knew the geography, and where the best water was to be found – the cisterns at the Kishon were proof of that. Yet it was his skill with languages that had Richard order him to his side late that night, long after we had finished hunting for tarantulas and scorpions. Curious, I went with him.

The king had decided to interrogate the prisoners taken that day himself. Realising his purpose as we came into his presence, I felt for Abu, who was still unaware. None of the captives were willing to talk, and Richard wasted no time. The least-important-looking Saracen was dragged forward and executed while the others watched. Then, directed by the stone-faced king, a grey-with-terror Abu told the rest that their fate would be far worse if they did not answer his questions. If they obeyed, their lives would be spared. Brutal but effective, this approach saw the prisoners sing like canaries. We did not find out much – none of the Turks were high-ranking – other than Saladin intended to harass our column as much as possible.

It did not matter how many times I whispered in Abu's ear that he was in no danger. The poor lad shook with fear throughout, and did not cease until we reached the safety of my tent afterwards. I offered him wine, but good Muslim that he was, he would not take it. I sat him down and told him again that he was under my protection, that his wellbeing was in my hands. The irony was not lost on me, that I should care for one of the accursed race, and yet be content to see others killed out-of-hand. But I was not alone. De Drune liked Abu; so too did Thorne. Even Rhys was being won over by his friendliness and easy manner. I had heard the pair deep in conversation outside the tent after I had retired on at least one occasion.

It did not take long to decide that when the time came to leave Outremer, I would free Abu. I told him as much the morning after Richard's interrogation of the prisoners, and was touched again by the tears that sprang to his eyes. He kissed my hand, oblivious to my discomfiture, and told me I was a kind and generous man.

'Jihad fi sabil Allah,' Abu repeated several times.

'What does that mean?' I asked.

'You strive in the path of God, sir.'

Uneasy, I said, 'I am not of your faith.'

He smiled. 'No, sir, but there is goodness in you. You try to do the right thing, praise be to God.'

I remembered Henry, whose throat I had cut to save my own skin, and thought, not always. Finding Abu's gaze still on me, I managed a stiff nod. 'You also have a kind heart.'

Pleased, he gave me a little formal bow. 'I merely act as God commands.'

I was struck by how similar, in some ways at least, his religion was to my own. And yet his people, the accursed race, and my own, the Christians, were locked in a bitter war, the outcome of which was still by no means certain.

CHAPTER XXIV

The next day, the twenty-sixth of August, recognising the travails endured by all, Richard ordered the army to travel only a short distance to Caïphas. It was frustrating to travel so slowly, he said to me, but the extreme conditions meant he dared move no faster. 'Now is the time for prudence. One rash decision could mean the end of the army, and that must not happen. Defeating Saladin and taking Jerusalem is all that matters,' he said grimly. 'We will wait at Caïphas for those who have lagged behind during the march, and the main body of the fleet. Then, rested, resupplied, our waterskins full, we will set out again.'

The two days afforded not just a welcome time of rest, but an opportunity for men-at-arms and knights to discard non-essential equipment. The foot soldiers especially had suffered during the march, carrying as they were not only food and water, but all their worldly belongings.

'If it cannot be eaten or drunk on this journey,' Thorne declared sagely, 'it is not worth having.'

'What about weapons and armour?' De Drune could always think of the awkward question. 'How will you fight the Saracens, let alone attack Jerusalem, with your bare hands?'

Thorne gave him an irritated look. 'We all need our war gear, obviously. I meant everything in addition. Mirrors, gewgaws, personal items, and so on.'

I thought of the lock of hair I had coaxed from Joanna before our farewell. As the fillet given me by Alienor had been for many years until it had sadly been lost, it was the most precious thing I owned. Light as a feather, it nestled always at my breast in a pouch of leather. Even if the golden strands had been made from lead, and a hundred times heavier, I thought, their burden would not have been too much. I imagined holding Joanna in my arms, and kissing her, and . . .

I put away the thought before it became too much to bear.

On the twenty-eighth of August, our march recommenced. To avoid the worst of the heat, we set out hours before dawn, and would make camp by sext, when the sun was at its highest. The formation was almost the same as before, two columns of infantry with the knights safely in the middle, but with one difference. Now, as it was to be on most days, the military orders rode in the vanguard and rearguard. Their discipline was second to none, Richard declared, and they knew the enemy like no other.

Saladin's army had suffered a setback during their ambush of the wagon train, but their resolve remained undimmed. Scouting troops of mamluks were never far from our lines, even at night, so news of our departure each morn was known from the outset. Attacks would begin almost at once. Continuous throughout the day, varying in strength from mild but annoying to full-scale, lethal efforts, they had all to be resisted with fortitude and determination lest the enemy sensed weakness and went for the kill.

Although our progress continued, casualties mounted little by little. Maddened by the oven-like temperature of their gambesons, some men-at-arms stripped down to their tunics. Inevitably, they were struck by well-aimed mamluk arrows. Others were unlucky, shafts finding unarmoured spots at top or bottom of gambeson. The majority of our losses, however, resulted from the brutal, unrelenting force that was the sun. If as a callow boy, someone had told me that men could drop dead from heat exhaustion, I would have laughed in their face.

That day I saw it happen a score of times at least.

The wretches who succumbed were given the swiftest of burials by comrades desperate not to be left to the mercy of the Saracens, and abandoned. No marker they had, no words said by a priest, just an unmarked grave in the middle of a barren wasteland. It was a poor end, I decided, for men who had given up their lives to help retake Jerusalem from the Saracens.

Our journey through this region was not altogether terrible. There was a profusion of wildlife – francolin and partridge, hares and even an occasional gazelle – amid the tall grasses and thorny bushes that covered the ground close to the sea. Astride our horses, knights could not avail ourselves of this bounty, but the foot soldiers, especially those in the shoreward column, had much sport with spear and bow. Dinner that night for many would be a feast.

Another advantage were the steep hills on our left, which prevented the Saracens from attacking us with the ease they did on flatter terrain. The road we followed was an old Roman way according to Abu, although long since fallen into disrepair. After passing around the foot of Mount Carmel, we proceeded towards Capharnaum, which had been destroyed by the enemy, and on to the castle of Destroit, built by the Templars. There we halted, weary beyond measure, and made camp.

As darkness fell, we suffered more 'attacks' from the dreaded tarantulas and scorpions. Thanks in part to Abu, men were now wise to an effective deterrent: noise. Each night then, a dreadful din arose from our camp, and went on for an age. Such a beating of helmets and headgear, of casks and saddles and heavy cloths, shields and round bucklers, basins and pots and pans – in short, anything a man could get hold of – was never heard in all of Christendom.

When silence finally did fall, and men began to think about retiring, the calm was broken by a nightly ritual. 'Sanctum Sepulchrum adjuva! Holy Sepulchre, help us!' It was the cry of a mendicant friar known to most, a man whose wits had long since been curdled by the sun, but his zeal was infectious. Thousands of voices would take up the cry, until our very camp seemed to be one great choir uttering the same one-line refrain. Three times it would rise up, and if one looked, it was possible to see by the light of the campfires, men with hands stretched skyward, and tears of religious fervour running down their faces.

Abu would stare at us during these moments with complete incomprehension, and Rhys was wont to say how the Saracens must be laughing in their tents.

I would nod and smile in agreement, and palm my gritty eyes, hoping the noise would soon end, that I might get some much-needed rest.

Two nights and two days the army rested at Destroit. The Saracens did not try to attack our well-defended camp, with its deep ditch and earthen rampart, which was manned at all times by triple the usual number of sentries. Supplies reached us from the fleet, along with men who rapidly became known as 'the lazy ones', soldiers who had previously managed to avoid setting out from Acre with the army, but since been rousted from hostelries. The injured and some of those exhausted by the heat and lack of water were loaded onto ships, that they might be transported in comfort further down the coast.

It was thirteen miles from Destroit to Merla, our next destination. I had been there already with Richard, who after one night's rest had been keen to spy out the land while the troops stayed in camp. A ball-tightening ride that was, and one that by rights should never have been undertaken, risking as it was deadly ambush by the enemy. It passed off without a hitch, however. Made late in the day and into the evening, to try and avoid the Saracens' attention, the king and I with ten score knights had travelled without a single casualty. We were seen by mamluks, but allowed to pass unhindered. They were scared of us, declared Richard, delighted. There was no way of knowing if he was right, or if Saladin had a trick up his sleeve, but it helped with my nerves.

After only a few hours' rest at Merla, we returned, reaching Destroit as the sun crept over the horizon on the thirtieth of August. While the sentries cheered us into camp, I pulled aside their captain and instructed him to spread the tale of what Richard had done far and wide. It would be a boost for morale, I said, thinking anything that helped men in this harsh world of scorching temperatures and death, baked earth and blood, was welcome.

When Garnier de Nablus heard the news, he came to remonstrate with the king, telling him that such risks were unnecessary, and jeopardised the entire campaign against Saladin. Mightily amused rather than angered, Richard slapped his thigh and told de Nablus that his life had never been in peril. Although we had come through unscathed, the king was lying. We all knew it, but his fearlessness and daring were an inspiration. He seemed invulnerable, which gave us confidence, and a belief that a final victory would be ours. His announcement to de Nablus, that together with the poulains we would lead the vanguard, delighted us all. Shouts of acclaim rose into the fast-brightening air.

De Nablus saw the passion in my face and those of the mesnie, and shook his head in resignation. 'May God keep his hand over you always, sire,' he said, and departed.

Richard's confidence and arrogance did have limits, however. Before the army moved off, he made his confession to Bishop Hubert of Salisbury and afterwards publicly asked for God's blessings on the day's endeavour. Hubert granted it right willingly, which lifted ordinary men's hearts, and sent crack-pated individuals like the chanting friar into ecstasies. Fresh cries of 'Sanctum Sepulchrum adjuva!' went up as the army marched from the camp.

The day's journey, our longest yet, was brutal, and a great deal worse than the one before. The never-ending sound of the Saracens' cursed drums, cymbals, horns, rattles, tambors and flutes – thanks to Abu, I could now distinguish the various types – was infuriating. Their attacks were frequent and disruptive, and arrows flew in such numbers that they darkened the sky. Our pace, which was never fast anyway, slowed to that of a hobbling greybeard. The temperature, which had not dropped much overnight, rose as the interminable hours passed, and by sext, it was hotter than the previous day.

Men-at-arms were dropping like flies in the columns on either side of us, not from arrows, but the heat. A number of knights had fallen, unconscious, from their destriers. They had had to be tied into the saddle, and rode now like nodding corpses. I myself had a pounding headache, which was not from wine, and felt as if I were being slowly cooked alive in my armour. Richard was also suffering – his sunburned face was drenched in sweat, and he spoke only when spoken to – but he remained in full control of the situation. Deciding that too many men were collapsing, he ordered a halt. The worst afflicted were helped to the shoreline, and from there ferried out by small craft to the fleet.

After that, the king commanded that the army stop to rest every quarter of a mile. Even a week before, in Acre, this decision would have seemed ridiculous, but now it was received with overwhelming approval. We knights were no less thankful than the men-at-arms. To conserve our destriers' energy, we dismounted during the halts. Abu, who had asked to travel with me on his mule – he was afraid of going with the wagon train, because of the danger of attacks by his own kind, but also because the drivers reviled him as one of the cruel, hated people – took the opportunity to express his opinion of the ordinary foot soldiers.

'I have seen men with ten arrows sticking out of their gambesons, sir.' Abu mangled the second last word, which made me smile. Typically, he repeated it a couple of times until he was happy with its pronunciation. 'Yet still they advance without leaving the ranks. I cannot help but admire the wonderful patience displayed by these men. They bear the most wearying fatigue without having any share in the management of affairs or deriving any personal advantage.'

'They have little choice but to continue,' I observed dryly. 'Stop for too long and a Saracen arrow will take them. That, or exhaustion and thirst.'

His teeth flashed white. 'You speak true, sir, but they are so resolute.'

'They *are* stout-hearted, but the king's leadership also inspires,' I said proudly. I was not alone in looking to Richard when my spirits wavered in the melting heat.

'Malik Rik is a true leader.' There was no mistaking the admiration in Abu's voice. 'But he takes a lot of risks. Your ride to Merla could easily have turned to disaster.'

I searched for the threat in Abu's words, or in his expression. There seemed to be none. He was not that devious, I decided. 'It could,' I admitted. 'It is not in his nature to avoid risk, however.'

'Do you not worry about him?'

I made a helpless gesture. 'Yes, but I cannot prevent him from acting as he does. All I can do is go with him, so I am there when the danger strikes.' I felt self-conscious saying the words.

'You would lay down your life for Malik Rik, sir?'

'In a heartbeat. As would the vast majority of his army.' I was embroidering the truth a little with the latter. Exceptions included the devious French, I thought, and probably most of the poulains.

Abu said nothing.

'If you were a soldier, would you die for Saladin?'

There was no hesitation. 'I would not.'

'And his men?'

'Some would, sir, I have no doubt – his bodyguard, and the best of his heavy cavalry. A number of the mamluks, perhaps. But not the rest. They are levied troops, most of them, not personal followers. That is one of the only advantages your king has over Salah al-Dīn.'

I bristled. '*Only* advantages? We have thousands of knights and disciplined foot soldiers. A huge fleet, and siege weapons that will batter down the walls of any city. Saladin has none of those.'

'No, sir. But he has that,' said Abu, and pointed at the sun. 'He also has the mamluks' stinging assault – the rush forward, shooting arrows, and the quick retreat – it is annoying, and effective, especially if your knights charge heedlessly after and the mamluk withdrawal becomes an attack. He can deprive your army of water too. When he realises that Malik Rik intends to march inland from what you call Ascalon, Salah al-Dīn will order every well on the road to Jerusalem poisoned.

How then will you march, even though it be just thirty-five miles?'

We stared at each other, I quivering with fury, he calm as a stone carving.

I would not strike him, I decided. He had spoken the truth after all. The weather was a brutal enemy to us, and the mamluks were potentially lethal every time they attacked. The king had chosen our route as the lesser of two evils, but what faced us after Ascalon might yet prove insurmountable.

'Richard will defeat Saladin before then. The way to Jerusalem will lie open,' I snarled. 'I am sure of it.'

'Yes, sir.' The shutters went down in Abu's eyes; his expression grew inscrutable.

I did not press him further; there was no point.

The discussion left me uneasy, however, and as the day dragged on, I came to the conclusion that the sooner we met Saladin in battle, the better.

Like the king said, though, it had to be on our terms.

Later that day, Richard took another calculated risk. A concerted Saracen attack had brought our advance to a standstill. Short charges by groups of knights had proved ineffective. He determined to lead forward the entire contingent of poulains, some four hundred strong. We in the mesnie were to be left behind, tired as we were, he said, after the ride to and from Merla.

I protested vigorously, and I was not alone. Our efforts were in vain.

Off they rode. The moment the enemy were close enough, the king charged with all the speed Fauvel could muster. The mamluks broke and fled, as he had expected. Laughing, Richard pursued them for a distance before he looked to either side. To his surprise and anger, he found himself alone. Sluggards, perhaps, wary of the enemy, more likely, the poulains had reined in some time before.

Unperturbed, the king had continued the attack alone, chasing the Turks half a mile into the hinterland. When Richard told me this upon his return, he alternated between laughter at the bizarre situation, and anger at the poulains' lack of spine.

I, on the other hand, was eaten up with worry. 'You could have been captured, sire, or killed.'

'I *was* almost taken,' he said, his sun-cracked lips quirking. 'If Fauvel were not so swift, I would now be sitting, a prisoner, in Saladin's tent.'

'Please, sire,' I said. 'You must not act so again.'

His eyes sparked. '*Must* not, Rufus?'

I bowed my head, but I continued, 'I speak from loyalty and concern, sire. If you were slain, this army would disintegrate. The same would happen if you were made captive.'

He made a sound of pure exasperation.

I hesitated, and then said, 'It would be a disaster, sire.'

'Sweet Jesu, am I always to be plagued by well-meant advice?'

I dropped my gaze, wary of his tempestuous anger, and waited.

'What you say is in all likelihood true,' he said after a moment. 'Art thou happy now, Rufus?' He was only partly jesting.

'I seek to ensure you remain uninjured and free, sire, no more.'

'I know.' He clouted me, hard, like an older brother does. 'I am grateful for it.'

Wanting to be sure, I risked asking, 'So you will not charge the enemy alone, sire?'

He laughed. 'I will not.'

Thankful, I relaxed. Too early, I found out an instant later.

'The poulains will not ride with me in future. It shall be the mesnie by my side when I charge the Turks again, eh, Rufus?'

'If you lead, I will follow, sire,' I said.

Another great clout, and a happy smile.

I smiled back, deciding that I should have known better. Preventing the king from entering battle, his natural element, was futile. Easier it would be to part the Red Sea, as Moses had once done.

By the afternoon, we had reached Crocodile River, so-called because two knights had apparently been devoured there some time before. I was a little disappointed to see none of the fearsome, scaled creatures, but the ordinary soldiers were not. Stripping down to their undergarments by the hundred, they flung themselves with delighted cries into the murky, blood-warm water.

The march was not so terrible, I decided, if the troops could end each day like this.

Another pleasant diversion came that evening when, with Abu as guide, I visited Caesarea, a former Roman city on the coast near Crocodile River. Never before had I seen an aqueduct, a circus where horse racing had long ago taken place, nor even an open-air swimming pool right at the sea's edge, built for some long-dead king. While Rhys lounged in the shade of an ancient, still-entire storage house close to the race track, I wandered with Abu, delighting in the incredible ruins.

My excitement and voluble descriptions were such that the next day, the thirty-first of August, Richard left off supervising the unloading of supplies from the fleet and came to see for himself. He too was impressed, especially by the circus. When several of the mesnie suggested a race there, he gave permission at once. The sight of four comrades – Thorne was one – galloping down the long, narrow track and around the sharp turn at the end, before pounding back towards us and sweeping around to continue the circuit – would long remain a favourite memory of our time in Outremer.

It helped that Thorne came in first, winning me fifty silver pennies from a disgruntled de Drune. He had bet on de Béthune, a wiser choice than mine, given his light stature and swift-footed rouncy. Disaster struck, however, when de Béthune's mount stumbled at the final turn, and was unable to regain the lead from a fist-waving, triumphant Thorne.

Harsh reality resumed on the first of September, when our journey resumed. The army broke camp long before dawn, and began to inch south. As the hours passed and the malevolent sun climbed into a cloudless sky, the temperature rose to heights to which I could never grow accustomed. Always the dust-laden air was thick with the smell of unwashed bodies, horse manure and human excreta. Preceded by the hideous clamour of their instruments, the Saracens' attacks began. They continued for the duration of the day's journey. Our soldiers died in large numbers, whether from arrow, heat, or thirst. The loss of horses, at whom the Turks aimed many shafts, was horrific, especially among the military orders. Despite the danger from the still-close mamluks, the men – famished from lack of food – stripped the carcasses to bare bones with the rapidity of starving wolves.

Over and again, the grand master at the rear asked leave to launch retaliatory attacks against the Saracens. Each time the king declined. When the right opportunity arose, and it was rare, Richard himself ordered and led a charge. The reprieves granted by these from the ever-attentive, gadfly-like Saracens were short, I am sad to say.

The distance covered this day was only three miles. My mind baked by the searing temperatures, my remaining purpose to keep the king from harm, while doing the same for myself and Pommers meant that day and the next became a blur. Some events stood out in my mind afterwards, though. How we camped at a place with the unwholesome name of Dead River. How I had the pleasure of watching de Chauvigny slay an enormous Turkish emir in single combat, a brute whose lance was twice as thick as an ordinary man's. When he fell from his horse, I swear the ground shook. As he died, we cheered, but the Saracens wailed and cried his name, 'Ayas Estoï!'

On the third of September, I think it was, forced by the impassable terrain close to the sea, we cut inland, searching for a road parallel to the coast. Wary of attack, the king had us march and ride in formation so close there was barely room to breathe, let alone wield our weapons. An apple or a plum tossed into our ranks could not have missed. The Saracens fell on us regardless, and we had a hard time of it. To relieve the pressure, Richard led a charge against the enemy, and was wounded in the side by a dart. I it was who seized Fauvel's reins and dragged his head around so that he would follow Pommers back to safety.

Praise God and all His saints, the king was not badly hurt. The arrow had punched through mail and gambeson, but had only caused a superficial wound beneath.

'The pain from the surgeon's vinegar hurts worse,' the king declared in a voice designed to carry.

The nearest men-at-arms, for whom the remark had been intended, cheered. 'Coeur de Lion! Lionheart!' The cry carried on down the column, audible despite the fearful din made by the Turks' cursedly never-silent instruments.

Richard, smiling, stood to receive the acclaim. Fussing, the surgeon wrapped a linen bandage around his middle. 'You must rest now, sire,' he said.

The king laughed. 'There will be time for that when I am dead.'

The surgeon blanched, quite a feat in the baking temperature. 'Please, sire, do not even think such thoughts.'

'I jest!' cried Richard. 'I am going nowhere – unless it be to Jerusalem!'

'Jerusalem!' shouted the men-at-arms. 'Jerusalem!'

Luckily, the lack of food did not affect we knights of the mesnie, who had access to the royal provisions. The ordinary soldiers were in dire straits, however, and desperate times see desperate measures. It had become the norm for knights whose horses were on the point of foundering to slaughter them, and sell the fresh meat to the troops. According to de Drune, the flesh was rich-tasting, and complimented greatly by cooking with bacon. I was not tempted.

There was trouble that evening, because the more unscrupulous knights with meat to offer had racked up the prices. The indignant, hungry soldiers fell to threatening the sellers, stealing meat and brawling among themselves. Such unrest was terrible for morale, and hearing of it, Richard acted at once. Orders were issued that any knight who gave over his dead mount without charge would receive a fresh horse from the king's own troop.

Peace restored, he considered the letter that had just come in from a mamluk bearing the white staff of a herald. It was a reply to his message to Saladin earlier that day, in which Richard had requested a meeting to discuss peace terms. Nothing but a ploy to stall the enemy's attacks until we cleared our next obstacle, the thick forest of Arsur, it was, according to the king, worth a try.

Clad in a short-sleeved tunic, he sat upon a three-legged stool outside his tent, and sipped fresh pomegranate juice. Where the fruit had miraculously come from, I had no idea. I was just grateful to be offered some by Philip. It tasted better than any wine.

'Saladin agrees to a meeting. It shall be the day after morrow.' Richard indicated the parchment at his feet. 'He will send his brother, as I asked.'

My interest pricked at the mention of Saphadin, whom I had liked. 'What else does it say, sire?'

'Just that. Saladin is a cagey one.' Richard drained his cup, and Philip moved in to refill it.

'Does he really think you mean to sue for peace, sire?' de Béthune enquired.

'I doubt it,' said Richard drily. 'But he is curious, and a delay may suit him also.'

I did not like to think of the reason for that: reinforcements. Abu seemed certain that more were coming from Egypt. 'Can I be one of the embassy, sire?'

'I see your eagerness, Rufus! You shall go. Bring that Saracen lad you saved also. Humphrey de Toron shall interpret for me, but it would be no harm having two sets of ears who understand Arabic.'

Surprised and pleased, I asked, 'You are going, sire?'

'After all the tales of Saphadin I have heard from you and the others, I would not miss this chance.'

'Do not forget de Chauvigny and me, sire,' said de Béthune.

'Very well,' said Richard. 'Six of us it shall be.'

A day of well-earned rest followed, the fourth of September, during which the majority simply lay in the shade and slept like dead men. I spent much of it tossing and turning, hot and sweaty. Do not let it be quartan fever, I prayed in the lucid moments. Rhys was concerned enough to fetch Ralph Besace. There was talk of bloodletting, but fortunately I had wits enough then to refuse the procedure.

'It is heat exhaustion,' I croaked, voicing my main hope. 'That is all.'

Besace tutted and protested, but Rhys had seen I was clear-minded, and ordered him away. The rest of the day, Rhys sat by my bed like a mother with a sick child, mopping my brow and giving me frequent drinks of fruit juice. By late afternoon, I am glad to say, I was much recovered, and even hungry enough to eat some bread and cheese.

The king, who had been setting all in order for the following morning, knew nothing of what had happened. Happy that I was restored to myself, I did not mention it when we gathered in the evening to dine. There was much talk of Saladin and Saphadin, and Richard's opinion had changed since the day before. The water of the Salt River, by which we had camped, was barely fit to drink. Supplies of food continued to run low. This was no place to remain should a peace deal be brokered, even if we had wanted to, and retreat was out of the question. Our journey, Richard said, must therefore continue, and that meant negotiations were pointless.

I suggested he cancel the meeting with Saphadin, but the king, amused, shook his head. 'If nothing else, we shall have some sport,' he declared.

For something so doomed to failure, the encounter – early on the morning of the fifth of September – began well. First came an exchange of pleasantries between Richard and Saladin's brother, relayed both by Humphrey de Toron and Saphadin's interpreter. Despite the language barrier, and the king's intention to give not an inch, both men seemed to take a liking to each other. Richard presented Saphadin with a magnificent sword, and made mention of knighting one of Saladin's sons when the opportunity presented itself. In return, Saphadin gifted the king with a curved blade such as the Turks wield, its gold-wrapped hilt and scabbard adorned with precious stones. He suggested hunting falcons together when cooler weather came.

After the courtesies and presents, Richard opened the proceedings. 'I am come seeking peace,' he said, apparently earnest.

Humphrey de Toron translated; Saphadin's interpreter did the same.

Saphadin's reply, through his interpreter, was as polite as you like. 'If you wish to obtain peace and desire me to act as your agent with the Sultan, you must lay out the conditions you have in mind.'

Richard cut to the meat and bone. 'The basis of the treaty shall be this. You must return all our territory to us and withdraw to your own country.'

The interpreter had barely finished speaking when Saphadin let out a loud, scornful laugh. His reply was short.

Humphrey translated. 'Is that all?'

'It is,' said Richard, as if he had merely asked to retreat to Acre unhindered.

Saphadin made a dismissive gesture as the king's reply was explained. His reply, through Humphrey, 'Those terms are unacceptable.'

'Should you not consult with your brother before you give such a definite answer?'

'I know his mind. He will never agree to such conditions.'

The two men stared at each other, their previous amity now absent.

'You are sure that Salah al-Dīn —' Richard made a decent fist of pronouncing the name '—will reject my terms?'

Humphrey listened to Saphadin's answer. 'He has never been more certain of anything in his life, sire.'

'It seems then that we have little left to talk about,' said Richard.

Saphadin's eyes glittered with sardonic amusement when his interpreter relayed the king's words. 'Nothing, I would say,' came his answer. 'Best return to your army, lest you be left behind.'

Richard chuckled. 'You knew that my soldiers set out hours ago.'

'Of course. Which proved you had no real intention to seek peace.'

'I might say the same of your brother. I wager he wanted to delay the battle so that his long-awaited reinforcements might reach him.'

Hearing the translation, Saphadin performed a mocking little bow.

Richard's lips pulled back from his teeth, but it was no smile.

Tension crackled in the already-hot air; it did not abate until we had ridden out of sight of Saphadin.

'We shall have battle, and soon,' Richard declared, his eyes alive with excitement.

CHAPTER XXV

By late afternoon, we were reaching the southern fringes of the forest of Arsur. It had taken the whole day to traverse, a hellish journey which set every man's teeth on edge. A rumour had begun in the morning – no one knew its origin – that the Saracens planned to set the tinder-dry trees alight with us among them. Unsurprisingly, the story had swept the army with the rapidity of the flames that might consume us all. So real did the threat seem that even Richard had been affected – I saw a rare uncertainty in his expression when he heard it. A brief consultation followed with his commanders.

In the end, though, the decision had been to proceed. As Richard said, we were between a rock and a hard place, and there was little choice but to continue. The rumour was probably just that, he said, hot air. We would place our trust in God, and march for the River Rochetaille, or as Abu called it, Nahr al-Fālik, the place of the Split Rock.

We saw almost no sign of the enemy, which was a cause of uniform relief. After the constant, stinging attacks of every previous day's march, it was inevitable that many saw this joyous absence as having divine providence. I grew weary of the cries of 'Sanctum Sepulchrum adjuva!' that rang out with monotonous regularity, but as we emerged from the forest into burning sunlight, I did offer up a prayer of thanks. Dealing with thorns and heavy vegetation had been easier, not to mention a great deal less lethal, than the cursed black swarms of Turkish arrows.

We camped close to the river, grateful also for the large, impassable swamp which protected our left flank. The next day, the sixth of September, was a day of rest. Throughout the afternoon, scouts brought word that the enemy host was drawing near. Amid the dust clouds swirling on the large plain beyond the swamp, we had views of approaching squadrons of horsemen and columns of infantry. They did not continue their advance, but appeared to set up camp. Even so, the news of their arrival swept through our soldiers, and a nervous tension was added to the heat exhaustion affecting us all.

As evening drew on, word came that two of our scouts, poulains, had been captured by the enemy. Entreated by Guy to intercede – one of the twain was a close friend of his – Richard sent a herald to the Turkish encampment, offering captives of ours in exchange. The news we heard back was brutal. When the pair had been brought into Saladin's presence, he had not bothered to interrogate them. Both were beheaded on the spot. The herald had seen their corpses, left out for the wild beasts like so much carrion.

The king began the meeting he had called by relating the fate of the two unfortunates. The general reaction was of outrage, as he had anticipated. Masterful, he waited until the noise subsided before telling those gathered that their fury was justified, wholeheartedly. 'But white-hot anger is not what will defeat the accursed race tomorrow – if it comes to a fight, messires,' he went on. 'We must be ice-cold in our purpose, and sharp-focused. Stray from it but a little distance, and disaster beckons.' Richard strode about before us, his relentless, threatening energy oozing from every pore. 'Battle must be joined only if the circumstances are right. Otherwise we merely march to Arsur.'

Into the lull that descended came the whine of mosquitoes, ever hungry for our blood. I could make out the call to prayer in the enemy camp, so close was it to our own lines.

'Hai ala-as-salah! Allahu-akbar! La ilaha illa'alah! Hasten to the prayer! God is most great! There is no god but God!' Despite the heat, gooseflesh formed on my arms to hear its hypnotic rise and fall. I took refuge in my cup of watered-down wine, and studied the men around me.

Everyone of importance was here. The grand masters of the military orders and their marshals. Guy de Lusignan and his brothers, and the poulain lords who followed them. Duke Hugh of Burgundy, young Henri of Blois, the valiant Guillaume des Barres, the bishop of Beauvais, portly as ever, and his bullnecked crony Drogo de Merlo. A dozen other French nobles of note. Barons and bishops from all over Richard's realm: England, Normandy, Maine, Anjou, Brittany and Aquitaine. We knights of the mesnie.

'The army will leave at dawn,' said Richard. 'Six miles it is to Arsur, and eleven more after that to Joppa. An unhindered journey would see us reach the former by noon. 'Twould be a miracle if that came to pass, however. The plain yonder—' he pointed over the river '—continues to run to the left of the road to Arsur and is perfect ground for horsemen. There are also sea cliffs to the south of here, which will force us away from the shoreline and raise the risk of being attacked on both sides. Saladin will not hold back from this opportunity. Expect full-strength attacks tomorrow from the outset. It is my belief that what we have endured thus far will pale in comparison.'

Grim expressions. Frowns. I saw fear, quickly masked, in more than one face, but the majority seemed determined.

'What then of your plans, sire?' asked Henri of Blois, one of those who seemed most eager.

'The wagons shall travel on the right of the army, protected on one flank by the sea. The host itself shall form five battalions, each of which will have squadrons of horse and foot, with the infantry marching nearest the enemy. In the van, leading us, shall be the Templars. Next will come the Bretons and Angevins; King Guy and his poulains with the Poitevins will make up the third battalion; the English and the Normans will guard the standard in the fourth, and the Hospitallers will comprise the fifth battalion, the rearguard. There shall also march a strong detachment of crossbowmen, for it is at the back that the hammer blow may fall.'

'Nephew, you shall command the left flank, the units of foot soldiers closest to the Saracens.' Henri of Blois smiled acknowledgement of this honour, and Richard went on, 'Duke Hugh of Burgundy and I will each lead a squadron of knights up and down the line, serving as protection where it is needed.' The king's tone grew unrelenting. Insistent. 'As I have said before, close order is vital. I want your horses nose-to-tail, and each man stirrup-to-stirrup with those on either side.'

'Easy prey for Saracen arrows,' said a French voice, but not loud enough for Richard to hear.

'No matter how severe the provocation, no matter how bad the casualties, discipline *must* be maintained,' said the king fiercely. 'There will perhaps be one or two chances to launch an effective counterattack. *I* will decide if and when that happens, and no one else. My order will come from paired trumpets in the front, middle and end of the column. Unless you hear them sound, *hold your position*.'

'What of the destriers, sire?' asked de Nablus. 'Lose too many to the Saracens' arrows, and we will be of no use to anyone.'

'My mind is made up, Grand Master.' Richard's tone was curt. 'Hold your position unless you hear the trumpets.'

'Very well, sire.' Despite his acquiescence, de Nablus did not look happy.

Nor, I thought, did some of his men. I knew two by name, William Borrel and Baldwin Carew, but distracted by de Béthune muttering something in my ear, I paid them no heed.

After a blessing by the bishops, Richard bade us goodnight, and amid a rumble of nervous amusement, told us to get what rest we could.

I lay for hours in the airless fug of my tent, staring open-eyed into the darkness, my mind racing.

I am sure I was not the only one.

I woke, coated in sweat, and wishing that I had lain out under the stars. Remembering the one night I had tried that, and how I had been eaten alive by mosquitoes and then had to suffer the fearful itch of the bites under my armour, I changed my mind. It was still pitch black inside, and I could see no light through the tent panels. Rhys, often the first to wake, was snoring. I lay back and tried to fall back to sleep.

It was a futile hope. My mind was already picturing how the day might unfold, and my heart rate was increasing. I clambered over Rhys, unlaced the flap and pushed my way outside. The air was fresh and, Christ on the cross, so cool. I luxuriated in the feel of it on my bare skin, and wished it would stay like this all day. I would fight the Saracens forever in temperatures this balmy.

Overhead, the stars were fading. There was a tinge of light on the eastern horizon; dawn was perhaps an hour off. It was a good time to rise, I decided, picking my way between the tents to the nearest latrine trench. The stench of it hit me from fifty paces out. Men were squatting there already, and from the horrendous noises, all was not well with their bowels. Grateful that I needed only to empty my bladder, I found a quiet spot and got on with it.

When I got back, Rhys was stirring.

'Rested?' I asked.

He looked at me, puzzled. 'Aye. Why would I not be?'

'Most men do not sleep like babes the night before a battle,' I said, a little irritated.

'Meaning that you did not.'

Instead of snapping, I said, 'Let us to the river, before the entire army gets there.'

In addition to filling our waterskins, and drinking our fill, we both had a quick dip – a delight before the furnace of the day. Refreshed, we walked back to the tent, letting the air dry us. Rhys, trencherman that he was, ate a hearty breakfast of bread, cheese and dried horsemeat. I ate sparingly and only because if I did not, I would not have the energy to fight well.

I began to dress and arm myself, Rhys helping when necessary. We did not speak. Today he was going with de Drune to the rearguard, liable to be one of the dangerous places in the army. He seemed unperturbed, while I wondered if I would ever see him again. In a lesser man, it could have been taken for lack of wits, that he did not understand the danger, but Rhys's mind was blade-sharp.

In the end, I could take it no longer. 'Are you worried?'

'About today?'

I gave him a great buffet. 'No, about the bad harvest at Striguil!'

A sloping grin. 'I will be all right.'

'How can you know that?'

'Death should have taken me that day at Acre, when I had the shooting competition with the Saracen named Grair.'

'A man can have more than one possible end,' I countered, thinking of the number of times over the years that I should have died.

He stuck out his chin, the way he did when his mind was made up. 'If Grair could not kill me, no filthy Turk can.'

I did not believe his brush with death at Acre made Rhys's chances of survival any better, but if it had given him confidence, it mattered not.

'And you?'

'I am scared,' I admitted. 'But that is nothing new.'

'You will fight regardless.'

'Of course. Like a lion.'

'As will I.'

'I know you will.'

He tightened his belt a notch, and adjusted the sit of his bollock dagger and quiver for his crossbow bolts. 'You have your way, and I have mine. Now, I had best saddle Pommers for you, and then rouse that slugabed de Drune. He will still be asleep, if I know him.'

'I will see to Pommers. You wake de Drune.'

We would not see each other henceforth until the battle was over. If we did at all, the devil in my mind said. There was every chance that at least one of us would be lying, arrow-riddled, in the hot sand by the day's end. Regret filled me, that I might never see Cairlinn or Joanna again. I felt equally sad at the idea of Rhys dying.

I stuck out my hand. 'Until later.'

Rhys took the grip, and we shook, hard. 'Until later,' he said. 'God be with you.'

'And you.' I walked away, lest he see the emotion twisting my face.

I passed the French tentlines on my way to Richard's pavilion. The portly bishop of Beauvais was blessing the assembled knights. I heard him exhorting them to visit God's vengeance on the accursed and evil hordes, to reap the people of circumcision like wheat. Turks, Bedouins, Persians and vile black men from the wilds of Sudan, all were to be slain. 'Let no living enemy escape the reach of your lance or your sword!' Spittle flew from his lips so wrathful was he, the fat capon.

I was tempted to stop and ask him to join the combat – I would have given a purse of silver pennies just to see his jowly face blanch at the suggestion – but I thought better of it, and continued on.

The king was in a fine mood when I found him. Already arrayed in his mail and surcoat, he was making the final checks on Fauvel himself as an unhappy-looking Philip stood by and watched. My friend's mood was not, as I discovered, because of Richard seeing to the stallion, but because he was not to be allowed to ride with the mesnie. 'It is not as if I have never been in battle,' he said to me in an aggrieved undertone. 'I proved myself at Acre!'

'A full-scale battle is not certain, you know.'

He gave me a look. 'Maybe so, but it has never seemed more likely.'

It was pointless trying to defend that weak argument, so I said nothing.

He bent my ear a while longer, before eventually asking – nay, begging – me to speak to the king on his behalf.

I wavered, torn between my loyalty to a dear friend, and a desire not to distract the king from his purpose. In the end, aware that Philip never asked for anything, I promised to see what I could do.

Philip pumped my hand, so thankful was he.

I decided to seize the moment. Leaving Pommers in Philip's care, I went over to Fauvel. Richard had finished checking every buckle and strap, and was stroking the stallion's head, and murmuring in his ear.

'May he bear you well today, sire,' I said.

The king smiled. 'Are you ready for the battle, should it happen?'

'I am, sire.'

'It has been long coming, and although I would prefer a location of my choosing, I will not avoid the confrontation. Defeat Saladin on the plain, and Jerusalem will fall.'

'God grant that it is so, sire.'

He gave Fauvel an affectionate rub, and cast his gaze over the knights gathered around. Many were mounted, or in the process of doing so. He called out that we should all be prepared to ride out soon.

I had to speak now. 'Sire, I have a request.'

'That you should ride on my right hand? It was already my intention.'

I bowed my head in thanks. 'I am honoured, sire. It was something else, however.'

'What then? Speak! Time is pressing.'

'It is Philip, sire. He is desperate to ride with the mesnie.'

Richard frowned. 'He has been at you too? I told him no.'

'He is a skilled swordsman, sire, and useful with the lance. He is also old enough to be a knight.'

'God's legs, between his sulky looks and your carping, I am to have no peace. Very well. Let him come with us, but he is to stay away from the front ranks, tell him. I want no heroics.'

'Sire.' Grinning, I went to tell Philip, who had been watching from a short distance away as he pretended to put a last burnish on the king's helm.

He pulled me into a fierce hug. 'Rufus, I cannot thank you enough!'

'Thank me by staying alive,' I said gruffly, hoping I had not done the wrong thing.

We rode out not long after, following the dust cloud sent up by the Templars, the Bretons and the Angevins. It was a beautiful morning, the sky cloudless, the sun just peeping over the hills that lay to the east.

Already it was damnably hot. Fighting the Saracens all day would be a herculean task. I wanted to be with the king, but he was busy with first one messenger and then another as they cantered up with queries from captains and officers along the line. I fell back, unnoticed, to Philip's position in one of the rearmost ranks.

We spent a pleasant time talking about the olden days, when Richard was still duke of Aquitaine. There was much mention of the young ladies we had courted, and of the nights spent drinking. Philip kept mentioning Juvette, his amour, and Alienor and Beatrice, at various times mine. I could only think of Joanna. In the end, the secret threatened to burst from me. I brought him into my confidence.

'Not a word of it must you breathe to anyone, do you hear?' I waved a threatening finger. 'Your life will not be worth living if you do.'

'I swear,' he said, beaming from ear to ear. 'Queen Joanna herself, no less! I thought I knew you, Rufus, but you have hidden depths.'

'I love her,' I said, my suppressed-since-Acre emotions rising to the surface. 'And she loves me. I would do anything to make her my wife, but—' My voice tailed off.

I did not have to explain why. Joanna's worth as a bride was beyond measure. Valued member of the mesnie though I was, I could not offer a strong alliance with another royal house. That would be the main quality sought by Richard when he had time to find her a new husband.

'I am sorry, Rufus.' Philip's expression was solemn.

'You and I both.' I turned the focus back to him, asking why he had not made more attempt to chase Joanna's or Berengaria's ladies. He laughed, and told me that he *had*.

'If you had not been so absent – and now I know where – I might have had time to tell you of my—' he paused before adding '—limited success.'

'You rogue!' I cried, delighted. 'What is her name?'

Time passed more easily while we were engaged in pleasant banter. Even the heat was less noticeable. The king guided us at a steady pace, slightly faster than the speed of march, between the lines of men-at-arms and knights, past the second battalion, and up to the first, the Templars. I saw him take counsel with the Grand Master, Robert de Sablé. The two pointed here and there to our left, no doubt considering where the enemy might attack from.

That done, Richard had us climb down from our destriers. There was little to no shade, and it was good for our mounts not to be ridden even for a short time. Not long after, the king led us at right angles, across the ranks of passing knights, and onto the other flank of the column, that nearest the coast. The lightest of breezes was discernible there, a blessed relief, but of the enemy we saw no sign.

So the first part of the morning passed. All along the army we rode, now and again taking brief rests. A complacent man or a fool might have let down their guard, but we knew better. Saladin *would* attack.

Perhaps three hours had gone by since we had broken camp – I judged it to be around the time of tierce – when I first heard the hideous, familiar racket of enemy instruments. Every musician in Saladin's army seemed to have been brought into play. I heard trumpets, horns, flutes, tambors, rattles and cymbals, all sounded together in a discordant cacophony that hurt my ears. With it came a fearful noise of shouting, baying and howling. If there was a tune to any of it, I said to Philip, its composer had been a lunatic.

I told him to fight well, and clasping his hand, declared that we would share a cup of wine that night and relive our experiences. He gave me a determined grin and agreed.

I went back to the king.

'Ha! Rufus! They are coming, the accursed ones,' he cried. 'Such a din they make! I declare God Himself could not thunder so loud.'

I pointed to the billowing dust clouds at our backs, all we could see from our position of the enemy movements. 'They are making for the rearguard, sire, as you thought.'

'Aye. This will test the Hospitallers' mettle.'

We stayed parallel with the third battalion, the one led by Guy de Lusignan, and many's the glance was cast over our shoulders as the battle raged far behind us. I wanted to ride back and join in, but there was a fresh threat. Over the plain to our left came riding serried ranks of Turks, thousands of them. Banners and pennoncels fluttered from their lances, and the ground shook beneath their horses' hooves.

I took a sup or two of water to wet my mouth, and donned my helm. Richard, everyone was doing the same. This was it, I thought. The full-scale battle with Saladin, the victor of which could take all.

Closer they came, the Turks. This mob were yelling and screaming too, and they had their own mad musicians and instrument players.

The officers among the men-at-arms shouted orders, and crossbows were spanned by the hundred. The speed of march slowed, but as the king had ordered, did not stop.

The first arrows came arcing up the sky, black darts that made my skin crawl. I rubbed Pommers' neck, and told him he was a good boy, and that no enemy shaft would hurt him. I was lying through my teeth, of course. Placed as we were between the foot soldiers and Guy de Lusignan's knights, we were well inside killing range.

Down the arrows dropped, into the men-at-arms. An instant later, they bristled out of gambesons, protruded from shields, and jutted from the earth like fletched, devil-sown plants. Cries there were, not a few, but to my relief they were mostly insults hurled at the Turks rather than screams of pain.

Closer came the enemy, mamluks, hollering and whooping like demons. Christ Jesus, but they were fine riders, I thought, and their mounts supremely well-trained. To shoot a bow from the back of a horse required two hands, which meant letting go of the reins, all the while pounding towards the foe in the midst of a close-riding horde of comrades.

Volley after volley of arrows were released now, until the whizz of them was like the buzz of swarming hornets and the blue of the sky was darkened by the shadow of their passing. Men-at-arms screamed, mounts went down, kicking. I heard the order, 'First rank, LOOSE!' and an instant later, the innocuous *click* sound of crossbow triggers. Godspeed, I thought, and was delighted as dozens of horses fell, taking their riders with them. Countless mamluks were hurled earthwards, so great was the force of the quarrels that ended their black, accursed lives. The Turks' front rank had dissolved as if punched by a mighty, invisible fist.

Hot air whipped in through the slit in my helmet, and I twisted to look down to my right. An arrow stood proud of the cracked earth, still quivering. It had missed me by a couple of fingers' breadth, and Pommers by the same.

'Second rank, LOOSE!'

Click, click, click. Hundreds more bolts flew. Another swathe of death sliced through the Turks. More great holes gaped in their formation. Saddles were emptied, horses smashed from their feet. It was too much for our foe. Still yipping and barking like wild dogs, with the frenzied musicians playing away to their rear, those who could wheeled and rode off at full tilt.

A ragged cheer went up from the men-at-arms, and one soldier cried, 'Sanctum Sepulchrum adjuva!'

Even I could not resent the chant this time.

A few dozen men-at-arms had been wounded, and four slain, and the mesnie had lost eight horses. These casualties were not terrible, but they were disheartening, not least because we had barely seen to the wounded and organised burial parties for the dead when the Saracens came back. Richard warned us that we might charge this time, if the opportunity presented itself.

In the event, we did not, because the mamluks were supported by infantry. Agile, fast-running men, black as soot, they were armed with bows and crossbows. Their combined assault was so heavy that it came to hand-to-hand fighting. Unable to load and shoot fast enough, with the enemy pressing ever closer, sections of our men-at-arms broke ranks and ran forward with shields and spears. A fearful struggle followed, with the advantage swaying back and forth every few moments.

We knights risked injuring our own soldiers if we advanced, but Richard, seeing how delicate the balance was, led us slightly off to the right. He had spied a gap in the Saracen ranks. Orders were relayed, and the men-at-arms pulled apart so we could canter through. Emerging on the other side, the king organised us into a narrow line and charged at once. We couched lances and galloped into the space he had seen. Those few Turks in our path panicked and fled. We rode them down, and pounded on. To our left and right now were hundreds upon hundreds of enemy infantry, black men all, pressing forward to reach the men-at-arms. Heads were turning in our direction, mouths opening in alarm, but there was no reaction. Yet.

Some five score paces in, Richard slowed our momentum, wheeled us left, reformed our ranks, and from a distance of perhaps thirty paces, charged into the side of the enemy formation.

We broke them apart as a stamping foot breaks puddle ice. Every lance skewered a black man. The destriers, battle-trained, trampled with bloody abandon. Swords flashed as they were drawn and in the same movement, scythed down to remove heads and arms. At one point, occupied with one opponent and unable to reach around with my blade, I even kicked a foeman in the face. Weighted by my mail hose, my boot smashed every tooth in his head and sent him cartwheeling out of sight.

Onward we pressed, while the enemy wailed and ran and bled and died. To left and right I hewed, until my right arm was coated in blood and ichor to the elbow, and the muscles were screaming for a rest. I was startled then to find open space in front of me. Instinctively, Pommers slowed, and as the red mist fell away from my eyes and reason crept back in, I realised that we had punched right through the black men. There was fighting a little way off, but it was a different group of Turks, assailing the men-at-arms in another section of the column.

'To me!' It was Richard. 'To me!'

We gathered round him. I noted de Béthune's device, and de Chauvigny's, and was relieved. Thorne was there too. Fewer of us there were than had charged, but our losses were light, considering we had shredded an entire unit of the enemy into mangled pieces of flesh and bone. The ground over which we had ridden was thick with bodies, most still, but some thrashing about. Cries of pain and unintelligible sentences of whatever barbarous tongue the black men spoke carried through the baking hot, windless air.

'We ride back to the army,' said Richard loudly.

Some knights were staring at the nearest enemy, no doubt thinking that we had only to fall on them from the side to wreak the same havoc for a second time, but not a single voice questioned his authority.

We withdrew in good order, to be greeted by the delirious shouts of the sunburned, perspiring men-at-arms. A word from Richard had us salute them in turn with our swords, recognising their courage and stalwartness in withstanding the savage and powerful assault.

We were still removing helms and supping greedily from our waterskins when a Hospitaller came galloping up the line with a message from de Nablus for the king. The rearguard was under an intense, prolonged attack by the accursed race. The grand master begged for permission to charge with his knights and relieve the pressure on the rest of the beleaguered troops.

I thought with a pang of Rhys and de Drune, who were in the midst of the storm, and hoped they weathered it unharmed. I could do nothing for them, though, for I knew what the king's answer would be.

'Tell the grand master to be patient. His men must continue to hold tightly together.' The king was also helmet-less now. Red-faced, his hair slicked to his head with sweat, he still exuded leadership and royalty. 'There is to be no charge unless I give the order.'

The Hospitaller's expression was dismayed, but he dared not argue with the king. He bobbed his head, and with a quick, 'Sire,' pulled his horse's head around and set off for the rear of the column.

The men-at-arms weathered a fresh attack by the mamluks; of the fearsome black men there was no sign. That was some cause for relief; the next arrow storm rained down on us was hard enough to endure. Again the concerted crossbow volleys caused terrible slaughter among the enemy; again they withdrew. We did not chase after this time – there were only so many charges in a destrier in these unbearable conditions – and they vanished into the shimmering heat haze that coated the plain.

Another Hospitaller came from de Nablus requesting permission to lead his knights at the Saracens. Once more the king refused. The time was still not right, he said to me.

Word came of fighting on the seaward side, towards the middle of the column. Mamluks who must have moved into place under cover of night had emerged from wooded areas and launched themselves ferociously at the men-at-arms. Duke Hugh and his squadron were on their way to help drive back the attack. We continued to move up and down the line, ready to respond to any sign of the enemy on our side.

It was not even close to sext, midday, and I had drained one waterskin. Fearfully thirsty still, I longed to start on my second. With an effort, I held off. Many hours of daylight remained, and the fighting seemed set to continue. I set up my leather trough, however, and gave Pommers and Fauvel a good drink. They too were parched, and would have consumed far more than I gave them. They whickered and shook their heads over the dry trough, clearly requesting more, and my heart twinged. I promised them both a bellyful later, and hoped they understood.

The sun inched upward. Its heat assailed us with baleful force. Men collapsed from overheating, from exhaustion, from their wounds. The riders of weaker horses had to get down and walk, else their mounts would have foundered. Clouds of flies plagued us. In this grim fashion, our journey continued, slow and plodding. We knights of the mesnie rode hither and thither with the king, charging short distances to drive back the Turks and allow the poor men-at-arms a break from the constant clouds of arrows.

Word came from the vanguard that they were nearing Arsur but it would take hours for the entire army to reach the relative safety of the fortress there. Enemy attacks continued, and in ever greater force. Whether we could reach our destination was yet uncertain.

I heard one soldier say that we were surrounded, like a flock of sheep in the jaws of wolves, that we could see nothing but the sky and our wicked enemies on every side. It was hard to argue with the sentiment. Our fate, and the outcome of the battle were very much still in the balance.

De Nablus came himself the next time, with two of his serjeants for protection. Richard bade him welcome, and listened as the harassed-looking grand master laid forth his case.

'Things are desperate, sire. We are harried shamefully and wrongfully. The ranks of men-at-arms who are rearmost are forced to march facing backwards, that they may see the enemy come, and fight against them. I do not know how long they can endure.'

In my mind's eye, I could see Rhys and de Drune pacing side-by-side, their backs to the front of the column, their crossbows aimed at the endless waves of enemy riders and infantry who swarmed in their direction. Sweet Jesu, I prayed, watch over them.

'So many arrows are falling that every knight is in danger of losing his mount. Some of the accursed ones have dismounted to shoot better, while others run at us with heavy clubs. Let us charge, sire!' de Nablus begged. 'We are being taken for cowards! Such shame has never been seen, nor was our army ever put under such reproach by the infidel and, if we delay in defending ourselves, we may delay too long.'

Richard was in no mood for the holding of hands or giving out of sympathy. 'The order to charge will come if and when I deem the time ripe. Listen for the trumpets, Master, and put up with the enemy's stinging,' he said, curt as you like. 'No one can be everywhere at once.'

De Nablus pleaded and argued to no avail. Richard was obdurate.

Frustrated and angry, but forced to accede to the king's wishes, the grand master went back to his knights.

'Do you think they will hold, sire?' I asked, worry nipping at me.

'I hope so, Rufus. I believe so!'

I was not wholly convinced by his bluff tone. We could not control the Hospitallers. We had to rely on their discipline and resilience, something the military orders were famous for. And to give them their due, the Hospitallers did obey Richard's orders for almost another hour.

By then, the king was close to committing to battle, to ordering an all-out charge by the entire body of knights. The Turks were attacking not just the rearguard now, but the middle of the column too. Let them just assail the front, Richard said, and Saladin would have sent his whole host to the fray. Not fighting back risked utter defeat, but an almighty blow delivered at that point by thousands of knights and their destriers would smash the enemy host.

Then, disaster. A messenger on a lathered horse, carrying the news that two Hospitallers had ridden out at a pair of Turks who were taunting them.

'*Who?*' Richard's voice was poisonous with rage.

'William Borrel and Baldwin Carew, sire.'

My memory jolted by the names, I remembered their earlier discontent at the king's order.

'And the rest of the Hospitallers?' demanded Richard.

'All of them have charged, sire.' Quailing, the messenger added, 'Henri of Blois has also ridden forth, and the French knights with him.'

'God's legs, they will be the ruin of us!' Richard roared for the trumpeter, and bade him sound the charge. Then, to us, he cried, 'To me! We ride for the Hospitallers' position, with all speed! Dex aie!'

We rode, my heart swelling with pride that more than a hundred knights were at my back. Heat – overbearing heat, enveloped me. Sweat stung my eyes; I blinked it away as best I could. The great weight of my helm pressed down on my skull. My ears filled with the clarion sound of trumpets and the thunder of hooves. Dry as a piece of tinder, my tongue stuck to the roof of my mouth. Right in front of me, Pommers' head rose and fell as he galloped, and a short distance beyond that, I could see the king. Dust clouds obscured everything else beyond thirty to forty feet.

Down the column we rode, and the men-at-arms, catching sight of us through the swirling dust, cheered until their throats cracked. Down the column we rode, eager to find the enemy and kill him by the thousand. Visibility was poor – it would be hard to tell friend from foe until close up – but that did not sway our resolve. I began to think of us as avenging angels, sent by God to smite the vile pagans who plagued this land of Outremer.

The king couched his lance, and seeing him, I did the same. Snugly fitted into my armpit, its shaft tight in my fist, I kept its tip directed over Pommers' right ear, ready to aim at an enemy. With no warning, we burst out of a gap in the all-encasing dust. To our right, hundreds of enemy riders and Hospitallers were locked in a fierce battle. To our left, mamluks on foot were shooting arrows at battered groups of men-at-arms. The messenger had been correct, I thought. They *had* dismounted to use their bows better.

Richard aimed straight at these enemies, hard and fast.

Most of the Turks never saw us coming. We smashed into their ranks like a hammer-driven wedge splitting a log. We cut them down in droves, impaled by our lances, cloven, maimed, and slain by our blood-hungry swords, or trampled by our iron shod destriers. Panicked, wailing in fear, calling on their god for help, they did everything but fight, which made the slaughter all the simpler.

I urged Pommers this way and that, slashing the upraised arm of a Turk as he struggled to rise, and beheading another who lunged at me with a mace. With the king, I charged a bunch of six or eight. They scattered like pigs escaping a pen, going in all directions. The last pair were too slow; Richard killed one, and I the other. The enemy was so plentiful there was no point pursuing the others, so we rode to the aid of a knight who was battling three Turks alone.

I split the skull of one, and the king drove his sword clean through the back of the second, and out through his ribs on the other side. Free to deal with the last Turk, the knight lopped off his right hand, and then, as the horrified man stared at the blood spraying from the stump, he stabbed him through the chest.

'Thank you, sire!' shouted the knight – it was Thorne.

Richard saluted him with his blade, and after a moment to assess the situation – the mamluks on foot had broken utterly, allowing the men-at-arms to surge forward again – he was off, urging Fauvel towards the main body of the enemy, which was engaged with the ground-to-a-halt Hospitallers. 'Dex aie!' he roared.

'Come on!' I roared at Thorne, and drummed my heels into Pommers' sides so that I might follow. To my left and right, I sensed riders joining us – more of the mesnie. Where they went, the rest would follow, I thought, secure in the discipline and training that ruled our existence.

We galloped after the king, and put a mob of Turks in our path – fifty at least – to flight. Then, with the battle madness in full control, we resumed our charge to aid the struggling Hospitallers. In among them we rode, and through and between them, to engage the ugly race, the accursed ones.

Dust and heat. Sweat and blood. Men's screams and the ring of blade on blade. Constant movement, Pommers charging, twisting, jinking, trampling. My right arm rising and falling, thrusting, hacking. My left arm with the shield, protecting, and my left hand, tight on the reins, controlling. These things framed my entire existence. I had no time for thought, could not consider what was next. My only purpose was to protect the king, and to kill Turks.

Our lightning strike, coming as it had out of the shrouding dust and out of the ranks of the Hospitallers, caught the mamluks completely off guard. Light cavalry never have much of a chance against heavy anyway, and the immense force with which we struck smashed the enemy like a rowboat on the rocks during a winter storm. Any semblance of formation disappeared. Discipline entirely left the accursed ones, any desire to fight was gone. All that remained was the primeval desire to survive.

They broke and fled, heedless of the injured or the comrades whose horses had fallen, disregarding of the dead who lay thick as sheaves of wheat on the hard, baked earth. They rode over men with hands raised in supplication, and cut down their own if they blocked the path. We chased after, fierce, eager, uncaring of the heat and the sweat drenching our bodies. Never had I felt the bloodlust run so thick and strong through my veins. It shamed me to think of it afterwards, but in the moment, I exulted as I slew enemy after enemy, rapacious as a night-creeping fox taking hens in a coop. Encased by a world of blade and blood, I would have ridden on to Jerusalem had the king not signalled a halt.

I was close to him, as I had been for the whole fight. Thorne was there, and de Béthune, de Chauvigny, and a dozen more. My heart rose to recognise so many of those I called close comrades, and as my breath slowed and sanity returned, I saw us properly for the first time. The surcoat of every man could scarce be described as such any longer, so marked and stained was it with dust, blood and gore. The rest of us, from our helms to our boots, were little different.

God help me, but it felt wonderful.

'Enough.' Richard's voice was a rasping croak. 'These foes are beaten, Christ be thanked, but we are needed elsewhere. Saladin will have sent men to attack other parts of the column. Before we go, every second man is to un-helm and take a drink. When he is done, every other man will do the same.'

Thorne and a few others were sent to relay the king's command to the Hospitallers and the knights under Henri of Blois. Again we rode, this time at a slower pace. Back up the army we travelled, along the way meeting groups of Bretons, Angevins and Poitevins. They had charged after us, and joined in our battering-ram assault on the enemy. Rallying to the king, they fell in behind us in dozens and scores. Reaching the fourth battalion, that of the English and Norman knights, Richard ordered them to follow. We were now a great mass of knights, more than eight hundred strong, riding in a file fifteen to twenty wide, with the king and I at the very front, and the mesnie with us. I felt all-conquering. I felt no thirst, no hunger. My sweat-stung eyes were bright, and my right arm felt fresh as if I had just drawn my blade. Pommers, the wonderful beast that he was, gave no sign of weariness, but stepped out as smartly as if we were to parade before Queen Berengaria.

Hidden by the dust for a second time, we surprised the Turks who had come at Saladin's behest to attack the centre of the column. Quickly forming a much wider line, we charged. Hooves drummed the ground. Even more dust rose. Richard roared something, but I could not hear. He pointed his sword at the enemy, and urged Fauvel to even more effort. The magnificent stallion surged ahead, faster than a crossbow bolt.

Every knight saw it. Every knight spurred his own destrier mercilessly, eager to show his desire to fight, concerned lest the king be caught on his own. I remember screaming a wordless war cry, an inchoate, animal noise that promised death. No one noticed it in the chaos, but if they had, I tell you it would have turned their bowels to water. Pommers, sensing my desperation, strained every muscle in his great body, and caught up with Fauvel.

Side-by-side with Richard, my battle brother, we hit the enemy.

Again we smashed the Turks' lines. Again we killed them in numbers impossible to count. Sunlight bounced off our swords. Blood gouted, sprayed, was drunk greedily by the parched earth. Sparks flew from helmets struck by iron blades. Heads tumbled from shoulders. Weapons dropped from severed hands. Guts, hot and steaming, spilled out of bellies. Horses reared and fell, or were sent tumbling by the cart-heavy weight of a full-charging destrier. Not a man among the Saracens could stand before us, so overwhelming was our force, our hunger to kill, dare I say it, our God-given might.

The pursuit went on for a lot longer this time. Right to the base of the hills whence they had come we chased the enemy. All of us would have gone further, but the Turks were broken, and Richard did not want to lose men unnecessarily.

Reining in Fauvel, he took off his helmet, and drained an entire waterskin. 'God's legs, but that was the sweetest draught I have ever had,' he said, chuckling.

We all laughed, for the taste of water from the oiled leather, cooked in the sun, was beyond vile. Then we did the same. Never had *I* enjoyed a drink so much. We watered the destriers too, from our leather troughs, and I hugged Pommers' broad neck, and told him he was the finest mount a man could ask for, better even than Fauvel. I whispered the last, in case the king heard and was offended.

After a short rest, Richard led us back to the column. Helmet dangling from his saddle bow, he rode with sword laid across his lap, ready to use, and his back stiff and upright. Brightly he greeted every noble he saw, loudly he commended the men-at-arms who were moving over the slaughter-field, dispatching the enemy wounded and taking what they could find.

'Richard! Coeur de Lion!' they cheered, saluting him, and running in alongside his horse to kiss his feet and clasp his hand. 'Richard! Coeur de Lion!'

'They think we have won,' the king said to me in an undertone.

'But we have, sire!' I cried, shocked. 'You have.'

'Not in the way we needed to, Rufus.' He gestured at the ground over which we rode, which was littered with corpses and horse carcasses as far as the eye could see, and said, 'These are but a small part of Saladin's army, sadly. Think of the size of the camp we saw from the River Rochetaille. The enemy has been beaten, it is true, but he is not destroyed.'

'If it had not been for those two Hospitallers . . .' I said bitterly.

'Even so, Rufus.' And now, for the first time, there was weariness in the king's voice.

'Will you punish them, sire?'

A laugh. 'What point would there be in that? It shall be shame enough for them that their rashness, their indiscipline, cost us complete victory.'

He is shrewd, I thought. That knowledge will be a harsher punishment for them.

Despite the battering we had given the Turks, the day's fighting was not over. Most of the army had reached Arsur and was setting up camp when a sudden attack came on the extreme rearguard. So close was it to the tentlines that the shouts and cries of the combatants were audible to us. Richard, still in his war gear, leaped to horse, and ordered those around him to follow. Fifteen knights we were, and the king, riding to fight any number it could have been of the accursed race.

Not a man hesitated.

'God and the Holy Sepulchre, help us,' Richard shouted as he galloped towards the camp entrance. 'The Turks are at hand!'

Men-at-arms leaped up and seized their crossbows and spears. Knights called for their destriers. Guillaume des Barres, roaring at his countrymen to join him, came riding towards us. I glanced over my shoulder, and was heartened to see a huge mob of men following on foot and on horse.

Whether it was the noise of our coming – our horses pounding the dusty earth, the shouts and cries of the soldiers, the trumpets' peals – or the memory of the humiliating defeat they had just suffered, I know not, but the Turks immediately ended their fight against the rearguard. We had no need even to break them; instead we hunted the enemy down yet again, and harried him all the way to the forest of Arsur.

It was a glorious end to a glorious day.

Only much later, when the king asked me where Philip was, and I did not know, did the first inkling of the day's worst loss sink home.

There was no sign of him anywhere. I had last seen him hours before, during one of our charges, but we had been swept apart by the chaos of battle. Richard was the same. Worryingly, no one had clapped eyes on Philip since. Dark had fallen, so we could not go out to search for him.

Although I was exhausted, I slept barely a wink that night. Before first light, I had donned a gambeson and saddled my rouncy. I dared not use Pommers, so spent was he from the battle. Richard caught me before I left with Rhys, Thorne and a score of others from the mesnie – he would have ridden with us, but gave in to our request that he avoid the risk, however small, of riding through the slaughter-field in a small group. We were also to seek the body of James d'Avesnes, a Flemish noble loyal to the king who was also missing. De Drune came too – he would have it no other way – perching awkwardly on a mule he had contrived to borrow from a wagon driver.

We were gone for much of the day, baking again in oven-like temperatures, sweating only a little less without our armour. Our faces were covered with dampened cloths, which helped a little with the stench, for the carcasses of horses and bodies of men that lay strewn across the miles-wide battlefield were already ripe. Bellies were swollen, flesh blackening, tongues and eyes falling victim to the multitudinous vultures and other carrion birds. There was no sign of the accursed race, which was a mercy.

We came upon James d'Avesnes first. Three of his kinsmen were with him, and they were surrounded by a circle of fifteen or more dead Turks. They had given a great account of themselves, which boded ill for Count Robert de Dreux, who had been close by during the fighting and had claimed afterwards that James and his kin had been quickly slain. Setting a lance with a pennant at its tip in the ground so that we might find them again, we continued our search for Philip.

Rhys it was who discovered him, lying by his destrier – one of the king's. Philip's mail had been pierced in numerous places, and one arm smashed, by a Turkish mace, like as not. Guilt lashed me, that I had asked the king to allow him to ride out with us, and that I had not been with him when he needed it most. Five dead Saracens lay close by, evidence that Philip had fought like a champion of old before the numbers grew overwhelming. Together we might have prevailed, I thought bitterly, even though I well knew that my primary duty always was to stay with the king.

'He fought well,' said Rhys, his voice unusually thick.

'Aye.' I could barely speak. Philip had been the first to extend the hand of friendship when I took service with Richard. For a decade, our lives had been intertwined as only those of brothers-in-arms can be. Now he was dead, and I had not been there with him.

Even de Drune, for whom it was rare to show much emotion, was grief-stricken. I caught him dabbing his eyes when he thought no one was looking. Other knights of the mesnie were no less affected; Philip had been well-liked.

Thorne stayed calmest, perhaps because he had known Philip for the shortest time. He it was who wrapped the poor lad in a linen shroud – we had thought to take several with us – and draped him across the saddle of a spare horse. My own tears came when Philip's sagging corpse had been tied hand and foot so he did not fall off as we rode. The finality of his death hit me like a thunderbolt. Lying surrounded by his slain foes, I had been able to picture him battling bravely, alone, never giving in until at last his strength had failed him. Now I could not deny that my oldest friend but one – Rhys – was gone forever.

The blow was made all the more grievous because I had not – given Philip's usual role – anticipated it.

CHAPTER XXVI

Outside Joppa, mid-October 1191

It was a warm, pleasant day, and incredible though it seemed, I was lazing in the shade of a row of lush green vines, upon which hung juicy clusters of black grapes. My belly full from a good lunch of bread, olives, cheese, figs and grapes, washed down by local wine, I was drowsy and content to half-listen to my friends' conversation. Now and again, I thought with a pang of Philip, buried on the battlefield with James d'Avesnes and his kinsmen, and asked God to look after him. I had already visited his grave on several occasions.

Rhys was sitting close by with de Drune and Thorne. Abu was there too, watching bemused as the three others played at dice, and gossiped.

'A three and a one. Your turn, Thorne.' Rhys's voice was disgusted.

'When is the king due back from Acre?' This from de Drune.

I pricked an ear, for Joanna would be with him. My heart warmed at the thought.

'Any day. It will not take him long to roust the rest of the "lazy ones" from the brothels and taverns,' said Thorne. 'Two threes.'

'Guy de Lusignan proved to be as useless at that as he was at Hattin,' observed Rhys.

Richard had sent Guy to fetch the malingerers some days prior, and he had abjectly failed, leading the king to go himself. He also wanted to find out what Conrad of Montferrat was up to, because rumours had reached him that the devious Italian was engaged in secret negotiations with Saladin.

'The king will not fail, but when the "lazy ones" arrive, they shall be quick to fall into their old ways. There are nearly as many whores in Joppa as in Acre,' said Thorne as the others chuckled. There had been a mass influx of such women in recent days, come in search of business. 'Roll, de Drune,' urged Thorne. 'Else we shall be here all day.'

Much had happened since our victory at Arsur, I thought, and much had not. Sapped by the effort of the victory over Saladin, the army had rested for three nights before moving on to Joppa. Finding it heavily damaged – the enemy's attempt to render it useless to us – Richard had ordered camp set up in an olive grove outside the walls. Sunburned, parched, exhausted, and grieving for our dead, it had been a joy to find orchards of almond, pomegranate and fig trees, as well as vines such as those in whose shade I luxuriated. The fleet had arrived the same afternoon with much-needed supplies of grain and dried meats. Once these had been unloaded, we had done nothing but eat, drink and sleep for a sennight.

A cry of delight.

'Two fives,' said Rhys with evident displeasure.

'I know not how you do it.' Thorne sounded no happier.

'Hand over your money,' de Drune ordered.

The chink of coin followed.

'Another round?' asked de Drune.

The others acceded, but with little enthusiasm. I smiled to myself. De Drune had a knack for winning most games he played.

'We ought to be marching,' said Rhys abruptly. 'Not here in the shade, gambling.'

Thorne snorted. 'I am happy enough to stay in Joppa.'

'And I,' added de Drune.

'Rhys is right,' I said. 'Have you forgotten our purpose here?'

'I thought you were asleep,' said de Drune.

I ignored him. 'The army should have journeyed south the moment we were recovered.'

I fell to brooding about what had happened. Richard had decided that taking Ascalon, the gateway to Egypt, took priority over Jerusalem. Hearing rumour soon after our arrival that the city's fortifications were being torn down on Saladin's orders, he had sent Geoffrey de Lusignan down the coast by ship. A worthy knight recently come to prominence called William de l'Etang went with him. When they returned, confirming the rumour, the king demanded an immediate march on Ascalon.

'Move fast, and we shall seize it ere all the defences are destroyed. Astride the main route to Egypt, we will have our boot on Saladin's throat,' Richard had cried, but the schisms between the different contingents had immediately opened up again. Commanded by the

French, a majority of the leaders voted that Jerusalem was our objective, not Ascalon. 'Why bother with some godforsaken fortlet in the desert?' Hugh of Burgundy memorably cried.

Richard's arguments – that Saladin's greatest fear was the army marching on Ascalon, that the supply lines would be impossible to keep safe once we moved inland – had fallen on deaf ears. Sensing that the unity of the coalition was at stake, the king agreed to the vote, albeit with great reluctance. He had set to work at once, overseeing the rebuilding of the fortifications destroyed by Saladin.

It had not all been hard work and no play. Hunting and hawking were the chief sources of enjoyment for both the king and the mesnie. Such expeditions were not without danger. Two weeks prior disaster had struck when Richard's party was ambushed by Saracens miles from the camp. But for the quick thinking of a knight called William de Préaux, who had shouted out that he was Malik Rik and thus been seized captive, Richard would have suffered the same fate. It was something I would have done, had I been there, but deep inside, I was glad not to be Saladin's prisoner.

As for myself, I had duties – patrols, overseeing the unloading of some supplies and so on – but leisure time took up a good part of each day. That was why I was lying in a vineyard, even if it did not help our cause.

'I am glad we stayed here,' announced de Drune. 'It has been most pleasant.'

Leaning up on an elbow, I snorted. 'Is that because of how much you have been drinking, or the whores?'

'Both,' said Rhys, and dodged a blow from de Drune, whom, I noticed, did not deny either charge.

'As if you have not sampled either,' said Thorne to Rhys.

'Ha!' cried Rhys. 'As if you have not?'

'How dare you address a belted knight so, thou pup!' cried Thorne.

'Do I not speak the truth, sir?' Rhys laid exaggerated emphasis on the last word.

Thorne, who had been supping from his costrel, spluttered wine everywhere.

Rhys's expression remained blank, but I could tell he was fighting not to laugh.

A chuckle of my own escaped me, not just because of Thorne's coughing fit. Rhys's ability to remain familiar with his social superiors never failed to amaze.

Abu was indifferent to the banter. 'When are we to see Saphadin again, sir?' he asked.

Contact had recently been reinitiated between Richard and Saladin. Relations remained cordial, but nothing of substance had been agreed.

'Soon,' I said, explaining, 'The king first wishes to be reacquainted with his wife, the queen.' I ignored the winks and nudges Rhys and de Drune gave each other, and thought longingly of Joanna.

'Nothing much happened at the first meeting, eh?' This was Thorne, directed at Abu.

'There was a lot of talk,' said Abu. 'Both sides said much and . . . meant little.'

The truth was frustrating, but that did not stop everyone from laughing. I made mention of how both sides were playing games. Saladin wished to delay Richard from attacking either Jerusalem or Ascalon, because once winter arrived – it was not long off – he would have to suspend hostilities until the spring. The king, on the other hand, wanted to convince Saladin that he meant to invade Egypt. Do that, he reasoned, and Saladin would offer generous terms to prevent it.

It was a sea change for Richard to seek a negotiated settlement, and born from multiple causes. Prominent among them was the brutal time we had had travelling from Acre; another was the fifteen months that had passed since leaving Chinon, with no foreseeable end in sight to the campaign. The king was growing increasingly concerned about his kingdom, and the threats posed to it by Philippe Capet and his own brother John. No word had come from England in months, but that signified nothing. As the king said, his brother John had never been one to sit on his hands.

'We Franks and the Muslims are bleeding to death,' he had said to me, words he intended to write to Saladin upon his return from Acre. 'The country is utterly ruined, and too many goods and lives have been sacrificed on both sides. The time has come to stop this. The points at issue are Jerusalem, the Cross, and the land. Come to an agreement on them, and I shall achieve my purpose here. We can go home, Rufus.'

Home, I thought. For him, maybe, but not yet for me. It was an old refrain in my head, and one that had weakened, although I hated to admit that. Returning to Cairlinn had been my purpose since the day I had first landed at Striguil twelve years before. To admit that I had little reason to go back there – my immediate family was long dead – seemed tantamount to denying what I was, a proud Irishman. Yet if I imagined sitting in the hall in Cairlinn by a smoky fire as the wind and rain howled in off the sea, as it did for close to half the year, my heart no longer swelled. Those few comrades in Ireland who had survived the brutal English attack on my family's lands – an event that had taken place while I was hostage in Wales – would be long used to living under the invader's yoke.

Lord of broken men I would be, I thought, ruler of a barren little patch of ground ever torn between Leinster and Ulster. I berated myself for even birthing the thought, so traitorous did it seem, and yet I could not deny the truth in it. As Richard's loyal companion, I had wealth, position and respect. There were few who sat as high in the king's favour. I had also the love of his sister Joanna. There was no reason this situation could not persist for some time. If I left the mesnie, on the other hand, I would take the title Richard had promised, Lord of Cairlinn, and whatever riches he granted. Everything else would be lost.

I was unsure if that was a price worth paying.

The king returned early that evening with a massive fleet. He had failed to win over Conrad, who was still refusing to have any part in the campaign, but had otherwise used his brief time at Acre well. Hundreds of 'lazy ones' had been cajoled back into the army, and Richard had also come to a new agreement with the Genoans. If his plan to attack Egypt was ever to become reality, he would need more ships than he had had during the journey to Joppa. Eager to make the most of this potential, the Genoans had committed to his cause.

I cared little for the new vessels, and the singsong Italian of their crews. I was pleased to see the king again, but the only person I was really interested in was Joanna. It was harder than ever to conceal my feelings as she disembarked with Berengaria, a delighted Richard preceding the pair down the gangplank and with outstretched hand, helping them onto the quay.

She was a vision, her blonde hair turned iridescent by the light of the setting sun, and her golden skin tanned even more than it had been before. Laughing at something the king said, she did not see me at first, standing as I was amidst the welcoming party. My breath caught in my chest; I felt like a lovestruck youth, rendered dumb by his passion.

Self-conscious, I looked instead at Berengaria, who seemed genuinely pleased to be with Richard. With God's blessing, I thought, she would get with child in the quieter months to come.

The king greeted us; a chorus of welcomes rang out in answer.

My attention drifted inexorably to Joanna. I could not stop a smile from forming.

She saw me, but her expression changed not a bit. There was the slightest dip of her chin, and that was all. Immediate concern knifed me, even as I told myself she was acting as I should have done. A lifetime at court meant she was expert at concealing emotion.

I burned to see her alone; on the ride back to the camp, my mind raced with ideas of how to engineer that possibility. Joanna was to lodge with the king, in the recently re-roofed and part-reconstructed bailey, which lay inside Joppa's walls. Getting into her chamber would prove tricky indeed.

In the event, several frustrating days passed without a single opportunity presenting itself. I managed to have a few words with Joanna one morning, when she came with the king on a falcon hunt; it was enough to reassure myself that she still cared for me, and for me to tell her of my undying love, but there were too many people about for a proper conversation. Physical contact, which I ached for, was out of the question.

Richard, free to do as he wished, spent less time with Berengaria than I might have thought, rising early and seldom making time for her in the day. I told myself that as long as they lay together each night, it did not matter, yet there was a coolness in the way he dealt with her. I do not think he even noticed the yearning in her expression when he took his leave. He seemed far more interested in the negotiations with Saladin than dallying with his young wife.

On the seventeenth of October, Saladin sent his secretary Ibn an-Nahlal to see the king rather than Saphadin. The meeting I would long remember, so unpleasant was it.

Ibn an-Nahlal was a short, dumpy little Saracen with a black beard. Earnest and intense in the manner of scribes and men of letters, he spoke some French, but still required an interpreter. Richard received him in the repaired and refurbished great hall, a smaller chamber than the one at Acre, with similar high-placed windows and a flagged floor. A low dais at one end had several high-backed chairs on it. Thick walls kept out much of the heat, and I was no longer in armour, but the air was warmer than I liked.

It was not a large gathering. The king was there, and Humphrey de Toron. I had brought Abu at Richard's request. De Chauvigny and de Béthune completed the tally. Ibn an-Nahlal had only his interpreter; his mamluk guards had been forced to remain outside.

After brief introductions and courtesies, the king began. He repeated the sentiments expressed to me, about the grievous loss of life on both sides, and the ruinous cost of the war on Outremer. Ibn an-Nahlal, rubbing his beard, agreed wholeheartedly, and asked if Richard had any suggestions.

'I have,' said the king. 'Jerusalem is for us an object of worship that we could not give up even if there were only one of us left. The land from here to beyond the River Jordan must be consigned to us. The Cross, which for you is simply a piece of wood with no value, is for us of enormous importance. If you will return it, we shall be able to make peace and rest from this endless labour.'

The interpreter did his work, after which there was a long silence, during which Ibn an-Nahlal did much rubbing of his beard.

Richard's only sign of impatience was his right foot, which twitched now and again.

He had demanded a lot, I thought, quite possibly more than Saladin would be disposed to grant.

At last Ibn an-Nahlal spoke through his interpreter. 'I cannot know Salah al-Dīn's mind completely, sire, but I am confident that his answer would be something along these lines. Jerusalem is as much ours as yours. Indeed it is even more sacred to us than it is to you, for it is the place from which our Prophet made his ascent into Heaven and the place where our community will gather on the day of Judgement. Do not imagine that we can renounce it. The land also was originally ours, whereas you are recent arrivals and were able to take it over only as a result of the weakness of the Muslims living here at the time.' This last was a reference to the war, a century before, when the Christians had seized Jerusalem from the Saracens and founded the kingdom of Outremer.

Richard's face was a mask as Humphrey translated, and Abu confirmed his words.

He cannot have been surprised, I decided, but he is not pleased either.

'And the Cross?' asked the king.

'Its possession is a good card in our hand, sire, and could not be surrendered except for an item of outstanding benefit to Islam.' Ibn an-Nahlal's tranquillity seemed to indicate that Richard owned nothing of such value.

I racked my brains, could think of no holy treasures captured at Acre or here at Joppa.

Again a quiet fell. Now it was the king who was deep in thought.

He is playing for time, I thought, but I was wrong.

'Ask Saladin if the hand of my sister is precious enough. What if she were to wed his brother Saphadin? Together they could rule the land, with Jerusalem as their capital.'

Ibn an-Nahlal's eyes narrowed as the interpreter spoke quietly to him.

I stared at Richard, brimming with shock and anger. My stomach turned at the thought of Joanna taken unwilling to wed Saphadin, one of the accursed race, a man old enough to be her father. Alone among unbelievers, her existence would be an indescribable torment, to last for the rest of her days. It was a fate I would not wish on an enemy, less still on the woman I loved.

He, oblivious, was focused on Saladin's secretary. 'Well?' the king demanded.

An-Nahlal spoke, and the interpreter asked, 'Is your offer genuine, sire?'

'It is.' Richard's voice was low but confident.

Ibn an-Nahlal was a born negotiator; his expression gave no indication if he believed the king or not. 'In that case, sire, I shall relay your proposal to Salah al-Din. He will be most interested to hear it.'

Arrangements were made to meet again within the next day or two, and Ibn an-Nahlal took his leave.

He was barely out the door when I turned to the king. I calmed myself as best I could, which is to say, not much. 'Do you truly mean to marry Queen Joanna to Saphadin, sire?'

Busy cleaning his fingernails with his dagger, an unpleasant habit of his, he did not see my face. 'If it means peace with Saladin, why, yes.'

I was aware of Rhys giving me a warning look, but I could no more stay silent than prevent the tide from turning. Reining in the violent protest I wished to shout, I said evenly, 'It would not be right, sire, to treat any woman so, still less a queen.'

Richard laid the dagger in his lap, and regarded me. His face was cold and hard. 'Do my ears deceive me?'

Panicked – terrified – by the idea that Joanna would be consigned to such a fate, I flailed for something plausible to say. 'Your sister is a devout Christian, sire, and despite all his graces, Saphadin is a vile Saracen. Your offer would condemn her to spend her entire life among the defilers, the accursed race. Unable to worship God, bereft of friends and family, it would be a fate worse than death. Place her in a prison cell, sire – that would be kinder!'

Richard rose to his full height, which was several inches taller than mine. His expression, at first perplexed and a little irritated, was now incandescent with rage. The dagger in his right hand pointed at me. 'How dare you speak to *your king* so?'

Unwilling to back down, but acutely aware that my next words might see my neck on the executioner's block, I stitched my lip. We locked eyes, each refusing to look away. How I hated him in that moment, the sheer arrogance of him, the assumption that his will superseded mine.

'Is the king within?' Berengaria's voice carried from beyond the portal.

A sentry muttered an answer, and the door swung inwards with a creak, bringing with it a blast of sunlight and heat.

'Queen Berengaria and Queen Joanna, sire,' the captain of the guard announced.

'God's legs, am I to be eternally plagued?' Richard muttered to himself. Giving me a murderous, *I will deal with you later* look, he smoothed his features, and called out, 'What an unexpected surprise!'

Everyone but he bowed as the women approached. Joanna was radiant, clad in a sky blue gown that emphasised the glory of her hair. Berengaria, bless her, was dowdy in comparison.

The latter spoke first. 'Was that Saladin's emissary I saw leaving?'

'It was indeed,' said Richard. Casually, he changed the subject. 'To what do I owe the pleasure?'

'Have you found any common ground, brother?' asked Joanna.

'In theory,' the king answered.

'Will that mean peace?' Her eyes were bright. 'Say it is so!'

'There is much still to discuss.' Richard's hand waved in the air. 'Berengaria, let us walk the shaded avenues in the gardens. Lass, will you come?'

'Fie on you, Richard,' said Joanna. 'Do you think so little of your women? Speak.'

The king looked a little strained. 'It is not that, lass.'

'What then?'

He did not answer, but moved to take Berengaria's arm. 'Let us go,' he said.

Joanna's gaze, frustrated, moved to mine, and the last of my resolve vanished. It was beyond me to remain silent. 'If Saladin agrees, madam, the king means to marry you to his brother,' I said. 'Saphadin.'

She blanched; her hand rose to her mouth.

Richard spun to regard me. I swear, if looks could have killed, I would have fallen down dead.

'Richard?' Joanna asked.

The muscles in his jaw worked, but he said nothing.

'Husband?' Berengaria asked. 'Can this really be your plan?'

'Tell me!' Joanna's horror had vanished. There was iron in her demeanour now.

'It was only a suggestion,' said Richard. He glanced at her, and incredibly – for I had never seen it before – there was guilt in his eyes. 'I would not have gone through with it without your consent, lass.'

'So you say! When would you have told me – the very day of the wedding?' cried Joanna. Her pretty face twisted with disappointment and anger, she hurried to the door.

Berengaria followed, paying no heed to the king's request that she stay.

I went too, my purpose not to speak to Joanna – she needed a woman's solace first – but to leave Richard, whose company I could not for the moment bear. Abu scurried after me, petrified.

'Rufus!' the king roared.

I ignored him.

'Rufus, get back here!'

I was near the entrance. The sentries were goggling; they had never witnessed such a scene. One made to block my path. I shouted at him with such venom that he almost fell over in his haste to stand aside.

Richard could have ordered them to seize me, but he did not.

I heard his angry shouts all the way to the main gate.

The day passed. No summons from the king arrived. No message from Joanna came. I brooded in my tent, and raged to Rhys – the only person I could confide in – of the injustice of it all. He listened with sympathy, but could offer no solution. I was powerless before the king, and we both knew it. The following morning, news reached me of a magnificent horse sent as a gift to Saphadin by Richard. It did not augur well for my hopes that he would have seen fit to rescind his shameful offer. There was no contact with the king. I went about my duties, and tried and failed to think of ways of thwarting Richard, and seeing Joanna in private.

The king and Saphadin met in person the day after, with Humphrey de Toron again interpreting. De Chauvigny and de Béthune also went, but I was not invited; nor was Abu. I was like a caged beast while the meeting went on in the great hall. The first moment I could speak to de Béthune afterwards, I did so. I could tell by his unhappy face that he did not bear good news.

'Did he take back his offer?' I demanded.

De Béthune shook his head.

'The craven bastard.'

'Hush!' De Béthune looked up and down the corridor. 'It is dangerous to speak so.'

I snorted. 'Tell me all.'

'It was simple enough. Richard offered Queen Joanna's hand in marriage to Saphadin, who seemed most complimented. He accepted on the spot, and asked for more details.'

I ground my teeth. 'Go on.'

'Joanna's dowry will include the coastal cities and lands taken by the king since his arrival. For his part, Saladin is to give over to Saphadin all the lands west of the River Jordan. The villages in these territories shall belong to the Hospitallers, and the castles to Joanna and Saphadin. The couple will reside in Jerusalem, which will be safe and open to visits by Christians. The Holy Cross will be returned and the prisoners held on both sides freed. Lastly, the king is to leave Outremer and go back to England.'

'Was Richard serious?' I demanded, scarcely believing what I had heard.

'I do not think he can be. There would be uproar in all Christendom to hear of a Christian queen wed, even willingly, to a Saracen.'

'Why does he even suggest it then?' I cried bitterly.

'He is playing games with Saladin. The army is not quite ready to march, as you know, and the king wants to strengthen further the defences at Joppa, as well as marshalling the Pisans and Genoese in case the chance to strike at Egypt should come.'

'To use his sister so is vile,' I said, but the intimation that the king's offer had not been genuine was beginning to make me regret my outburst two days before. 'What did Saphadin say?'

'That the terms were not disagreeable, but that Saladin would also have to concur. He left, promising to have an answer by tomorrow.'

'And if Saladin accepts?'

'We shall see, but I cannot see the king allowing the marriage to proceed. He has not admitted as much – he is saying nothing to anyone – but de Chauvigny feels as I do.'

This was good news, more than I had hoped for. Whether there was any chance of a rapprochement with the king, though, I was unsure.

'De Chauvigny and I are of one mind, Rufus. Marrying Queen Joanna to a Saracen is a barbarous idea, and unacceptable. The notion seems to have affected you a great deal more than us, however. There is more to this than meets the eye.' De Béthune gave me an enquiring look.

In my mad desperation, I had not considered how my behaviour had seemed to others. I stared at him, wordless.

'I saw the way you looked at her in Sicily, Rufus.'

'You see through me,' I said thickly. 'It is the queen. I love her.'

'Does she feel the same way?'

From nowhere on the storm-tossed sea in which I was drowning, a spar. I pushed it away, and trusted that de Béthune was as true a friend as I judged. 'She does,' I whispered.

'Sweet Jesu! Does the king suspect anything?' De Béthune shook his head. 'No, he cannot, else he would have cut off your head. You walk a dangerous path, Rufus.'

I managed a cracked smile. 'Love's arrow cares not who it strikes.'

'That is true,' he said with an amused nod. 'Well, Richard shall not hear it from me – you have my word.'

I muttered my thanks.

'I shall endeavour to dampen the king's anger towards you, but I warn you, it will be no easy task. The mere mention of your name sends him into a towering fury.' Clasping my hand, de Béthune took his leave.

Miserable, unable to see a solution to the crisis my outburst had caused, I donned my armour, then went to the stables and saddled Pommers. It was easy to find a sparring partner on the open ground close to the walls; there were always knights training.

I would take out my frustration on whoever accepted my challenge.

Bells were ringing compline from a rebuilt church – a welcome sound, for despite my liking for the wailing muezzins, it felt more natural, more Christian – and I was sitting in the darkness outside my tent. There was no need for a cloak, but a small fire glowed at my feet; it was starting to grow chilly at night. Hundreds of other tents were dotted around me. There was noise of music, and singing, and from somewhere off to my right, the sound of men having a drunken argument. Dragging a reluctant Abu, Rhys had gone off with de Drune in search of wine. Thorne, de Béthune, de Chauvigny and half a dozen more of the mesnie were in the best of the town's taverns. Weary from my exertions against half a dozen knights, nursing several large bruises, I had declined an invitation to join them. I was alone, and content to be so. A costrel of wine lay in my lap, and I had every intention of draining it ere I took to my blanket.

Dark thoughts consumed me. If the king did not go through with his offer to Saladin, as seemed likely according to de Béthune, I would have spoken up for nothing, fractured our long friendship without reason. It was hard to see how I could remain in the mesnie if things continued as they were. I might even have to leave Outremer, to take ship for I did not know where.

Over and again, I berated myself for speaking out, for not having the wit to anticipate that Richard's offer had merely been a gambit in the chess game he was playing with Saladin. When I thought of Joanna, my anguish grew even worse. Any chance of secretly visiting her had diminished further.

My mood spiralling downward, I attacked my costrel, gulping down great mouthfuls of wine. It would bring but temporary solace, and I would pay for it on the morrow – that did not stop me. I wanted to forget, if only for a few hours.

'Beware the man who drinks alone.'

Startled, I leaped a foot in the air. The soft voice, a woman's, was known to me. 'Joanna?' I asked, trembling, careful to pitch my voice low.

Into the dim glow cast by my fire she came. Back went the hood of her mantle. A vision she was, even in the plain dress of one of her serving women. She smiled. 'I judged it too difficult for you to reach my room unhindered.'

Leaping up, I stood, drinking her in. 'Are you alone?'

Her head turned, and I spied two figures in the shadows whence she had been. 'I wish to have privacy. Back to the keep with you,' she said. One of the women began to protest, and Joanna said, 'I am safe here, and will not return unaccompanied. Go!'

The pair bowed and left us.

Nervous – we had spent long months apart, and she was *so* beautiful – I stared in silence at her.

'Art not glad to see me?' she asked.

The dam broke. 'God and all His saints, I am delighted! Knowing you were so close has made every hour since your arrival a torment.' Wanting more than anything to touch her, I hesitated. She was a queen, I a mere knight.

Reaching out, she drew me into a lingering kiss.

When we pulled back – our faces were still close – she said throatily, 'How I have missed you, Ferdia Ó Catháin.'

'And I you, madam,' I said, and kissed her again.

We retired to my tent, where little more was said for some time.

We lay together on my linen sheet, close as lovers, who, having partaken of each other's bodies, do not yet want to separate. Our hands roamed, caressing, touching, getting to know one another again. We kissed. Laughed. Teased. Slept for a time. Coupled again. Drank wine. Joanna pronounced it 'acceptable'; I told her, teasing, that it was the best that could be found, the royal quartermaster having bought up the rest.

She made a face, and before taking another mouthful, said, 'In that case, it will have to suffice.'

Mention of the king had stirred my disquiet; knowing Joanna again stoked my determination that Saphadin should never have her.

'Have you spoken to Richard about his offer to Saladin?' I asked.

She stared into my eyes. 'Several times.'

'And . . .?'

'There was more to my brother's ploy than it seems. He offered me to al-'Ādil'—' she made a fine fist of the name belonging to the man I only ever called Saphadin '—trying to drive a wedge between the brothers. Saladin is eight years the older, and not well. His oldest son is but one-and-twenty, and shows none of the aptitude for leadership that Saphadin has. Richard's plan was to entice Saphadin with the idea of wedding me, and becoming a king. That in turn might tempt him to hatch plans to seize power from Saladin. If dissension broke out in the Saracen camp, our cause would be strengthened.'

'Even if he did not mean to honour the offer, it is an over-elaborate scheme with almost no chance of success,' I grumbled.

'That was my thinking also.' A line creased her perfect brow. 'As if I would ever be part of a harim! Believe me, Richard is well aware of my displeasure. So is every person in the keep, according to one of my ladies. The shouting would have brought down the walls of Jerusalem, she maintained.' Joanna looked rather pleased with herself.

I chuckled, delighted that Richard should have been browbeaten by a woman.

'I am surprised you did not hear it. At need I have a real harridan's screech.'

'Incredible, from one so beautiful.' I ran a finger along the line of her jaw, marvelling as ever that she loved me. Me.

She caressed my face. 'Ah, Ferdia. What am I to do with you?'

Marry me. I bit the inside of my cheek to stop myself from saying those words. An instant later, I tasted warm copper. I must have winced, because she asked if aught was wrong.

I shook my head, thinking, I cannot mention it again. Powerful enough she is to tear Richard down to size over his putative arrangement with Saphadin, but she cannot resist him forever. He is the king. He shall decide whom she shall marry. Cherish the happiness you have with her now, I told myself, because it will come to an end. When that day comes to pass, nothing you can do will stop it.

'So Saphadin will not have you?' I asked.

'Never!' Her nostrils flared. 'I took Richard to the keep's chapel and there made him swear it on holy relics.'

The image made me snort with amusement, but I was still troubled by the rift in my relationship with the king. 'Has he spoken of me? He must be furious still.'

'He said you were a bull-headed Irishman with more courage than sense. There was something else, about your stubbornness and insufferable nerve.'

'What did you say?'

'I sympathised with his position, that is all. I gave nothing away.'

I sighed, picturing Richard raging about me, still unwilling to see reason, less still, prepared to build bridges.

Her mouth crooked. 'He will come around, Ferdia.'

'How do you know?'

'I will not rest until he does. Secondly, I know my brother. When he has done wrong – and he *knows* he has – he will act to put it right.'

'I hope so, madam,' I said, and pulled her to me.

CHAPTER XXVII

Casel Moien, November 1191

Thick grey cloud hung over the land, threatening rain. It was Saint Leonard's Day, the sixth of the month, and I was wrapped in my cloak against the autumn cool. A short distance away, Richard was supervising the rebuilding of the small fortress of Casel Moien, which lay several miles from Joppa and the coast. Some three weeks had passed, and we had come no further inland. In addition, and despite Joanna's optimism, the king and I had not repaired the rent in our friendship.

I was still part of the mesnie; I continued to share duties with the other knights, but I did not attend to Richard or spend time in his company, as de Béthune and de Chauvigny were this very instant. If we locked eyes, the king would look away, and he did not speak to me unless it was unavoidable. It was a heavy burden to bear, as I oft said to Joanna during our night-time trysts. Her gentle response was always the same, that I should give him time. 'He is a proud man, Ferdia. It is not easy for him to admit that he was wrong.'

I took her at her word, for there was little I could do about the situation.

The king was deep in conversation now with a gnarly featured stonemason from Wells in Somerset called Arthur, who served as a man-at-arms. He had been called into service at first in Arsur and then Joppa, to help repair the damage done by Saladin's army. Here at Casel Moien he was also needed; the stronghold was small, but sitting as it did on the pilgrims' path to Jerusalem, it was an important defensive point against Saracen attack. Richard had declared that both it and the Casel of the Plains – Abu indignantly called it Yāzūr – which lay some two miles away, should be restored before the army continued its march east. It made sense, but it was frustrating.

In typical fashion, the king had thrown himself into learning about stonemasonry. He would talk about cutting techniques, the best way of lifting slabs of stone, and other things that bored me to tears. I was glad not to be close to him as he loudly discussed with Arthur the quickest way of repairing the large holes in the fortress walls. Instead Thorne and I were playing dice, using a great carven block of granite as our playing board.

It was I who first spied the Templar spurring towards us. Down the road he came, mud and stone chips flying. The way he was bent forward over the destrier's neck spoke of one thing alone.

'Trouble,' I said, feeling a thrill of fear and excitement both. Early that morning, protected by fifty Templars, a hundred squires and men-at-arms had gone seeking grass and fodder for the horses and baggage animals – in the very same direction from which the rider was coming.

Thorne, cupping the dice, lifted his head. 'Where?'

'The Templar, there. Look.' I thought of Rhys and de Drune, and was glad they were in the camp.

Thorne, ever with an eye to winning coin, glanced, and then rolled. 'Two sixes! I win!'

I paid him no heed, but stepped forward with a raised hand so that the Templar might see me. 'The king is here!' I called.

He came thundering towards me, slowing as he neared the blocks of stone that lay strewn everywhere.

'What news?' I asked, offering to take the reins of his sweat-lathered destrier.

'An ambush! Hordes of mamluks appeared from nowhere and all but surrounded us.' He slipped from the saddle and ran towards Richard.

Thorne and I were close enough to hear the Templar's dramatic tale. The squires and men-at-arms had spread out thinly, as was their wont when looking for grass. The Templars had been unable to watch over every single one; that too was normal enough. Nothing untoward happened for some time, but near the village of Bombrac, four troops of Turks, well-drilled, launched a sudden attack. A number of squires and men-at-arms were killed before the Templars managed to deploy. Thanks to the overwhelming enemy numbers, they had soon been forced to dismount and fight on foot.

'How many mamluks, would you say?' demanded the king.

'Six, eight hundred, sire, maybe more. We beg for every assistance you can provide.'

My heart thumped. This was just the kind of action I lived for.

'André,' said the king to de Chauvigny. 'Take as many of the household as can be gathered quickly and ride there at once. De Béthune, you accompany him.' His gaze roved over those who were close by; it rested on me, and my hopes rose.

He said not a word.

The snub cut like a knife. Furious, I glanced at Thorne, who gave me a 'what can we do?' shrug.

De Béthune, the stout heart, acted. 'Rufus is there, sire, and Thorne. Should they not also come?'

'They can remain for the moment.'

De Béthune seemed about to protest, but Richard gave him a look, and he subsided.

'And you, sire?' asked de Chauvigny.

'I shall send the earl of Leicester and the Count de Pol after you – they are not far away. I will follow on should I be needed. Now, go to, lest the accursed ones wreak a slaughter!'

'Why is the king being like this?' Thorne muttered to me as de Béthune and de Chauvigny ran, shouting for their squires, with the Templar following. 'There should no longer be any quarrel between you.' Negotiations with Saladin continued despite our advance eastward, but Richard had taken the proposal about Joanna off the table.

'I know not,' I said, fighting bitterness.

'You are one of his best men. He is cutting off his own nose to spite his face,' said Thorne.

Cheered by his solidarity, I gripped his shoulder.

At this juncture, Thorne reminded me that I owed him a silver penny for our last, interrupted game of dice. I offered him double or nothing; he accepted, and lost. Undaunted, he challenged me to another game. In this manner, we managed to distract ourselves, partly at least, from the commotion as de Chauvigny, de Béthune, the Templar and a score of others assembled and rode off at top speed.

It was noticeable that the king was paying less attention to Arthur the stonemason, and that his gaze often strayed in the same direction as ours. A short while later, there was more excitement and noise as the earl of Leicester, a doughty fighter, and the Count de Pol, an excitable, talkative type, galloped off with their large retinues.

I could scarcely concentrate on the dice, my mind full of what might be unfolding on the road to Bombrac. I lost to Thorne time and again. Finally, I could take no more. I gave him his winnings.

'I am going to arm myself.'

Thorne immediately declared a wish to do the same. 'Better to be prepared than not,' he said, as we helped each other into our hauberks.

I laughed upon our return to the spot where we had been standing. 'Look at the king.'

Thorne chuckled.

Richard had clearly ordered his young squire, a lad of fifteen or so, to fetch his war gear. Still talking to Arthur, he was donning his gambeson. His heavy mail coat lay on a nearby slab, and his squire stood by with sword, belt and dagger.

We had all done the right thing, it turned out. The block and tackle had lifted only two fresh blocks to the breach in the wall when a Flemish knight called Guillaume de Caieux came riding as if every demon in Hell was after him. The first attack, he reported, had been a ruse. First de Chauvigny and de Béthune had ridden into the trap, and then the earl of Leicester and the Count de Pol had been surrounded as well.

'There must be four thousand Turkish cavalry on the field, sire,' said de Caieux. 'Our comrades face annihilation.'

His dramatic arrival had seen the work on the fortress walls cease. Now, at his doom-laden words, men muttered prayers. Like an ill omen, a northerly wind whistled around the corner of the half-rebuilt gate tower.

'Let us go,' said Richard, striding towards his destrier.

De Caieux hurried to keep up.

Giving Thorne a nudge, I made for Pommers.

'Is this wise?' Thorne asked, even as he joined me.

'I heard no order forbidding us from riding with the king. Did you?'

Thorne was smiling as he worked his helm into place and pulled it down onto his head. Muffled, he said, 'In truth, I did not.'

We left at once, riding hard and fast, in a triple file, not quite fifty of us. The king knew, as did we all, that every moment's delay risked sealing the fate of our brothers-in-arms. If there was to be any reaction, it needed to be instant; the thousands of knights in the main camp were near, but also too far.

Our own fate we did not think about, at least not until we drew near to the battle, which was raging to and fro across the dirt road to Bombrac. Richard halted, the better to assess what was going on.

It was not easy; all was confusion. I could see little circles of men on foot – the squires and men-at-arms, and with them, the Templars – being assailed from every side by a myriad of mamluks. Loosing volley after volley of arrows, the enemy riders rode around their prey, whooping like devils. Mounted knights – those led by de Chauvigny, the earl of Leicester and the Count de Pol – charged denser groups of mamluks, but these fled, separating into twos and threes so they could not be caught. The moment the knights reined in and began to withdraw, the mamluks regrouped and attacked their rear.

'Twenty to one, the Templar estimated?' said Thorne grimly. 'I would hazard thirty to one.'

It was hard to argue with his guess. This battle was already lost, and our comrades doomed. Enter the maelstrom, I thought, and we had no chance of surviving.

I was not alone in my assessment. Although I held my peace – I did not want to seem afraid – voice after voice, knight after knight, entreated the king not to press home the assault. The situation was dire, they said. Too dangerous. It was not worth the risk.

De Caieux it was who made the most eloquent plea. 'We do not judge it would be safe to engage such a large force with a few knights, sire. Perhaps you think that you should risk it, but you will not be able to sustain the enemy's attack. Less damaging it would be, sire, if those who are surrounded perish alone, rather than allow the Turks to swallow you up with them, for then the hope of Christendom would perish and its confidence be destroyed.'

Richard listened in silence. When de Caieux was done, he said, 'I can no more ride away from this field than worship the Devil Himself.'

'But, sire—' began de Caieux.

'I sent those men here,' said Richard, couching his lance. 'If they die without me, I do not wish to be called king any longer.'

Heart-stirring words they were, and my love for him, my regard for his loyalty and fearlessness, swelled anew in my breast. I will die beside you, I thought, readying myself for the coming charge. When he asked who was with him, I was first to speak.

'I am here, sire!' I saluted him with my lance.

'Rufus!' Incredibly, he laughed. 'Ride with me, you and every man who would follow!'

A loud cheer rose, and then, knee-to-knee, destriers racing one another, we charged.

It was pure, unadulterated madness. We should have died, all of us, wiped out by the mamluks. They, bursting with confidence, jeered and hurled insults as we rode at them.

We hit with the power of a Biblical flood, punching a great hole in their ranks. Skewered by lances, mamluks were hurled like puppets into the air. Horses stumbled and went down, their riders toppled from saddles. Our destriers trampled indiscriminately. Out came our swords, and we cut fresh swathes through the enemy, few of whom even landed a blow. Arms were sliced off, heads too. I saw a leg, the foot still in a shoe, tumble to the dirt. Blood arced, sprayed, gushed, spattered. Now and again, I heard the king shouting, 'Dex aie!', and I echoed his call. There were cries, gurgles, screams, prayers, what I assume were pleas for mercy, and over everything, the metallic ring of arms. Of sword meeting shield. Of blade ringing, skidding off mail. Of mace striking helmet, and shield taking blow after hammer blow.

Death reigned supreme, and we were kings of it.

Deeper we pushed into the mamluks, slaughtering, maiming, sowing panic.

They could not stand before us, numerous as they were.

We had come to kill, and nobody could, would stand before us.

As a flock of birds neatly changes direction, guided by some internal impulse, the mamluks turned and fled. I heard no command to withdraw, no signal. One moment I was surrounded by foes, and the next, I could only see men's backs, and horses' rear ends. I blinked away sweat, and the gap between me and the nearest mamluks had doubled. Another blink, and they were a hundred paces from us. To either side, their fellows were doing the same. Mingled with my relief and exhilaration was a powerful desire to chase after and redden my blade again.

'Flee!' Richard was close by me, on my left. 'Flee, you defilers!'

'Victory, sire,' I cried. 'You did it!'

His red-crested helm turned. 'We did it, Rufus,' he said. 'We.'

Heart full, I saluted him with my blade. His acknowledgement mattered far more than our against-the-odds victory.

Out of the blue, he said, 'I would never do anything to harm my sister.'

'I understand, sire.' This, I decided, was the closest I would get to an apology.

My friendship with Richard was restored, just like that. Whether he had any suspicions about me and Joanna, I had no idea, but nothing was said. All was well with the world, and I told myself that the days following the fight on the road to Bombrac would be, if not as glorious, then trouble-free.

If God heard my prayers for such, He laughed.

It started raining on the seventh of November, and did not stop. Thick grey clouds came so low to the ground they felt like shrouds. They drenched, showered, and hailed on the army. They saw fit to dump snow on a number of occasions. Gales battered us by day and tore our tents at night. The roads, already muddy, turned to quagmires in which no wagon could travel, unless there were a dozen strong men to heave it from one area of sucking morass to another. We were fortunate if the host made two miles in a day. Often it was less.

By the last week of November, negotiations with Saladin had ground to a halt and by unspoken mutual assent were not renewed. The enemy leader had gone into winter quarters at Jerusalem, and we had reached the town of Ramla, less than halfway to that city. There the army was to stay for more than a month; it seemed possible we might remain until spring. The terrible conditions did not ease, nor did the downpours. The rain and endless damp sickened men and animals, mildewed clothing and food, rusted weapons and armour. Even the salt pork rotted in its barrels. Incredibly, the troops' morale remained buoyant. The priests who accompanied the army spoke, loud and eloquent, of the rewards that would be ours within weeks, in Jerusalem. Word spread to Joppa, and the halt and the sick who were lying there began travelling to our camp in wagons, expecting soon to be able to worship in the sacred shrines.

The Holy City was less than twenty-five miles from our camp, I often heard men say, continuing that the final objective lay almost within our grasp. I grew weary of the refrain, 'A sennight's march, is all!' It seemed that many could not see what was in front of their faces: the roads made impassable by deep mud, the shortage of food and supplies for man and beast, and the shocking weather, which would not improve for months.

Every discussion held between Richard, his commanders, and the grand masters of the military orders came to the same conclusion. Even if we reached the tall, high, well-manned defences of Jerusalem, we had not enough soldiers to encircle it. Any attempt at a siege therefore risked defeat, either at the hands of the Turks, or through disease and hunger. In the unlikely event that we took the Holy City, we diced with failure as well. At least half of the army, their promises to God complete, would immediately return home. At a stroke, its garrison dangerously under strength, the city would be in grave peril of falling to the first Saracen force to arrive before its gates.

Although most men did not yet see it, Richard and his closest advisers had come to the grim realisation that our best option was to withdraw to the coast, and there rebuild Ascalon. To block Saladin's main supply route would grant a vital breathing space, and the sending of urgent messages to every kingdom in Christendom. Thousands more men needed to take the cross; only their arrival would make an attempt on Jerusalem feasible.

The French and other contingents could not be swayed, however, and a stalemate developed. We did not march east, nor retreat west, but remained at Ramla, wet, cold and miserable.

The nightmarish conditions did not put a stop to scouting, raids and skirmishes. Probe was followed by counter probe, ambush by surprise attack. Five days before Christmas, the count of Leicester was taken prisoner in a vicious little scrap that fortuitously ended in victory for our knights and his being freed after a few short hours in captivity. De Chauvigny suffered a broken arm during the skirmish, but was fortunate not to have been slain, as several others were. Tension eased not long after with the news that Saladin had disbanded his army until the spring. Two days before Christmas, Richard ordered his court eight miles south to Toron des Chevaliers – Abu called it al-Latrun – and the ruined Templar castle there.

Our dirty, mildewing, vermin-infested camp was no place for gentlewomen – Berengaria and Joanna were with us still – so Richard decided to make the Yuletide festivities memorable. A grand feast was laid on, or as grand as could be produced in tents with constant rain drumming off the canvas. The food was good at least, and the wine flowed in torrents. I also managed to sneak into Joanna's tent unseen that night, something that had been proving tricky, what with the sucking mud and greater than normal number of sentries everywhere. Warmed by braziers, we lay naked on her bed, laughing and talking quietly for hours. We did other things too, pleasurable and memorable in equal measure, telling each other as we did, of our undying love.

Too brief are such moments in life. Too soon does cold reality return.

Several days after Christmas, using the opportunity of a short dry spell, the army marched to Bait Nūbā, a mere twelve miles from Jerusalem. There was much rejoicing, and wild expectations that we would drive the Saracens from the city by the middle of January. I even heard claims that if we but attacked in force, the enemy would flee, allowing us to enter the Holy City, triumphant, on New Year's Day itself.

We did nothing of the sort. The weather grew even more brutal. Gales came shrieking down from the mountains, ripping tent panels and causing landslides that threatened the peripheries of the camp. Torrential downpours saw the mud knee-deep and worse. The stories of men drowning in it were just that, stories, but many wagons had to be abandoned, so deeply enmired were they. It was some good fortune, I suppose, that their unfortunate mules could then be slaughtered for food.

By the eleventh of January, the year of our Lord 1192, Richard had endured enough. With Berengaria and Joanna safely back in Joppa – she and I had had a bittersweet parting – he could, with my help, focus entirely on a withdrawal to the coast.

The French, everyone knew, would not take the king's decision well.

It was even possible that the army would break up.

That afternoon, I waited with Richard in his tent for the leaders of the various contingents to arrive. The antechamber was carpeted throughout, and half a dozen braziers did their best to raise the temperature, but the howling wind outside found every crevice and gap. Chill currents of air kept licking at my ankles and the back of my neck, making me glad of my thickest woollen tunic.

De Béthune was also present, but de Chauvigny was on his way to Rome, his mission to find out all he could about John. As the king said, knowing something of what was going on was better than nothing.

Richard paced about, musing aloud. ''Tis a sad day, Rufus.' He saw my face. 'Aye, I hate the notion of retreating. Withdrawing, maybe, is better.'

'After this long, sire, it feels . . . *wrong*.'

'If we stay, things will get a lot worse. You heard what Ralph Besace said. Cholera and dysentery will become rampant as the winter grinds on. Hundreds, if not thousands will die from those diseases alone, not to mention those who succumb to hunger and other maladies. There is not enough food for the horses and mules either. Losses among those would also be severe.'

'Yes, sire.' I sighed. Without our destriers, we had no chance of defeating the Saracens.

'Come the spring, Saladin's men would arrive in his camp well-fed and content after months spent by the fireside. They would smash us like so much kindling.'

His argument was powerful, and he carried the day in the meeting held soon after. It helped that both de Nablus and de Sablé were of the same opinion, and also Guy de Lusignan. Three times the gathering heard that withdrawal to the coast was the sensible option, that a siege risked all, that our supply lines were already stretched and brittle. Only the French, who had entered the meeting thinking that Jerusalem might still be taken, continued to argue.

Richard was well-prepared. Ordering a map of the Holy City to be drawn, he proved beyond doubt that the army's numbers were not great enough to span the circumference of the city. 'If we cannot even surround it, messires,' the king had argued eloquently, 'That pack of curs will break out at will, and food and materiel will enter the city in the same manner.'

Henri of Blois, who had been nodding while the king spoke, was first to break ranks with his fellow Frenchmen. He won over des Barres, who in turn persuaded Duke Hugh of Burgundy that Richard's plan made sense. After that, the rest of them folded, albeit with poor grace.

I wish I could say that the ordinary soldiers took the news better. As the order to quit Bait Nūbā was disseminated through the camp, such a wailing and crying was never heard. An air of utter despondency descended. I saw men throwing themselves down in the mud with despair, and declaring this the worst day of their lives. The perennial cry of 'Sanctum Sepulchrum adjuva!' was heard loud and frequent until long after darkness fell.

Although he had got what he wanted, the king was in sombre mood that night. He looked worn out with grief and toil, like I had never seen him. Together with de Béthune, I stayed with him for hours. We sat around a brazier, drank far too much wine, and swore owlishly to each other that we would return to take Jerusalem at the first opportunity.

'If my cursed brother John does not prevent us,' said the king towards the end.

I turned bleary eyes on him. 'Sire?'

'There has been no word from Longchamp for months.'

'That could be a good thing, sire,' I ventured.

A worn smile. 'You do not know my brother John as I do. He never rests, the whelp, never ceases from conniving and scheming. It is the winter weather and the danger to shipping that have prevented fresh letters reaching me, that is all.'

De Béthune, who had served Richard's father Henry first, and spent a lot of time with John in the process, did not look in the least surprised.

The king stared for so long into the glowing ashes I began to wonder if he was falling ill again. To any question he was asked came a curt yes or no.

At length, de Béthune asked leave to retire. I was left alone with Richard. We sat in silence for some time. I did not know how to offer advice or comfort – I was no statesman or politician. I would have taken John's head years before, and yet that was no solution either, for to do so would have left a tiny child, Richard's nephew Arthur, as his only heir. The risk to his kingdom from that would have been even greater than leaving the weaselly John to his treachery.

The king broke the silence at last. 'It would be an ignoble end to the campaign if I had to leave Outremer because of my brother, eh?'

'Surely it will not come to that, sire,' I protested.

'I hope not,' said Richard, but there was a hollow sound to his words.

CHAPTER XXVIII

Ascalon, April 1192

I lay curled up with Joanna in her bed, her head on my shoulder, her golden tresses falling down over us like a coverlet. It was night-time, and although I had not been in her tent long, we had already sated our passion. The novelty of being with each other had not palled even a little; we had seen precious little of each other for three months.

She had not been with the army when we slogged through the mud and driving rain from Beit Nūbā to Ramla. There all the French had abandoned us save Henri of Blois and his men, and surprisingly, Duke Hugh of Burgundy. Nor had I seen her as we continued to Ascalon, because we had bypassed Joppa to reach the coast faster. A brief re-union of a few days in mid-February came about when the king broke his journey north to meet Conrad of Montferrat, but I had not seen her again until the end of March.

It was unsurprising then that, disregarding the risk, we had spent almost every night together since. I say night, but well before each dawn, Joanna would force me – with many's the kiss – to leave.

It was wonderful, but it could not last forever.

Soon we would be on the move; our work of the last three months, rebuilding Ascalon, was almost complete. Thorny issues, among them Saladin and Jerusalem, which had been laid aside, had again to be addressed. Negotiations had recently restarted, but already agreement seemed improbable. War threatened once more, and thanks to the rivalry and infighting within the army, our forces were weaker than they had been six months before.

I let out a long, slow breath.

'That was a big sigh.' Joanna's hand moved across my chest, a gentle, possessive gesture. 'What is it, my heart?'

I chuckled. 'Where to begin?'

'At the start?' There was a teasing lilt to her voice, but the sentiment was genuine.

'It is nothing we have not discussed before.'

'If you are troubled, the subjects bear airing again.'

I squeezed her to me. 'The Pisans. The Genoese. Conrad of Montferrat. Duke Hugh of Burgundy. Guy de Lusignan – I could go on.'

She pushed up on an elbow, the better to look at me in the honey-yellow candlelight. 'Acre is at peace now – Richard forced the Pisans and Genoese to lay down their arms.'

The animosity between the two factions was always close to the surface; she was referring to the latest round of hostilities, which had erupted in February. Word had reached us of the Genoans' approach to Conrad; the rogue was quick to come to their aid. Duke Hugh had joined him, and a fresh siege of the city started, with the Pisans inside and the Genoese, Conrad and Hugh outside. Richard, already on the road north to the meeting with Conrad I had recalled, had diverted to the city. Wary of his wrath, the pair had scuttled back to Tyre.

'Do not worry about Acre.' She turned my chin with a forefinger so that I looked at her.

'Aye, I suppose.'

'Next, Conrad of Montferrat and Duke Hugh. They are troublesome men, I cannot argue, and all the more so since they leagued themselves with each other.'

I nodded, remembering how I had ridden with the king to see Conrad at Casel Imbert, north of the city, after the status quo in Acre had been restored. 'He is a scheming dog. The meeting with Richard was an exercise in futility.'

'Conrad refused any suggestion that he join with us, if my memory serves, and the two of them argued bitterly.'

'Aye.' I could still hear them shouting.

'When you got back to Acre, therefore, Richard directed the council to deprive him of all future revenue,' said Joanna. 'It was a symbolic gesture more than anything else, given the kingdom's empty coffers, but it was to prove fateful.'

I nodded. 'He went scuttling to Duke Hugh, who recalled every French knight in the king's army. Seven hundred knights, plus their squires, men-at-arms and crossbowmen. More than a thousand men.'

'A grievous blow, but Duke Hugh has made his play now. There is little else he can do in Tyre.'

'Conrad, though—'

'Yes, he is a different creature. Ruthless, manipulative, and popular.'

'Treacherous too. Do not forget his efforts to forge an alliance with Saladin.'

According to the king's spies, it had not borne fruit only because of Saladin's demand that Conrad had first to take the field against Richard. To do so would have been tantamount to suicide, and the potential alliance had for the moment foundered.

'Untrustworthy he may be, but Conrad would still make a better king than Guy de Lusignan.'

'True, my heart. That is the crux of it,' I said, kissing her hand.

Military matters aside, this was the most awkward dilemma facing Richard. He had backed Guy since Cyprus. It had been a natural choice then, but our time in Outremer had revealed an unpleasant truth.

'Guy will always be the man who lost Hattin. If the poulains, the Templars and Hospitallers have no faith in him, he can never rule effectively. From the moment of Richard's departure, therefore, the kingdom will be in great peril. His good works could be lost to Saladin in a matter of months.' Joanna smiled. 'It is simple, Ferdia. Conrad must be king.'

'But Richard gave his word . . .'

Again she interrupted, but gently. 'He did, but every man has a price, including Guy.'

'You are right,' I admitted.

'Am I not always?'

I tickled her, making her laugh in the most unqueenly way, and asked, 'What is Guy's price, then?'

'Cyprus.'

'The king sold it to the Templars,' I said, recalling the transaction and the fact that they had only paid forty thousand bezants so far. Another sixty thousand was outstanding, and their recent imposition of a heavy tax on the population – their intent to raise the rest of the monies – had of recent days caused a rebellion. Intuiting the king's reasoning, I chuckled. 'But Cyprus is too troublesome for the Templars – they have enough to deal with in Outremer. Let Guy give them what they paid the king, and they can wash their hands of it—'

'—providing Guy de Lusignan with an island kingdom,' she said, finishing. 'I deem that a better prospect, not to say a more secure one, than being ruler of a precariously held territory with enemies to north, east and south.'

'It was your idea!' I cried in surprise.

Her expression grew mischievous. 'Let us say I planted the seed in Richard's mind.'

I tickled her again. 'When were you going to tell me?'

A coy look. 'Women's ways are not those of men. You know now. Is that not enough?' She leaned in close.

She was always a step or three ahead of me, I thought, drowning in her eyes.

Before all reason left me, I remembered that we had not spoken of John, another thorn in the king's side. It was perhaps better that way, I decided. I felt sure that Joanna would side with Richard, but for me to criticise John, her flesh and blood, would not be wise.

The king's politicking had to wait. Easter fell in the sennight that followed, and there was great celebration in Ascalon. One of the more remarkable events was a knighting. As part of the negotiating process, and the exchange of gifts that had taken place, Richard had seen fit to ennoble one of Saladin's sons. It was an act frowned on by the bishops, but no one dared argue with him.

Easter was barely over when he led a reconnaissance force south to Gaza, destroyed by the Saracens the year before, and Dārūm on the coast, which was still held by the enemy. I was with him when we surprised the accursed ones at Dārūm, and fortuitously freed twelve hundred Christians who had been taken prisoner at Acre and other places. Although the fortress remained in Saracen hands, our spirits were high as we returned to Ascalon on the afternoon of the fifteenth of April.

I had only one thing in mind, seeing Joanna, but my plans were soon thrown awry.

Scarce had we ridden into the camp than a squire found us. Thorne's he was, a stolid but reliable type whose name I could never recall. 'A messenger has come, sire, from England,' he said, running alongside Fauvel.

Richard's attention was instantly on him, like a far-above hawk spying a mouse. 'Who?'

'The prior of Hereford, he is, sire,' answered the squire, a tall lad of perhaps eighteen years. 'He bears a letter from the chancellor, William Longchamp.'

Richard's feet came out of the stirrups. He swung down from Fauvel, throwing the reins to the startled squire. 'See that he is fed and watered,' ordered the king. I leaped down from Pommers and hurled my reins as well. 'And this noble beast.'

Leaving the squire open-mouthed behind me, I chased after the king, who was making for his tent with giant strides.

Robert the prior of Hereford was waiting for us. A short man with protuberant eyes and a self-important manner, he nonetheless bowed deeply to Richard.

'Welcome to Outremer,' said the king.

'My thanks, sire, I—'

Richard was in no mood for social niceties. 'You have a letter from Longchamp?'

'Yes, sire.' Robert proffered a rolled parchment sealed with wax.

Usually, the king's secretary read his letters aloud, but not today. Richard read the message, his lips moving silently with the words. De Béthune entered with the earl of Leicester, another man Richard trusted; Bishop Hubert of Salisbury, also highly regarded by the king, was not long after the pair.

At length, the king finished. He let the parchment roll itself closed. 'Do you bear any other letters?' he asked Prior Robert.

'One from your lady mother, Queen Alienor, sire.' He hurried forward.

Silence again reigned as Richard digested the contents of the second parchment.

He came to the end, and still he did not speak. His face could have been carved from stone, so unreadable was it.

I glanced at de Béthune, who seemed as unsettled as I felt. I could bear it no longer. 'What news, sire?' I asked.

To my astonishment, he laughed. 'There is so much, I do not know where to start.'

De Béthune and I exchanged another look. Bishop Hubert whispered in the earl of Leicester's ear.

'It started in September,' said Richard. 'The week after the battle of Arsur, my half-brother Geoff took it upon himself to sail for England.

Hearing the news, Longchamp sent word to his brother-in-law, the constable of Dover, who duly arrested Geoff for breaking his oath. He was dragged, archbishop or no, his head bouncing off the cobbles, to the castle, and there imprisoned.' He went on, 'It was stupid of Longchamp, for at one pass he alienated every priest and bishop in England. By the time he freed Geoff a sennight later, the harm had been done. Longchamp was an outcast, reviled by all. Fleeing London, he attempted to cross to Normandy, but was caught and detained for a number of days. Although he was soon freed, John was already busy whipping up bad feeling against him. My brother also saw fit to raise an army, take Windsor as his base, and march on the capital.'

So much for family loyalty, I concluded, murderous thoughts towards John racing around my mind. I wondered too about FitzAldelm, who would have reached Normandy by now. What devilry was he up to? He might even have crossed to England.

'A meeting was convened in St Paul's in London on the seventh of October,' the king went on. 'There John and Archbishop Walter stripped Longchamp of his position. John seemed about to make a claim for power. Before he could, Walter revealed the authority granted him by me, allowing him to take supreme control of the kingdom. Thwarted, John had to be content with the post of *summus rector*.' Richard's smile was lean, and not in the least friendly. 'It grants him the trappings of Regent, without the power. According to Longchamp, he was spitting with rage, and was pacified only when those present swore that he should become king if I died before returning to England.'

'What of Longchamp, sire?' asked de Béthune.

'He made his way to Flanders, and sent word to the Pope, complaining of his ill-treatment. The response from Rome was swift. Longchamp is still the papal legate, while Archbishop Walter, four of the justiciars and two other bishops have been excommunicated. Geoff has been busy stirring things up in York, fighting with de Puiset and then excommunicating him, and soon after, John also, because he spent Christmas with de Puiset.' Richard made an exasperated noise. 'At this rate, there will hardly be a Christian left in England.'

Even Prior Robert laughed at this.

My dislike of John meant that I had no difficulty in believing Longchamp's letter, but Bishop Hubert needed convincing.

'Might Longchamp not be exaggerating things, sire, to make your brothers appear the malfeasants, and his own position seem more tenable?'

'It pays to be wary,' said Richard to Hubert, 'but the letter from my mother confirms what Longchamp described, more or less to the letter.'

Prior Robert smiled.

Richard gave him a flinty stare. 'Be not so smug. Well it is said that you hold yourself in no small esteem, and moreover, meddle gladly in matters in which you have no business. I suspect it was for your own benefit that you sent word to my mother, informing her that you were to travel to Outremer. It was *you* who contacted her, am I not right?'

Paling, Robert mumbled, 'Yes, sire.'

Richard snorted.

'The prior's self-seeking has worked to your advantage then, sire,' said Bishop Hubert.

'It seems so,' the king admitted.

Robert's expression grew hopeful. He looked most disappointed when Richard dismissed him.

'But for my mother's letter,' said Richard, 'I would have hesitated to believe the speed with which that losenger Philippe made overtures to John, and the rapidity with which *he* replied.'

I ground my teeth. Richard's ability to see only the good in someone, even when the bad was in plain sight, amazed me. It was a character flaw he shared with his late father.

'What did Philippe offer your brother, sire?' asked Bishop Hubert.

'The hand of his sister Alys—' here Richard made a droll face '—as well as all my continental territories: Normandy, Brittany, Anjou, Maine and Aquitaine.'

'John is already married, sire,' said Bishop Hubert with great disapproval.

'That would not stop him! He was to sail for France in February, and a meeting with Philippe, when, merci a Dieu, my mother landed from Normandy and stopped him.'

'How did she force him to stay in England, sire?' I asked.

'She told the whelp that he would have no castles or lands left to come back to if he went,' Richard revealed with satisfaction.

How good it would have been to see that altercation, I thought, with black amusement. The arrogant princeling brought to heel by his aged mother.

'Ah, Queen Alienor,' said Bishop Hubert. 'What a woman she is!'

'She is an example to us all,' said the king with great feeling.

'So the kingdom is secure, sire.' This from the earl of Leicester.

'For the nonce, although Philippe's hope of invading Normandy has not gone away, and John is still discontent. He will continue to scheme, and thanks to his treacherous whisperings about my imminent demise on this campaign, he has a decent base of support among the nobles. Archbishop Walter, my mother, The Marshal and the other justiciars will keep matters in hand for now, but she warns me that I should not linger in Outremer. *Your realm is in peril – make no mistake about it.* Those were the parting words of her letter.' Richard roamed to and fro, the caged lion impatient to act.

'If only you had Saladin and Saladin alone to deal with, sire,' I burst out. Everyone turned to stare, making me feel self-conscious. I flushed like a callow youth.

'You mirror my own thoughts, Rufus,' said the king, chuckling. 'A simple battle between me and Saladin, my army and his – how tempting that is. Much to my frustration, it seems destined never to come to pass.' He brandished the letters. 'Here is hard evidence that I may soon have to quit these shores. It makes the choosing of a new king even more important. A Turkish onslaught will surely follow on the heels of my departure.'

'And Guy is not that man, sire?' asked de Béthune.

'He is not.' Richard laid out his intention to offer Guy the island of Cyprus.

'An intelligent move, sire,' said Bishop Hubert.

'Presuming that Conrad shall be the new king, sire, what of your own plans?' Bishop Hubert posed the question that was in all our minds.

'Reluctant though I am to admit it, I must leave for England; sooner rather than later. I see no other way.' Richard's pacing continued, but his restless mien had been replaced by a rare, harried expression.

A cold truth sat unspoken. Conrad or no Conrad, the poulains and the military orders would surely be defeated by Saladin inside a twelvemonth once Richard and his large army departed.

De Béthune made mention of it, discreetly, and the king revealed that three hundred knights and two thousand men-at-arms would remain, and be paid from the royal treasury. Whether that number of troops could guarantee the future of Outremer, it was impossible to say, but even their cost was crippling. It was hard to see how Richard could do more.

Soon after, the king bade us to leave. He wanted to be alone, I thought, to consider his options. I glanced over my shoulder at the entrance. He was perched on a stool, his back hunched, staring into the distance.

It was an unhappy stance, that of a man who feels, despite all he has done, on the verge of defeat.

CHAPTER XXIX

Richard's plan bore fruit. On the sixteenth of April, Conrad was designated the new king of Jerusalem. The only dissenting voices were those of the de Lusignans and the grudge-holding Humphrey de Toron; nobody paid any heed to them. Count Henri of Champagne, trusted by the king and the French, was sent to Tyre bearing the good tidings. Conrad, he reported upon his return, was so overcome with emotion to hear them that he fell to his knees, thanking God and asking Him to allow his accession to the throne only if he was worthy.

Finally, Richard would have all the poulains behind him, for Reynald of Sidon and Balian d'Ibelin, Conrad's most prominent supporters, would bring their knights and men-at-arms south with the new king. It was even possible that Duke Hugh might return the Frenchmen to the fold. A delighted Richard declared that united, they had an excellent chance of vanquishing Saladin. I hoped so.

A period of fine sunny weather had been with us since Easter, mercifully without the searing heat of the months to come. Conrad was to be crowned within a sennight, and soon after he and his allies would sail to join us. Preparations began for another raid to the south. The king was set on taking Dārūm, the fortress he had previously attacked without success. Rebuild it and Gaza, and the Christians would have, with Ascalon, a triad of strongholds controlling the road to Egypt. With his main supply route cut off, Richard reasoned that Saladin would be forced back to the negotiating table, and there have no option but to agree to his demands.

There was much to do, but also time for leisure. One of my favourite pastimes was to hunt in the surrounding countryside with the king's hawks – Richard was especially fond of this pursuit – another to ride Pommers on the beach. At night, I whiled away the hours with Joanna. The friendship that had slowly developed between Rhys and Abu continued. The pair were as thick as thieves, although try as he might, Rhys could not persuade Abu to drink wine. De Drune caroused every hour of the day and night when he could, which was much of the time, and Thorne was often with him.

When we met, I got much abuse for not joining them, to which I made little reply. This inevitably brought down an attempted interrogation, to find out the name of the lady I was courting. My regular absences had been noted, and suspicions were running high. My resistance was stout, however, my lips sealed. I trusted both men with my life, but not with a confidence like this, and when they had drink taken. I felt bad not trusting them as I did Rhys, but my affair with Joanna *had* to remain secret.

And it did. For a few short weeks, I was blissfully happy.

On the last day of April, André de Chauvigny arrived on a ship from Rome, which heartened us all. De Béthune and I were with Richard, sitting outside his great tent, when de Chauvigny appeared. The news he carried, of Philippe Capet's trickery, was less welcome.

'From the moment of his departure, sire, the French king spun a web of lies and deceit about you,' de Chauvigny revealed. 'He was forced to leave the Holy Land against his will; you are a monster and a deceitful ingrate, a man who met secretly with Saladin to evil purpose.'

'Whose ears did he pour his poison into?' Richard demanded.

'Most important, sire, were the Holy Roman Emperor Heinrich, and Pope Celestine.'

Richard looked a little surprised. 'The emperor would have been suspicious of Philippe's dealings with Tancred, however.'

'He may have been, sire, yet he was cozened enough to form an alliance with Philippe.'

Richard grimaced. 'And the Pope?'

'Told of your "forcing" Philippe to leave the Holy Land, sire, he saw fit to release him and his followers of all oaths made after taking the cross.'

Richard raised his clenched fists to Heaven in fury. 'Now Philippe will claim no longer to be bound by his vow not to attack any of my territories! And as for the still-current papal ruling that forbids Christians from harming the property of any lord still fighting the Saracens, or travelling home. . .' He made a loud sound of disgust.

We glanced at one another, waiting.

'I see three choices,' said the king. 'The first is to return to England at once to deal with Philippe's machinations and my recalcitrant brother; the second to stay until the year's campaign has played out, in the hope that Jerusalem will be taken. The third is to remain even longer, thereby ensuring this kingdom's stability. Given the letters from Longchamp and my mother, I see this as the riskiest option.' He threw an enquiring glance at us, not something he often did.

I threw caution to the wind. 'When Conrad and God willing, Count Hugh, bring their forces south, sire, you will have a fine opportunity to confront Saladin, whether it be at Jerusalem or at Dārūm. Leave before then, and you will always regret it.'

Richard threw back his head and guffawed, that belly laugh that made his whole body shake. 'You know me well, Rufus! I can think of few worse things than hearing of Conrad and Hugh leading their army to victory six months from now, and I not there to share in the glory.' He looked at the others.

'You said yourself, sire, that the third choice is perilously risky,' said de Chauvigny. 'In my mind, that leaves you but one option, the second.'

De Béthune and I were in complete accordance.

Richard was pleased. 'You confirm my own thoughts. So be it. I shall stay until early to mid-September, which will still leave time for a sea voyage back to England. I shall box John's ears, and Geoff's, and Berengaria will experience a Christmas feast such as she has never seen.'

On this optimistic note, the meeting was concluded.

The next day was the first of May, a glorious, blue-skied day with balmy temperatures. The king had decided to go hunting, and was persuaded by Berengaria and Joanna to take his hawks rather than seek wild boar, his favourite quarry. I played along with Richard's quiet grumbling, but was secretly delighted, because now I would spend time with my love in public, and without fear of discovery.

Noise and excitement filled the horse lines as we made our preparations. Rouncys and palfreys stamped, and whickered their eagerness to ride out. Squires were making last adjustments to saddles and bridles. Rhys was there too, readying my mount, and my spare for himself. The falconers were ready; the birds hooded and tethered on their gauntleted arms. Huntsmen stood with leashed, whining sight hounds. A squadron of Templars in full armour waited by their destriers; protection against sudden Turkish attack. Richard would not have taken them, but the queen and Joanna both had insisted. There had been too many narrow escapes.

I was talking to de Béthune and de Chauvigny; we were betting which falcon of the king's would make the first kill, when Rhys spoke.

'Sir. A horseman.'

His tone made me look. A man was riding towards us from the direction of the coast as if his life depended upon it. My guts twisted. Whatever news he carried would not be good. I made for the king at once.

Richard was in full flow about the saker he had recently bought. Berengaria and Joanna were listening; the former with less interest than the latter. Joanna noticed my approach, however, and she gave me a warm look.

'Your pardon, sire, but a messenger is arriving,' I said.

Hearing the pounding hooves himself now, his expression became curious. 'Let us hope it is not more news of John,' he said to Joanna, his tone half-joking, half-serious.

The rider drew nearer, and I remarked in surprise, 'It is the Count of Champagne, sire.'

'My nephew rides as if the Devil himself is on his tail,' the king said, frowning.

Henri thundered up, and reined in right in front of us. 'Sire, terrible news. Conrad of Montferrat is slain! Murdered!'

Richard swore savagely. The queen let out a cry of anguish; Joanna, her face horrified, put an arm around her. Shock consumed me. I cared not an ounce for Conrad, but his death threatened the very existence of the kingdom.

'Tell me,' ordered the king.

Dismounting, bowing swiftly to Richard and the women, Henri began. 'It happened almost three days ago, sire, early on the afternoon of the twenty-eighth of April. Conrad was to dine with his wife Isabella, but she was taking so long at her bath that he decided to call on his friend the bishop of Beauvais, in the hope of dining there.'

Utter silence had fallen; every man within earshot was listening.

'The bishop had already eaten, however,' Henri went on. 'He urged

Conrad to stay nonetheless, telling him his servants could soon prepare some food, but Conrad decided to return home. Isabella would soon be back, he said; they could dine together as previously planned. He and the two knights escorting him left. Near the Exchange, they were approached by a pair of men dressed as monks. Producing hidden daggers, they attacked Conrad, stabbing him many times in the stomach. He fell from his horse, mortally wounded.'

'Sweet Jesu,' I heard Joanna say.

'And the murderers?' demanded Richard.

'One was killed, beheaded on the spot, sire, by Conrad's knights. The other fled to a nearby church, but was caught and interrogated. He confessed to being an Assassin.'

A ripple of shock. Like most, I had heard of the Assassins, but knew only a few details. A mysterious sect of Saracens, they lived high in the mountains northeast of Outremer, and were renowned for their ability to murder at will. To hear of their involvement in Christian politics was alarming and unnerving, to say the least.

'That is most strange,' said Richard. 'Why would the Old Man want Conrad slain?'

'The Old Man?' asked Joanna.

'Rashīd ed-Din Sīnān, madam,' Abu piped up. 'The leader of the Assassins, a man famous for his ruthlessness.'

I was worried that Richard would be annoyed by the interruption, but he gave Abu a nod.

'Well, would he?' the king asked again.

'It is possible, uncle. Last year, Conrad seized a ship off Tyre,' said Henri. 'The cargo belonged to the Assassins. Conrad kept it, and drowned the Old Man's agents. This could be the result.'

'The throne is yet warm from Guy's rear end, and already its prospective occupant is dead.' Richard shook his head in disbelief, and again when Henri related how Duke Hugh had tried to seize Tyre the next day.

'Only Isabella's foresight – she had the citadel gates locked against him – prevented it,' said Henri. 'Hugh demanded she surrender. Her reply was that she would do so only to you, uncle, or the rightful King of Jerusalem.'

'Still only a girl, but she has spine,' said Richard in approval.

'Uncle, there is more,' said Henri, his tone apologetic. 'The bishop of Beauvais and Duke Hugh are both saying that the second Assassin, the one who was tortured, alleged that you paid for Conrad to be killed.'

Richard snorted in disbelief. 'You jest.'

'Sadly, no, uncle. They are spreading the story far and wide.'

'If I want a man killed, I will slay him myself, or have my executioner do it,' Richard said coldly. 'Christ on the Cross, I do not send skulking, murderous Saracens to do my work. How does it serve me that Conrad is dead anyway? A fool can see it does not!'

'I know, uncle,' said Henri. 'All of us here know that.'

'I can hear Philippe spinning the tale already,' said Richard.

For some reason, I thought of Duke Leopold, and his rage over the standards on the ramparts of Acre. He too would enjoy seeing the untruth spread far and wide.

'You can do nothing about the lie right now, Richard. You can, however, ensure that a new king is chosen without delay.' Berengaria's voice was pitched for those close by.

'She is right, brother,' said Joanna, her gaze moving to Henri.

Richard saw her intent, and chuckled. 'Wise women, both of you. Nephew, come.'

I managed to get to Joanna's side as the king and Henri walked off, their heads bent together. There was so much commotion that no one noticed me whisper in her ear. 'Conrad's body is still warm, and you would have Isabella marry again?'

'She cannot rule by herself. A man must sit on the throne – that is what the poulains need, the kingdom needs. The woman's wishes in the matter – Isabella's – are irrelevant.' Joanna's eyes were sad. 'This is what I have been telling you.'

I stared at her, mute. The pain was like a blade turning in my flesh. She could never be mine. She had always been destined to wed another.

I said nothing to her – could say nothing. She left a moment later, returning with Berengaria to their tent. Richard summoned me then, and I went to him, more heartsick than I had ever been in my life. I cared not who would be king of Jerusalem, nor indeed whether Saladin seized all of Outremer.

Everything seemed futile.

*

Henri of Blois married Isabella of Jerusalem less than a sennight later. He was a popular choice. Having led the siege of Acre for a year before our arrival, he was respected by the poulains, and the French liked him because he was one of their own. Richard approved also, for his nephew was loyal to him more than to Philippe. At one ruthless stroke, insensitive to Isabella's wishes, and less than two weeks after Conrad's murder, the kingdom again had a ruler. Even I, still downcast, could see that that was a good thing.

Richard summoned Henri and the French south to join him in his attack on Dārūm, but impatient to prosecute the siege, he left before their arrival. We took the city on May the twenty-second; they reached us a day later. Richard handed control of Dārūm to Henri at once, sealing his authority as the new king.

A decision about where the army would march next – east to Jerusalem, or south to Egypt – had not been made by the twenty-ninth of the month, when we were returning slowly to Ascalon. The army was camped close to a stronghold called the Castle of the Figs, and another messenger arrived for the king. John d'Alençon was the Archdeacon of Lisieux and a former vice chancellor of England. He was a man trusted by Richard, and had travelled with us from Vézelay to Lyons the year before. The news he carried was most unsettling.

The king's half-brother Geoffrey's feud with de Puiset had not been laid to rest; Geoffrey was also refusing to listen to Queen Alienor's advice on the matter. John had seized Wallingford Castle in addition to Windsor. He continued to spread the rumour that the king was dead, and seek allies among the nobles. He and Philippe were still in league with each other; messengers travelled frequently between their two courts. The French ruler's attempt to invade Normandy had failed, but only because of his nobles' reluctance to invade the territory of a man who had taken the cross; it seemed probable that another attempt would be made before long.

John d'Alençon also brought letters from Queen Alienor, The Marshal and the royal council. All said similar things, but his mother's message put it best. If he did not deal with 'the abominable treachery, there was a danger that very soon England would have been taken from your authority'. She went on to say that Richard should return home at the earliest opportunity.

The news cast the king into a sad, downcast mood, the like of which

I had rarely seen. He took to his tent for the next two days, seeing no one save Berengaria or Bishop Hubert, and rarely, Joanna. During her first visit, she was concerned enough to summon Ralph Besace, telling me afterwards that Richard seemed so out-of-sorts, even a little confused, that she wondered if his quartan fever had returned. To our immense relief, Ralph declared the king's health not to be at risk, prescribing an infusion to help with his melancholia.

This news brought me some relief, but I was still troubled by not being allowed to see Richard. With little to do in the camp, and having no interest in hunting or even going on patrol – I had done this a hundred times – I kicked my heels each day, waiting impatiently until dark fell and I could creep into Joanna's tent. By unspoken agreement, we had not spoken about our future; instead we both endeavoured to savour every moment together.

I was sharpening my sword late on the afternoon of the thirty-first of May, with Rhys watching, disgruntled – in his mind, that task was his – when de Drune appeared round the corner of my tent. He had the rolling stride and crafty expression I knew well; it signified he had something of interest to tell.

I set down blade and oiling stone. 'De Drune.'

'Rufus.' He cast a look at Rhys. 'Should you not be seeing to your master's weapon instead of standing by while he toils over it?'

Rhys was well-used to his mischief-making, but could not help himself from glowering.

His job done, de Drune chuckled.

He wanted me to ask if he had any news, so I did nothing of the kind, picking up my sword again.

My ploy worked a treat. De Drune made some idle chitchat, including the tale of his latest drinking session with Thorne, and I grunted or made no reply. Rhys, still irritated with him, kept silent. It did not take the eager-to-share de Drune long to crumble.

'There is a real to-do going on in the French part of the camp,' he declared.

I pretended not to have heard.

He tried again. 'I said, the Frenchies are up to something.'

'Oh yes?' I used my most bored voice, while sighting down the blade to spy any nicks I had missed.

'Hellfire, Rufus, are you not interested?' At last, a trace of annoyance.

Behind him, Rhys was grinning – he knew what I was at.

I stared at de Drune, wide-eyed. 'Interested in what?'

He let out a foul oath.

'What is up with you?' I asked, and then I could hold it in no more. I roared with mirth until tears came to my eyes. Rhys joined in, as de Drune, his face as sour as curdled milk, looked on.

'Finished?' he asked as we regained control of ourselves.

That set us off again.

His expression grew blacker.

'It is what you do to us,' I said at length, still chortling. He grunted, only a little mollified, and I continued, 'You have news. Spit it out.'

'Hugh of Burgundy has called a council meeting. They are all gathering at his tent.'

'All?'

'Not just the French and the poulains. I saw many Normans, English, Poitevins, men from Anjou and Maine.'

'And Richard knows nothing of this,' I said.

'Just so. That is why I came to tell you,' he answered sulkily.

'In the most indirect manner possible,' I retorted, but I reached up and touched his arm. 'You did well. I shall go and see what mischief Hugh is up to. You and Rhys should come too.'

It was as sly a move as the French had made during our time in Outremer. Duke Hugh had sensed the mood of the army, which was buoyant thanks to the warm, dry weather and the recent capture of Dārūm, and acted while the king was avoiding company. Of the senior commanders, the only faces absent were the grand masters of the military orders, Henri of Blois and Richard himself.

Hugh's proposal that the army should march on Jerusalem without delay, regardless of whether the king stayed or returned to England, was carried with barely a word raised in protest. But the duke saved his most devious move for last. I did not see him give the order, nor see the messengers slip from his side, but when I heard later that night that the troops had been told, there was no doubt in my mind that it was he who was responsible. A general euphoria descended; the soldiers drank, sang and danced long into the night.

*

I went straight from the meeting to the king's tent, where I cajoled and threatened his guards until they gave in and admitted me. Richard's reaction was of complete frustration.

'The only thing that has changed since we were at Jerusalem's door in December is the weather,' he said. 'We still do not have enough men to encircle the city, and our supply lines will be stretched perilously thin.'

'Duke Hugh made no mention of those facts, sire.'

'Of course not, the losenger.' Richard thumped a fist off the table. 'Even if by some miracle they take Jerusalem, there will scarce be enough men to garrison it inside a twelvemonth. Saladin will need only to knock on the gates and enter. Why should I lose my kingdom aiding and abetting a cause that will so clearly fail?'

To my delight, our brief meeting had restored the king's spirits, and I was summoned to his tent at least once a day thereafter. The meeting called by Duke Hugh had not banished his indecision, however. It lingered for several more days, as the army reached Ascalon and preparations were set in train for the march on Jerusalem. He talked; I listened, hoping it would help him to reach a decision.

To leave, Richard said, would make him no better than Philippe, a quitter, a breaker of oaths taken. He would also be abandoning his nephew Henri of Blois, whom he had just helped to the throne of Jerusalem. There was a significant risk too that his departure would cause the army to break up – and yet the risk of staying was immense. An attack on Jerusalem was potentially disastrous; in England, meanwhile, John was wreaking havoc and conniving with Philippe, who was intent on invading Normandy.

More than once, I heard the king mutter, 'Do I give up my own throne in order to save Henri's?'

It was a hellish quandary he faced; I was glad it was not my own.

A few days later, Richard emerged from his period of gloomy contemplation, having decided to stay in Outremer until Easter of the following year. He was drained-looking and gaunt, but his mood was brisk. 'I cannot put a price on my conscience, Rufus,' he said to me. 'It will not allow me to leave without making another attempt to win this cursed war.'

The announcement that he was to remain with the army was received with general rapture. I had my doubts about Duke Hugh's reaction, but for the nonce, that did not matter. In high spirits, we set out for Jerusalem on June the sixth. A mere five days later, we had reached Bait Nūbā, a journey that had taken two months the previous winter. Of the Saracens, there was no sign; the only casualties were a couple of men lost to snakebite. Nonetheless, Henri of Blois went back to Acre for what reinforcements could be spared, or dragged from hostelries and brothels.

I was with Richard a day later when we waylaid a group of Turks intent on ambush. The group of us, thirty of the mesnie, slew many, and drove the rest of the curs pell-mell from the spring of Emmaus. Into the peaks that formed a protective girdle around Jerusalem, we pursued them. Atop the peak of one hill, a vista opened out, and instinctively, we all reined in.

'Sweet Jesu,' I heard Thorne say.

To my astonishment, I saw in the distance a city ringed by a great wall. There was no question what it was, and where we were. 'This is Montjoie,' I said.

'The mount from which the first Christians saw the Holy City a hundred years ago,' muttered Richard in reverent tones. 'There it lies, less than five miles away.'

My heart beat faster, and I imagined seizing the city, and seeing the Church of the Holy Sepulchre, holiest of all Christian shrines. Having done my uttermost to complete archbishop Walter's penance, to visit that sacred place, and there beg forgiveness for Henry's murder, would see my crime completely forgiven.

To be utterly cleansed, you must regret killing him, said the little devil in my head. And you do not.

I cursed the devil, and told myself that no Christian could do any more to atone for his sins.

'A wondrous sight, is it not?' Richard's tone was contemplative. 'Will we ever find ourselves any closer, I wonder?'

Locked in my own misery, I did not have an answer.

CHAPTER XXX

Acre, late July 1192

It was late afternoon, the hottest part of the day, when the sun's heat radiated not just from the sky, but from every building and the very paving stones of the street. Once I would have hated the oven-hot temperatures, but here in Acre it had become my favourite time, because it was when I met with Joanna in the same inn, deep in the Genoese quarter. While I perched on a stool in our room and waited, Rhys was on watch outside, as ever.

Almost six weeks had passed since Richard and I had been atop Montjoie. I sighed at the memory, for it had been our only sighting of Jerusalem, and was not one likely to be repeated. The penance I had thus far completed would have to suffice. Negotiations with Saladin had reopened yet again, and possession of the Holy City was not one of the bargaining points. Christians might be allowed to visit, but it would remain in the Turks' hands.

I fell to brooding. The end of our hopes had come soon after the twenty-ninth of June, when Henri of Blois – now the uncrowned King of Jerusalem – had arrived at Beit Nūbā with his reinforcements. At an army council held the next day, Richard demanded a decision be made on the best way to proceed. There were two choices: to try and take the Holy City, or to abandon the attempt in favour of an attack on Egypt. Twenty men had voted: five poulains, five Templars, five Hospitallers and five Frenchmen. With the majority well-versed in waging desert war, the result was a foregone conclusion: fifteen to five in favour of retreating from Jerusalem, the five all being Frenchmen.

After the council meeting, Hugh and his followers had split from the army. Taking Jerusalem was the only thing that mattered to the French. It mattered not that attacking Egypt, or taking Beirut – Richard's latest plan – would both weaken Saladin considerably, thereby making an attempt on the Holy City more realistic. Despite his breaking away, Hugh and his contingent had travelled with us from Beit Nūbā to Joppa, and thence to Acre. He, the bishop of Beauvais and his senior nobles now quartered a few streets over from the inn, while the majority of his troops camped outside the walls – separately from the rest of the army.

A soft knock. I padded to the door and opened it. Joanna stood on the threshold, her cheeks a little flushed from the heat. In my mind, she looked divine. I bowed low, as if we were in court, and bade her enter.

We embraced; kissed. More would have happened, much more, but for the sudden distraction of shouting on the street close by.

'Saladin!' The voice was clearer now. 'Saladin has taken Joppa!'

We stared at one another, astonished. I peered through the shutters, but the press of people outside was too great for me to see who was speaking.

An excited Rhys came hammering up the stairs a few moments later. He bore a little additional information – that our enemy had sprung a sudden attack on the city. Outnumbered, with little chance of holding out, the garrison had sent a frantic plea to Richard here in Acre.

I turned to Joanna. 'Forgive me, my love, but I must attend the king.'

'Of course.' She laid a lingering kiss on my lips – ignoring the embarrassed Rhys – and shoved me towards the door. 'Go!'

Ere the sun had gone down, we had sailed from Acre's harbour, taking fifteen ships – as many as were fit to leave at such short notice. On board were Pisan and Genoese men-at-arms by the hundred, fierce-eyed, their enmity set aside for the duration, and the English and Angevin knights. Sadly, we had not a single destrier or rouncy with us: there had not been enough time to load them. Rhys was with me, and de Drune had sneaked on board as well. Henri of Blois, the new king, had set out by road, leading a large force of Templars and Hospitallers.

Richard was at the prow, his eager eyes searching the darkening horizon as if he could spy out Saladin along the shore. A rising breeze tore at us, snapping the royal pennant attached to the main mast. I stood by the king's side, content that we were going to war again.

Politics and negotiations, alliances made and unmade, all were things that left me cold. I loathed the constant niggling hostility with the French, the duplicitousness from men like the now dead Conrad of Montferrat and the fact that I could not simply engineer a fight to the death with FitzAldelm the next time we met. I much preferred the black-and-white of war, the blood-hot simplicity of it. The king and I on one side, the enemy – Saladin – on the other.

A chuckle. I turned my head. 'Sire?'

'Even as Saladin and I negotiated for peace, we were both plotting an attack. Mine on Beirut, his on Joppa. Ironic, is it not?'

'Aye, sire. After we have driven his forces from the city—' like the king, I would not countenance defeat '—will the negotiations resume?'

Another chuckle. 'Undoubtedly. At this point, Saladin must be as weary of this war as I am. We shall come to agreement sooner rather than later.'

'Will you give him Ascalon, sire?'

This had been the sticking point during the recent talks. The two rulers had settled everything else: the Christians allowed to visit Jerusalem, and to keep the coastal strip from Tyre to Joppa, Saladin to have Jerusalem and the castles of the interior, the land between there and the sea shared. Ascalon, however, was a step too far for Richard. Saladin wanted it destroyed; the king had refused even to consider this. The very demand had caused him to strengthen the garrison there.

'I will not.' Richard's jaw jutted, his habit when he was at his most stubborn. 'A fortune it cost to rebuild, and it finished little over a month ago!'

I jabbed my stick at the hornets' nest. 'How then will you reach an accord with Saladin, sire?'

Instead of a snapping retort, a rueful glance. 'In truth, I know not.' Then, in an undertone so that not even the close by sailors heard, 'I must have peace. If Ascalon be the price for a settlement that allows me to return to England, I *will* consider it.'

I did not like this choice any more than he, but I also had had enough of this hot and unfriendly land. With the king's realm at significant risk, we had to leave soon. If we could not beat Saladin in battle, I thought, then a treaty offered the best way forward.

The distance between Acre and Joppa was sixty-odd leagues by sea. An uneventful voyage it should have been, lasting no more than a night and a day. Struck by contrary winds off Mount Carmel, however, our fleet was first separated and then battered for three full days and nights. Not until late in the evening of the thirty-first of July did the fortifications of Joppa heave into sight. Seven ships only, huddled together at anchor, waiting for the dawn, and every man on board hoping that we had come in time.

A new day, the first of August, brought us little indication of that. The shoreline was thick with Turkish soldiers, the town swarming with them. At the sight of us they sent up volleys of arrows, but we were out of range, and laughed our contempt. Despite our catcalls, the scene boded ill. Thinking that all Christian resistance had ended, Richard fumed and stamped about, cursing the weather that had delayed us.

'Seven ships,' he said. 'How many knights and soldiers is that?'

De Béthune did a quick calculation. 'Perhaps three score knights, sire, and five times that number of men-at-arms.'

Richard made an exasperated noise. 'Not enough to take the city.'

Even he could see that the danger was too great to risk an assault, so we remained safely at anchor, a quarter of a mile out, and waited for the rest of our ships to appear. Time passed. The sun rose in the sky. We ate dry bread and cheese, and engaged in desultory small talk. The watchman hanging from the top of the mast made no sound, let out no welcome shout of, 'Sails!'

'They will not come,' said Richard, restless, impatient. 'And by the time Henri arrives by road, the curs will be well settled in. It will be the same as last summer, when we came from Cyprus!'

I had come to the same grim realisation. With Joppa in Saracen hands, the Christian territory would be split in two, its security dangerously undermined. We *had* to retake it, whatever the cost.

'Christ on the cross, look,' said Thorne.

My gaze followed his outstretched arm to a point on the citadel walls. A figure was standing on the very lip of the rampart, and as we watched, it jumped. Feet first it plunged, landing in the sea. The splash carried through the hot, still air. A head bobbed in the water, and the man began to swim towards us – the red-painted royal galley with the dragon at its prow making it easy to know Richard's location.

We cheered the swimmer all the way. Pulling him on board with a rope, it was evident from his robe that he was a priest. Amazed, for it was rare for men of the cloth to possess much courage, we congratulated him heartily.

The priest knelt before the king. 'Sire, I bear some good news. The outer walls and the town are in Saladin's hands, but a group of stout-hearted Christians yet fight on. Good king, those who await you here are lost, if you and God do not have mercy.'

'What?' cried Richard. 'Do some still live, my friend? Where are they?'

'In the citadel, my lord, where they await their death.'

Richard roared for the captain, and gave the order to row for the shore with all speed, and to pass the same command to the other ships. 'Prepare yourselves,' he told us, grinning with delight.

Having expected battle, we were already in our hauberks. I was about to don my mail hose, but noticing, the king bade me leave them off. 'Do not bother with your helmet either. The beach is near, and we cannot tarry even a moment for anyone who sinks, Rufus.'

I nodded, my heart thumping.

Fast and sure, the galley scythed through the water. The oarsmen prayed as they rowed. Seeing us come, the Turks screamed and shouted. Drums and cymbals began to play, that hideous cacophony so reminiscent of Arsur.

Richard stalked up and down, a Danish axe in his fist, issuing orders. The men-at-arms were to start loosing as soon as we came within range, aiming at the spot where the ship would beach. 'Reload and shoot again. Reload and shoot, as fast as you possibly can,' he cried. 'You will clear the path for us. I will go first, and my knights will follow, then you men-at-arms. God is with us!'

'God, and the Lionheart!' shouted de Drune.

We were still roaring that as the prow grated off sand, the ship slowed and came to a stop. Amid the frenetic clicking of crossbow triggers, I held Richard's heater shield as he clambered onto the ship's side. I handed it over. 'Be careful, sire.'

He laughed, and jumped.

Up I went, Rhys giving me my shield. He was wearing his gambeson and had every intention of joining in the battle. I balanced, spying the king waist-deep in the sea, wading ashore. Dozens of Turkish bodies lay on the sand there, victims of the crossbows, but countless more were waiting for him.

Us, I thought, and leaped myself.

The sea was pleasantly warm on my legs as I caught up with the king. 'With you, sire!' I yelled.

'Dex aie!' Richard's voice, loud and proud. Sunlight flashed off his axeblade.

I was dimly aware of splashes behind me, but all my attention was on the foe before us. We were outnumbered hundreds to one; it was pure folly to act as we were, but when I looked at the red-golden-haired giant on my left, I felt no fear. Richard was born for situations like this; he throve on them. Rather than slow his pace as we came out of the shallows, he broke into a lumbering run.

I went with him.

There must have been men with us – I was told afterwards by de Drune that de Chauvigny and de Béthune were close behind with Rhys, as were two other knights, Geoffrey du Bois and Peter de Préaux, with more leaping off the ship – but it felt as if we two alone were charging the entire Saracen army.

I am not sure which emotion ran higher in me, fear or exhilaration, as we closed with the enemy. Dense rank upon rank of them there were, with pointed helmets, round shields and long shields, mail shirts and lamellar cuirasses. Armed with spear and bow, mace and sword, they were legion. Never had I faced such terrifying odds, nor felt such joy. Richard and I would carve our destiny together, I decided, and slaughter as many of the accursed race as we could before they cut us down. I would die by the king's side, with Joanna's name on my lips.

A better end I could not think of.

'Dex aie!' Richard cried again.

Utter astonishment took me then, because rather than stand and fight, the nearest Turks took to their heels. Faces contorted with terror, wailing in their own tongue, they jostled and shoved, frantic to escape our hungry blades.

We reached them. Richard's axe came down swinging, and split a Turk's head in twain. My sword lopped off an arm. Again the king's axe rose and fell, and another foeman died. I stabbed a Saracen in the back, and gloried in it. On we pushed, killing at will. Not a man tried to fight us, so infectious was the panic infecting the enemy. Screaming with fear, ruthlessly trampling their own, discarding weapons and shields, they were no longer an army but a panicked mob.

We few had put them to flight, I thought, my blood fizzing with delight and pride.

After a short distance, Richard paused to draw breath, and to gather what men were close by. Sixty-odd knights we numbered by now, and almost three hundred men-at-arms, Pisans and Genoese. 'More than enough,' the king told us, grinning.

Under his confident direction, we swiftly built a rough palisade out of the debris on the shore: barrels, beams and planks, pieces of a smashed-up barge. Angled across the sand between us and the main body of the Saracen host, it would afford some protection in the event of a counterattack.

The moment it was done, we rampaged into Joppa. Most of the Saracens within the walls were yet oblivious to our arrival, so swift had the assault been. We fell on them like avenging angels, and for a long while thereafter, the air echoed with screams while blood ran down gutters, and pooled in the streets.

When the defenders in the citadel realised we had come to their aid, they sallied forth, hitting the enemy from behind. Within a short space of time, there was not a living Turk inside the city.

Richard let us rest long enough only to slake our thirst, and then he led the entire force out onto the plain, straight at Saladin's camp. Our arrival came as the final blow to the already-fearful Saracens. On foot and on horse, they retreated, abandoning their tents, supplies, food, weapons and booty. Everything was left in the blind panic, down to the pots of stew bubbling over the fires. We chased them – on foot – for a mile and more, until, laughing still, the king brought us to a halt.

'I think they have learned their lesson,' he declared, upending a skin of wine he had snatched up in the enemy camp. His throat worked several times, and then he looked at the skin with new respect. 'God's legs, but this is good! Here, Rufus!'

It came flying through the air.

I saluted the king, and drank, and passed it to Thorne. He took a mouthful, and gave it to de Béthune.

We were a band of brothers, I thought with fierce pride. Bound by friendship and blood.

And this was our hour.

*

For all that Saladin was a courteous enemy, he could be ruthless, and his men were savages. Upon our return to the city, we found that the Turks had slaughtered all the pigs they could find – pork being an unclean meat to Muslims – and piled their carcasses on the middens. In a calculated insult, they had afterwards thrown the bodies of slain defenders on top of the putrefying pigs. Outraged, Richard ordered the Christians' bodies given proper burial, while the Saracen dead were heaped and left to rot with the animals they so despised.

We built a camp outside the walls. Despite our requests, Richard was completely unwilling to shelter inside Joppa. 'Let Saladin come and find me,' he declared.

Over the course of the next three days, we laboured, king, knights, ordinary soldiers, to repair the shattered defences. Covered in stone dust, burned by the sun, the ends of our fingers split and bleeding, we worked from dawn to dusk. Henri of Blois arrived by ship with part of his force, surprising us. It seemed his way south had been blocked by the Saracens at Caesarea, forcing him to take to the water. Like Richard, he also helped to rebuild the walls. The troops loved them both for it.

With the two sides eager for breathing space, negotiations were re-opened. They did not progress far, ending after Richard indicated to Saladin that if peace were concluded within six days – leaving him in possession of Ascalon – he would have no occasion to spend the winter here, and would return to his own country. Saladin's barbed response was that it was impossible for him not to have Ascalon, and that Richard would be obliged to overwinter in Outremer anyway, because if he did not, Saladin would reconquer all the lands he had taken.

By the fourth of August, the fortifications were starting to look as if they could withstand a siege – something which appeared to be coming. Like jackals drawn to carrion, the Turks had come creeping back from the hills into which they had been driven. Thousands upon thousands were now encamped about a mile from our position. We were fearfully outnumbered. The eight remaining ships had not yet appeared; nor had the remainder of Count Henri's force. As for horses, the city had been ransacked from top to bottom; fifteen had been found. Such a collection of broken-down, half-starved hacks you have never seen, but they were all that were to hand. Richard ordered padded caparisons made for each one, to provide some protection against the Saracen arrows.

I remember asking – even begging – the king that day to leave the camp, and shelter behind the relative safety of the walls.

'I will not,' he said, eyes sparking. 'I am the master of this field, not that mongrel Saladin.'

'You are, sire, but—'

He cut me off. 'Do not waste your breath, Rufus.'

Infuriated by his stubbornness, his unnecessary risk-taking, I stitched my lip and decided to take matters into my own hands. I found Rhys and de Drune, and told them that – in addition to the king's guards – we were going to keep watch in case the accursed ones launched a night attack. Rhys laughed and said they were too craven to try such a thing. Arrogance is one of the things that will see a man slain in battle, I told him. We were going to do it, whether he liked it or not.

Rhys grumbled and muttered, but he was the first to offer to stand sentry as the sun went down. I told him I was proud to have him as a comrade, and the last of his bad mood dissipated. He supped at his wine – watered down, he said – and told me that he would remember the fight here to the end of his days. I clasped his hand, full of emotion, and told him I felt the same way.

De Drune relieved Rhys after a few hours, using the church bells sounding matins as a guide. At lauds, he woke me from a deep slumber, reporting that there had been not a sound from the enemy's positions. Drowsy-eyed, he left me to it. I rose quietly, and dressed in gambeson and hauberk. Rhys was snoring at the foot of my blanket; he did not stir as I picked up my crossbow and quiver.

The eastern sky was still dark and decorated by a million stars as I paced towards the king's tent. The sentries there only noticed me when I was within killing range. I warmed their ears viciously with a few quiet words, and left them standing bolt upright, staring all around. I did the same at the barricade, warning the hapless men-at-arms on watch there that I would have their ears and noses cut off if they were caught dozing again. Pausing to cock and load the crossbow, I stole around the end of our barricade and towards the enemy camp. I waited, listening, but heard only the eerie screech of a night bird.

Fifty paces I went, and a hundred. I took a knee, and with the crossbow resting on my thigh, peered into the blackness. A long time I stayed there, until content at last that the Turks were sleeping like our men, I returned to the barricade.

I stayed by its seaward limit, because that lay closest to the king's tent.

Hours passed. I paced about, enjoying the blessed cool, and the gentle sound of waves lapping the shore. The stars faded, and the eastern sky gradually lightened. It was so peaceful and quiet that I confess to letting down my guard. I had not checked on the sentries in a while, and my head might even have begun to nod when the tread of footsteps behind me brought me swinging around, my crossbow aimed.

'Who comes?' I hissed, my forefinger on the trigger.

'Do not shoot,' said an Italian-accented voice. Out of the gloom came a sleepy-faced Genoese man-at-arms. 'I go . . . piss, yes?'

'Aye,' I said, feeling guilty that I had almost shot one of our own.

Off he went around the end of the barricade, stretching and yawning. I stared after him, my gaze searching for movement. I saw nothing, the entire duration of my watch had been the same. I was being over-suspicious, I decided. Saladin was not quite the fox I had thought he might be.

Back came the Genoese man-at-arms. He smiled, baring his rotten teeth, and asked, 'You . . . look for . . . Turks . . . all night?'

'Not quite,' I said, feeling at last the weight of the hours spent awake. It was time to seek my blankets and get what rest I could before the camp came alive.

'You good man.' He twisted, and stabbed a forefinger towards Saladin's position. 'Turks bad—' He stopped.

I came back to full alertness. I peered past him, and whispered, 'What do you see?'

He pointed. 'Sun flash . . . something out there.'

I swear my guts did a double somersault. Left to right, and back again, I raked the scrubby bushes, the undulating ground, with a fierce gaze. Then, about half a mile away, a bright wink, and another – sunlight off metal. There were horsemen out there, I decided, and they were not ours.

CHAPTER XXXI

'You have keen sight,' I told the Genoese. 'The Turks, the accursed ones, they come. Understand?'

He nodded, nervous but resolute.

'Go and bestir your comrades. In fact, waken everyone – loud as you can!'

'Yes. And you?'

I grinned. 'Why, I will do the same, and rouse the king while I am at it.'

He laughed, the brave bastard, and we ran the first distance together, shouting the alarm in French and Italian. A strange chorus it was, but it worked. Men came stumbling from their tents, shouting questions. The enemy was coming, I replied, in what numbers I did not know. My throat grew hoarse from crying, 'Arm yourselves!'

Richard had heard the clamour. I found him outside his tent in nothing but his underclothes, the Danish axe in his hand. Unshaven, his expression hawkish, he resembled a god of old. That, or a mad Viking warrior.

One I would be glad to have at my side, I thought with a fierce rush of love.

'What news, Rufus?' he demanded.

I explained what the Genoese man-at-arms and I had seen.

'Saladin, the rogue!' Richard leaped into action, issuing orders even as his squire helped him to don his gambeson and hauberk. Any soldiers who were ready to fight were to go out beyond the barricade at once. Meanwhile, the fifteen horses were to be saddled, and held in readiness out of missile range. When there were enough men ready, we would form a line in front of the barricade, knights in front, and the men-at-arms with their crossbows behind.

'God be with us, Rufus,' said the king. 'Now get you out there. I shall be with you soon.'

'Sire!' Needing only my shield, I ran to my tent, there finding Rhys dressed and armed. De Drune was with him. I snatched up the shield, and told them to follow me.

As we emerged, the scale of the Turkish 'surprise' attack became evident for the first time. In dense formation, hundreds upon hundreds of enemy horsemen were formed up a third of a mile from the barricade. For reasons unknown, they were not making an immediate advance.

Which was as well, for we were the only men facing them.

Nonetheless, every hair on my neck stood on end.

'Mary, Mother of God,' said de Drune.

Rhys's face had gone pale as that of a frozen corpse, but he said not a word. Instead, he spanned his crossbow and set a quarrel in place. He raised the weapon to his shoulder for a moment, before lowering it again. 'The dogs are not in range yet.'

'Lucky for us,' I said with feeling.

Two knights came into sight then, de Béthune and Thorne. I had never been more glad to see them.

'Five of us against that lot, eh?' Thorne snorted. 'This should be easy!'

A cracked laugh left my lips. 'We need to leave a few for the king, else he will not be best pleased.'

'There will be plenty for everyone,' said de Drune, cocking his crossbow.

Ten men-at-arms, the Genoese I had met among them, came haring up with broad grins on their faces. They were the first drops in the flood. Next were five more knights, then a score of men-at-arms, and a positive rush of knights, some not even properly dressed or armoured. There were numerous men-at-arms wearing only tunics. I smiled to myself, for it did not matter whether a crossbowman had a bare arse or not.

The king appeared, and we let out a great shout. He smiled, and bade us form a half-circle with the barricade at our backs. Knights and men-at-arms with spears formed the front rank – I was in it, with Thorne on one side and de Béthune on the other. We knelt and interlocked our shields, then jammed the ends of our lances into the earth and angled them towards the enemy. The bristling points made a fearsome obstacle. Behind us stood the rest of the men-at-arms, in pairs. One would shoot, the other reload, Richard ordered. He strode about behind us, crying that all we had to do was hold fast.

'They will break upon us like waves on rocks,' he cried. 'Let them come!'

'Lionheart!' It was de Drune again.

We cried his name again and again, taking courage from his confidence and determination. Somehow we would resist the overwhelming tide.

With the advantage of surprise gone, and the threat offered by our 'armoured hedgehog', the Saracens were in no hurry. They walked their horses within a hundred paces and then halted.

Richard sensed the temptation. 'Do not shoot!'

Not a bolt was loosed.

The Turkish officers and captains harangued their men, and pointed at us. Finally they urged their mounts forward, shouts and ululating cries rising into the air.

'There are so many,' said a quavering voice – one of the men-at-arms.

Christ, I thought. That is all we need. Fear spreads faster than a blaze in a haybarn.

'I know,' said de Drune, his tone droll. 'And for once, we have the knights in front of us, instead of the other way around. Best make the most of it!'

A burst of nervous laughter broke the tension.

I licked my dry lips, and wished I had drunk some water.

'Ninety paces,' said the king. 'Do not loose!'

The mamluks had also been waiting until they were in close range, I saw. Some were raising their bows. 'Sire,' I said.

Eighty paces.

As was so often the case, he had already noticed. 'Loose!' he shouted. 'Loose!'

Head ducked behind my shield, I peered along the length of my forward-pointing lance. Score upon score of bolts blackened the air, covering the distance to the enemy in the blink of an eye. Suddenly, there were gaps in the Saracen front rank, men and horses punched earthwards by the quarrels' terrible force.

Fifty paces.

Behind me, the men-at-arms exchanged their crossbows for loaded ones. They took aim and shot again. More Turks and steeds fell, but now they were loosing too. Clouds of arrows shot up in a graceful arc, coming down with lethal speed. I looked at the ground, eager not to take a shaft in the eye, as King Harold had at Hastings.

Forty paces.

There were a few cries of pain, but the enemy arrows had not the force to penetrate our mail and gambesons. Only those unlucky enough to have a hand or foot struck had been hurt. Again our men-at-arms shot and shot.

Thirty paces.

The Turks galloped closer, riding thigh to thigh. They were cut down in huge numbers, man and beast both, by the unrelenting crossbow volleys.

Twenty paces.

By the time they got to us they were a ragged line, bloodied and dismayed. Unwilling to close with our lances, they dextrously pulled on the reins and turned their horses sideways. We speared any who came within reach, easy prey, and the men-at-arms shot them side-on from ten paces. Dozens of the curs died, and even more of their horses. Not a single Turk reached the shields.

They broke and rode away, and we jeered our contempt, hurling abuse after them.

The men-at-arms continued to work their crossbows without pause, calm and measured. They shot the retreating mamluks in the back, and killed their mounts, over and again.

Richard had them cease when the enemy was out of range. He ordered groups of men-at-arms out onto the corpse-riddled ground, half to guard against the Turks, half to pick up every quarrel that could be found. The small number of injured were seen to, and he ordered us all to drink water. He was in excellent mood, striding about, clapping soldiers on the back, and praising individual knights.

'I swear, if he told us to charge the Saracens now, we would do it,' said Thorne, beaming from ear to ear.

'With fifteen horses?' De Béthune looked doubtful.

'I would not put it past him,' I said, chuckling.

A fresh squadron of mamluks – at least a thousand strong – charged us a short time later. Again the crossbows exacted a deadly toll, and again the Turks' horses would not close with our bristling lance points. Once more they swerved across the front of our line, and then retreated, leaving a fearful number of dead and injured men and beasts behind. Out rushed the parties of men-at-arms to retrieve quarrels, but they had not gone far before the curs showed signs of coming at us again. A disorganised, slightly panicked retreat to our position ensued.

Insults rained down on the running men-at-arms, hurled by their comrades [illegible] was too slow. Whose genitals were flapping about as he ran. W[illegible] like an old woman's.

Everyo[illegible] laughter, Richard loudest of all.

Indign[illegible]ng faces scarlet with effort, the men-at-arms reached u[illegible]eir turn. They cursed us, knights and their fellows, to[illegible] again.

We lau[illegible]er.

And th[illegible]e mamluks were drawing near, we focused on the task a[illegible]mors in the earth beneath my feet. The air, thick with the t[illegible] of hooves and hideous war cries. That charge broke as well. So did the next, and the one after that. Then I lost count.

For four sweltering hours the hedgehog withstood the Turks – we knew what time it was, roughly, by the incongruous sound of church bells ringing inside Joppa.

We had suffered casualties. There are only so many times a man can stand below a cloud of descending arrows and not be hurt, but our numbers were not greatly diminished. Grievous among the losses was Thorne, who was unlucky enough to take a Turkish arrow in the mouth. Shot from a great distance, which was why we did not see it coming, the shaft struck while he was talking to me. Transfixed from his lips to the back of his neck, he choked to death on his own blood even as we tried desperately to remove it.

Rhys had a flesh wound. An arrow had glanced off the top of his scalp, and thunked into the part of his gambeson protecting his shoulder. He was bleeding all over himself and de Drune, who was next to him, but he would not leave his position. Only when Ralph Besace intervened, in the main because de Drune, irritated by being bled over, had fetched him, did Rhys allow it to be seen to. Returning with a neat line of sutures in his hair, he bore our ribbing about not wearing a helmet with his customary grumpiness.

After a particularly vicious charge by the mamluks, which the crossbow volleys had broken again, Richard decided the time had come to charge. He called me out from the front rank, as well as de Chauvigny. Poor de Béthune had a slight wound to one hand, but he would not be left behind. The fifteen horses had been led around from behind the barricade. We eyed them with some apprehension: ribby, humpbacked, spavined, they looked as far from destriers as could be found. Two were at once determined to be over-weak for the exertions we were about to ask of them, which left thirteen.

Richard, undeterred, took the best one, a sturdy-enough chestnut, and told us to agree between ourselves who had what. Henri of Blois selected his next, and then Robert, the earl of Leicester. André de Chauvigny chose one, and de Béthune. So did Bartholomew de Mortimer, and Ralph de Mauléon, who never had enough of fighting. Henry Teuton, who proudly bore the king's lion banner, got a decent-enough nag, and mine did not look altogether terrible. Henry de Sacey was on the poorest hack of all, while William de l'Etang had a clearly exhausted horse, and the mount of Gerard de Furnival, a doughty knight if ever there was one, was lame. Hugh de Neville, a man-at-arms, with us because he was favoured by Richard, had a horse that looked old enough to be grandsire to the rest.

'See them?' The king pointed at the broken remnants of the mamluks, who were straggling back to the main body of their fellows. 'They are not even looking this way. We have the advantage.'

'The advantage, uncle?' Count Henri's voice was gently mocking. 'We are thirteen, and they number in the thousands.'

'They are beaten, though, nephew, and therein lies the difference.' Richard pricked spurs, and rode off. 'We will form a wedge, as Alexander did of old with his Companions.' It was evident he would be at the point, the most dangerous place in the formation.

We formed up behind him. I took one of the two positions at his back, without asking if anyone else wished to be there. If any man wanted my place, he could try to take it, I decided fiercely. We were in grievous risk of dying, which meant I *had* to be close to the king. De Chauvigny came in beside me, for which I was glad. The earl of Leicester seemed content to be behind us, with Henri of Blois and de Béthune completing the third rank. The rest came after them.

A signal from Richard, and we couched our lances and charged. It was not far to the enemy, less than half a mile. A tiny wedge we were, pounding over the blood-soaked earth, nothing like the hundreds of Companions who had ridden with the man they called the Great, but by Christ, I no longer cared about the odds we faced.

I went with Richard, and that was all that mattered.

Perhaps half the distance had flashed by before the Turks noticed us. The effect from then on was truly remarkable. There was no counter charge. No volleys of arrows. No attempt by officers to rally their men. No individual brave mamluks prepared to ride out against us.

Instead they continued to retreat, gaping over their shoulders at us, staring like lackwits. Because we were galloping and they were not, the gap between us narrowed with every passing moment.

Again the king's battle cry rang out.

With one voice, we shouted it.

And we struck them, the thirteen of us, like the hammers of Hell.

My lance punched into a Turk's side. Its point smashed his one arm, drove right through his chest, and into the arm on the other side, and out again. Up into the air he rose, ripped from the saddle, a dead man before he even realised. I dropped the lance, massively heavy now, and trying to spy the king, hauled out my sword.

Richard was twenty-five paces and more ahead. He was also without a lance now, laying about him with his blade. I saw him split a mamluk's head from the crown to the teeth, and with the back swing of that stroke, slice off another enemy's hand. He did not look in the least need of help, but I spurred after him regardless.

Deep into the Turks' formation we punched. We spared neither man nor beast, for a steed cut down meant one less foe to fight. Arrows hummed in at us, shot at close range. They shinked off our mail, lodged in our horses' caparisons, but miraculously, considering the number of them, killed none of us.

The earl of Leicester's mount stumbled then, and unbalanced, he toppled from the saddle. Like cursed gadflies, the nearest mamluks saw his plight, and in a flash, retreat became attack. On foot, alone, he faced a dozen enemies. Richard, twisting around to spy where everyone was, saw. Turning his chestnut, he rode like a demon and entered the mêlée. Light bounced off his sword, the portion of it that was not coated in crimson, as he killed and maimed and killed again. I joined him with de Neville, and we drove the mamluks back. The earl of Leicester, by some marvel unhurt, was able to grab the bridle of a riderless Turkish horse and clamber onto its back.

Laughing, the king told us it was time to return to our own lines, else our poor nags would collapse beneath us. We chuckled inside our helmets, for there was no mention of the gathering horde of mamluks not a hundred paces away.

Without a backward glance, he led us from the field.

Worried that we would be struck from behind, I could not help from glancing over my shoulder at the enemy. They outnumbered us a hundred, a thousand to one, and would have trampled us into the dust with a concentrated charge.

Instead they sat on their horses and watched us go.

Another three hours, marked by the bells, went by. We endured several more attacks – they came less frequently now – and still the accursed ones could not break our formation. A messenger brought word from the shore. The ships' crews were panicking, and threatening to put to sea. Richard rode thence at top speed, and restored order as only he could. Stripping the vessels of all but five guards on each, he brought the shirking crewmen back to stand with us.

Another assault came. There was a grisly protective barrier before the front rank now, a mass of dead horses and men, which meant our enemies could not close with us even if they had wanted to. Secure behind it, the men-at-arms shot down the mamluks and their steeds without mercy.

Click, pause, scream. Click, pause, scream. Those sounds would fill my dreams for nights afterward. Never before or since have I seen the deadliness of the crossbow exhibited to such effect as that brutal day in August. Such a simple weapon it is, a length of wood the thickness of a man's forearm, with a span of curved steel laid across, a thick string, a hook and a lever trigger. Yet it is utterly lethal.

The sun was falling in the sky – at last – when another Turkish attack came. Vicious, powerful, it threatened us as few of the previous efforts had done. Perhaps it was the mamluks' attempt to salvage their pride, or the desperation of men who have been threatened by their commanders. The stock of quarrels had been diminishing through the day, and during this assault, they began to run out. Suddenly, our spearmen in the front rank became one of two things between us and annihilation. The other, macabrely, was the horse-and-man corpse-barrier that lay before them.

Our foes were as exhausted as we. Despite our men-at-arms' lack of bolts, they could not press home their numerical advantage. No longer whooping and shouting, they broke off and rode away. A ragged cheer went up from our position.

Standing with the dozen others who also had mounts, I laid my head on my horse's neck and closed my eyes. It was over, thank God. We had won, just.

'Prepare yourselves!' Richard's voice was cracked, but still loud.

I lifted my head in wonderment.

He was on the chestnut, shoulders back, helmet off so that we could all see and hear him. 'One more charge, messires.'

I glanced at de Béthune, who grinned in a *what else is he going to do?* kind of way.

'One more charge, and the Turks will flee the field, I tell you.'

We did it once, I thought. We can do it again. I ignored the little voice in my head that was saying there were only so many times a man can tempt the devil and escape unscathed.

Richard's eyes went to Henri, then the earl of Leicester. On they moved, lingering on each and every one of us, the thirteen. We nodded, dipped our chins and muttered our acceptance. As my gaze met his, he smiled. Overwhelmed by emotion, feeling the gooseflesh proud on my arms, I returned the smile.

'From this day to the ending of the world, messires,' said the king, 'but we in it shall be remembered, we few, we happy few, we band of brothers. He today that sheds his blood with me shall be my brother. So I swear, with Christ as my witness.'

I yelled, 'I am with you, Coeur de Lion!'

'And I!' 'I am here!' 'Coeur de Lion!' Our voices rose to the bright blue sky.

We charged. Thirteen men against ten thousand, our battleground a crimson-stained patch of ground outside the walls of Joppa, in the sun-wasted land they call Outremer. In baking temperatures, through the soup-thick air we rode, heedless of our own safety, glorying in the moment. Following the Lionheart.

We should have died, been shot down like mad dogs, hacked into butcher's pieces of meat.

Instead, after a short but vicious clash, we put an entire army to flight.

Not a single man of us was slain, or even injured. It was remarkable. God-given. Some would have called it a miracle. Indeed in later years, I heard it referred to as such. I was always quick to point out that although God had been on our side, we had won because of Richard, and Richard alone.

At the end, it was clear that the Saracens had had enough. We had had to rein in our exhausted horses as they retreated, and the enemy were making no move to attack us, even though we were now a mile or more from our soldiers. The king was not done, however. Instructing us on pain of death to remain where we were, he rode straight towards the Turks. He had a lance, picked up from the ground somewhere, but he was alone.

My heart was in my mouth. I prayed, do not let him be slain now, o Lord, *please*.

Lance-end balanced at his stirrup, point towards the sky, Richard rode up and down before the enemy. One man. One sweat-lathered horse. Thousands of the accursed ones watching him. 'Is there any man who will fight me?' he cried in French, and then an attempt at that in Arabic. 'Fight me!'

Not a single horseman came out to meet him.

Not a single arrow was loosed in his direction.

'Sweet Jesu.' De Béthune's voice trembled with awe. 'You and I will never see such an incredible sight again.'

I was so spent, I could only croak an aye, but my heart was singing.

Of such things are legends made.

CHAPTER XXXII

Only for a short time can men step outside themselves and fight like the great heroes of history and legend: Achilles, Alexander of Macedon, Judas Maccabaeus. The white-hot flame of invincibility in battle burns as well as protects. As if to prove this, Richard fell gravely ill a few days after we had defeated the Turks.

It was the same accursed quartan fever that had affected him in Italy, Sicily, Cyprus and Acre. That it came on was no particular surprise. The battle had drained Richard's energy, leaving him spent, grey with exhaustion, and our camp was beside the battlefield with its thousands of stinking, rotting corpses, dense swarms of flies and carrion birds. He was not alone in being afflicted. Disease had also broken out among the ordinary soldiers. Rhys was ill, and de Drune too. I had to tend to them, as well as visiting the king as often as I could. It was a miserable time.

Worrying all of us, Richard sank fast. Rarely conscious, he suffered bouts of fever and bone-aching cold one after another. Ralph de Besace being in Acre, a local surgeon, much recommended, cared for him. We knights of the mesnie drew lots and took turns sitting by his side, wiping his sweat-covered brow and pouring sips of water and medicine into his mouth. He suffered terrible nightmares, and when he was half-waking, visions too. Through all of them, he cursed Philippe and John in equal measure. Saladin was barely mentioned. Sometimes he called for his mother, or Joanna, and even, once or twice, for me or de Chauvigny. Sad to say, Berengaria's name never crossed his lips.

He was lucid enough at times to be apprised of the situation – Saladin's army had again closed in on the city – and to issue a few orders. He dispatched Henri of Blois to Caesarea to fetch the French who had first accompanied him on his mission to join us, and who, through their own sloth, still remained there. They refused to come, bar a few brave souls. The only good news Henri came back with was that Hugh of Burgundy was ill, and had had to return to Acre.

When Saladin sent a message to say that he was coming to take Joppa, and Richard too, if he dared to wait in the city, the king's reply was curt. 'I will wait here for you, and as long as I can stand on my feet, or hold firm on my knees, I will not flee from you the distance of one foot.' Despite this bravado, Richard could not have fought off a three-year-old boy with a stick, and we all knew it.

Weeks after the battle, our plight seemed to be growing worse. The king remained very ill. Rumour stalked the camp that he was dying, dragging morale into the dust. Disease was killing men by the score every day. The enemy forces around Joppa outnumbered us many times. Almost no reinforcements had come to Richard's summons; bafflingly, even the Templars and Hospitallers would not obey his commands to strengthen the garrison here or at Ascalon.

Brooding over these things one sweltering afternoon, I sat beside the king's sickbed and watched him sleep. Although he seemed restful, it was distressing to see the profound effects the quartan fever had wrought on him. His mane of hair was matted and stuck to his skull with sweat. An unhealthy grey-yellow colour tinged his skin, and great pouches were carved out beneath his eyes. His cheeks were gaunt as a starveling's, and the arm that rested on the coverlet was shrunken and wasted-looking.

If he recovered – when he recovered, I told myself fiercely – it would take months for him to regain his full strength. Meanwhile, we sat on our hands even as the wolves – mamluks – prowled around our camp. Although all was not well with the enemy – Abu had been busy talking to Saracen merchants who dealt with both sides – Joppa was at considerable risk of falling again, and we taken or slain with it. Negotiations with Saladin continued, but in a desultory fashion, with Ascalon still the stumbling block. And as for the cursed French, who would not help in any way, I thought . . . but bring the fat bishop of Beauvais, their acting leader while Hugh was ill, before me, and I would wring his fleshy neck with pleasure.

I found myself savagely chewing a thumbnail. These were only the problems Richard faced here in Outremer. All was not well at home, either. I pictured the snake-eyed John meeting with Philippe, plotting, scheming, with FitzAldelm by his side.

'Ferdia.' A whisper.

Drawn from my reverie, I glanced at the king. His eyes were open, and thank God, clear. 'You are awake, sire.'

A rueful smile. 'I seem to be. What day is it?'

I had to think for a moment. 'The twenty-seventh of August, sire.'

'More than three weeks I have lain here.' Resignation oozed from his voice.

'Yes, sire.'

'I can scarce remember any of it.' He licked his lips.

I brought the cup I had ready up to his level. 'Some fruit juice, sire?'

'Made from the peaches and pears sent by Saladin?'

'Even so, sire. The snow has melted, but it is still cool. Another delivery will come tomorrow, I am told.'

He took several small mouthfuls, then lay back, closing his eyes. 'That is delicious. Saladin may be a stubborn dog, but he is fair courteous.'

'Indeed, sire.' He was right. The baskets arrived every few days, even though the snow came from Mount Hebron, far to the northeast.

'His brother too, Saphadin.' Richard looked at me. 'Are the Arabs well?' During a lull in the fighting, Saladin's brother had sent Richard two magnificent horses in appreciation of his bravery.

'Thriving, sire. You will be able to ride them soon,' I said, hoping my lie sounded convincing.

'It will be a while yet, for in truth I am as weak as a newborn kitten. God's legs, but this illness is hard to throw off.' He lay back.

A little time passed. I thought he had fallen asleep again, but then he spoke.

'The Templars and the Hospitallers, have they arrived?'

He was still feverish, I realised, or at the least, his wits were still scrambled. It had been weeks since the grand masters had sent word. They would not occupy a stronghold unless Richard was there as well. With the king needing to go to Acre to recuperate, that ruled out here – Joppa – and Ascalon. 'No, sire. They will not come,' I said gently.

'And that losenger Hugh of Burgundy – is he still unwell?'

'Word came this morning from Acre, sire. He is dead.' And no loss, I thought.

Richard's head came up off the pillow. His eyes were bright. 'Truly?'

I nodded.

'Some good news at last.' He seemed much strengthened. 'Is Saladin's host still close by?'

'Yes, sire.'

'And our strength?'

I would not lie – I owed him that. 'It is not good, sire. Disease is rife in the camp.' I thought of Rhys and de Drune, and thanked God they were recovering.

A deep sigh. 'How has it come to this?'

'I know not, sire.' The same question was in my own head. Our victory had been so comprehensive. Now defeat was staring us in the face.

'I must have peace, else I will never leave this place. What are Saladin's conditions?'

It was wretched to hear the tone of resignation in his voice. 'They remain much the same, sire. Do you remember—'

'Aye, I do. They are acceptable, except the last. He insists that Ascalon must be destroyed.'

'Yes, sire.' You must give in to that demand, I thought, or we may all die here.

'God forgive me, I have not the strength . . .' His voice tailed off.

He sounded wretched. I longed to clasp his hand with my own, but it was not my place. I ventured, 'There is no shame in giving up Ascalon, sire. It cannot be held long after our departure anyway: the poulains and the military orders do not have enough men to garrison it properly. If you do not give it to Saladin, he will take it in any case.'

Silence fell. Having said my part, I held my peace. Richard had to make up his own mind.

He was quiet for so long that I again began to think sleep had taken him. When he spoke, however, his voice was clear and crisp. Determined. 'Have Humphrey de Toron brought to me.' He had continued as the king's principal messenger during the on-off negotiations with the enemy. Richard continued, 'I want word sent to Saphadin. He is the most sympathetic to my position. Let him wrest from his brother the best terms possible.'

'Yes, sire.' I was amazed. No ultimatum. No declaration that Ascalon must remain in Christian hands. Instead, a request, through Saladin's own brother, for terms. Hope flooded my heart.

Perhaps peace was not impossible.

*

So it proved. Saphadin welcomed Humphrey de Toron, and agreed to do as Richard requested. Not a day had passed when his brother Saladin's offer came. Ascalon's fortifications were to be destroyed, and not rebuilt for at least three years, but Richard would be compensated for the vast sums he had spent on their construction. The coastal strip from Tyre to Joppa was to remain in Christian hands. Pilgrims would be free to visit Jerusalem without hindrance; Christian merchants could also trade there. These terms would last until Easter three years hence, the year of our Lord 1196. No mention was made of the Holy Cross, and the king did not bring it up.

Nor did I, or Henri of Blois, de Chauvigny or any of the others who were present as these terms were delivered. Another obstacle was the last thing anyone wanted.

'Tell Saladin I accept,' Richard said to Humphrey.

Fierce, relieved grins were exchanged all round. Not only did the king seem on the road to recovery, but we had peace.

We could leave Outremer at last.

The treaty was concluded several days later, on the second of September. Richard's strength had recovered enough for him to rise from his sickbed and ride through the camp, heartening the soldiers greatly. Soon after, many set out for Jerusalem, desperate to fulfil their pilgrimage. Three large groups went, de Chauvigny leading one, and Bishop Hubert of Salisbury another.

I longed to go also. In the Church of the Holy Sepulchre, I could have asked for final forgiveness of Henry's murder. But I stayed with Richard, who had declared he would not enter the city while it remained in Saracen hands. My reason was not his, although that was what I told any who asked. To seek absolution in the holiest shrine in Christendom, when in my heart I was unrepentant for murdering Henry, would have been a step too far. And so I stayed with the king, telling myself – as Richard said – that we would come back to Outremer once the period of the truce was up.

One day we would defeat Saladin once and for all.

EPILOGUE

Acre, late September 1192

The twenty-ninth of the month dawned bright and sunny. A light wind carried from the southeast, from Jerusalem. It was a good omen for a long sea voyage, men said. I hoped it was true. Today most of the fleet was leaving for Marseilles. My friend André de Chauvigny was in command, and the queens Berengaria and Joanna were to be in his care.

I was heartsore and having slept little, bone-weary. All through the long hours of darkness, I had tossed and turned, alone. My hopes of a final night with Joanna had been dashed. There were too many people about, she had decided, and the king was forever coming to her rooms with a question about this, or a request about that. Our last tryst, therefore, had been two nights before. Although it had been tinged with sadness and more than once, tears, I would treasure the memories to my dying day.

'Remember me, Ferdia,' Joanna had said. 'As I will you.'

'We will see each other again,' I had protested. 'We can—'

Her finger on my lips had silenced me. 'Do not say the words. We know not what the future holds,' she had murmured, and bent to kiss me.

Sweet Jesu, I thought. Give me the strength to see this morn through. Given a choice, I would have preferred to have charged the Turks again at Joppa, just the thirteen of us. I did not have that option, however, so I went to the baths with Rhys and then made ready as best I could.

The appointed hour came far too soon. I had taken great effort with my appearance, wearing a triple-dyed dark blue Flemish tunic, my finest, and a new pair of hose. My belt and shoes had been polished by Rhys until the leather shone. It was all for Joanna, of course, who was leaving.

Grief-stricken, but with great effort, blank-faced, I accompanied the king's party to the harbour, where crowds had gathered to bid farewell to the two queens. Joanna's gaze had drifted over me as I stood with the others of the mesnie – my mien had cracked, and I had smiled – but she had given no sign of recognition. It stung, although I knew she meant nothing by it.

Poor Berengaria was inconsolable, telling the king over and again in her accented French that she wanted him to come with her. Ill at ease, as he rarely was, Richard patted her hand and told her that there was much business yet to be concluded here. When she protested that his captains could deal with it, he told her that honour bound him to see at least one thing through to its conclusion.

'William de Préaux willingly gave himself into captivity, my love, in order that I should remain free,' said Richard. 'I cannot leave this place until he is released. I will not. The negotiations seem promising, but until I see him with mine own eyes, I cannot rest easily.'

Seeing his resolve, Berengaria asked then to stay until the king was also ready to depart. A sennight more mattered not, surely. On this too, Richard was immovable. It was already late in the season to sail across the Greek Sea; every day of delay risked high winds and storms. Her safety, and Joanna's, was more important than waiting to sail together as man and wife.

My eyes on Joanna, I wanted to take Berengaria's part, and plead with the king to do as she wished. I did nothing of the kind, however, instead hardening my heart as best I could. I had business of my own too: Abu had to be set free.

When Berengaria had calmed down, Richard kissed her fondly, almost absentmindedly, and told her they would be reunited by the New Year. He commended her to the care of de Chauvigny, who bowed and swore to guard the queen with his life. Richard turned to Joanna, and opened his arms. Her reserve cracked, and she threw herself at him, sobbing like a young girl.

'Ah, lass, lass,' said Richard, his voice uncharacteristically full of emotion. He hugged her tight.

'Richard.' Her voice wobbled.

I was consumed with jealousy and sorrow. I would have given anything to have exchanged places with him, to have been able to embrace her in public.

'We will see each other again soon,' said the king, stroking her hair.

She pulled back, her beautiful, tearstained face staring up into his. 'You swear it?'

'I do.' His voice was sincere.

She nodded. Then, an unexpected and oh, so welcome addition. Her soul-devouring eyes moved to rest on mine. 'And you, Sir Rufus – do you swear to watch over and protect your lord the king until he returns safely to his own realm?'

There was more to her words and her look, much more.

'I do, madam,' I said loudly. 'I will guard him with my very life.'

'Thank you.'

Her radiant smile lit the darkest corners of my heart. The strength I took from it bore me up as the queens went down the steps to a large rowboat, and from there, were carried out to their ship.

De Chauvigny went last, exchanging a few final words with the king, and then a farewell to me and de Béthune. He leaned close as we clasped hands, and whispered, 'Joanna will come to no harm, you have my word.' I gave him a grateful nod, glad that I had finally brought him into my confidence.

Glancing back, Berengaria raised a hand. After a moment, Joanna did the same.

Richard waved; standing as I was behind him, he did not see me do the same.

We stood for a long time in silence, watching the ships weigh anchor, and then, each pulled by several oar-powered lighters, slowly move towards the harbour mouth. Not until they reached open water would they raise sail.

I was surprised to feel a weight lift from my shoulders as the royal craft edged past the encircling wall. Joanna was gone. God willing, I would see her again in Normandy or England, but until then, my only duty lay with the king.

I was not altogether surprised to see the same relief in his face as he turned away. He clapped me on the shoulder. 'Ten days, perhaps, Rufus, and we shall begin the same voyage. The losenger Philippe and my conniving little brother await us at its end.' He chuckled, the fighter in him already relishing the struggles to come.

'I will be with you at every step, sire,' I said.

AUTHOR'S NOTE

In the author's note to *Lionheart*, I miswrote a sentence that has come to haunt me a little since. I stated that my publishers had asked me to move into a non-Roman period, a detail some readers took to mean that I was pushed into it, perhaps kicking and screaming. Nothing could be further from the truth! Rome is a culture that holds a special place in my heart, but I have wanted *forever* to write about different civilisations and times in history. I have so many ideas for such novels that I will probably never get to write them all. Know also that there have been occasions prior to *Lionheart* where books set in a non-Roman period were on the table: *The Eagles of Rome* trilogy was originally supposed to be a Hundred Years War series, for example. My then publisher decided it might not be a good idea, however, so I stuck with Rome. Orion, my current publisher, had a different view when I joined them, hence the move to the medieval period.

In some ways, this book almost wrote itself. There are so many contemporary accounts of the Third Crusade, three from the Christian perspective and two from the Muslim, that I was always going to be faced with more incredible, fascinating facts than I could fit into the story. And despite my best efforts, I still ended up with more than my editor felt happy with. Story is everything, and the arc of the tale cannot be slowed down by too much detail, however fascinating I find it! This book was more than fifteen per cent longer than it is now before I took my editing scalpel to it. What remains is chock full of historical facts. Essentially, the entire tale is true, except for Rufus and Rhys's presence in it. Some of the details follow, but not all. Richard did indeed strip England's cupboards bare to fund his crusade. He held a conference about Alys Capet's future, and met with King Sancho of Navarre to arrange marriage to Berengaria. He journeyed from Vézelay to Marseilles, laid out draconian punishments for bad behaviour on his ships, sailed in leisurely fashion to Italy, fell gravely ill then (and a number of other times during the crusade), risked his own life for a falcon's, and sailed into Messina in grand fashion. The medieval author al-Jahiz described mamluks as I did.

Richard's dealings with Tancred, freeing of his sister Joanna, the taking of Messina, jousting with Guillaume des Barres, and confrontations with Philippe Capet all happened. He lay naked before a church altar to ask forgiveness for his sins, asked his mother to chaperone Berengaria to Sicily, and then took his prospective bride and Joanna with him on crusade. His meetings and clashes with Isaac Comnenus, the lightning fast campaign to take Cyprus, and his marriage there are all recorded. So too is the stallion Fauvel, whom Richard rode in the Holy Land, the fight with the Saracen ship off the coast, the king's arrival at Acre, and the detailed subsequent events that saw the city taken. I described Acre and the citadel as I found the buildings that still stand there; they are dated to the early thirteenth century. As you may have guessed, apples of paradise were bananas. Rufus' near-death experience when at his toilet happened to an unnamed knight earlier in the siege – I could not resist using it! The prisoners taken at Acre were massacred – men only, not women and children as some texts state. This atrocity is regarded by many as Richard's darkest deed, but was a pragmatic decision, I believe, and one most Christian war leaders of the time would have taken.

The brutal march south along the coast unfolded as I related, down to the mist that obscured the last part of the column, the description of arrow-peppered men-at-arms looking like hedgehogs, soldiers dropping dead of heat exhaustion, the cries of 'Sanctum Sepulchrum adjuva', the selling of horse meat, and Richard's reconciliation with des Barres. The place names are all original, as are countless numbers of the minor characters and the Christian terms of abuse for the Saracens; the dates are as the medieval chroniclers recorded. Even some of the speech comes direct from the sources. The site of Richard's greatest victory was called Arsur at the time, not Arsuf as it is now known. Baruth is nowadays called Beirut; Joppa is modern-day Jaffa. I invented the collapsible water trough, unable to think how else knights might have watered their mounts during the march. The battle of Arsur was Richard's greatest 'if only moment'. His failure to achieve a conclusive victory over Saladin, thanks in part at least to the two hot-headed

Hospitallers who broke the lines, led to the fizzling out of the campaign over the following twelve months – all of which unfolded as I described – and the peace treaty that ended the war and allowed Richard to return home. The incredible tale of his sailing to the relief of Jaffa in July 1192, the priest swimming out to his ship, followed by the king's storming ashore with only a few men against overwhelming numbers of the enemy, is all true. So is the scarcely credible account of the battle outside Jaffa a few days later, when some of his men fought naked below the waist, and he and a dozen companions charged Saladin's entire army. Rufus's incredible lance strike during this clash is a word for word description of a Saracen slain by a knight, which was witnessed by a comrade. We know that Richard rode up and down in front of the Saracen host, demanding single combat against any man in it, because both Christian and Muslim historians wrote about it. The scene shouts Hollywood fiction, but it is not!

Although the ultimate goal of capturing Jerusalem was not attained, the Third Crusade was successful in seeing the Christian kingdom in the Holy Land endure for another century. Not until 1291 was Acre again taken by the Saracens. While this book is titled *Crusader*, the term was not in usage in the twelfth century. 'Taking the cross' was the most common phrase of the time. It is worth noting that English crusaders wore white crosses on their surcoats, the French red crosses and the Flemish green. I hope you can forgive the use of a red one on the book's cover! While Richard's credentials scream out from the details of his battles – he was a supreme leader, charismatic general and peerless warrior – I truly hope my story has revealed him to be more than that. Imbued with a strong moral sense, he was full of humour and great kindness as well as arrogance and cruelty. Learned, a lover of literature and music, he was capable of great diplomacy – even if the offer of his sister Joanna's hand in marriage was not genuine, it was something that none of his own kind would have contemplated. He was remarkable also in showing the Saracens respect, not just by negotiating with them but by knighting one of Saladin's sons, and forming friendships with more than one Muslim nobleman.

Many of you will know that Richard fell foul of Duke Leopold of Austria and the Holy Roman Emperor Heinrich on his way back to England. His captivity lasted for more than a year, during which time his brother John and the French king Philippe were up to all kinds of mischief. Full details will be in book three, working title *Lionheart: King*, which should hit UK bookshops in May/June 2022, and other English-speaking countries not long after. If you read the Lionheart books in other languages, you will likely have to wait until late in 2022 or even 2023 for this, the final volume in the trilogy. Look out too for my compilation of short stories, *Sands of the Arena and Other Tales*, which publishes later in 2021.

Readers familiar with my books will know that I make every effort to represent historical events as best as can be done, using accounts of the time and textbooks on every subject under the sun. While writing *Crusader* I consulted contemporary or near contemporary medieval accounts by Ambroise, Roger of Howden, Gerald of Wales and Ralph of Diss, as well as the Muslim authors Behâ Ed-Din, Usama Ibn Munqidh and Ibn Jubayr.

An incomplete list of texts that I used during the writing of this book includes *The History of the Holy War* (Ambroise's *Estoire de la Guerre Sainte*), trans. Marianne Ailes, *The Crusades: The War for the Holy Land* by Thomas Asbridge, *The Crusaders in the Holy Land* by Meron Benvenisti, *Richard the Lionheart* by Antony Bridge, *The Travels of Ibn Jubayr*, trans. Roland Broadhurst, *The Canterbury Tales* by Geoffrey Chaucer, *William Marshal* by David Crouch, *The Conquest of Jerusalem and the Third Crusade*, Sources in Translation by Peter W. Edbury, *The Kingdom of Cyprus and the Crusades 1191–1374* by Peter W. Edbury, *The Life of Saladin* by Behâ Ed-Din, *Deeds Done Beyond the Sea: Essays on William of Tyre, Cyprus and the Military Orders* presented to Peter Edbury, ed. Susan B. Edgington and Helen J. Nicholson, *Life in a Medieval City*, *Life in a Medieval Village* and *Life in a Medieval Castle* by J. and F. Gies, *Richard the Lionheart* by John Gillingham, *The Normans* by Gravett and Nicolle, *Food and Feast in Medieval England* by P.W. Hammond, *Knight* by R. Jones, *Crusader Castles* by Hugh Kennedy, *The Medieval Kitchen* by H. Klemettilä, *Medieval Warfare* by H. W. Koch, *Daily Life in the Medieval Islamic World* by James E. Lindsay, *Saladin: The Politics of the Holy War* by Malcolm Cameron Lyons and D.E.P. Jackson, *Lionheart and Lackland* by Frank McLynn, *Medicine in the Crusades* by Piers D. Mitchell (here I must thank Dr Mitchell for his help), *The Book of Contemplation / Islam and the Crusades* by Usama Ibn Munqidh, trans. Paul Michael Cobb, *Saladin: In His Time* by P.H. Newby, *The Chronicle of the Third Crusade*

(*The Itinerarium Peregrinorum et Gesta Regis Ricardi*), trans. Helen J. Nicholson, *The World of the Crusaders* by Joshua Prawer, *The Annals of Roger de Hoveden*, trans. Henry T. Riley, *Crusading Warfare, 1097–1193* by R.C. Smail, *Henry II* and *King John*, both by W.L. Warren, *Eleanor of Aquitaine: Lord and Lady*, ed. Bonnie Wheeler and John C. Parsons, numerous Osprey texts and articles in *Medieval Warfare* magazine.

I am indebted to Dr Michael Staunton of the School of History in University College Dublin, Ireland, for his generosity and time. A specialist in the twelfth century and the House of Angevin, he kindly answered my questions throughout the writing of the book. He also read the entire thing, checking for inconsistencies and errors. *Go raibh míle maith agat* for a second time, *a Mhícheál*. I travelled to Israel in January 2020, and was fortunate enough to visit the breathtaking thirteenth-century city that lies beneath the centre of old Akko (Acre). I then drove down the coast, following Richard's line of march, visiting Roman Caesarea, the medieval castle of Arsuf, and the approximate area where the biggest battle against Saladin took place. Exciting archaeological news in late 2020 suggests that the exact site of the battlefield may have been found. Lastly, I went to Jerusalem, a city Richard only ever saw from a distance. I also had the privilege of visiting the staggeringly impressive Roman-era fortress of Masada, something I have wanted to do for nearly forty years.

I do not just write novels. Seek out my recent Kickstarter-funded digital short stories *The March* (which follows on from *The Forgotten Legion* and reveals what happened to Brennus), and *Eagle in the Wilderness* and *Eagles in the East* (both featuring Centurion Tullus of the *Eagles of Rome* trilogy). There is also *Centurion of the First*, a standalone tale. All but the last will feature in *Sands of the Arena*. Don't own an e-reader? Simply download the free Kindle app from Amazon and read the stories on a phone, tablet or computer. Interested in seeing Pompeii and Herculaneum with me as your guide? Google Andante Tours (tinyurl.com/yc4uze85). Enjoy cycling with an historical twist? Take a look at Bike Odyssey (bikeodyssey.cc) and Ride and Seek Bicycle Adventures (rideandseek.com). Both these companies run epic trips (Hannibal, Lionheart, Venetians, Napoleon, Julius Caesar) that I am involved with as an historical guide.

I am a passionate supporter of the charities Combat Stress, which helps British veterans with PTSD, and Médecins Sans Frontières

(MSF), responsible for sending medical staff into disaster and war zones worldwide. To raise money for these worthy causes I do eccentric things like walking Hadrian's Wall in full Roman armour. In 2014 I marched 210 kilometres in Italy with two author friends, all the way to the Colosseum in Rome. The documentary about it is narrated by Sir Ian McKellen – Gandalf! The 'Romani walk' is on YouTube: tinyurl.com/h4n8h6g – if you enjoy it, please spread the word.

I also fundraise for Park in the Past, a community-interest company which is building a Roman marching fort near Chester in north-west England. Its website is: parkinthepast.org.uk. Thanks to everyone who has contributed thus far. You may know that I auction minor characters in my books to raise money for the charities mentioned above. (If you are interested in this, please email me; contact details below.) Three readers 'acquired' by this method appear in this book. Rufus's friend Philip is based on the wonderful Bruce Phillips, someone I greatly wish to have a beer with. Richard West is the man behind Richard de Drune, and Richard Thorne is based on . . . Richard Thorne! Gratitude, all three. The name of FitzAldelm's terrier – P'tit – is 'small' in English; this happens to be the name of my family's dog.

Every writer needs a good editor, and I am blessed in that regard. Francesca Pathak at Orion Publishing, thank you for all your input and support during this most strange of years, 2020. I'm also indebted to my foreign publishers, in particular Aranzazu Sumalla and the Ediciones B team in Spain – *gracias* – and Magdalena Madej-Reputakowska and the Znak team in Poland – *dziękuję ci*. Thank you, Charlie Viney, my agent, and Chris Vick, masseuse extraordinaire. In this troubling year, with a great deal more than COVID-19 to deal with personally, friends and family have *never* been more important. Heartfelt thanks to my mother and father, brother Stephen, Killian, Shane, Colm, Camilla, Will and Kelly, Philip and Anna, Matt, Nick and Sophie, Jamie and Jo, Andrew and Jane. Know that I will always be available for a chat, beer or more, should you need it. And so to you, my amazing readers. I have been a full-time author for twelve years now, thanks to you! I love receiving your emails, and comments/messages on Facebook, Twitter and Instagram. Look out for the signed books and goodies I give away and auction for charity via these media. I also do regular (every two to three weeks) 'Blades and Banter'* events via Zoom, often interviewing or talking with other authors. Email me or make contact via social media to join the shield wall [*Thanks to Simon Scarrow for that name!], or go to eventbrite.co.uk and search for 'Ben Kane', clicking on the Follow button to make sure you are updated with all new events.

Now that you have read this book, leaving a short review on Amazon, Goodreads, Waterstones.com or iTunes (or all of the above!) would be of enormous help. It has never been more important. Sad to say, historical fiction is currently a shrinking market, and times are a great deal tougher than they were when I was first published. An author lives and dies on their reviews, so a few minutes of your time would help a great deal. Thank you in advance.

Last and most importantly, I want to thank my children Ferdia and Pippa, whom I love more than I can say. I am truly blessed to have you both in my life. Yah!

Ways to get in touch:

Email: ben@benkane.net

Facebook: facebook.com/benkanebooks

Twitter: @BenKaneAuthor

Instagram: benkanewrites

Soundcloud (podcasts): soundcloud.com/user-803260618

Also, my website: benkane.net

YouTube (short documentary-style videos): tinyurl.com/y7chqhgo

CREDITS

Orion Fiction would like to thank everyone at Orion who worked on the publication of *Crusader* in the UK. And so would Ben!

Editorial
Francesca Pathak
Lucy Frederick

Copy editor
Steve O'Gorman

Proof reader
Kate Shearman

Contracts
Anne Goddard
Paul Bulos
Jake Alderson

Design
Rabab Adams
Tomas Almeida
Joanna Ridley
Nick May

Editorial Management
Charlie Panayiotou
Jane Hughes
Alice Davis

Rights
Susan Howe
Krystyna Kujawinska
Jessica Purdue
Richard King
Louise Henderson

Finance
Jasdip Nandra
Afeera Ahmed
Elizabeth Beaumont
Sue Baker

Audio
Paul Stark
Amber Bates

Production
Hannah Cox

Publicity
Virginia Woolstencroft

Marketing
Cait Davies
Lucy Cameron

Sales
Jen Wilson
Esther Waters
Victoria Laws
Rachael Hum
Ellie Kyrke-Smith
Frances Doyle
Georgina Cutler

Operations
Jo Jacobs
Sharon Willis
Lisa Pryde
Lucy Brem

KING

Get ready for the final instalment in the Lionheart trilogy …

Warleader. Captive. Negotiator. King.

Autumn 1192. Richard the Lionheart will face not just his archenemy Philippe Capet of France, but also his treacherous younger brother, John. Taken prisoner and handed over to Henry VI, his year-long captivity fans the flames of unrest in England and beyond. The extortionate sum demanded to free the king empties the treasury and bleeds England dry. Crowned a second time, Richard restores order in England. Forging clever alliances, building strategic castles and when obliged, waging war, the Lionheart carves a unique path into history.

Coming April 2022

Turn the page to start reading early …

Prologue

I was standing in the courtyard of the great castle at Chinon. Bright sunlight lanced down from a vast expanse of blue sky; birds sang happily in the trees beyond the walls. I could hear the excited cries of a child mixed with the barking of a dog. Rhys was nowhere in sight; I was alone, in fact, which struck me as odd. I could see no pages scurrying by on errands, no men-at-arms patrolling the walkway. There were no washerwomen gossiping with servants. Not even a single groom or a stable lad was visible outside the stables.

As my eyes moved to the keep doorway, the king came striding out. I smiled and my mouth opened in greeting, but, to my consternation, black-haired Robert FitzAldelm was right behind him. Another close companion of Richard's, he was my greatest enemy, and had tried to murder me more than once. My greatest desire was to see FitzAldelm dead, but I had sworn not to kill him.

The king approached, his usually friendly expression absent.

Stay calm, I told myself. You have no reason to worry.

'Good morrow, sire,' I said, bending a knee.

There was no reply, and fear spiked me. I stood, but gave no greeting to FitzAldelm. He smirked. Although my mind swirled with the violence I would like to do to him, I kept my face blank.

'Robert here is making grave accusations against you, Rufus.' Richard's tone was cold.

My heart lurched. There was only one thing it could be, but I was damned if I would admit it. FitzAldelm had no proof – Rhys and I had seen to that. I put on my best questioning expression. 'Indeed, sire?'

'He says that you foully slew his brother Guy in Southampton ten years ago.' Richard's gaze switched to FitzAldelm, who nodded, then came back to me. 'Hours after you and I met.'

When you saved my life, and I yours, I thought, but could not say it.

'Well?' demanded the king.

'It is not true, sire.' I acted in self-defence, I wanted to shout.

'He lies!' said FitzAldelm. 'He murdered Guy, sire, for certes.'

'I did no such thing, sire, and Rhys will say the same. He was with me the whole night.'

There was a trace of what I thought was doubt on Richard's face now, but an instant later, my hopes were dashed.

'Robert says he has a witness,' the king grated. 'Someone who saw you in the stews, drinking in the very same inn as his brother.'

'A witness, sire?' I could not help but scoff. The man-at-arms Henry was long dead. I had slain him in cold blood, as I had not FitzAldelm's brother – slit his throat, and with Rhys's help, buried him deep in a midden. The chances of finding another person who remembered me, so many years afterwards, was remote, I told myself. Impossible.

Richard turned to FitzAldelm, as did I.

'Henry!' he called. Loud. Confident.

No, I thought in horror. Surely not.

A man appeared in the gateway. Even at a distance, his beard was evident. Closer he came, and the spade shape of it could not be denied. His face was also familiar.

I began to tremble. You are dead, I wanted to shout. I slew you with my own hands, and buried your corpse. With snaking dread, I watched Henry take a knee six paces from the king, and bend his head.

'Sire.'

'Rise,' Richard ordered. To FitzAldelm, he said, 'This is he?'

'Yes, sire.'

A curt nod, and he glanced at the newcomer. 'Name?'

'Henry, sire. A man-at-arms I am, from Southampton.'

To me, the king said, 'Do you know this man?'

'No, sire,' I lied, somehow keeping a quaver from my voice.

'You did not see him in the inn the night Sir Robert's brother was slain?'

Relieved, I said truthfully, 'No, sire.'

'He saw you, however. Is that not correct?'

'It is, sire,' said Henry, meeting my gaze.

Nausea swept up my throat. Henry was dead, buried, rotted to bone and sinew, yet here he stood, his testimony about to seal my fate with the surety of an enemy's blade.

'Look well,' Richard urged. 'It was many years ago. Men change.'

'I am certain, sire,' Henry answered. 'His mop of red hair is unmistakeable, and his raw-boned face. This is the same man, and I will swear so on a reliquary.' There was no more sacred oath he could offer to take.

FitzAldelm's eyes glittered with triumphant malice.

'Tell us what you saw,' said the king.

'He took great interest in a pair of men who had been swiving a whore, sire. When they left, he slipped out after them. One of them, sire, was Sir Robert's brother.'

'How do you know?' said the king sharply.

Henry glanced at FitzAldelm. 'They are – were – as like as two peas in a pod, sire.'

'They were ever so, it is true.' Richard's gaze bore down on me. 'Well? What have you to say?'

Uncertain, panicking, I began, 'Sire, I –'

'Were you in the tavern?'

I looked at Henry, at FitzAldelm, at the king. I felt like a rat in a trap. Stupidly, I said, 'I . . . I was, sire.'

'I knew it!' crowed FitzAldelm.

Richard's mien was thunderous now. 'And you followed Guy and his squire?'

I considered lying, but my face – already flushing bright red – was betraying me. I did not wish to condemn myself further. 'I did, sire, but that does not make me a murderer! How could I do such a thing, one man against two?' I hated my tone, which was as shrill as a fishwife's.

'Because your lowlife squire was waiting outside to help you!' cried FitzAldelm. 'Sire, I have another witness who saw Rhys leave the royal lodgings not long after Rufus.'

A black, bottomless chasm opened at my feet. In its depths, I glimpsed a reddish-orange glare. Hellfire, I thought, waiting to swallow me. Consume me, because of what I had done.

I stood, numb with shock, as a bristle-headed groom was summoned, a man I did not remember but who was known to the king. His account was damning. He had seen Rhys steal after me and, the following morning, heard us talking about my injured arm.

'Well?' Richard roared. 'What say you now?'

I had nothing to lose. 'I did kill Guy FitzAldelm, sire, but it was in self-defence.'

'You stole after him into the alley, and then he attacked *you*?' Scorn warred with the disbelief in the king's face.

'Yes, sire,' I protested.

Richard paid no heed. He was calling for his guards. Burly men-at-arms in royal livery, they appeared with the speed of those who had been waiting to be summoned.

I was dragged away, still proclaiming my innocence. Deep in the bowels of the keep, I was hurled into a windowless, fetid, stone-flagged cell. The door slammed shut with an air of finality. I hammered my fists on the timbers. 'Let me out!'

An uncaring laugh was my reply. It was Robert FitzAldelm – he had followed the men-at-arms.

I pounded on the door again. 'I am no murderer!'

'Tell that to the executioner.'

'The king will never issue such an order!'

An amused snort. 'You know him less well than you think, then. The date has already been set.'

More than once in my life I had seen men punched in the midriff just below the ribcage, the sweet spot that when struck expelled all the air from their lungs, and sent them floorward, slack-jawed and half unconscious. FitzAldelm's words hit me with the same force. My legs gave way, and I slumped to the stone flags. I leaned my head against the thick-timbered door, dimly hearing through it FitzAldelm's footsteps as he walked away.

It was more than my strength could bear to hold me upright. Placing a hand behind me so I did not fall and strike my head, I lay down. Wanting the blackness to take me. Wanting never to wake up and face the cruellest of fates, ordered by my liege lord, whom I loved like a brother.

I closed my eyes.

A hand gripped my shoulder, sending stabs of terror through me.

I woke, sweating, frantic. Instead of cold stone beneath me, I felt planking. Heard the creak of timbers and the gentle slap of water off the hull. My senses returned. The blackness around me was that of night-time, not a windowless cell. I was at sea, returning from Outremer, and it was Rhys who gripped me.

He was crouched by my side, his face twisted with worry. 'Shhhh,' he hissed. 'Someone will hear.'

But to my great relief, nobody had. The confrontation with Richard and FitzAldelm had been a vivid nightmare. My dark secret was safe.

For the moment.

CHAPTER I

The Istrian shore of the Adriatic Sea, December 1192

Cold seawater squelched in my boots. My tunic and hose, also soaking wet, clung to me. Shivering, I tugged my sodden cloak tight around myself, and turned my back on the south, wishing in vain that that would stop the icy wind from licking every part of my goosebump-covered flesh. Of the king's score of companions, I was the only unfortunate who had fallen into the sea as we disembarked from our beached ship. Richard stood a dozen paces away, haranguing the pirate captain who had delivered us to this benighted spot, a featureless stretch of coastline with no villages or settlements in sight. Marsh grass and salt pools extended as far as the eye could see, suggesting a long walk inland.

'Change your clothes now, while you have the opportunity.'

My sour-faced attention returned to Rhys, who had laughed at my immersion as hard as the rest. In truth I could not blame him, nor anyone else. The water had not been deep; I had come to no harm, other than a soaking. And after the travails of the previous few weeks, God knows we needed a moment of levity. Nonetheless, my pride was stinging. I gave him a non-committal grunt.

'You will catch cold ere we find a place to spend the night.' Now Rhys's tone was reproachful. He had already contrived to go through my wooden chest, and was proffering a bundle of dry clothing. 'Take it – go on.'

Teeth chattering, I studied the group. Few men were paying any attention, busy as they were with selecting whatever gear they could carry. We were all soldiers, I thought. We had suffered and sweated and bled in Outremer together, had seen countless comrades fall to Saracen arrows, or die of thirst and sunstroke. We had cradled our friends' heads in our laps as they left this life, choking on blood and asking for their mothers.

In the face of that, baring my arse did not matter.

Stripping off my boots and clothes, I gratefully tugged on the new garments, ignoring the comments of Baldwin de Béthune, who noticed what I was at. He was a close friend and, like me, one of the king's most trusted men. I thought with a pang of de Drune, another friend who would not have missed this chance to jibe. But the tough man-at-arms would poke fun no more. He had been swept overboard during the first of the storms that had battered us since our departure from the Holy Land almost two months before. I hoped his end had been swift.

'Two hundred marks, and *this* is where they brought us to land?' Richard's volcanic temper showed no sign of abating. He threw a murderous look at the pirate captain, who had wisely retreated to his vessel. When the tide came in, as it would that evening, he and his crew would do their best to push the long, low shape into deeper water. We were not waiting to help.

The pirate was a rogue, I thought, and the price he had charged for our passage was extortionate, but he was not to blame for the beach where we stood. 'He could do little about the storm, sire.'

Richard glared at me, but I had spoken the truth.

Ferocious autumn gales had battered our large buss all the way from Outremer; we had been fortunate not to drown. At Sicily, the king had decided the open seas were too dangerous, so we aimed our prow for Corfu. Our plan had been to voyage up the more sheltered Adriatic, but further bad weather and an encounter with the pirates had seen Richard drive a bargain with the corsair captain. His two galleys were more seaworthy than the fat-bellied buss which had carried us away from the Holy Land. Or so we thought.

High winds – the bora – had struck soon after our departure from Corfu, and driven us, helpless, up the Adriatic. Three days, or had it been four? My memory could not be relied upon, so exhausted and sleep-deprived was I. Ceaselessly thrown up and down for hour upon hour, from side to side, forward and back, I had vomited until it seemed my stomach itself would come up my red-raw throat. There had been snatched, uncomfortable periods of rest, but never enough. I had forgotten the last time food had passed my lips. When the ship had run aground in the shallows, I had felt nothing but relief. Eager for dry land beneath my feet, paying not enough attention as I prepared to disembark, I had fallen into the sea.

'Aye, well, there's nothing to be done about where we are now,' said the king. 'And standing around will not get us to Saxony any sooner. Let us go.'

He was not now the godlike figure he had so often been in Outremer. There was no bright sun to wink off his mail, no high-prancing stallion to set him high above us. Even in plain tunic and hose, Richard remained an imposing and charismatic figure. Several inches taller than six feet and broad-shouldered with it, his handsome face framed by windblown red-gold hair, he *looked* like a king. He acted like one too: fierce-tempered, regal and fearless.

When he led the way, we twenty willingly followed.

I was unsurprised that Rhys was the first with a question. In an undertone, he asked, 'How far is it to Saxony?'

'I do not know. Hundreds of miles. Many hundreds.'

I had told him this before, but Rhys's expression darkened anyway.

'It will not all be on foot. We will buy horses.'

He rolled his eyes. 'I would we had left earlier. We might have sailed all the way.'

'That was never a possibility.' I explained again to him how the winds and currents that had helped us east across the Greek Sea were too powerful to permit westward travel through the narrow straits that separated Spain from Africa.

Rhys fell silent and, downcast myself by the long journey before us, I began to brood. Landing on the French or Spanish coast might have been an option, but it was precluded by Richard's long-running enmity with the Count of Toulouse, who, with his Spanish allies, controlled the region. We could not travel up through Italy either, because most of its rulers were in league with the Holy Roman Emperor. Heinrich VI, one of the most powerful monarchs in Europe, historically held no love for Richard because of *his* support for another Heinrich, der Löwe, the former Duke of Saxony. Recently, the divide between Richard and the emperor had deepened. The French king Philippe Capet had met with Heinrich VI on his way back from the Holy Land, winning him over and forging a new alliance.

Thoughts of Heinrich der Löwe made me remember, wistfully, Alienor, the blonde beauty who had served Matilda, his late wife and Richard's sister. It had been years since I had seen Alienor, but the mere thought of her quickened my blood. There was even a chance we might meet. Once our roundabout route had taken us through Hungary, we would travel to Saxony, ruled by Richard's nephew, and further north-east to the lands of Heinrich der Löwe. I prayed that Alienor was alive, and in Heinrich's service. Then, guilt-ridden for thinking of her while still in love with Joanna, the king's sister, I put her from my mind.

It was as well that I had elected not to wear my second pair of boots. For an hour or more we trudged through a sandy marshland, its only inhabitants the seabirds that lifted, screeching, at our approach. We waded through saltwater pools; it was my turn to laugh at de Béthune and the rest as they sank to their knees, cursing their own soaking boots. Reaching the shore finally, we came upon a collection of run-down hovels that would struggle to be called a hamlet.

While Richard hung back – a man of his size and stature would stick in anyone's memory – de Béthune and I went with the royal standard bearer, Henry Teuton, to find out where we were, and to buy any horseflesh that might be on offer. Thanks to the soldiers we had met in Outremer, de Béthune and I had some Italian, and Henry Teuton was fluent in his father's language. Between us we managed; the silver coins I proffered also loosened tongues. The area we found ourselves in was the county of Gorizia. I thought nothing of the name, but I caught de Béthune's expression as its ruler, Meinhard II, was mentioned.

Telling his apprentice to fetch out the horses he had, the smith explained that Meinhard co-ruled with his brother, Engelbert III, the lord of the nearest town, also called Gorizia. It lay some miles away, at the foot of the mountains.

As we haggled over the nags, de Béthune risked much by asking about Meinhard's and Engelbert's relationship with emperor Heinrich VI. The smith twined a forefinger and middle finger, indicating they were close allies, and my concerns rose.

But the king laughed when de Béthune told him what we had heard. 'We are in enemy territory from the outset,' he declared. 'As it was in Outremer, when Saladin's men threatened us at every turn.'

Our confidence bolstered by his, we grinned at one another.

William de l'Etang, another of the king's close companions, frowned. 'I remember the name Meinhard, sire.'

'Speak on,' urged the king.

'I am sure he is related to Conrad of Montferrat, sire – his nephew, I think.'

De Béthune and I gave each other a look; Richard's expression tightened.

Conrad had been an ambitious Italian nobleman who rose high in Outremer society. Crowned King of Jerusalem the previous spring, he had been murdered within the week. Everyone in the Holy Land at the time knew that the Assassins – a mysterious Muslim sect – were behind Conrad's slaying, but malicious gossip spread by Philippe Capet and his followers since had been remarkably effective. Conrad's family were not alone in believing that Richard was responsible.

'Better that we should *not* pretend to be Templars,' Richard declared. This had been his initial plan. 'We would draw unwanted attention; our heads must be further below the parapet. Pilgrims, we shall be, then, returning from the Holy Land. Hugo of Normandy will be my name. There is no need for you to have a false identity, Baldwin. You shall act as the military leader of the party.'

This seemed a better ploy, I thought. My relief was momentary, for with his next breath the king ordered Henry Teuton to take one of the four new horses and ride ahead to Gorizia. There he was to ask the authorities for safe passage, a guide and treatment according to the Truce of God, a Church ruling that protected those who had taken the cross from physical violence. Pulling off a magnificent ruby ring, Richard handed it to Henry with the declaration that this should be a mark of his good faith.

Their thoughts on roaring fires and hot meals, few of the group took notice.

I could not believe the risk-taking, however. 'This is his idea of travelling in secret?' I whispered to de Béthune.

'I agree with you, Rufus, but he is our lord.' He saw my face, and said, 'Cross him at your peril. He is in a fey mood.'

I saw that de Béthune was right. The king's bonhomie on the ship had been genuine enough, but the beaching of the vessel in the middle of nowhere, our long trudge to an armpit of a village, the swaybacked, spavined horses – all that had been on offer – and Meinhard being Conrad's nephew had hit Richard hard. If he could not be a proud Templar, the next best thing was a rich and influential pilgrim. And by his haughty expression, his mind would not be changed. I decided on another course of action.

'Sire, let me go also.' Adding that I wanted to improve my German and that Henry was a good teacher was enough. Richard even gave me one of the three remaining nags, a ribby chestnut.

We set off at once. The interrogation began before we had ridden a hundred paces.

'You vant to learn Tcherman?' Henry had a thick, hard-to-understand accent.

'Yes.' I was not about to admit my main purpose. Henry was a no-nonsense, direct type I could see marching into the castle at Gorizia, loudly asking for all of Richard's requests. I hoped for a more discreet approach and, if at all possible, that the ruby ring should stay hidden.

I could tell Henry none of this – dutiful and rigid, he would fulfil the king's orders to the letter – and so my punishment was to endure a prolonged, finger-wagging lesson in basic German that lasted for the entire ride to Gorizia. I sound ungrateful; Henry was in fact a half-decent teacher, and I learned more in those miles than I had during the entire voyage from Outremer.

Gorizia stood at the foot of a hill upon which perched the castle, Engelbert's stronghold. The town had its own wall; there were guards at the main gate, but to my relief we passed through unchallenged.

'Do not look around so much,' Henry said in an undertone.

I checked my enthusiasm. After the guts of two months at sea, with the only interlude being at Ragusa, even an inconsequential place like Gorizia had me gazing about like a wide-eyed child. Although Henry was right to bring me back to our mission, I thought, we were not in so much of a hurry that I could not visit a nearby bakery. Tired of mouldy bread and salted pork, the smells emanating from it were too much to resist. Hurling my reins at a protesting Henry, I strode inside, emerging soon after, triumphant, four honeyed pastries in my grasp.

'Two for you and the same for me,' I said, prepared for his outburst. 'We can eat and walk towards the castle at the same time.'

Won over, Henry ceased grumbling, and set to with a will.

The guards at the castle entrance were a slovenly crew, their mail covered in brown rust spots; they paid us as little attention as their counterparts at the town gate. Their lack of interest was explained by the crowds in the courtyard beyond, where we discovered – happily – that Count Engelbert was holding court in the great hall.

We left our horses in the charge of a stick-thin, sharp-featured boy of perhaps twelve years. Eyes fixed on the two silver pennies Henry brandished as his reward afterwards, the lad swore that he would guard the horses with his life.

'See that you do,' Henry warned him quietly, 'or we will hunt you down and open you from balls to chin – as we did with many a Saracen.'

Pale-faced, the lad nodded.

We joined the queue of petitioners, locals come to plead their cause with Engelbert, who sat with his feet up on a table, playing idly with a dagger. He was the picture of boredom. The line advanced at a snail's pace, but eager not to draw attention, we dared not jump it. If we talked, it was in low tones; the fewer people who heard either French or my bad German, the better. Time dragged by. I listened in to the conversations around me, trying to understand. To my frustration, I recognised only words here and there rather than the full meaning of what was being said. There would be plenty of time for further lessons from Henry on our long journey, I told myself.

Two cases had been dealt with when I heard church bells in the town tolling one. My hopes began to fall. There was no obligation on Engelbert to hear the case of everyone in the queue. He could call a halt whenever his patience ran thin. To our good fortune, however, he flew into a rage with a hand-wringing peasant. According to Henry's amused translation, the wretch was lamenting the theft of his hens – by a neighbour, or so he claimed. Unconvinced by the claim, Engelbert ordered the unfortunate peasant from his sight. He refused to hear the petition of the next man as well – a merchant whose stammer annoyed him – and reached a decision about the next case the instant it had been explained to him. Moved up the queue three places, we drew near enough to watch Engelbert.

Perhaps thirty-five, he had thinning brown hair and a prominent forehead. Although he had lost his temper with the peasant, his face was amiable, and he was laughing now at whatever the latest plaintiff had said. This was no reason to let down our guard, however, I thought. Engelbert was an enemy.

Our turn came at last. Bored, cold from standing around – for like all great halls, the room was as draughty as a barn – I marshalled a humble but enthusiastic expression onto my face as, urged by a steward, we advanced towards Engelbert's table. Both of us bowed deeply, as we had agreed. Flattery could only help.

His initial glance was disinterested. Then, taking in our muddy, travel-stained clothing and our daggers, which marked us out from the other supplicants, his expression sharpened. Not only were we strangers, but armed ones. An eyebrow rose, and he said something in German.

Henry replied, and I heard the words for 'Holy Land', taught to me on our ride to Gorizia. He was telling Engelbert we were returning pilgrims.

The count's face came alive. He asked a question, and then another and another. I heard mention of Jerusalem, Saladin, Leopold and Richard.

Henry's answers, calm and measured, took some time. I stood by his side, wishing I understood more of what he was saying. The less he gave away, I had told Henry as we waited, the better. Plead our case simply, I said, and do not mention de Béthune and the merchant Hugo unless you have to. Henry had not liked that, but conceded it might be awkward if Engelbert, interested, demanded to meet these pilgrims. The ring, I warned, would also attract too much attention. On this Henry had balked, stubbornly saying that the king had ordered it be offered to Engelbert. Anxious, I had managed to persuade him not to offer the priceless gift unless he felt it absolutely necessary.

The count asked another question, and Henry replied. This time, I heard 'Acre' and 'Joppa'. My mind filled with memories of our brutal march from the first to the second, and the titanic battle against Saladin outside Arsuf. I cast a look at Henry, whose face had grown animated. He too had been there. I began to worry that he might inadvertently reveal something about Richard. Keep it simple, I thought.

A messenger approached Engelbert, affording me an opportunity to speak with Henry. 'Have you asked for safe passage?' I said. 'Has he granted it?'

'I did at the start, yes, but he began asking questions at once. He is fascinated by the campaign against Saladin. What can I do but tell him?'

I had no answer. Refuse to answer Engelbert, and we risked his denying us safe passage and a guide. Offer too much detail, and he might glean that our master was not de Béthune but someone far more important. We had put into enough ports on our voyage for word of the king to have spread this far.

His business with the messenger concluded, Engelbert returned his attention to Henry. Now there was mention, several times, of '*Herr*', the German for master or lord. Henry replied; he said 'de Béthune' and 'Hugo'. He asked for safe passage again, I could understand that, and after a heartfelt '*bitte*', or 'please'.

Alarmed that he sounded too desperate, I casually turned my head towards Henry. He did not see me. I slid my boot sideways and, touching his, kicked him.

He glanced at me, and I mouthed, *Do not give him the ring.*

His brow wrinkled. His lips framed a 'What?'

Christ, I thought.

A question from Engelbert; he was frowning.

Henry did not immediately reply.

I threw caution to the wind. 'What is he saying?'

'He says he can offer safe passage and the Truce of God, but guides with knowledge of the mountains are hard to find. He wants money, I think.'

A grim look passed between us. We had only the silver coins in our purses; enough to buy food, but nowhere near the sum required to win the favour of a man like Count Engelbert.

Henry was like me, ever a man of action. The muscles of his jaw bunched, and then he was reaching into his purse. Out came the ring.

Engelbert could not conceal his avarice. The ruby at the ring's heart was deep red, the size of a large pea. It was worth a fortune by anyone's standards. He held out a hand. There was silence as he examined it and, after a tense few moments, a broad smile.

Henry and I glanced at each other in relief.

The count thanked Henry, and then said something else. The only words I understood, and they were enough, were '*König*' and 'Löwenherz'. My blood ran cold. King. Lionheart.

'He says that no nobleman, still less a merchant, would offer so rich a gift,' muttered Henry.

'He is right,' I hissed, wishing that I had stood up to the king, and asked for a purse of gold bezants instead of his magnificent, far-too-obvious gift. 'But you must persuade him otherwise! Tell him the ring was taken from a dead Turkish noble on the battlefield.'

Henry did his best, his tone eloquent and persuading.

He was still mid-flow when Engelbert placed the ring on the table with an empathic, metallic clunk. '*Nein,*' he said. '*Nein. Ihren Herr ist ein König. König* Richard.'

Henry fell silent. My eyes shot to the guards lounging behind the count. I fully expected them to be ordered to arrest us. We had no chance of fighting free, unarmoured and with daggers as our only weapons. I cared nothing for us, but the king *had* to be warned.

Rather than issue a command, Engelbert smiled. It was an open smile, with no hint of malice. He spoke fast then, earnestly. I heard the words '*Kaiser*' and Heinrich. Breathing fast, sick with tension, I waited until he had finished, and Henry could translate.

Henry grinned at me. 'He insists that our master is Richard, and he holds the king in great admiration for what he did in Outremer and has no wish to do him any harm. The same cannot be said for his brother Meinhard, or the emperor Heinrich.'

'Can Engelbert supply us with a guide?'

Henry shook his head. 'There is no time to find one. We must leave Gorizia today.'

'Are things that bad?' I asked, my hopes of a comfortable bed in a warm inn dwindling.

'So he says. Meinhard would pay a huge sum to anyone delivering the Lionheart into his hands. No one in the town can be trusted.'

We thanked Engelbert and took our leave. At the door, I looked back. The count had not called forward the next petitioner but was talking intently to his steward. Then, as if he discerned my stare, he turned his head. Our gaze locked for a heartbeat. Engelbert smiled, but his eyes were as cold and calculating as a falcon's.

I told Henry what I had seen. It was likely, we decided, that Engelbert would send word to Meinhard about the king's whereabouts.

'*Tadhg an dá thaobh*, he would be called in Ireland,' I said.

'*Tie-gh on daw* . . .?' Henry mangled the words. 'I do not understand.'

Chuckling, I explained, 'Timothy of the two sides. He has a foot in both camps.'

Henry looked downcast. 'You were right. I should not have offered the ring to him.

'Look on it as a blessing,' I said. 'If you had not, we would have sought accommodation here in Gorizia and, like as not, had our presence reported. But for Engelbert's warning, we might have been taken while here.'

This realisation was scant solace as we set out southwards to find our companions. The wind was sharp as a knife. Yellow-grey clouds threatened snow; even as I lifted my gaze upwards, little skirls came falling from the sky.

Only God knew if we would find shelter that night.

The first instalment in the epic Lionheart trilogy . . .

MADE IN BATTLE. FORGED IN WAR.

1179. Henry II is King and the House of Plantagenet reigns supreme. But there is unrest in Henry's house. Not for the first time, his family talks of rebellion.

Ferdia – an Irish nobleman taken captive – saves the life of Richard, the king's son. In reward for his bravery, he is made squire to Richard. Crossing the English Channel, the two are plunged into a campaign to crush rebels in Aquitaine. The bloody battles which followed would earn Richard the legendary name of Lionheart.

But Richard's older brother, Henry, is infuriated by his sibling's newfound fame. Soon it becomes clear that the biggest threat to Richard's life may not be rebel or French armies, but his own family . . .

Available to buy now